Ashfall

Helen York

Published by Helen York, 2024.

This is a work of fiction. Similarities to real people, places, or events are entirely coincidental.

ASHFALL

First edition. November 13, 2024.

Copyright © 2024 Helen York.

ISBN: 979-8230078814

Written by Helen York.

Chapter 1: Ignition Point

The heat pressed down on me like a vice. I could feel it crawling over my skin, the air thick with smoke, the stench of burning wood and something more—something metallic, like iron. My lungs ached with every breath, but I refused to leave. Not now, not when my father's shop was hanging by a thread. I couldn't even see it through the haze, but I knew it was there, hidden beneath layers of chaos. There were too many memories in that place, too many pieces of my childhood, to let it go without a fight.

I was so focused on the burning building that I almost missed him.

The first thing I noticed was the way he moved. Fast, efficient, with purpose. A tall silhouette against the orange backdrop, his black firefighting gear swallowing him whole, save for the flash of his helmet as he ducked under the line of flame. His boots crunched against the charred earth, the sound sharp, the only thing clear in the midst of the inferno. And his eyes—dark, stormy, a contradiction to the fire raging around him. I couldn't see much more than that, but it was enough.

He barked orders, a voice so steady it could have soothed the flames themselves. "Move that ladder!" "Clear the back entrance!" He didn't raise it, didn't need to. There was an authority in his tone that felt familiar—like someone who knew exactly what they were doing, who had seen this kind of destruction too many times before. I froze in my spot, just far enough away from the building's edge to stay out of the fire's reach, but close enough to feel its heat, to taste the burning dust in the air. The world felt like it was collapsing, and yet this man, this stranger, made it seem like he was holding everything together.

When his gaze met mine, I stumbled back, almost knocking into a fire extinguisher. He didn't pause in his work, didn't even break stride, but there was something in that look—something that made my stomach flutter and my heart stutter. There was no recognition. No warmth. Nothing. Just that steely focus, the way his eyes briefly lingered before moving on to the next task.

He hadn't seen me in years. If anything, I probably didn't even register as more than another face in the crowd.

But I remembered him. I remembered the way he used to be—quiet, thoughtful, and more than a little reckless. He was the kind of guy who would disappear without a word, leaving everyone to wonder what went wrong, what had changed. I hated that about him. And now, here he was, back in my life, standing in the midst of a crisis like some kind of hero.

I shoved the thought away. I had no time for this.

I started toward the entrance, my boots crunching over the gravel, my mind whirring with a thousand things I needed to do. There was no room for sentiment, no space to think about how this town had once been his, how he had once been one of us. He'd left us, left me, and that was something I couldn't just forgive. Not after everything.

The fire crackled louder, a growl echoing from the heart of the building. It sounded like it was moving closer, and panic rose in my chest. The antique store was my father's lifeblood. His pride and joy. The walls that had once stood as silent witnesses to generations of history, now threatened by a force no one could control.

I reached the front of the building, but the fire trucks were clustered in front, blocking the way. The sound of water hissing against flames mixed with the frantic shouts of the other firefighters. My gaze found him again—Rafe Quinn, moving with the precision of someone who had been born into this life. He was climbing a ladder, directing streams of water from the top of the truck with ease, his entire being focused. But even in the midst of it all, he managed to look... untouchable.

I hated how he could still affect me like this.

"You shouldn't be this close," a voice called, pulling me from my thoughts. A firefighter stood in front of me, his face hidden behind the mask, but the voice was familiar. "Get back, it's too dangerous."

I blinked, taking a half-step back, my body reacting before my brain caught up. "I'm not going anywhere. That's my father's store."

He eyed me, scanning my face as if trying to figure out whether I was worth arguing with. "Fine. But stay out of the way. You're a liability out here."

I nodded, already turning away before he could say anything else. I wasn't about to be dismissed again. Not today.

But as I glanced back toward the flames, toward the tall, dark figure in the distance, something shifted in my chest. A crack. A subtle, almost imperceptible change that I couldn't place. He was saving the store. No matter what had happened between us, Rafe Quinn was saving a piece of my father's legacy. And that, in some strange way, made it impossible to ignore him.

For now, I'd let him do his job.

But that didn't mean I had to forgive him for walking away all those years ago.

I couldn't escape him. Even as the fire continued to rage, consuming everything in its path, his presence anchored itself in the chaotic backdrop. He was everywhere—his voice steady, his movements deliberate, as if the world had slowed down just for him to make sense of it all. He barked orders to his team, his gestures sharp, but there was no panic in him. He was a master of the storm, and I hated him for it.

I hated the way he'd just slipped back into town like nothing had changed, like he hadn't abandoned us all those years ago. When he left, it had felt like the town was swallowing itself, the void he'd left behind more crushing than any fire could ever be.

People had spoken of him like a ghost, as if he'd been a hero in some other life.

But me? I knew the truth. Heroes didn't leave. They stayed. They fought.

And now here he was, a hero again, in the very place where he'd been a ghost, where he'd left me to pick up the pieces of his absence.

I tried not to look at him. I really did. But when he stepped down from the ladder, his figure moving fluidly through the smoke, I found myself watching, unable to look away. There was something hypnotic about the way he worked, like he was in his element, a place where nothing could touch him. The heat of the fire had nothing on him, and somehow that made the anger burn all the fiercer in me.

The fire was starting to die down now, the worst of it under control. But that didn't stop the smoke from billowing into the streets, turning the air into something thick, something that clung to you. I made my way toward the back of the store, where the flames had been the least threatening. There were no firefighters here, no one to stop me. I had to see the damage. Had to know how much my father's life's work had been reduced to ash.

The door creaked open, and the smell hit me—charred wood, melted glass, the sour sting of plastic. My eyes watered as I stepped inside, and I could feel the burn of it on my skin, like a second degree. The store was dark, the windows covered in soot and smoke, but I could still make out the once-pristine shelves that had held my father's collection. The brass knobs, the faded velvet-lined boxes, the delicate porcelain that had been my father's pride and joy.

Most of it was gone. Burnt. Ruined.

I wanted to scream, but the sound stuck in my throat, lodged there with the frustration and grief that had been building for years, ever since he left. My father, who had put everything into this shop, who had built it up with his hands, now standing on the edge of losing it all.

And who was there to help him? Rafe Quinn. Of course.

"Rafe," I muttered under my breath, the word slipping out like a bitter pill.

I wasn't ready for him to show up.

And I certainly wasn't ready for him to find me standing in the wreckage.

"You shouldn't be here."

His voice was low, rough, a hint of that same calm authority I'd heard earlier. My stomach did a strange flip, not because of the way he spoke, but because of how familiar it felt.

I turned, heart pounding in my chest, and there he was, standing in the doorway, silhouetted against the smoky light, his helmet in hand, the rest of his gear hanging off his broad frame. His expression was unreadable, but there was something about the way he looked at me, like he was seeing me for the first time in years. Like he didn't know what to make of me either.

"You're not supposed to be here," I repeated, my voice a little stronger this time, though the words felt like they were coming from somewhere far away. "This is my father's shop. I can handle it."

He didn't step closer, but I could see the conflict in his eyes. That same unspoken tension I hadn't realized had always existed between us. "You don't have to do this alone," he said softly, the words a challenge I wasn't ready to hear.

I scoffed, a sharp sound that cut through the thick smoke. "And what? You're back to play the hero again? I don't need you, Rafe."

He flinched, but only for a moment. He was good at hiding things, that much was clear. "I'm not here to save you. But I'm not going to let this place burn down either."

I stared at him, unsure of what to say. Of what I could say. It had been so long, and yet here he was, standing in the middle of the wreckage, offering me help I didn't want, didn't need.

"Then what's your plan?" I snapped, crossing my arms over my chest, trying to create distance, even though I knew he could close it in a single step. "You're going to fix it all, just like that? All the things you left behind, all the things you broke?"

Rafe's eyes darkened. For a moment, it almost seemed like he might step closer. But he didn't. Instead, he sighed, the sound deep and resigned. "I never meant to break anything."

The words hung between us, thick and heavy, like the smoke still swirling around the room. I swallowed, my throat tight, as the weight of them hit me harder than I expected. "Then why'd you leave?" I whispered, though I hadn't meant to.

He hesitated. It was a long, painful moment. "Because I wasn't the person you needed me to be."

The silence stretched out, and in that moment, I wasn't sure if I was angrier with him for leaving or for coming back.

His words lingered in the smoke-filled air like a challenge I wasn't ready to confront. I could feel the pulse of something hot and angry spreading through my chest, not from the fire but from the weight of his presence. Rafe Quinn, standing there like he'd just dropped out of the past, leaving behind his ghost with the ashes of this place.

"You weren't the person I needed you to be either," I said, my voice raw, a little sharper than I intended, though it wasn't like he hadn't earned it. "You disappeared. Just like that. You didn't even say goodbye. You didn't even leave a note."

The air between us crackled. I could see the muscles in his jaw tense, the flicker of something too complicated to name in his eyes. But he didn't flinch, didn't apologize. That was Rafe. Always so sure of himself. Too sure of himself.

"I didn't disappear, Allie," he said, his voice lower now, almost a growl. "I left because I needed to figure out who I was. I couldn't be here... not like that. And you, you didn't need someone who was still trying to figure it all out."

"Maybe I didn't need you at all," I muttered, pushing past him. The words came out before I could stop them, thick and cutting, but in that moment, I meant them. I didn't need anyone—least of all him. Not now, not after everything.

I moved deeper into the wreckage, dodging a shelf that had collapsed under the weight of its own age. The smell of burned paper and varnish filled my nostrils, making my eyes water, but I kept going. I had to. I had to prove to myself that I could still hold it all together, even if the world around me was falling apart.

"Look, I didn't come here for this," I heard Rafe's voice again, closer now, his footsteps echoing off the charred floorboards. "I came to make sure the shop wasn't a total loss. To make sure you're okay."

I scoffed and turned back to face him, the words spilling out before I could even think. "I'm fine. What, you think I'm going to break down now, after all this?" My hands clenched into fists at my sides. "Well, guess what? I'm not. You should've stayed gone, Rafe. This... this place is mine now. And you have no claim on it."

He studied me for a long moment, his eyes tracing every line of tension in my face, the way I was standing like a wall between him and the remnants of the store. A wall he couldn't break down. "I didn't want to be the one who came back," he said, his voice a little softer now, like he was finally talking to the person he remembered instead of the one standing before him. "But I didn't think I'd find you here, trying to fix things on your own."

"I'm not fixing anything," I snapped, too quickly. "I'm just dealing with it. And I don't need you to tell me how to handle it. I've been doing fine without you."

Rafe looked at me like he wanted to argue, to keep pushing, but then something in his posture shifted, as if he realized the futility of it. His eyes softened, just for a moment, before he turned away, surveying the damage. "You're not alone in this, Allie," he said quietly, almost to himself.

I wanted to laugh. I wanted to rip his words apart, throw them back at him like the shards of glass on the floor. But I didn't. Instead, I turned and walked toward the back of the store, my boots heavy against the creaking floorboards. I was so sick of hearing that line. So tired of the same empty promises wrapped up in a bow.

But something gnawed at me, something deeper than my anger. His words, his presence, the fact that he hadn't just walked away like he had before—it wasn't sitting right with me. Not because it was a relief, but because I wasn't sure how to handle it. I didn't know how to handle him.

I stopped when I reached the back counter, a piece of oak that had once held my father's best treasures. It was scorched, the top split from the heat, the edges curling like burned paper. My hand hovered over the remnants of a glass display, the last piece of my father's legacy I could salvage. My heart thudded painfully in my chest as I tried to focus on something, anything, that would keep me from falling apart.

"You know," Rafe said behind me, his voice close again, "there's no reason for you to do this alone."

I didn't turn around. I couldn't. "How many times do I have to tell you?" I said, my voice tight. "I don't want your help. Not now, not ever."

He sighed, a deep, exasperated sound that made me feel like I was the one who was lost. "I get it," he muttered, almost too quietly for me to hear. "I do. But you can't just carry this on your own forever, Allie."

I felt the words settle over me like a weight, but I refused to acknowledge them. I was fine. I didn't need him. I didn't need anyone.

But then the air shifted, and it wasn't the usual smothering weight of smoke or the charred dust in the air. It was something else—something cold, something wrong.

"Do you hear that?" I whispered, my breath catching in my throat. My eyes darted to the door at the front of the shop, and the feeling hit me like a punch to the gut.

Rafe's eyes flicked to the door, and his posture immediately went rigid. Without saying a word, he moved, his footsteps silent but swift as he crossed the room toward the front.

My heart started to race, panic flooding my veins as I followed him. I knew something was wrong.

The door crashed open just as we reached it.

Chapter 2: Smoke and Mirrors

I wasn't sure what I'd expected when I stepped into the diner that morning—maybe a moment of clarity, a sharp answer to the swirl of questions that had been gnawing at me for days—but it certainly wasn't this. The bell over the door jingled as I entered, the familiar scent of fried eggs and sizzling bacon curling into my nose, mixing with the faintest hint of stale coffee. The chatter from the few regulars—farmers, truckers, the occasional tourist—seemed to pause, like they could feel the storm brewing in the air. My boots clicked against the floor, each step carrying the weight of all the memories I'd tried so hard to bury.

Rafe Quinn sat at the counter, of course, looking like he belonged there, even though he hadn't set foot in this town in years. The place hadn't changed, but he had. Time had carved a few lines into his face, the skin darker now from years in places I couldn't even imagine, and his shoulders were broader, more solid than I remembered. His dark hair, always a little too long, was now streaked with silver, the kind of silver that looked like it had been earned, not just passed down with age. He wore that damn leather jacket, the same one that made him look like trouble when he was twenty, and somehow, it fit him even more now.

He didn't even look up when I approached, like he'd known I was coming. Maybe he had—he always had this uncanny ability to know when I was near, even when I was trying my best to avoid him.

"Quinn," I said, my voice a little sharper than I intended. His name felt like a blade on my tongue. "I didn't expect to see you here."

That got his attention. His head tilted slightly, just enough for me to catch the glimmer of something in his eyes—something too dark to name. A moment of recognition, maybe, or just a flicker of curiosity. He set his coffee cup down, slowly, deliberately, and turned on the stool to face me. The movement was fluid, the kind of grace that came from years of doing things in a way that didn't let the world know just how much you had to fight to make it look easy.

"Didn't think you'd come here either," he said, his voice low, like it had been dragged through some hard places. He studied me, really looked at me, as if he was seeing the girl he once knew and the woman I'd become, all in the same breath. It unsettled me more than I cared to admit.

"Why did you come back?" I blurted, the question slipping out before I could think better of it. "After all this time, after everything, why now? What's the point of showing up if you're just going to leave again?"

He shrugged, a smooth, almost effortless motion that made the tension in the room tighten. "Sometimes things aren't what they seem."

I didn't know what that meant, but I could feel the sharp edge in his words, like he was cutting through the space between us and revealing something neither of us were ready to confront. I took a breath, fighting the urge to punch the counter, to do something—anything—that would make him stop looking at me like that. Like he knew what I was thinking, like he could see all the things I kept hidden.

"Is that supposed to make sense?" I said, the words a little too bitter. "That's your answer?"

He didn't flinch, didn't move a muscle. He just looked at me, those dark eyes boring into mine like they could see right through all the walls I'd built around myself. "No," he said, his voice steady. "It's not an answer. It's a question."

I blinked, thrown off by the way he said it. A question. But I didn't have time to process it before he spoke again, his gaze softening just a fraction. "I didn't come back for you, Ellie. I didn't come back for anyone. But things aren't always as simple as they look."

The diner felt suddenly smaller, the air heavier. The clink of silverware against plates, the low hum of the jukebox in the corner—all of it faded into the background, leaving just the two of us, caught in the middle of something we couldn't quite define. I wanted to scream at him, to ask him why he'd left in the first place, why he'd disappeared without a word, why he'd never looked back. But the words caught in my throat, tangled up in everything I didn't know how to say.

"So what now?" I finally asked, my voice rough. "You just show up, drop a cryptic line, and expect me to be okay with it?"

His lips quirked, just a hint of a smile, but it didn't reach his eyes. "I don't expect anything, Ellie. Not from you, not from anyone."

I could feel the walls of the diner pressing in around me, the smoke from the kitchen mixing with the tension in the air. The heat from his body, the warmth of his presence, made everything feel too real, too close. My heart hammered in my chest, but I didn't look away. Not this time. Not when the question he had thrown at me was still hanging there, waiting for an answer.

"Well, I'm not playing your game," I said, but even I could hear the lie in my voice. Because somewhere deep down, I knew that this wasn't over. That no matter how hard I tried to walk away from him, he would always be there, like smoke and mirrors—faint, elusive, impossible to catch—but always lingering in the air around me.

It felt like the town itself was holding its breath, waiting for something—anything—to break the uneasy silence that had descended ever since Rafe Quinn showed up. Every time I walked down the main street, there was that flicker of recognition from people I'd known my whole life, but their gazes always lingered just a second too long, shifting uncomfortably when I caught them watching. It was the same at the grocery store, with the butcher pretending not to notice Rafe as he grabbed a cart. Even old Mrs. Wilkins, the sweetest woman in town, barely spared me a glance, her lips pressed tight like she was afraid I might burst into flames at any moment.

It was all too much. Too much for a place that had spent years pretending the past was just a shadow we could ignore. But shadows had a way of crawling back into the light when you least expected it.

I couldn't escape the constant reminder of him. And the worst part? He hadn't even said goodbye when he left. He just vanished. Like smoke. I'd spent half my childhood chasing him, begging him to stay, to not go off to places that were a world away from this tiny town. The day he left, I'd told him I hated him. I hadn't meant it, of course, but the words had slipped out, fueled by a mixture of heartbreak and confusion.

But it didn't matter. He had still walked away.

The day after our conversation at the diner, I took the long way around to the post office, avoiding the small crowd gathered at the café. The sunlight was bright, almost too bright for a fall morning. It painted the streets in shades of amber and gold, giving the whole town an illusion of warmth that didn't quite reach my skin. My mind, however, was sharp, picking apart the fragments of our conversation, trying to make sense of something that had never made sense to begin with.

I heard the crunch of gravel underfoot, followed by the familiar sound of Rafe's voice. It made my stomach drop.

"Ellie."

I stopped in my tracks, not sure what I was more annoyed by: the fact that I couldn't outrun him or the fact that I still cared whether he was following me.

I didn't turn around. "What is it, Quinn?"

"You're avoiding me," he said, his voice too calm. It made my skin itch.

"I'm not avoiding you," I shot back, my heart hammering in my chest as I fought to keep my pace steady. "I'm just... busy."

It was a lie, but it sounded convincing enough.

"You know, it's funny," he continued, his voice sliding closer, teasing. "For someone so determined to get away from me, you sure do keep finding ways to run into me."

My fingers tightened around the strap of my purse. He had a way of making me feel like I was on the edge of something dangerous, something that could turn everything upside down. Maybe that was why I hated him so much. Or maybe it was because I couldn't stop thinking about him. Even now, I could feel the weight of his presence, the heat of his gaze lingering behind me like a storm waiting to break.

I couldn't resist the temptation to turn around. "What is it you want, Rafe?"

He was closer now, close enough that I could feel the heat of his body, the scent of fresh soap and something earthy that must have been his cologne—or maybe it was just him, a blend of memories and things I couldn't forget. He stood there, his hands shoved in his pockets, his jaw tight, like he was ready to break something.

"I just want to talk," he said, but his voice was different now, softer, as though he were trying to tread carefully. It made the hair on the back of my neck stand up. I didn't like this version of him. The one that didn't have an answer to the questions I kept asking, but still made it sound like he did.

"Talk?" I scoffed. "About what?"

He didn't respond right away. Instead, he stepped closer, as though the distance between us had become some kind of invisible barrier he was eager to breach. "About what happened. About why I left. About how I didn't mean to hurt you."

The words fell between us like stones in a pond, and for a moment, everything was still. I wanted to be angry, to tell him I didn't care, that he had no right to explain himself after all this time. But the way he said it, the way his eyes softened for just a split second—it was enough to make the ground feel a little less solid under my feet.

"You didn't mean to hurt me?" I repeated, incredulous. "Rafe, you broke my heart. You disappeared without a word. You think saying you didn't mean to hurt me makes that okay?"

He winced, but it was so fleeting that I almost missed it. "I never wanted to hurt you, Ellie. I left because I had to. I thought I was doing what was best for you."

"Best for me?" I couldn't help the laugh that escaped me, a bitter sound that tasted like ash. "You thought abandoning me was what was best for me?"

Rafe stepped back, his expression hardening again. "I wasn't the person you needed me to be. I wasn't the person I thought I was, either." He paused, his eyes flashing with something I couldn't quite read. "But maybe that's why I came back."

The weight of his words hung in the air between us, heavy and charged. I wanted to yell, to scream at him that I didn't need him, that I had built a life without him and I was fine. But in the silence that stretched between us, there was a small, dangerous part of me that wanted to know the rest of the story. To understand why he was here, standing in front of me, trying to explain the impossible.

But I didn't know if I was ready for the truth.

I turned away from him, but the pull was too strong, like gravity had shifted and I couldn't resist it, no matter how much I wanted to. He took one step forward, closing the gap between us just enough that I could feel his breath, warm and uneven against the back of my neck.

"You really think it's that simple, don't you?" he asked, his voice lowering. "You think I just left and never looked back? Like it was all easy for me?"

I didn't answer, my lips pressing tight together, fighting the words that threatened to spill out. "You left," I managed, the simple truth hanging in the air like a fog. "You don't get to just come back and play the martyr."

He didn't flinch, didn't even look away. "I'm not asking for forgiveness, Ellie. I'm not even asking you to understand." He was closer now, just inches from me, and I had to force myself not to step back. "But you want me to explain myself like it's going to change anything. Well, it's not."

I opened my mouth to argue, to scream that it was going to change something, that I needed answers, but the words stuck in my throat, tangled up in the mess of emotions I'd buried for so long.

Instead, I stared at him, all the years of resentment and confusion swirling in my chest like a storm. "Then why come back?" I finally asked, quieter now, but no less intense. "Why come back to a place where you know nothing's the same anymore? Why come back to me?"

"Because I didn't know where else to go." His words were raw, almost too much for me to take. "I've made a mess of everything, Ellie. I don't expect you to fix it. But I can't undo what's been done. I can only show up and hope you'll let me explain."

He paused, letting that last sentence sink in. There was a vulnerability in his tone, something I hadn't heard in years, and it made my heart ache.

But no. I couldn't let him do this to me again. I couldn't be the fool who let him waltz back in like everything was fine. Like we could just pick up where we left off.

"You think showing up is enough?" I said, biting the words out as if they were made of glass. "You think that's going to undo all the damage you've done?"

Rafe's expression flickered, just for a moment, but it was enough to make me second-guess myself. The hardness that had been there before—the indifference, the anger—dissolved into something softer, something almost human. And damn it, I hated that I noticed it. I hated that it made me want to listen.

"You don't get it, do you?" he said, his voice lower now, rough around the edges. "I'm not asking you to forget, or to forgive me. But the world isn't black and white, Ellie. Sometimes people do things they think are right in the moment, only to realize later they were wrong. Sometimes people leave to protect others, even if it means breaking their own heart."

"Protect me?" I couldn't help the laugh that burst out, a laugh that felt more like a sob caught in my throat. "From what? What could you possibly protect me from, Rafe? The only thing you've ever protected me from is you."

He winced, and for the first time since I'd seen him again, I saw the cracks in the facade he'd built. His eyes, dark with memories and guilt, softened just a fraction. "I never meant to hurt you, Ellie. Never. But sometimes we do the worst things with the best of intentions."

"Great," I snapped, shaking my head. "So now you want me to buy into this whole martyr act? Is that it? You're here because you feel guilty?"

Rafe took a deep breath, like he was holding back something, his fists tightening at his sides. "It's not about guilt, Ellie. It's about trying to make things right. Trying to figure out what's left after everything's gone to hell."

I didn't know what I expected—maybe anger, maybe more of the indifference that had surrounded him for years—but it certainly wasn't this.

I took a step back, shaking my head. "You can't just waltz in and expect everything to fall into place. There's no 'making things right' after this. You don't get to undo the past just because it suits you now."

Rafe's face hardened, and for a moment, I thought he might walk away, might retreat like he always had, but he didn't. Instead, he took another step toward me, his jaw clenched, his eyes never leaving mine.

"Then what do you want from me, Ellie?" he asked, his voice raw with frustration. "What am I supposed to do? How do I make up for something that can't be fixed? You think I've forgotten what I left behind? You think I don't live with that every damn day?"

I opened my mouth, ready to deliver a cutting response, but the words stuck in my throat. The truth was, I didn't know what I wanted from him anymore. I didn't know what he could do that would fix what had been broken between us.

For the first time, I felt the weight of my own uncertainty. It was like a door had opened in front of me, and behind it was a future I wasn't sure I was ready to face.

"Maybe I'm not here to fix things, Ellie," he said, his voice low, steady. "Maybe I'm just here to give you a choice."

The air between us thickened, and I suddenly felt like I was standing on the edge of something—something I wasn't sure I was ready to fall into.

"Choice?" I echoed, my voice barely above a whisper.

Rafe nodded slowly, his eyes never leaving mine. "Yeah. A choice. To either keep running from this... or face it."

The words hung in the air, thick with possibility, with something I couldn't quite name, and for the first time in years, I wondered if I was strong enough to choose.

Before I could speak, the sound of a car screeching to a halt nearby sliced through the tension. I turned just in time to see a familiar face step out of a black SUV—someone I never expected to see. Someone who could change everything.

Chapter 3: Ashes of the Past

The air outside was heavy with the smell of charred wood, a scent that clung to the back of my throat like a secret I wasn't quite ready to face. I stood in front of my dad's store, watching as the fire trucks packed up their hoses and began to disperse, the flickering orange lights fading into the night. The damage was done. Another fire, another ruin in the heart of the town. Only this time, it wasn't my dad's fault. No, this time, it was a little too familiar, a little too purposeful to be an accident.

I'd seen that look in my dad's eyes before. The one where his jaw tightened and his hands clenched into fists at his sides. But now, as I stood there in the aftermath, it wasn't just the charred remains of his livelihood he was staring at. It was the ghost of something darker, something older. I knew the stories—the ones about the fire years ago, the one that took down the old mill, along with half the town's savings and all of its trust. The one that burned too hot, too fast, and left more than just ash behind.

And then there was Rafe Quinn.

The name alone stirred something in the pit of my stomach. I hadn't seen him in years, but that didn't mean I hadn't heard about him. Rafe Quinn—the boy who had burned bridges and buildings alike. The one who'd survived the fire of the mill, the one everyone had written off as a bad memory, a casualty of his own recklessness. But here he was, standing at the edge of the ruins, his eyes locked on the burned-out remains as if he were searching for something in the blackened mess.

I didn't plan on going up to him. In fact, I had every intention of doing what my dad told me to do and staying far, far away from the man. But something about the way he stood there, the stillness of him, made it impossible to ignore. And when I caught his gaze, sharp and unblinking, there was no turning back.

"Why?" I didn't even know what the word meant when it left my mouth, but it felt right. I wasn't asking why he was here; I already knew that. I was asking why he cared. Why he was still poking around in a town that had turned its back on him, a town that had turned its back on everyone who had anything to do with the mill fire.

His lips curled into something like a smile, but it wasn't a smile. It was a mask, a brittle piece of armor that didn't quite hold up against the weight of whatever he was carrying inside.

"You've got a lot of questions, don't you, Harper?" His voice was low, rough around the edges, like he hadn't used it in a while. Like he was still testing the waters to see if the world would listen.

"I'm just trying to figure out why you're back," I said, stepping closer, my shoes crunching on the gravel as I moved toward him. "After all these years, after everything that happened, why now?"

He tilted his head, studying me for a long moment. I could feel the heat from the smoldering remains of the fire, but it wasn't the only thing making me sweat. The way his eyes tracked me felt invasive, like he could see straight through me, through all the walls I'd built up around myself. The walls I'd spent years reinforcing.

"Guess I'm not as easy to get rid of as you thought," he said, his words carrying a note of amusement that didn't quite match the intensity in his eyes.

"You never were," I muttered under my breath. The words came out before I could stop them. I didn't know what it was about him, but every time I saw him, I was reminded of how small and confined my life had gotten since he'd left. Maybe it was the way he moved, with that fluidity, like he didn't have a care in the world, like he didn't know what it was to be stuck in a place like this.

He smirked. "Still bitter, Harper? You should let it go. That fire was years ago."

"I haven't forgotten," I shot back, though I couldn't tell if I was talking about the mill fire or the way he'd walked out of my life without a word.

His face flickered with something I couldn't read, something raw, before he looked back at the fire. "Neither have I."

I couldn't keep standing there, letting him control the conversation. "You know, this isn't the first fire in this town," I said, my voice colder now, my resolve stiffening. "The mill fire wasn't the last. You can't tell me this is all some coincidence. You're back for a reason, and I want to know what it is."

Rafe didn't move for a long time, didn't even blink. And then, with a shift in his posture, he finally spoke. "Maybe I came back to finish what I started."

I felt the ground shift under my feet. The words hit me like a punch in the stomach. The memories, the questions, the mystery of it all—suddenly, it wasn't just a ghost from the past anymore. It was something real, something dangerous. And I was standing right in the middle of it.

"Finish what you started?" I whispered, my pulse quickening. "What does that even mean, Rafe?"

His gaze never wavered. "It means I'm not done with this town. Not by a long shot."

And then, just like that, he turned and walked away, leaving me standing in the ashes of the past, not sure what had just happened—but knowing for sure that everything had just changed.

The sun had barely begun its descent when I trudged up the narrow staircase to my apartment, the heavy weight of the night pressing in from all sides. I should've been used to this town by now—the thick, suffocating heat that clung to every corner, the way everyone seemed to have a story about someone else's mistakes. But something about tonight felt different, sharper. Rafe Quinn had a way of making everything feel ten times heavier, as if the very air around him had more substance than it was meant to.

I kicked the door shut behind me with a thud and dropped my bag on the floor, my fingers running through my hair as I tried to shake off the lingering feeling of being watched. It wasn't just Rafe. No, there was something else here, a familiar twinge of unease that seemed to echo from the depths of my own memories. I wasn't sure what it was—something gnawing at the back of my mind, too elusive to name, but too persistent to ignore.

I went straight to the kitchen, the fluorescent lights flickering as I opened the fridge, grabbed a bottle of water, and unscrewed the cap. The cool liquid felt like an anchor, steadying my racing thoughts. I needed to think. I couldn't let myself get swept up in whatever this was, whatever Rafe Quinn was dredging up.

The man had a way of sticking with you, like gum on the bottom of your shoe. He'd walked out of this town with no explanation, no apology, leaving behind nothing but whispers and bad blood. And yet, now here he was, looking at the remnants of another fire as though he were some kind of expert in destruction. Was he back to finish what he started? Was he trying to burn this town to the ground—again?

I shook my head, trying to clear the fog that clouded my thoughts.

Rafe Quinn was a mystery, and I wasn't the type of person to go looking for answers in places I didn't belong. My dad had made that perfectly clear. "Stay away from him," he'd warned, his voice rough with years of regret. "He's trouble."

But trouble had a magnetic pull, didn't it? And if I was being honest, I'd never been particularly good at listening to my father's warnings—especially not when they involved Rafe.

I closed the fridge door with a little more force than necessary, the sound reverberating through the small kitchen. That's when I noticed it—the faint scratching noise coming from the other side of the room, just beyond the kitchen. It was subtle, almost like the sound of nails dragging across wood. I froze, every muscle in my body tensing.

The scratching grew louder, more persistent. I wasn't sure if I was imagining it, but the hairs on the back of my neck stood on end. Slowly, I turned around, half-expecting to find a cat clawing at the door or something equally mundane. But when I looked, there was nothing.

Then the air changed. It wasn't just the quiet. No, it was something else. A shift in the space around me, like the room itself was holding its breath. My heart began to pound in my chest, each beat echoing too loudly in my ears.

I took a step toward the hallway, my pulse quickening with each soft creak of the floorboards beneath my feet.

And then I saw it.

A shadow in the corner of the room, stretching long and thin across the floor. But it wasn't just any shadow. It was familiar—too familiar—and for a moment, I couldn't breathe. There, standing in the doorway, half hidden in the darkness, was Rafe. His eyes gleamed in the dim light, the same haunted intensity I'd seen earlier at the fire site.

I didn't know whether to scream, laugh, or punch him in the face. So instead, I just stared. "You've got a lot of nerve," I finally managed to croak out, my voice shaking slightly.

"Do I?" He stepped forward, his boots making a soft noise on the floor as he crossed the threshold into my apartment. "I thought you were the one who was curious."

"Curious?" I said, my eyebrows shooting up. "Curious about what, exactly? How you plan to ruin everything again?"

He didn't flinch. Instead, he leaned against the doorframe with a nonchalance that made me want to throw something at his head.

"No. Curious about why you're so afraid of what's coming. Everyone else in this town is. You just haven't figured out why yet."

"I don't know what you're talking about," I snapped, but the words didn't carry the weight I'd hoped. I was trying to act like I wasn't rattled, trying to hold onto the threads of control, but it was hard when everything felt like it was slipping through my fingers.

He studied me for a long moment, as if he could see right through the layers I'd wrapped around myself. "You're not stupid, Harper. You know exactly what I'm talking about. This fire? It's not an accident. It's just a warning."

"A warning?" The words were bitter on my tongue. "A warning for who? You? Me? Or is this just your idea of making a grand reentrance?"

Rafe's eyes darkened, and for a moment, the man who stood before me seemed less like the careless boy who'd left and more like someone who had seen things he wasn't supposed to see. "For everyone. This town's been living on borrowed time, and you all know it."

I couldn't even begin to process what he was saying. It was like he was speaking in riddles, and I was too tired to try and decipher them.

"I don't need your warnings," I said, trying to regain some composure. "You should leave before things get any worse."

He smiled, a small, almost imperceptible curve of his lips. "Too late for that."

And just like that, he was gone, slipping back into the night like a shadow fading before the dawn. But his words lingered, swirling in the space he'd left behind. This wasn't just about the fire. It was about something bigger—something that, for once, didn't have an easy answer.

I spent the next day in a haze. It wasn't just the lack of sleep that made my eyes heavy, or the constant buzz of the town's gossip that seemed to permeate every conversation. No, it was Rafe's last words, echoing in my mind like an ominous drumbeat. "Too late for that." It didn't matter that I had no idea what he meant—those words felt like a warning, something I couldn't ignore even if I tried.

I found myself walking to my dad's store that afternoon, my feet moving with a purpose I couldn't quite explain. The store wasn't much to look at—just a dusty old building wedged between two newer, slicker shops that seemed out of place in a town like this. But it was my dad's, and it had been here long before any of those fancier storefronts had gone up. That counted for something, even if most of the people around here had forgotten it.

The door creaked as I pushed it open, the familiar scent of leather and wood polish hitting me like a blanket. My dad was behind the counter, as usual, his back to the door as he rearranged the tools he sold to farmers, builders, anyone who still knew what it was like to do work with their hands. It was his world, and I didn't expect anything to shake it.

But then again, Rafe Quinn had a way of shaking everything.

"Hey," I said, trying to sound casual. "How's the store?"

Dad didn't turn around. "Not much business today," he muttered. "Too hot for anyone to be out shopping. Not like back in the day."

I leaned against the counter, my eyes scanning the shelves. "You talked to Rafe lately?"

At the mention of his name, Dad stiffened, his hands pausing mid-motion. Slowly, he set the tool down, turning to face me. His eyes, usually so calm, flickered with something I couldn't quite place—anger, fear, maybe a bit of both.

"Why are you asking about him?" he asked, his voice low.

"I saw him yesterday," I said, my words tumbling out before I could stop them. "He's been hanging around the fire site. He's...

acting strange, Dad. He's not just back for some nostalgia trip. There's something going on."

Dad's face hardened, and for a long time, he didn't say anything. His hands clenched around the edge of the counter, his knuckles turning white.

"He's trouble," he finally said, his voice hoarse. "Always has been."

"Is that all you're going to say?" I pressed, trying not to let the frustration creep into my voice. "He's been gone for years, and now he's back, poking around like nothing happened. You know what he's capable of. Don't tell me you're not worried."

Dad sighed and ran a hand through his graying hair. "I warned you before. Rafe Quinn isn't someone you get involved with, Harper. You have no idea what he's really capable of. He was never the same after the fire. And neither was this town."

The words hung in the air like smoke, thick and suffocating. I wanted to press him for more, to demand that he tell me everything he knew, but something in his expression stopped me. Whatever had happened all those years ago, whatever Rafe had done to this town—it was a wound Dad had never let heal.

I stepped away from the counter, pacing the small space. "You're not giving me anything here. I need to know what's going on, Dad. If Rafe's back, then something bigger is happening. Something we can't ignore."

He looked up at me, his face softening just a fraction. "There's nothing you can do, Harper. It's too late to fix what's been broken."

But I wasn't listening anymore. I couldn't. My mind was already elsewhere—back on Rafe, back to those eyes of his, that look that spoke of things long buried. I wasn't going to sit by and let whatever was happening pass me by. If my dad wouldn't help, then I'd have to figure this out on my own.

I left the store in a hurry, the door slamming shut behind me as I stepped out into the heat of the afternoon. The town felt quieter than usual, the sound of distant conversations muffled by the weight of the air. I headed straight to the edge of town, to the charred remains of the last fire. The place had been roped off by the fire department, but there was still something unsettling about the sight of it. The blackened earth, the twisted metal, the ghost of what had been—there was something off about all of it.

I didn't expect to find anything, but my gut told me I wasn't alone. The hairs on the back of my neck prickled as I moved closer to the center of the wreckage. And then I saw him.

Rafe Quinn, standing just beyond the ruins, his hands in his pockets, staring out at the devastation like it was a canvas and he was deciding what to paint next. His back was to me, but I knew he felt my presence the moment I stepped into the open.

"Not planning on burning anything else, are you?" I called out, the words slipping out before I could stop them. I didn't know why I'd said it, or why my heart had started to race the moment I saw him. Maybe I was just sick of pretending I wasn't curious, sick of pretending this wasn't something I needed to figure out.

He turned slowly, a half-smile playing at the corners of his lips. "If I was, I wouldn't be standing here, would I?"

"You always have a way of being cryptic," I said, stepping closer, trying to ignore the way my pulse quickened with each step. "Why are you here, Rafe? You're not just here for a stroll down memory lane. What's going on?"

His smile faded, replaced by that same dark look I'd seen before. "You should stop asking questions you don't want answers to, Harper."

My throat tightened. "And if I don't?"

Rafe's eyes glinted, and for the first time, I saw something darker in them than I had ever expected. "Then you'll find out the hard way."

Chapter 4: Beneath the Surface

The sound of children's laughter filled the air as I stood in the doorway of the school's main entrance, watching the chaos unfold. A fire drill was nothing new. Every month, like clockwork, the school would empty its hallways and classrooms, sending children in a noisy procession toward the playground. There were always the same handful of kids who would argue about who was first, who was last, and who had the most impressive exit form. But today, something felt different. It was the way Rafe moved through the crowd, his tall frame cutting a path through the children, his presence as commanding as it was unnoticed.

I didn't expect him to show up at all. Sure, he was on the team, but I hadn't seen him for a few weeks. He'd been on some other assignment, or maybe he'd just been avoiding me. Either way, I'd gotten used to the quiet absence of his voice, the weight of his eyes, always hovering at the edges of my thoughts. The last thing I expected was to see him here, but there he was, gliding across the tarmac like a man with a purpose. It was unsettling, how easily he belonged in a place like this, in a crowd of wide-eyed children and impatient teachers.

My stomach tightened. It was the same reaction I had whenever I thought about him—tight and twisted. I wasn't sure when the knot had appeared, or why, but I had learned to ignore it. Until now, when I had no choice but to watch him move through the drill, seemingly without breaking a sweat.

The principal, Mrs. Marshall, called for the last group of children to line up as I walked toward the center of the playground, ready to usher them back into the building. I saw Rafe across the yard, bending down to speak with one of the little girls who had stopped in the middle of the field, looking lost. His hand was on her shoulder, steady and reassuring, and his voice was low, smooth like a promise.

I wasn't sure what was more surprising—the fact that he had taken the time to talk to her so gently or the fact that it was so effortless for him. It had been a long time since I'd seen anyone handle a child like that, with so much patience, so much care. My father was the same way, the same calm demeanor, the same self-assurance in the face of chaos. But Rafe wasn't my father. He was something else entirely, something I still couldn't quite figure out.

I made my way toward the group, making sure the kids were returning to their classrooms in an orderly fashion. The last thing I wanted was to get caught up in the tension that seemed to hang between us, but somehow, there I was, pulling myself toward him. It was as though some invisible force had drawn me in, no matter how hard I tried to stay away.

"Everything okay here?" I asked, pretending not to notice the way my voice faltered slightly. He straightened up, glancing at me for a fraction of a second before his gaze swept back to the kids, making sure they were all accounted for.

"Yeah, everything's fine," he said, his voice low, almost distracted. I hated how easy it was for him to sound so in control, so unruffled. It was a stark contrast to my own sudden burst of nerves, the way my heart fluttered whenever I was near him. I swallowed hard, forcing myself to focus on the task at hand. The drill was nearly over, and I could almost taste the relief in the air.

"Thanks for stepping in," I added, trying to make the words sound casual. It was ridiculous to feel this way—like a student trying to get approval from a teacher—but there it was, that creeping discomfort.

"Of course," he replied with a slight smile. It was small, barely noticeable, but I caught it. And for some reason, it made my stomach turn even more. There was something behind that smile, something I couldn't quite decipher. I wasn't sure I wanted to.

Rafe turned back toward the kids, his movements easy and fluid, like he had done this a thousand times before. Maybe he had. I knew enough about him to understand that he had a history with firefighting, a history that no one liked to talk about. Not at the station. Not in public. It wasn't until I overheard my father and another firefighter discussing it one afternoon that I even had a glimpse of what Rafe had been through. He'd seen things, things that I couldn't even begin to imagine.

I forced myself to look away, to focus on the kids, on the routine that had become so familiar to me. But the memory of that conversation lingered like smoke in the back of my mind. It was like one of those half-formed thoughts you couldn't shake, no matter how hard you tried. My father had said Rafe had been through a fire. But it wasn't just any fire. It was one of those fires that change you, that break something inside you and make you see the world through a different lens. It was the kind of fire that left scars, whether you could see them or not.

Rafe's voice broke through my thoughts as he called out to the last few children, guiding them toward the entrance. His tone was firm but kind, the kind of voice you trusted when you were lost, when you needed someone to lead you out of the smoke. It was the voice of a man who had lived through things that would have broken most people, but somehow, it had only made him stronger.

I couldn't help but watch him as he worked. There was something magnetic about him, something that pulled at me even when I didn't want it to. It wasn't just his presence; it was the way he moved, the way he seemed to be in complete control of every situation. It was the calm in the middle of the storm.

I shook my head, trying to clear it. I couldn't get caught up in whatever this was. I had a job to do. The kids needed me. And

Rafe... well, Rafe was just a man. Another firefighter with a past, a past I didn't need to understand.

The morning after the fire drill, I found myself at the local coffee shop, staring into the dark swirl of my latte like it could provide me some answers. The usual hum of early-morning chatter filled the air, but it felt muffled, like the world outside was happening in a separate universe. My mind was firmly anchored on one thing: Rafe. There was something about the way he had been with those kids—something unsettling in how naturally he slipped into that role. A firefighter's hands, rough from the work of saving lives, holding a trembling child so gently. It was like he could carve out softness in the hardest parts of his day.

I knew better than to fall for the quiet allure of someone who carried more weight than they let on. It was the same lesson my dad had taught me my entire life. "People show you what they want you to see," he'd say. "You never really know what's beneath the surface." It was advice I'd lived by, both in my work and my personal life. But when it came to Rafe, I couldn't seem to shake the feeling that there was something hidden underneath that smooth surface. And as much as I wanted to ignore it, that something gnawed at me.

"Coffee looks suspiciously lonely over there." The voice was familiar, so familiar that it sent an involuntary shiver down my spine. I didn't have to look up to know it was him.

Rafe slid into the seat across from me without waiting for an invitation. His scent—the earthy, woodsy smell of smoke and something more—was like a balm I didn't know I needed, and it settled over me like an unexpected comfort. His hair, messy in the way only a man who didn't care could pull off, framed his face in a way that made him look like he'd stepped out of some rugged magazine spread. I fought the urge to roll my eyes. He had that effect on people—on me, in particular.

"You know, you're an awful stalker," I said, trying to keep the irritation out of my voice, though I was secretly glad he was here. It was all complicated, this push-pull I'd been feeling every time I saw him.

"I prefer 'persistent,'" he replied, leaning back casually in the chair as if this were the most natural thing in the world. "Persistent with a touch of grace. I'm like a cat that just keeps coming back."

I smirked despite myself. "You're more like a dog with a bone. Stubborn, relentless."

He chuckled, that low, rumbling sound that could send ripples through a room even when it was almost imperceptible. It was disarming, like a quiet storm you didn't realize you were caught in until it was already too late. "I'm going to take that as a compliment."

"Don't," I said, lifting my mug in a mock salute. "The dog comparison? It's all about loyalty and slobber. Not really my thing."

"Fair enough," he said, eyes twinkling. But then, just like that, the smile softened, and for the first time in our conversation, something flickered behind his eyes—something darker, maybe even reluctant. "You seemed... different yesterday. During the drill. Is everything okay?"

I froze, my fingers tight around the handle of my mug. Rafe had always been a little too observant for my liking. He noticed things that most people didn't, and I hated how it made me feel exposed. "I'm fine," I said quickly, a little too quickly. "It was just a drill. Kids are always chaotic."

"Right," he said, his voice quiet as if weighing my words. "I saw you with them. You're good with them. You didn't seem shaken at all."

I shrugged, trying to dismiss it. "I've done it a million times. Besides, it's not about me. It's about the kids."

"Still," he pressed, his gaze unyielding. "There's more to it than that. You've got this fire in you, something that drives you. I can see it."

I could feel the heat in my cheeks, and it wasn't from the coffee. I could never lie to Rafe—not in the way that mattered. He could see through the facades people put up, and God help me, I had a whole arsenal of them. But I wasn't about to crack open that door. Not now, not when I still didn't know if he was someone I could trust.

"I guess that's why they keep me around," I said lightly, but the words felt too heavy. "It's what I do."

He leaned in slightly, his elbows resting on the table, eyes searching mine like he was looking for something he couldn't find. It made me uncomfortable, but I couldn't bring myself to look away. "Maybe," he said slowly, "but I don't think that's all of it. I think there's something more that you're keeping locked away."

I swallowed hard, my pulse ticking in my throat. There was that prickling sensation again, like his words were too close to a truth I didn't want to acknowledge.

I opened my mouth to respond, to shut him down the way I always did, but nothing came out. I wasn't sure why I couldn't get the words out. Maybe it was the way he made everything feel so real, so raw. Or maybe it was because, deep down, I knew he was right.

But then, just as quickly, Rafe seemed to retreat into himself, that quiet intensity in his eyes shifting into something more distant. A shadow flitted across his face, an expression so fleeting that I wasn't sure I'd even seen it. He was good at that—masking what he didn't want to show. A little too good, in fact.

"I should go," he said abruptly, pushing his chair back. "Don't want to keep you from your latte."

I blinked, momentarily stunned by the sudden shift in him. "Rafe—"

"Don't worry about it," he said, standing up and offering me a half-smile. "I'll catch you later, Chief."

And just like that, he was gone. His presence, once so tangible, vanished into the buzz of the coffee shop, leaving me with nothing but the echo of his words and the unsettling feeling that he had seen far too much.

It had been two days since Rafe had slipped out of the coffee shop like a shadow, leaving me to stew in my own thoughts. Since then, everything felt slightly off. The air was thicker, somehow heavier, and I couldn't shake the feeling that something was looming just beyond my reach, waiting for the right moment to make itself known. I hadn't expected Rafe to just disappear like that, to leave me hanging with my own half-formed questions, but that was exactly what he'd done. And I hated it.

I had been keeping busy, of course. The usual things: work, family, the endless cycle of fire safety programs and community outreach. The kind of tasks that were simple, straightforward, and in their own way, comforting. But whenever I tried to focus, my mind would inevitably wander back to him. To that half-smile, the unspoken understanding that passed between us in the moments before he walked away. The way his eyes had searched mine, like he was waiting for me to reveal something—something I didn't want to admit, even to myself.

I was standing at the back of the firehouse when my phone buzzed, pulling me out of my thoughts. The screen lit up with a message from my dad: Rafe's on the call list. Keep your head down.

The words were simple, but they struck me like a cold splash of water. Rafe was on the call list. It wasn't unusual—he was a member of the team, after all—but my dad's words had a weight to them. The "keep your head down" part was never a good sign. It was a warning, plain and simple, and I had learned long ago that when my dad sent messages like this, there was always something lurking beneath the surface. Something he wasn't telling me.

I chewed on my lower lip, staring at the message for a long moment. The idea of getting involved in another one of Rafe's messes—if that's what this was—didn't sit right with me. I wasn't part of the front lines anymore. I had my own role now, running drills, keeping the community safe, making sure people didn't burn their houses down over something as simple as leaving a toaster plugged in overnight. It was a comfortable existence, one I had worked hard to build. The last thing I needed was to get wrapped up in whatever storm was brewing in Rafe's world.

But that nagging feeling, the one that had been with me ever since our conversation in the coffee shop, wouldn't let go. What was Rafe hiding? What had my dad meant by keep your head down?

I couldn't ignore it. Not this time.

I slipped my phone into my pocket and grabbed my jacket, throwing a quick look over my shoulder at the firehouse door before I made my way to the garage. As much as I wanted to avoid this, I had to know what was going on. And if it involved Rafe, well, I wasn't about to let it slip by.

When I reached the truck, I was surprised to find it empty. My heart skipped a beat before I saw the familiar figures of the crew huddled around the table in the back office, discussing the upcoming shift. They were all here, except for one.

Rafe.

I wasn't sure if I felt relieved or disappointed. There was something about him that made the air around him crackle with tension, something that made every moment spent in his presence feel like it was charged with a thousand unspoken things. The absence of that charge left me feeling disoriented.

"Chief." One of the younger firefighters, Ryan, waved me over as he flipped through a set of papers on the table. "We've got a situation. A call just came in. They need backup."

My heart sank. I didn't have to ask what kind of backup they needed. The urgency in Ryan's voice said it all. The call had to be serious. "Where are we heading?" I asked, trying to keep my voice steady.

"Downtown. Big fire. The kind that needs more than just a few hands. We're all going out together."

I didn't need any more details. I had seen enough fires in my life to know when things were bad. And something told me this was one of those times. As I turned to grab my gear, the door creaked open behind me, and I didn't have to look to know who had just entered.

Rafe.

I didn't have time to acknowledge him, not yet, as I pulled on my helmet and checked my equipment. The room seemed to hold its breath as he approached, his footsteps firm and deliberate. His presence was as heavy as it had ever been, but there was something different this time—something that seemed almost... resigned. I didn't know what to make of it.

"You're going?" His voice broke the silence like a thunderclap.

I glanced up, meeting his gaze for the first time since our encounter at the coffee shop. His eyes were intense, unreadable. "Yeah, looks like it."

Rafe didn't say anything for a long moment. He just stood there, watching me. I could feel the weight of his gaze pressing into me, like he was trying to read my mind. It made me uneasy, the way he could always seem to see past whatever mask I was wearing.

"Stay safe," he finally said, his voice softer than I expected.

I nodded, though the words didn't feel quite right. There was too much left unsaid between us. Too many questions I couldn't bring myself to ask. But for some reason, I didn't have the strength to walk away from him just yet, not when the storm was closing in, not when everything felt like it was about to change.

I was about to turn away, to get in the truck and drive off to whatever nightmare awaited us, when the silence was shattered by a shout from the front door.

"Chief!" It was Ryan again, his face pale. "You need to see this."

My stomach dropped as I turned toward the door, instinct kicking in. I didn't know what was happening, but the urgency in Ryan's voice told me we didn't have much time. Rafe followed me as I ran outside, my heart racing in my chest.

When I reached the front of the firehouse, my eyes locked onto the scene unfolding in front of me. The smoke. The flames. And in the distance, a figure I never thought I'd see again.

Rafe's past, it seemed, had finally caught up with him. And now, it was coming for all of us.

Chapter 5: Cinders and Sparks

The firehouse smelled of smoke and sweat, the sharp tang of burned wood lingering in the air like a secret. The walls, stained and cracked from years of heat and turmoil, were a silent witness to the battles fought, both within the flames and the hearts of those who worked here. I could feel the heat even as I stood across from Rafe, the space between us charged with something I couldn't name. I stood still, my fingers brushing the edge of the doorframe as I leaned in slightly. He didn't move.

"You're not answering my question," I said, my voice deliberately even, though inside I was a tempest, waves of confusion crashing against each other. I had asked him about the fire, about the one that had changed everything—the fire that had sent him away without a word, leaving me to sift through ashes, both literal and emotional. But here he was again, standing in front of me as though nothing had happened, his broad shoulders filling the space between us, and that same half-bitter, half-ashamed look in his eyes.

Rafe shifted his weight, the slight motion barely perceptible, but I saw it. I always saw him.

"I told you once, Emma, I don't talk about that. Not to anyone." His voice was gravelly, low. It was the voice of someone who had lived too many secrets. Maybe that's why it sounded familiar, comforting even, in a twisted, broken way.

"Why not? What's so wrong with the truth?" I bit back the words, but they were already slipping from my tongue before I could stop them. Truth. I wanted answers, and he knew that. But every time I thought I might reach something, some crack where I could slip my hand in and pull out the truth, Rafe closed up even tighter, like a safe whose combination was just out of reach.

"I'm not the one who's afraid of the truth, Emma," he said with a crooked smile, one that didn't reach his eyes.

I laughed, but it was a hollow sound, too brittle to be real. "You're right. That's my job, isn't it? To dig, to poke and prod until I find whatever's left of the truth to hold on to. But you, you're just content to let me flounder, aren't you?"

The silence stretched between us, thick like fog, but there was something else there now. Something more than just frustration. I didn't know what it was, not yet. But it was real. He was real.

"I don't want to hurt you, Emma," he said finally, his eyes dark and intense, like the smoldering coals in the bottom of a fireplace. His words were sincere, but there was something underlying them—something that made the hairs on the back of my neck stand up. What was he really saying?

"Then stop pretending I don't exist," I shot back, stepping closer. My chest tightened. I wasn't sure if I was angry or if it was something else entirely. I had spent so long avoiding this moment, trying to push him out of my life, trying to let the past remain in the past. But it didn't work like that. Not with him. Not with Rafe.

His jaw clenched, and for a moment, I thought he might say something else. But instead, he just stood there, staring at me with a mixture of anger and something softer, more confused.

I was about to say something else, something sharp and final, but then he moved, and everything shifted. He took a step closer, so close I could feel his breath against my cheek, warm and familiar. For a second, I couldn't breathe. It was like the air around us thickened, pressed in on me from all sides, until the space between us felt almost unbearable.

"Emma," he whispered my name like a prayer, like a confession.

I should have pulled back. I should have slapped him, told him to get out, that I never wanted to see him again. But I didn't. I stood there, rooted to the spot, as he leaned in just a little more, his hand brushing against mine like it was the most natural thing in the world.

And for a moment—just a brief moment—I let myself believe that maybe, just maybe, things could be different. That maybe we could go back to before everything fell apart. Before the fire.

But then I remembered. I remembered the note. The cryptic words. Ask him about the fire. It was like a bucket of ice water over my head.

"Why did you leave?" The question slipped out before I could stop it, and this time, there was no hiding the desperation in my voice. I needed to know. More than I needed air in my lungs, more than I needed to hold on to the pieces of my pride, I needed to know why Rafe had left without a word, why he had disappeared into the smoke and shadows, leaving me to pick up the pieces.

Rafe's face softened for a split second, but just as quickly, it hardened again, the walls going up around him faster than I could see.

"You wouldn't understand," he muttered, stepping back. His eyes darkened, his hands clenched at his sides, as if he was holding himself together by sheer force of will.

"Try me." My voice was quieter this time, less sure, but the challenge was still there. Because I needed him to try. I needed him to give me something—anything—so that I could stop feeling like I was chasing ghosts.

But instead of answering, Rafe did something I didn't expect. He stepped back again, this time moving to the door. He paused, just for a moment, his hand on the handle.

"I don't think you want the truth, Emma. Not the way it really is."

With that, he was gone, leaving me standing in the firehouse, alone once again, my heart racing in my chest, the unanswered question hanging in the air like smoke.

I watched the door swing closed behind Rafe with a finality that rattled my bones. The faint echo of his boots hitting the floor still lingered in the air, like the last note of a song that's too beautiful to forget but leaves you with a melancholy ache. I could still feel his presence, thick and undeniable, like a storm cloud hovering just outside the window, threatening to break with a flash of lightning.

"Damn it," I muttered under my breath, kicking a stray boot across the firehouse floor. It hit the far wall with a satisfying thunk, but it didn't help. The space around me felt empty now, too quiet in a way that made my skin prickle. There was no comfort here, no reassurance. Just the remnants of the heat he'd left behind.

I stood still for a moment longer, my fingers twitching at my sides, the weight of the unanswered question pressing on my chest. Why? Why had he left all those years ago? And why come back now, only to retreat into that same cold, impenetrable silence?

The note—the one with the cryptic, maddening message—pressed into my mind, its words flashing behind my eyes. Ask him about the fire. As if I needed another riddle to solve, another thread to pull on in this tangled web he'd left me to untangle alone.

"Stop it," I told myself, but the words felt hollow, as though I was trying to convince someone else and not the woman in the mirror. Because it wasn't just about the fire anymore. It wasn't even just about him. It was about me, about the years I'd spent in the dark, piecing together fragments of a story I wasn't sure I wanted to hear but couldn't stop needing to know.

I pushed the thought aside and grabbed my jacket, my hands shaking only a little as I pulled it on. The night was already turning cooler, the kind of chilly that makes you wish for a cup of something hot, but there was no time for warmth. I had questions, too many of them, and I couldn't let him slip away again. Not without at least trying to get something real from him. Even if it killed me.

I drove in silence, the hum of the engine the only company I had as I headed out to the place I'd tried to forget for so long—the old mill. The one that had burned to the ground all those years ago, the one that had taken everything from us, including Rafe. And I had no idea why I was going there. It felt like some sort of twisted pilgrimage, a return to the scene of the crime.

The mill was still standing, though barely. The brick walls were scarred and blackened, remnants of the fire still etched into the mortar. No one had been there to fix it, to make it whole again. The whole place had been abandoned after the fire, left to rot, left to become a monument to loss.

I parked my car a few yards away, the headlights casting long shadows over the overgrown grass. The place was quiet, eerily so. The world felt like it was holding its breath. For what, I couldn't say, but there was something about this place that made every step heavier, every breath more labored.

And then, as if the world had been waiting for this very moment, I saw him. Rafe.

He was standing by the old steel door that had once been the mill's entrance, his figure outlined against the fading light. There was something almost ghostly about him here, like he was part of the ruins, a shadow among shadows.

He didn't turn when I approached, but I wasn't sure whether that was a statement or just him pretending not to care. "I thought I'd find you here," I said, my voice sharper than I intended. The words felt like they came from someone else, someone angry, someone who wasn't sure whether they were done with the past or ready to face it.

Rafe didn't answer at first. He just stood there, staring at the half-burned remnants of the building, as if it held all the answers he'd been running from. The silence stretched, thick and unyielding, until it almost became unbearable.

"I know you're angry, Emma," he said finally, his voice low, like it didn't want to disturb the quiet. "But you don't know the whole story. You never will."

I took a step closer, the dry grass crunching under my boots. "Then tell me. I don't care what happened, I just want to know. You owe me that much."

He turned to face me then, his eyes—those damn eyes—locking onto mine with an intensity that made my heart stutter. For a moment, I thought he might finally say the words I'd been waiting for. I thought he might give me the truth, the real truth, the one that had been hidden from me all these years.

But instead, he just looked at me, like he was seeing me for the first time in a long time. His gaze softened, and for the briefest of moments, I thought I saw something else—something vulnerable, something human—but then it was gone, replaced by the cold, hard wall I was so used to.

"I didn't leave because I wanted to, Emma," he said, his voice barely above a whisper. "I left because I had to. And there's no coming back from that."

I wanted to scream, to shake him, to make him understand that it wasn't enough to just leave and expect me to pick up the pieces. But I didn't. I couldn't. Instead, I just stood there, staring at him, trying to make sense of the man who had once meant everything to me and now seemed like a stranger wearing a mask.

"I think you're lying," I said softly, almost as if the words were coming from somewhere deep within, a place where the truth was still a stranger.

Rafe flinched, just for a second, and that was enough. Because even though I didn't have all the answers, I knew one thing for sure.

He was hiding something. And I wasn't going to stop until I found out what it was.

The night wrapped itself around the mill like a dark cloak, the cool breeze stirring the overgrown grass as if urging us to speak, to finally tear down the walls we'd built. But as much as I wanted to, as much as I could feel the weight of his silence pressing on me, there was something—something about him, something about this place—that made me hesitate.

"You didn't answer me, Rafe." The words came out before I could stop them, sharp, impatient, like a demand for something I knew I might regret asking for. "Why did you leave?"

His eyes narrowed, his jaw tightening in a way that made my heart skip. I didn't know whether he was about to say something that would break me or tear him apart. Maybe it was a little of both.

"You don't get it, do you?" he said, his voice rough, as if every word was a battle. "I didn't leave you. I left because I had no choice." He ran a hand through his hair, looking away, as if that could somehow shield him from whatever was coming next.

I clenched my fists at my sides, trying to keep the tremor from my hands. "No choice? You always had a choice, Rafe. You could have stayed. You could have fought for us. But instead, you left, and we were stuck with nothing but questions. And a fire that still burns."

His eyes flashed, a spark of something deep inside him catching fire. "You think it was that simple? You think it's all just—" He broke off, his voice low, almost dangerous. "You have no idea what it cost me to leave, Emma. What I lost."

"Then tell me," I shot back, stepping forward, needing him to finally give me something—anything—so I could make sense of the years of silence between us. "Tell me what you lost. Because for me, it was everything. You disappeared, and I was left to pick up the pieces of a life I didn't even recognize anymore."

The words hung in the air, thick and heavy, like smoke that refused to clear. I expected him to step back, to push me away again, but instead, he took a single step forward, closing the distance between us. The tension crackled, thick and charged, like a storm waiting to break.

"I lost you," he said, his voice barely more than a whisper, but it felt like a confession, like something too heavy for him to carry alone.

For a heartbeat, I froze, not sure if I'd heard him correctly. My breath caught in my throat, and for the first time in years, I felt something in my chest loosen, a faint flicker of hope rising from the ashes. But before I could respond, before I could even process what he'd said, the sound of footsteps shattered the fragile moment.

Someone was coming.

I turned instinctively, my pulse quickening, my body going on high alert. In the distance, I saw a shadow move, flickering between the trees at the edge of the property. My stomach dropped. This was the last place I wanted an interruption, especially now, when Rafe had just—had just—

"Emma," Rafe said, his hand reaching out as if to stop me from running, but I was already moving, already taking a step toward the shadow in the dark. The sound of boots on gravel was unmistakable, and there was no mistaking the tone of the voice that followed.

"You two are quite the picture."

I spun around, my heart thudding in my chest, to see a man standing just beyond the edge of the headlights, a smirk on his lips. He was tall, lean, with dark hair that curled at the edges, his face partially hidden by the shadows. The unease that crept up my spine wasn't just from the sudden appearance of this stranger. It was the way he looked at us, like he knew something we didn't.

"Who are you?" I demanded, my voice trembling despite myself. "What do you want?"

The man laughed, the sound low and menacing, like a predator toying with its prey. "I think the better question is, what do you want, Emma?" He took a step closer, the faint glint of something metallic flashing in the moonlight. A gun, maybe. Or a knife. I couldn't tell, but I didn't like it.

Rafe moved to stand between me and the man, his stance protective, but there was something about the way he held himself—something stiff, something... resigned—that didn't sit right with me.

"Stay back," Rafe said, his voice hard, but there was a flicker of doubt in his eyes. He wasn't just worried about me. He was worried about the man in front of us, too.

The stranger raised an eyebrow, as if he were enjoying some private joke. "Oh, I'm not here to hurt you, sweetheart. Not yet, anyway." He looked between me and Rafe, his eyes gleaming with something far darker than amusement. "But you're both in deep now. And I'm not sure either of you can get out unscathed."

Rafe stiffened, and I could feel the shift in the air, like something heavy was about to fall. "What do you know about the fire?" I asked, the words slipping from my mouth before I could stop them. But it was too late to take them back. The moment the words were out, I saw a flicker in the man's eyes, a shift in his posture. He knew something. And now, so did I.

The man's smile widened, and the tension that had been building between us all night snapped. "You really want to know?" he asked, his voice dripping with mockery. "Well, maybe I'll tell you. But first, you both need to understand something. This fire? It wasn't an accident. And neither of you—" He paused, savoring the moment, before adding, "Neither of you are leaving here until you figure out what that means."

Before I could respond, before I could even process what he'd just said, he turned and vanished into the shadows, leaving us standing in the dark, the air heavy with unanswered questions.

And just like that, the world I thought I knew began to shift once again.

Chapter 6: Embers of Truth

The old library was a place of dust, shadows, and silence—the kind of silence that presses in on your chest, suffocating yet strangely comforting. I made my way down the narrow aisle of weathered shelves, the scent of aged paper and musty leather curling around me like an old friend. There was something about the place that reminded me of forgotten things—memories that had slipped from people's minds but refused to let go of the corners of this building. Maybe it was the way the light came through the tall windows, fading into a dim glow, or how the stacks of books seemed to whisper if you listened close enough. But it wasn't the faded romance novels or half-completed encyclopedias I was interested in today. It was the town's history, the kind that got buried when the earth shifted beneath everyone's feet and made them forget what came before.

I ran my fingers along the rows of records, trying to ignore the thudding of my heart. It felt like I was trespassing in a place where even ghosts were afraid to linger, but I couldn't stop now. The fire had changed everything. Rafe had told me that much, though he hadn't said much more. For years, people whispered about it in hushed tones, the flames that swallowed whole blocks, the screams that echoed down the streets, and the lives lost. Rafe's sister was among them, her name reduced to a hushed prayer, her memory locked away. But there had to be more. There had to be a reason, something beyond just a tragedy.

I finally found it—the entry buried in a tattered ledger, the ink faded but legible enough to send a chill down my spine. The fire had begun, the report said, late at night on the east side of town. The cause was listed as "undetermined," but a note scribbled hastily beneath that stated: "Possibly arson." My fingers trembled, the weight of the words pressing on me. A spark, a flicker of suspicion, and I knew that this was where my search had to begin.

There was no going back now.

I turned the page, but the sound of a door opening behind me startled me enough to snap the brittle paper in half. I winced, quickly pressing the pages together as a pair of boots clacked across the wooden floor. "You should be careful with that," a voice said, sharp and low. I froze. I knew that voice.

Rafe.

He was standing at the end of the aisle, his dark eyes fixed on me with a gaze that could strip away the thin veneer of calm I had been holding on to. His broad shoulders filled the space between the shelves, and his presence—his whole being—felt like a storm waiting to break. I could feel the tension in my bones, a quiet storm of its own, but I held my ground. "I'm just looking for answers," I said, the words coming out sharper than I meant them to.

His lips curled into a half-smile that didn't reach his eyes. "I told you before, you're digging in the wrong place. Some things are better left buried."

"And I told you," I shot back, standing taller, "I don't believe in leaving things buried. Not when people are still hurting, not when the truth is out there somewhere."

He walked toward me slowly, his movements deliberate, as if every step took effort. When he stopped in front of me, the air between us felt heavy, charged with the weight of everything unsaid. He glanced at the page in my hands, the records I had unearthed, his jaw tightening imperceptibly.

"Leave it alone," he said, his voice hoarse now, more controlled but thick with something else—pain, or maybe fear. "The fire took everything from me. It burned down more than just homes, it burned down lives, futures, memories that never had a chance to grow. What you're holding is a scar I've spent years trying to forget."

I swallowed, not sure how to respond. I knew he was right in some ways. The fire had taken so much from him, from everyone. But if I walked away now, if I left this unfinished, the grief would continue to echo, and nothing would ever change.

"I know it's hard," I said, my voice softening. "But you can't run from this forever. I need to understand, Rafe. We all do. What really happened?"

He let out a breath, a low, almost painful sound, and I saw it—the crack in his armor, the briefest flicker of vulnerability that he usually kept hidden beneath layers of anger and resolve. I wanted to reach out, to somehow ease that pain, but I knew better than to try. He had built his walls too high, too thick for me to tear down with one kind gesture or sympathetic look.

"I'm not asking you to," he murmured, the words quiet but heavy. "But I came back for one thing. To find out why. I need to know who did this, who took everything from me—and maybe from you, too."

I blinked, his words landing in my chest like a stone. For a moment, I didn't know how to respond. He was right. This wasn't just about him, about his sister, about the town. This was bigger than that. The fire had left marks on everyone, scars that could never fully heal.

"I want to help you," I said, before I even realized the words had escaped my lips.

Rafe's eyes flicked to mine, searching, as though he was trying to decide if I meant it or if I was just another person who couldn't understand the depths of what he had lost. For the first time, I wasn't sure if I could pull him back from the edge. But there was something about the way he looked at me in that moment, something raw and real, that made me want to try. Because if he was going to dive into this hell, I wasn't going to let him go alone. Not when I had a chance to find out the truth.

Rafe's gaze held mine for a long moment, the silence between us heavy enough to crush a hundred unspoken words. He didn't move, didn't give an inch, and I had a sudden, maddening urge to shake him. To tell him it was okay to be angry, to be raw, to stop carrying all that weight alone. But I didn't. Instead, I folded the pages carefully, tucking them back into the worn folder. The sound of paper sliding against paper felt like a betrayal, as if I were closing the door on a truth we were only beginning to uncover.

"You think you can fix this?" His voice cut through the stillness, quieter now, tinged with something I couldn't quite place—doubt, maybe. Or resignation.

"I think I can help find out what really happened," I said, meeting his eyes with a steadiness I didn't entirely feel.

His lips tightened into a line, his jaw muscles working as he seemed to wrestle with something. He took a step back, hands sliding into his pockets, his posture suddenly defensive.

"You've never had to look this far into the dark, have you?" he asked. The question wasn't an accusation, but it landed like one, and I swallowed the retort that hovered on my tongue.

I wanted to say no, that I'd never faced a truth this sharp and dangerous. I wanted to tell him that he was right—that no one could really understand what it was like to live with that kind of grief, with the kind of hollow ache that never really goes away. But I wasn't sure that was true anymore. I'd seen what it had done to him, how it had worn away the parts of him that had once been lighter, easier.

"I've been in the dark before," I said, my voice softer now, tempered by the truth I didn't want to confront. "I know what it's like to want answers no one else can give you."

Rafe's eyes flickered, something shifting in them like a storm cloud breaking. "Maybe you do," he murmured, but his tone was gentler, almost regretful, as if he were trying to apologize without saying the words.

"Why don't we find out together?" I suggested, the words tumbling out before I could stop them.

He studied me for a long moment, like he was weighing whether to trust me or push me away. The tension in the room thickened again, but this time, it felt less like a wall between us and more like the thin thread that held us on the same side. I watched him exhale, a quiet, defeated sound that echoed too loudly in the silence.

"You don't know what you're asking," he said finally, but there was no heat in his voice now. It was a simple statement, a fact that neither of us could deny.

"I know more than you think," I shot back, the words sharper than I intended. "I'm not asking for your permission. I'm asking for your help."

He raised an eyebrow at me, a flicker of amusement—or maybe something darker—lighting up his eyes. "You sure you're not asking for a favor?"

I didn't flinch. "I'm asking for the truth," I said, my voice firm, as if saying it aloud might make it real.

Rafe gave a low laugh, the sound bitter and humorless. "Truth," he repeated, as though the word itself were foreign to him, like it had betrayed him one too many times. "You're brave. I'll give you that."

"I'm stubborn," I corrected, crossing my arms. "And I know when to pick my battles."

For a beat, we just stood there, exchanging a look that spoke volumes without a single word being exchanged. Then, with a resigned sigh, he shoved his hands deeper into his pockets and glanced toward the door. "Fine," he muttered, though I could see the tightness in his shoulders, the way his muscles tensed as if bracing for something. "I'll take you to where it started."

It was the kind of offer I hadn't expected—no grand speeches, no explanations. Just a tacit agreement that the past would be dredged up again, and once it was, there would be no turning back. I nodded without a word, feeling the weight of it settle on my chest. I wasn't sure if I was relieved or terrified, but either way, we were about to open a door that could never be closed again.

Rafe led the way out of the library and into the cold, late-afternoon air. The streets were quieter than usual, as though the town itself was holding its breath, waiting for something to happen. The wind carried the scent of old wood and rust, a reminder of the years of neglect that the town had suffered, the pieces of its soul scattered like debris in the wake of the fire.

He didn't speak as we walked, the distance between us stretching further than I would have liked. I tried to think of something to say—anything that might bridge the gap between us, but the words felt hollow, meaningless. I could feel the pull of the past dragging at us, and I didn't know if Rafe was running toward it or away from it.

We turned onto a side street, one I hadn't been down in years. The buildings here looked different, less cared for, more weathered, as if they too had been touched by the fire but had somehow managed to survive. There were remnants of the old neighborhood everywhere—the faint outline of where walls had once stood, the charred remains of what used to be homes. But there was something else, something far more chilling: the silence.

Rafe stopped in front of a building that had long since been reduced to a blackened skeleton, the outline of a roof barely visible against the gray sky. His eyes softened for a split second, and I saw the vulnerability that he so carefully guarded from everyone else. "This is where it started," he said, his voice almost a whisper.

I stepped forward, feeling the pull of history, of grief, and of something more. And as I took my first step onto the ashes of what once was, I couldn't shake the feeling that this was just the beginning.

We stood there, surrounded by the ruins, the wind picking up, sending ash-like fragments swirling around our feet. I could feel the weight of Rafe's silence pressing down on us. He had led me to the edge of the destruction, but not the heart of it. The place that had been ground zero for all that pain. I could see it in the way his eyes were fixed on the charred remnants of a wall, as if the past had a grip on him so tight that it left no room for anything else. The air was thick with the smell of burnt wood and something darker—regret, perhaps, or even something more sinister that I couldn't yet name.

"This is where it all began," Rafe said, but his voice barely reached me, as though he were speaking to the ashes themselves. There was no bitterness now, no anger. Just weariness. And maybe something else—guilt.

"I don't know if I can even imagine what this was like," I said, taking a step forward, careful not to disturb the debris around us. I had no intention of speaking flippantly, but the truth was that I couldn't wrap my mind around it. People had died here. Rafe's sister, among them. And yet, the place felt eerily quiet, almost peaceful, as if the ruins had long since exhausted their grief.

"Good," Rafe muttered, turning to face me. His expression was unreadable, but I saw the flicker of something there. Something that wasn't entirely cold. "I wouldn't wish that on anyone."

There was a long pause before I gathered the nerve to ask the question that had been burning in me ever since I'd found the town records. "Rafe... why did you come back? After everything?"

He didn't answer at first, and I wasn't sure if I was asking for myself or for him. Maybe I wanted him to finally say it out loud—to admit the part of him that still felt tied to this place, to the memories, to the unanswered questions.

"I don't know," he finally said, his gaze flickering to the twisted remains of a nearby lamppost. It had once been a beacon of light, and now it was nothing but a jagged silhouette against the overcast sky. "Maybe I thought I could find something that could make sense of it all. Or maybe I thought that if I came back, it wouldn't feel like I was running away from it anymore."

The words landed like a weight in the pit of my stomach. There was no bravado, no sense of control. Just a man caught in the middle of a storm that never seemed to stop. "And have you found it?" I asked, the question almost too soft to break the tension hanging in the air.

He shook his head slowly. "Not yet."

The wind howled around us, picking up the remnants of what had once been the heart of a thriving neighborhood. It was strange, the way the destruction felt so final, yet there was something alive about it—like the past wasn't just buried here. It lingered. Watching.

"Are we really going to find answers here?" I asked, more to myself than to him, my eyes scanning the jagged remains of the building that had once been someone's home. It was easy to get lost in the haunting sense of history, to feel as though time itself had stood still here, trapped beneath the rubble.

Rafe didn't answer right away, and when he did, his words were careful, deliberate. "Maybe the answers aren't what you expect. Maybe you think there's some big conspiracy or someone to blame, but sometimes, the truth is just... messy."

I frowned, unsure of where he was going with this. "Messy?"

He turned to face me fully now, his posture stiff, his eyes sharp. "The fire wasn't just some accident. It wasn't some random act of nature. It was deliberate. But the why, the who... that's where it gets complicated."

The weight of his words hung between us. Deliberate. Not an accident, not a tragedy, but something intentional. My heart skipped a beat. I had suspected something like this, but hearing it out loud sent a chill down my spine. If it was deliberate, if someone had set that fire with intent—then we were dealing with something far more dangerous than a tragedy. We were dealing with a lie.

"You think someone set the fire?" I asked, my voice trembling ever so slightly, despite my best efforts to keep it steady.

Rafe's jaw tightened, and for the first time, I saw a flicker of anger behind his eyes. "I don't think. I know." His gaze shifted, narrowing on the remains of what had once been the heart of the neighborhood. "But finding out who did it... that's the part no one wants to talk about."

I swallowed, trying to grasp the weight of his words. It was one thing to suspect, but another to hear it said so plainly, with so much certainty.

"Who doesn't want to talk about it?" I pressed, my curiosity pushing through the layers of grief and anger between us. "Is it the town? The authorities? Or is it someone close to you?"

Rafe's lips curled into something that could have been a smile, if it weren't so grim. "You're persistent, I'll give you that," he said, his voice barely above a murmur. "Maybe too persistent for your own good."

I didn't know what he meant by that. But I wasn't about to back down now. Not when I was so close. "I want to know, Rafe. The truth. No more half answers."

For a long moment, he didn't speak. The wind howled again, sending the ashes swirling in front of us like ghostly dancers. And then, with a sudden movement, he stepped forward, his voice lowering to a dangerous whisper.

"I'll take you to him," he said. "But I don't think you're ready for what you'll find."

The words were a promise. And a threat. I followed him, my pulse racing, the weight of what we were about to uncover bearing down on me like a shadow.

Chapter 7: Heatwave

The heat settled over the town like a blanket too heavy to shake off. By noon, the asphalt shimmered, blurring the horizon and the sun hung like a stubborn weight in the sky. The air itself felt thick, cloying, sticking to the skin, leaving a slickness that couldn't be scrubbed away no matter how much you tried. And Rafe? He was everywhere. Unavoidable, like the sun. Or, perhaps more accurately, like a shadow stretched long across the ground, lingering just a little too close for comfort.

I had never been good at avoiding things I didn't want to confront—especially not when they came in the form of a tall man with eyes like a storm cloud and a walk that suggested he was always ready to leave. He showed up at the diner most mornings, ordering the same black coffee and sitting at the corner booth like he had every right to be there. He didn't talk much, just stared into his mug like the answers to every question in the world were hiding in that dark liquid. I had tried, unsuccessfully, to pretend I wasn't watching him. To convince myself that my fascination was nothing more than curiosity. But it was more than that. I could feel the tension in the air whenever he was around, and it had nothing to do with the weather.

Today, though, I couldn't pretend. He'd come into the diner just after I finished a shift, his usual brooding presence impossible to ignore. Something in the way he looked at me—his gaze steady, like he was measuring me for something I didn't yet understand—made my stomach tighten in a way that was both unsettling and magnetic.

I moved to the counter, taking my place next to him. He didn't greet me, just took a sip of his coffee and set the cup down with a soft thud, eyes still fixed on me.

"Late night?" I asked, trying to sound casual, though I knew damn well he was up to something, something that had kept him busy for days. The town had been buzzing with talk of strange occurrences, of mysterious figures lurking in the shadows. And Rafe? He was digging. Hard.

"Yeah," he muttered, his voice rough, like gravel sliding over stone. "Couldn't sleep."

I smiled, knowing full well that there was no "couldn't sleep" about it. He never slept. Not for more than a few hours at a time, at least not since I'd known him. The restlessness in him was more than physical—it was in his bones, in the way he moved, like he was always running from something.

I sat across from him, a small part of me thrilled by the proximity, but most of me annoyed at how naturally he slipped under my skin. I had things to do. People to see. But none of that seemed to matter when he was near.

"So, what's keeping you up?" I asked, my voice softer than I intended.

His eyes flicked to mine briefly before returning to the cup in front of him. I could feel the walls go up, the familiar barrier between us. And yet, I couldn't stop myself from pressing on. It was like trying to unravel a mystery, only to find that the clues always led back to the same place—him.

"Nothing," he said, his lips curling into a half-smirk that didn't reach his eyes. "Just work."

I raised an eyebrow. "Work?" I repeated, incredulous. "The whole town's talking about you, Rafe. You're poking around places no one's been for years. You don't seem the type to care about old buildings or... police reports."

He shifted in his seat, fingers tapping against the side of his mug. He didn't answer right away, which told me everything. I wasn't going to get anything out of him today. And yet, I couldn't shake the feeling that he was waiting for me to push harder.

"Fine," I said with a soft sigh, leaning back in my seat. "I guess you'll tell me when you're ready."

His eyes caught mine then, dark and unreadable, but there was something in them—a flicker of acknowledgment, of something shared that neither of us was willing to put into words. His jaw tightened as if fighting a war inside himself, and I wondered for the thousandth time what it was that haunted him so thoroughly.

For a moment, silence settled over us, the low hum of the diner's air conditioning the only sound between us. I watched him, studying the lines of his face, the way he seemed to carry the weight of the world on his shoulders. There was a part of me that wanted to reach out, to offer him something—comfort, understanding, anything. But I knew better. Rafe wasn't the kind of man you helped. He was the kind who pushed people away, who refused to let anyone close enough to see the truth of who he really was.

And yet, despite all of that, I found myself drawn in. It was as if the more he resisted, the more I wanted to push against that wall, to break it down and see what lay beneath.

"I didn't ask for this," he said suddenly, his voice low and strained. "None of it. But it doesn't matter. It's here now. And I have to finish it."

I leaned forward, intrigued despite myself. "Finish what?"

He stood abruptly, the movement sharp and purposeful, like he was done with the conversation—or maybe with me. I wasn't sure. "Everything," he said, his gaze lingering on me for a beat longer than necessary. Then, without another word, he turned and walked out of the diner, leaving me to chew over his cryptic statement.

And just like that, he was gone, leaving a trail of tension in his wake, a promise of things left unsaid.

The next few days blurred together in a haze of heat and frustration. Mornings arrived far too early, and each one carried the same routine. I'd head into the diner for a cup of coffee that never quite tasted right, sit down at a corner booth, and wait for the inevitable. Rafe would show up—his presence like the start of a thunderstorm, predictable but always carrying the tension of what was yet to come. It was the only thing about this town that seemed to stay the same. And no matter how much I told myself I was over it, my pulse still quickened the moment he walked in.

I'd see him in the corner of my eye, that long, fluid stride, like someone who was never quite at home anywhere. He was always too restless, too much like a wild thing trapped in a cage that he couldn't quite break free from. He never spoke much, but there was always something in the way his eyes flickered to me, just for a second longer than was necessary, that made me feel like we were caught in something deeper than either of us was willing to admit.

But the real unraveling started the night we stayed late in the police station, going over files, maps, and old reports that smelled faintly of stale paper and desperation. The air inside was as thick and still as the night outside, the hum of the overhead lights the only sound that broke the silence. I'd long since given up on trying to push him, to coax the truth out of him with my questions and my carefully crafted arguments. It was clear by now that Rafe didn't trust anyone. Not even me.

"Why are we doing this?" I asked, glancing over at him from across the room. I could see his face in the dull light, the faint shadow of his jawline catching the light in odd angles. He was bent over a map, his fingers tracing lines that I couldn't quite follow.

"You don't get it, do you?" His voice was rough, but there was something else there—something quieter, almost sad. "There's something here. Something no one's talking about."

"I don't know what you're looking for, Rafe," I said, my voice softer now, leaning toward him unconsciously, drawn to the urgency in his tone. "You keep going over the same thing, retracing your steps, and it's not leading anywhere."

"You don't know that," he said, his eyes flicking up to meet mine, sharp and intense. He wasn't angry, not exactly, but there was a growing frustration there. "You haven't been where I've been. You haven't seen what I've seen."

I felt a spark of something—maybe it was stubbornness, maybe it was just plain curiosity—but whatever it was, it burned through me. I crossed my arms over my chest, the slight movement drawing him to my side of the table. "Then tell me. Stop dancing around it, Rafe. What are you looking for?"

He leaned back in his chair, rubbing his hands over his face, a gesture that felt almost like exhaustion, like he was too tired to keep up the pretense. "I can't tell you. Not yet."

The words hung between us like a weight, like something unsaid that we both knew, deep down, was the core of everything. I had the strange sensation that we were both standing on the edge of something—and that it wasn't just about the case. No, this was something more, something that had nothing to do with old files and maps.

He stood up suddenly, slamming his palm on the table. "I can't do this, not right now. I need—" He broke off, running a hand through his already messy hair, looking torn in a way that sent an unexpected jolt through me. I had never seen Rafe look so vulnerable, so raw.

"Need what?" I asked, barely above a whisper. It wasn't a question I expected an answer to. Not really. But sometimes, asking was all you could do. Just to fill the silence.

His jaw tightened, and for a moment, I thought he wasn't going to answer at all. Then, in a voice barely audible, he said, "I need you to back off. Just for a little while."

It felt like a slap, but not the kind that hurt. The kind that made you stop, made you think. And in that pause, I understood something in him had shifted. Whatever he was hiding, whatever he was running from, he wasn't ready to face it—at least not with me.

I couldn't ignore the sting, though, the sharp burn of being pushed away when I had finally thought, just for a second, that maybe we could be more than just two people caught up in the wreckage of something neither of us could understand. But there it was, plain as day. He wanted distance. He wanted me gone.

I pushed back from the table, my chair scraping harshly against the floor, the sound far too loud in the quiet room. "Fine. If that's what you want."

Rafe didn't stop me, didn't try to say anything else. He just watched me, those eyes of his unreadable and distant. I didn't wait to see if he'd follow me, didn't wait for the apology that I thought might come but never did. I left the station, stepping out into the oppressive heat, the night air thick with the weight of things unsaid.

The town was quiet at this hour, but there was something in the stillness that felt charged, like a storm waiting to break. And as I walked down the street, I couldn't shake the feeling that I had just been caught in the eye of it, the calm before the real chaos came. Something was about to change, I could feel it in my bones, but whether it was going to pull me in or push me further away, I didn't know.

But I would find out. And that, for better or worse, was something I couldn't stop myself from doing.

By the time the third day arrived, the weight of the heat seemed to press against me from all sides. I'd half-forgotten what it felt like to breathe without it clogging my lungs. The town was suffocating, a living, breathing thing caught under a blanket of relentless sun. But that wasn't the worst part. The worst part was Rafe's absence.

I hadn't seen him since the night in the station, and the silence that stretched between us felt heavier with each passing hour. For the first time in weeks, I found myself wondering if it had all been a mistake—if everything we'd shared, all the late-night debates and near-moments of connection, was nothing more than my overactive imagination. I hated myself for feeling the way I did. I hated how much his withdrawal bothered me. But it did.

I spent the afternoon pacing my small kitchen, the soft hum of the refrigerator the only sound filling the emptiness. My fingers itched to call him, to make sense of the space he'd created between us. But I knew that would only push him further away, so I did nothing. I folded laundry, sorted through old files, and waited.

Then, as the sun began to set, a knock echoed on my door.

My heart gave an odd jolt. There was no mistaking the heavy, deliberate sound. I didn't need to ask who it was. I already knew.

When I opened the door, Rafe was standing on the other side, his tall frame filling the space with a mixture of heat and tension. His shirt was rolled up at the sleeves, the fabric tight over his broad shoulders, and his expression was unreadable. He looked at me with a weight in his gaze that made my breath catch. The air between us crackled with everything we hadn't said, everything we had been too afraid to admit.

"Can I come in?" he asked, his voice low, almost hesitant.

I nodded, stepping aside to let him pass. The second he crossed the threshold, I felt the familiar sense of displacement. Like he didn't belong here, but still, something inside him drew him to this space, to me.

He didn't sit right away. Instead, he moved to the window, his hands resting against the sill as he stared out at the town bathed in orange light. The silence stretched between us, thick and uncomfortable. My pulse thudded in my throat. This was the part where I was supposed to say something, anything, to break the tension. But my mouth went dry, the words tangled in the mess of emotions swirling inside me.

Finally, he turned to face me. "I don't know what you want from me," he said, the words blunt, but there was a slight tremor in his voice that betrayed the mask of indifference he was trying so hard to wear.

"I don't want anything," I replied, a little too quickly. "I don't want you to explain yourself or tell me your whole life story. I just..." I stopped, shaking my head. "I don't know."

He watched me for a long moment, the weight of his gaze so intense it was as if he was searching for something in me—something I wasn't sure I even understood. "I'm not the guy you think I am," he said quietly. "You don't know what's at stake here. You don't know what I've been doing."

I stepped closer, despite the ache in my chest urging me to keep my distance. "Then tell me. I'm not asking for the whole story. Just—just give me something."

He shook his head, the frustration in his expression evident. "You think you can fix this? Think you can just waltz in and change everything? It doesn't work like that."

I stood my ground. "I'm not trying to fix you, Rafe. I'm trying to understand you." My voice softened. "I'm not going anywhere, not until you stop shutting me out."

His eyes flickered with something I couldn't place—something between guilt and recognition. Then, before I could say another word, he moved toward me, closing the gap between us with a step that felt like the world shifting beneath my feet.

He reached out, his hand brushing against mine, tentative at first, like he wasn't sure if I'd pull away. But I didn't. I let him take it, let him pull me into his orbit. And in that moment, the silence shattered.

"I don't know if I can do this," he murmured, his forehead resting against mine, his breath warm against my skin. "I'm not who you think I am."

"I don't care who you think you are," I whispered back, my voice barely a breath. "I care who you are when you let me in."

His eyes searched mine, and for a fleeting moment, I thought he might let go, let himself feel what had been building between us all this time. But instead, he closed his eyes and let out a slow breath, his grip on my hand tightening.

"I'm not the answer you're looking for," he said, his voice tinged with a quiet finality. "But I'm all you've got."

And then, before I could respond, before I could find the words to make him see that I wasn't giving up, the window slammed open, the gust of wind making everything in the room tremble. I whipped around, my heart racing.

The air had shifted. The tension—already thick—now felt suffocating, like something was about to break. And then, in the distance, a sharp, unmistakable sound reached my ears.

The screech of tires.

The crash.

And then nothing.

Rafe stiffened beside me, his face going ashen. Without another word, he grabbed my wrist and tugged me toward the door, his grip ironclad, dragging me out into the night as the sound of sirens began to wail.

"What's happening?" I asked, my voice trembling as I fought to keep up with him.

He didn't answer. Instead, he pulled me faster, toward the place where the darkness seemed to hold its breath.

And somewhere, deep within me, I knew that whatever was coming was far bigger than anything either of us had bargained for.

Chapter 8: The Burn Line

The smell of smoke still lingered in the air, faint but persistent, as if it had become a permanent fixture in the town's atmosphere. I hated the way it made my lungs ache, the way it hung in the back of my throat like an unwelcome guest. I wasn't sure when the smell had first seeped in, but now, it was impossible to avoid. Fires, the kind that scorched homes to their bones, weren't supposed to feel like a rhythm—something predictable and inevitable—but that's how they had settled into the cadence of our lives. And with every new one, the stakes seemed to grow higher.

"Are you sure this is where it started?" I asked, my voice barely above a whisper, the words catching on the wind. The charred remnants of the old building stood behind me, a skeleton of what had once been a grocery store, now reduced to an eerie, ashen shell.

Rafe was pacing, his boots thudding against the ground in a deliberate, unsettling rhythm. He had been on edge ever since the fire at the bakery, the third one in two months, and each time his face twisted with a deeper sort of fear I couldn't name. He was always good at hiding it—his layers of control like a fortress—yet I could see the cracks in the facade now, like pressure building behind a dam, begging for release.

"It's not about where it starts anymore," he said without turning to me, his voice strained. "It's about where it's going."

I crossed my arms, rubbing my bare skin as a chill crept up my spine. I could feel his eyes on me, even though I couldn't see his expression, and I wasn't sure if I was more afraid of the flames or of the quiet certainty that was creeping into his voice. "So, what? You think someone's targeting the town?"

He stopped then, pivoting so quickly I almost stumbled backward. His eyes locked with mine, and there it was—something too raw, too sharp, like he was standing on the edge of something and was afraid I might push him over. "Not the town, Chloe. It's you. All of this"—he waved a hand at the ruins behind us—"it's connected to you. I know it sounds crazy, but I can feel it."

I didn't know how to respond. Rafe had never been one for melodrama, but there was a sense of urgency now, a weight to his words that made my chest tighten. He wasn't just rattling off theories; he believed this.

"You're wrong," I finally said, but my voice wavered in a way I hated. "This is just... it's a string of bad luck. That's all. It's the dry season, and things happen. Accidents, maybe. Nothing more."

He stared at me for a long moment, and I saw the flicker of doubt in his eyes, quickly masked by something far darker. "I used to think that, too. But then I started looking at the patterns. It's too consistent to be an accident. It's intentional. And it's getting closer to you."

My heart stuttered at the words. They felt like a punch to the gut, and I hated that I could see the truth in them. The fires had been happening with alarming regularity, each one more devastating than the last. A handful of suspicious deaths had followed in their wake, and the townspeople were starting to talk in whispers—hushed voices, eyes darting toward shadows, always on edge.

"You're paranoid," I said again, but it didn't sound convincing even to my own ears. "Just because it happened here doesn't mean it's got anything to do with me."

Rafe's jaw clenched, and I saw the muscles in his neck tense like he was trying to hold himself together. "You really don't get it, do you?" His words hit harder than I expected. "This isn't about you, Chloe. Not in the way you think. It's about what's underneath it all. Whoever's behind this... they're sending a message. And you're the one they're sending it to."

A cold wave of realization washed over me. I hadn't considered it before—hadn't wanted to. But now, the idea of it was settling in, burrowing deep where I couldn't escape it. The fires. The accidents. The strange coincidences that were starting to pile up. They weren't just random events. They were happening for a reason.

I shivered, and it wasn't just the cold. It was the weight of his words, the way they reverberated in the air like the echo of something ancient and inevitable.

"I don't know what to do with that," I muttered. "I'm not a target, Rafe. I'm just a waitress."

His eyes softened for a split second, and in that moment, I saw the vulnerability he kept hidden so well. He looked at me like I was the only person in the world, and for a brief moment, I wished it were true. But the truth was, I wasn't sure I even knew who I was anymore.

"You're not just a waitress, Chloe," he said, his voice almost too quiet. "You're the one they're looking for."

I stared at him for a long moment, his words hanging between us like smoke—thick, suffocating, impossible to ignore. It would have been easier to dismiss it all, to laugh at the ridiculousness of it. After all, I was just Chloe, wasn't I? Just a girl who'd spent most of her days behind a counter, hands busy with orders, smile fixed, pretending she didn't care when the world outside went up in flames. But now, the lines of what I thought I knew were blurring in ways that made my head spin.

"I don't want to be part of this," I said, shaking my head as though doing so could clear away the creeping doubt. "It's not my fight, Rafe. I'm just here because I—"

"Because you're running from something, I know." His voice cut through my protest like a knife through silk, smooth but sharp. "I'm not asking you to get involved, Chloe. But whether you like it or not, you already are. This town's tangled up in something bigger than we both want to believe, and I can't do it alone."

The words were spoken with the kind of conviction that made me want to take a step back, to flee, to run far away from whatever was lurking behind that desperate look in his eyes. And yet, I couldn't. Not this time. Because when Rafe looked at me like that, when he finally allowed himself to drop the walls he built so carefully, it made my stomach tighten in ways that weren't entirely uncomfortable.

"I'm not the one you should be worried about," I said, taking a deep breath. "This is your problem, Rafe, not mine. You've been carrying it for years, haven't you?"

He didn't answer right away. He just let the silence fill the space between us, heavy and dense. I could almost hear the clattering of thoughts in his mind, the things he wasn't saying. And then, as though deciding it was finally time to speak the truth, he opened his mouth.

"I think... I think someone's been watching you," he said quietly. His voice wavered, the slightest tremor in it that was hard to ignore.

I blinked, the weight of his words crashing over me like a wave. "What?"

His eyes dropped to the ground, his hand running through his hair in frustration. "That fire? The one that happened last week? It wasn't supposed to be here. It wasn't meant to be this close to you. But there was something about it, something that felt wrong... like it was pushing us toward something."

I took a step back, my mind racing. "Pushing us toward what, exactly?"

Rafe's lips pressed together, his eyes darkening. I knew he wasn't going to explain. He never did. Rafe was one of those people who would hold the whole world inside himself until it broke apart, and even then, he would never let anyone in on the secret of what it all meant. I wanted to scream, to throw something at him, to tell him that none of this made any sense. But I didn't. I stayed quiet, the words lodged in my throat, too afraid to speak the truth.

"So, what now?" I finally asked, my voice barely more than a whisper. "We just sit here, waiting for the next fire?"

"Not just any fire," Rafe muttered, his gaze flickering back to the charred remains behind me. "There's a pattern. It's not random. And the thing is, I know how it ends." He swallowed hard, his throat working as though it were a difficult task, like he was choking on the weight of his own thoughts.

"Rafe," I said, my tone sharper now, but not entirely sure if I was angry or terrified. "You have to stop. This is a mess, and you're dragging me into it."

"I don't have a choice," he snapped, his voice suddenly filled with a rawness I wasn't prepared for. "If I stop, they'll think I'm giving up. But if I keep going..." He trailed off, rubbing his fingers against his eyes, a frustrated sound escaping his throat. "There's something happening here, Chloe. Something you're not seeing. Someone wants you to know. They need you to see it."

"I don't understand," I admitted, the words tasting sour in my mouth. "Why me? What makes me so special? I'm not a detective or a hero or anything like that. I just work at a café. I don't have any answers."

Rafe's gaze locked onto mine, and for a split second, everything else around us seemed to fade away. The fires, the darkened sky, the ruins of the town—it all disappeared, and I was left with the feeling that maybe, just maybe, I was in the middle of something I had no business being a part of.

"I know it's hard to believe," he said, his voice softening as though he were finally conceding a point to me, "but everything about this town, the fires, the things that don't make sense—none of it is random. You're the key to it, Chloe. The one piece I didn't understand until now."

A small laugh slipped from my lips, though it didn't sound at all like humor. "Well, that's a pretty terrifying compliment."

Rafe gave me the smallest of smiles, one that didn't quite reach his eyes. "I guess you could say it's the kind of compliment I wouldn't wish on anyone."

I didn't know how to respond. The tension between us was thick, almost suffocating. Whatever was happening here, whatever Rafe had gotten tangled up in, it was bigger than the both of us. And the worst part? I wasn't sure I could walk away from it, even if I wanted to.

I wanted to take a step back, breathe, pretend that the sharp edge of his words hadn't found its mark, but I couldn't. I felt the weight of his certainty settle in my chest like a stone, and the ground beneath me suddenly seemed less stable, as though something underneath was shifting, preparing to give way. I wasn't sure what frightened me more—his confession or the fact that I wasn't sure I could just walk away from this. Rafe was looking at me with eyes that seemed to say he had already walked through fire, and now, he was pulling me with him, whether I was ready or not.

"I didn't ask for this," I said, my voice tight with something that tasted a lot like regret. It was too late to turn back, too late to feign ignorance. "But you're not the only one with things to lose, you know?"

Rafe's eyes softened for a second before he caught himself. The man had mastered the art of concealing everything beneath a mask, but every now and then, I saw the cracks. Just enough to know he wasn't as untouchable as he liked to pretend. He rubbed his temples, frustration radiating off him. "I know. I'm not asking you to join me in some crusade. But this isn't just about us anymore. It's about everyone in this town. The people you've known your whole life. I'm trying to protect you from whatever this is."

"By pushing me into it?" I raised an eyebrow, crossing my arms defensively. "You don't get to protect me like that. Not anymore. I don't need saving, Rafe."

He stared at me, his jaw set, and I knew he was battling with something inside himself, something he hadn't yet shared with me. Whatever secret he was holding, it had to be bigger than either of us could comprehend. I could see the danger he was tiptoeing around, but I couldn't quite place it. The way the hairs on the back of my neck stood on end suggested we were on the edge of something far more dangerous than just fires and smoke.

"I'm not saving you," he finally said, his voice raw. "I'm just trying to make sure you don't get burned."

The words stung, even though I knew he didn't mean them that way. There was a flicker of something else beneath his protective instincts—something darker, more desperate—and it gnawed at me.

"What if I'm already burned?" I muttered, and he didn't have an answer for that. Neither of us did.

The night stretched on like a thread pulled taut between us, and though we were standing only a few feet apart, I could feel the distance between us growing wider with every unspoken word. I knew he was right, somewhere deep inside me, but I couldn't bring myself to admit it.

"I have to figure this out," Rafe said after a long silence, his voice low, almost to himself. "There's more to this than just the fires. There's something behind all of it, something bigger than arson or even the people causing it. And I think—no, I know—you're the missing piece."

I took a step back, my stomach doing something ungraceful. "I think you've been alone in this too long, Rafe. You're seeing things that might not even be there. Maybe it's time to let it go."

His laugh was hollow, bitter. "That's the problem, Chloe. I can't let it go. Not when I'm this close."

"Close to what? What are you really after, Rafe?" My voice broke, the frustration clear now, spilling out into the night. "What's going to change if we chase this down?"

He didn't respond right away. Instead, he turned away, walking toward the edge of the burned-out building. The wind whipped through his hair, carrying the smell of smoke still lingering in the air, and I wondered if it would ever truly leave this place. Would it be washed away with time, or was it already a part of us now, a stain that would never fade?

"You don't get it," he finally said, the words coming out like a confession. "This isn't just about the fires. It's about who's controlling them. Who's watching us from the shadows. And who's willing to destroy everything to keep it that way."

I moved closer, instinctively reaching out to him, but he pulled away before I could touch him. The space between us had become a chasm, and no matter how hard I tried, I couldn't bridge it.

"And why would they care about us? Why now? We're just—" I started to say, but I was cut off by a sound—faint but unmistakable—a crackling from the direction of the town's outskirts.

Rafe froze. His body tensed, every muscle suddenly on alert.

"Not again," he whispered, his breath hitching. His eyes darted toward the horizon, where the faint glow of another fire was beginning to light up the night sky.

I couldn't believe it. The fires had come again. But this time, it was too close. The intensity of it, the speed, the sheer urgency behind it—it wasn't just an accident. It was deliberate. Someone was sending a message, and I was starting to fear that message was for us.

Rafe was already moving, pulling me along with him, as though he had no intention of waiting to see how bad this would get. I followed him, too stunned to think clearly, adrenaline coursing through my veins, pushing me forward. We were running out of time.

We reached the top of the hill overlooking the town, and the sight that greeted me stole my breath. Flames shot up from the direction of the café, the very place I'd worked for the past two years. My heart stuttered as I saw the orange glow reflected in the sky, brighter than I had ever seen it before. The fire was everywhere, consuming everything in its path.

"Chloe," Rafe's voice cracked like the snap of a twig. "They're going after what you care about. You're the target."

I turned to face him, my stomach plummeting. The realization hit me like a freight train. I wasn't just a part of this—I was the reason for it. And as I looked down at the inferno below, I understood. Whoever was behind this... was coming for me.

Chapter 9: Flickers of Attraction

I hadn't meant for the evening to spiral out of control. I'd pictured the party—my dad's big send-off after twenty-five years of loyal service—like one of those old sitcoms where everyone sits around, clinks glasses, and laughs at the quirks of small-town life. A few harmless jabs, some local gossip, and then the world would feel right again. But that was before I made the mistake of inviting Rafe.

Rafe had agreed to come, but not without a sarcastic eyebrow raise that made it clear he thought the whole thing was a waste of time. His words were smooth and laced with that sharp edge of his that I hated so much. "Small-town politics, huh? That's your thing now?" he'd said when I asked him. But, to my surprise, he showed up. His suit was as dark as his mood, his presence as heavy as the tension in the air between us. And no, I didn't think about the subtle way his eyes shifted when he caught me standing by the punch bowl, or the way my heart seemed to do that annoying skip whenever his gaze lingered just a second too long.

We'd been on opposite sides for months, locked in a game where neither of us wanted to admit the stakes had changed. But tonight, in this room filled with clinking glasses and half-suppressed chuckles, the old rivalry seemed irrelevant. The music hummed softly, a sweet lullaby of familiarity, but the space between us crackled with something darker, more electric. I watched as he stood in the corner, exchanging words with my brother, his broad frame towering over everyone else like a storm cloud ready to burst.

It didn't take long for the inevitable to happen. My dad made his speech, cracking jokes that weren't funny but got the crowd laughing anyway, and there was that familiar wave of warmth spreading through me. There were no surprises there—just my dad, the man who always knew how to make everyone feel at home. But then Rafe had to lean in with that damn sarcastic smirk and say something about "the same old routine." I could feel my muscles tense before I even turned to face him.

"You really think this is all just one big joke?" I'd snapped.

"Oh, no, not a joke. Just...predictable," Rafe had replied, his voice smooth, like the sound of ice cubes tumbling into a glass. I felt my pulse quicken. I could already feel the shift in the air between us, that undeniable pull, the way his words made something inside of me itch and burn all at once. My irritation turned into something more volatile.

"What's your problem with small towns, huh? With my family? This isn't just some 'predictable' thing," I shot back, my voice louder than I intended.

He raised an eyebrow, that infuriating, frustrating, too-charming eyebrow. "Oh, right, because everyone here is so exceptional, right?" He waved a hand around the room. "Just like the greats. This town is a museum. I'm just a tourist passing through."

That was it. My patience snapped. I didn't care about the small talk, the smile everyone was expecting me to wear, the way my dad's eyes looked up at me in quiet concern. I grabbed Rafe's arm and yanked him outside, away from the chatter, the warm smiles, the too-sweet air of nostalgia.

The night outside was crisp, too crisp, like the chill was there just to remind me of how tight my throat had become. I had to swallow hard to keep the anger from spilling over. The air around us felt too still, the hum of the conversation fading into the background.

"You've got a way of showing up, don't you?" I said, my words biting, sharper than they should have been.

He crossed his arms, a little smirk curling on his lips. "Did you expect me to lie about it?"

"No," I shot back, exhaling harshly, "but I didn't expect you to act like everyone else here is just beneath you."

"I'm not," he said, but there was a flicker of something behind his words—something dark, something more than just the anger. His voice softened, just enough to make me pause. "You're the one who invited me, remember?"

The implication of it hit me harder than I expected, and I opened my mouth to respond, but my words caught. I hadn't invited him just to get under my skin. I'd invited him because I thought he could see what I saw—the heart of this place, the people, the reason I couldn't walk away from it, even when it suffocated me sometimes. But now, with him standing in front of me, the realization of how wrong I'd been hit like a slap.

"Maybe I made a mistake," I muttered under my breath, but I wasn't sure whether I was talking to him, or to myself.

"Yeah, maybe you did," he said quietly, taking a step closer. Too close, and yet not close enough. There was a flicker of something in his eyes, something that made me forget how much I hated him for a moment. His hand brushed against my arm, and my body reacted before I had a chance to stop it. That sharpness between us melted into something... softer, something dangerous. My breath caught. He wasn't supposed to make me feel like this. Not him. Not now.

For one brief moment, I thought about what it might be like to just forget all the reasons I shouldn't be this close to him. But then his hand lingered a little longer, and the thought was gone, snuffed out by the cold air, the burning in my chest, and the tension that had snapped taut between us.

It wasn't the first time I'd felt this way around him. But it was the first time I'd let myself admit it.

Rafe's touch lingered in the cold night air, and for a second, I almost let myself believe it wasn't a mistake. His fingers against my skin burned hotter than I wanted to admit, like they could brand me in the same way the town had. I pulled away, a little too sharply, and he didn't stop me. He just watched me, his eyes dark with something unreadable.

"What exactly are you trying to do here?" I asked, my voice coming out more raw than I intended, but I couldn't help it. My nerves were shot, and the tension between us was like a knot I couldn't untangle. He was too close. Too familiar.

Rafe raised an eyebrow, the corner of his lips twitching in amusement. "Trying to do what? You invited me to a party and then acted like I was the problem." He stepped back, but the distance didn't ease the pressure in my chest. "Seems to me like you're the one who's all over the place."

I shot him a glare, the words he said cutting deeper than I expected. "I'm not the one standing outside in the cold because they can't keep their mouth shut."

He laughed, low and almost gentle, and it made the back of my neck prickle. "You always this much fun, or is tonight just special?"

I couldn't answer that without sounding defensive, so I didn't. Instead, I stared at the ground, wishing for the millionth time that I could be anywhere else. I didn't want to deal with this—whatever this was between us. I didn't want to care.

We stood there, the quiet between us stretching thin like the fabric of a shirt too tight across the shoulders. I wanted to leave. Walk away and pretend none of this had happened. But I couldn't. Not with the way he was looking at me now, like he was waiting for something. A sign. A shift.

"So, what now?" I asked, my words a little breathier than I intended.

His gaze never wavered. "Now you tell me what you're so afraid of. Because it's not just me."

That stopped me dead. I didn't want to admit it, didn't even want to think it. But there it was—truth in the way he said it, like he could see through the walls I'd built around myself. "I'm not afraid of you," I said, my voice barely above a whisper.

"No?" Rafe's smile was small, but it held something that made my pulse pick up. "Then why do you look like you're about to run every time I get close?"

I didn't have a comeback for that, and he knew it. We both knew it. He was right, of course. Every time he came near, I felt like my entire world tilted. Like nothing made sense anymore, and I was standing on the edge of something too big for me to grasp.

But it wasn't just that. It was the way I wanted to stop fighting. The way, every time he spoke, I felt something pull me deeper into the mess we'd created.

"I'm not running," I said, finally lifting my eyes to meet his. "I'm just trying to figure out why I thought any of this was a good idea."

His eyes softened, a flicker of understanding crossing them. It was gone before I could blink, replaced by that familiar smirk. "You invited me, remember?"

I clenched my jaw. He had a point, but that didn't mean I had to like it. "Yeah, well, sometimes I make terrible decisions."

There was a long pause. Rafe didn't move, didn't say anything. For a moment, the world shrank down to the two of us standing in the dark. And in that moment, something shifted between us. It wasn't a reconciliation or an apology, but an understanding of sorts. Like we were both stuck in this mess we'd created, unable to look away.

"You're not as complicated as you think," he said, his voice suddenly serious.

I scoffed. "Oh, really? Care to explain that one?"

He tilted his head, studying me like a puzzle he was trying to figure out. "You don't know what you want, but you're scared to admit it. And in the meantime, you push everyone away because it's easier than facing it."

I opened my mouth to argue, to tell him he had no idea what he was talking about. But the words never came. Instead, I stood there, staring at him, realizing that he wasn't wrong. Not entirely, at least.

Rafe took a step closer, his eyes never leaving mine. "I'm not saying this is easy, or that it's going to be. But at least be honest with yourself." His voice was quiet, but there was a weight to it now, something that made my chest tighten. "Because the only person you're fooling is you."

I couldn't breathe.

The cold air seemed to bite harder, but it wasn't the weather that had me frozen in place. It was him. The way his words cut through me, the way he made me feel like he could see every single crack I'd spent so long hiding.

For a moment, I didn't know what to say. I didn't know what to do. I was too caught up in the pull of it all—the tension, the unspoken truth, the way he was looking at me like he wasn't sure whether he should kiss me or shake me until my teeth rattled.

I turned away, needing space, needing something to break the suffocating silence that had taken over. "I need a drink," I muttered, more to myself than to him.

Rafe's voice stopped me before I could walk away. "You sure about that? Because what I see right now? You're running again."

I didn't look back, but the words followed me like an echo in the back of my mind.

I walked away from him. At least, that was the plan. But with each step, the weight of my own hesitation pressed heavier against my chest. I could hear Rafe behind me, his footsteps following a beat too slow to be casual, but too quick to be indifferent. He wasn't done. Not by a long shot.

I reached the door to the house, a glassy reflection of a place that had seen too many of my mistakes, too many of my half-baked decisions. My hand lingered on the knob as I tried to control the tremble that had taken over my fingers. There was no denying it anymore. Every nerve was on high alert, humming with the electric undercurrent between us. I should have been smarter than this. I should have known better. But here I was, standing in the doorway, wondering what the hell I thought I was doing.

And then, his voice. Low and controlled, but cutting through the air like it was made of glass. "You're running again."

I could have ignored him. I could have walked inside, locked the door, and let the party continue on without me. But I didn't. I turned slowly, my back still against the doorframe, my heart pounding a little louder than I was comfortable admitting. "I'm not running."

"Really?" Rafe's eyes didn't leave mine as he took a step closer. "Because every time I get close, you do this dance—turning away, shifting the conversation, pretending it's something it's not."

I knew I should be furious. Maybe I should yell at him, tell him to back off, that I wasn't interested in whatever this was. But the words wouldn't come. Instead, I found myself standing there, stuck between wanting to yell at him and wanting to do something far more dangerous.

I couldn't make sense of any of it. This—us—wasn't something I understood, not even a little bit. And yet, here I was, standing face-to-face with Rafe, the one person I'd sworn to hate, feeling like maybe it wasn't so simple after all.

"I'm not doing anything," I muttered, my voice barely above a whisper. But it didn't matter. He heard it. And he was right.

"Stop pretending," he said, his voice softer now. The edge was gone, replaced by something far more dangerous—something that made my pulse race. "You can't keep running from this, no matter how hard you try."

I opened my mouth to argue, but the words got caught. Because the truth? It was right there, clear as day. He had me. He'd always had me, whether I liked it or not. But I wasn't about to give him the satisfaction of seeing it on my face.

"You think you know me, don't you?" I snapped, pulling my arm back from his reach, even though my body was begging me to do the opposite.

"I know enough," he replied, his gaze steady as a stormfront. "I know you're scared. Scared of whatever this is between us, scared of letting it go too far."

I blinked, taken aback by how much he had nailed it. The fight, the distance I'd put between us, everything. He was right. But admitting that would mean acknowledging the one thing I had spent my entire life running from.

"So what? You're going to psychoanalyze me now?" I asked, my voice rougher than I intended.

"No," Rafe said, taking another step closer, this time with a quiet certainty. "But you're doing a damn good job of psychoanalyzing yourself." His words hung in the air between us like smoke. "And that's the problem."

I was still trying to find my ground when I felt it—a flicker of something, something that wasn't just frustration or anger or confusion. It was something deeper. Something that made me feel like I couldn't breathe, like my chest had been hollowed out and filled with too many questions.

For a split second, it was like everything stopped. The party inside, the people laughing, the buzz of normality—it all faded. All I could hear was Rafe's voice, low and steady, wrapping around me like a thick fog. "You can fight it all you want, but I'm not going anywhere. You're going to have to face this."

It was his eyes. There was a flicker in them, something raw and unguarded, something that made me take a step back. "You're wrong," I said, shaking my head, as if I could force myself to believe it. "You don't know anything."

His gaze never wavered, and I swear, for the first time, I saw a hint of something—something like regret. Or maybe it was understanding. But before I could ask, before I could decipher the look in his eyes, he took another step closer, closing the distance between us. "I know more than you think," he said, his voice dropping to a whisper that felt like it was meant only for me.

I should have said something. I should have told him to get lost. Told him that whatever this was, it wasn't going to happen. But I didn't.

He reached out, his hand resting lightly against my arm, like he was testing the waters, like he wasn't sure whether I would pull away or lean into it. I froze, torn between wanting to push him away and wanting to let him hold me there. Let him take the tension away. Let him kiss me.

I felt the shift in the air between us before I heard his voice again. "You don't have to do this alone, you know. You don't have to pretend anymore."

His words were an invitation, soft but laden with something far heavier.

And just as I was about to respond, to tell him exactly how wrong he was, the door behind me creaked open, and my brother's voice cut through the moment like a knife. "Hey, what's going on out here?"

I turned, heart leaping in my chest, as Rafe's hand dropped away, like he'd been caught in the act. The sudden tension in the air shifted, everything snapping back into place—except I wasn't sure anymore what that place was. What was I supposed to do now?

My brother's voice again, clearer this time, breaking the silence between us: "You two okay?"

I opened my mouth, but nothing came out. And in that moment, I realized that everything—every single thing—I had been avoiding, had been waiting for this.

Chapter 10: Hidden Flames

The air in the study was thick with the smell of stale paper and old ink, the weight of forgotten secrets clinging to the yellowed pages I sifted through. I could barely remember the last time I'd felt comfortable in this room, and it wasn't because of the dusty bookshelves or the half-empty mug of cold coffee I'd been ignoring for hours. No, it was the creeping sense of unease, the gnawing sensation that I was getting closer to something, but I wasn't entirely sure if I wanted to uncover it. The blueprints, with their neat little diagrams and lines, felt more like traps than the solutions they promised. And the police reports? They were the final insult—detached, methodical, yet entirely incapable of explaining the darkness that had descended on my family.

I ran my fingers over the edges of the documents, each one a piece of the puzzle, yet none of them seemed to fit together properly. The fire that had torn through my family's estate had left more than physical scars; it had left a deep, insidious wound in the fabric of everything we knew. We'd spent years pretending it was over, that it was some terrible accident, a stroke of bad luck. But here, with the past unfolding before me, I knew better. The past was never finished. It was merely waiting, dormant, like a sleeper ready to wake up and claim what was rightfully its own.

"Did you find anything useful?" Rafe's voice cut through the silence like a knife, his words thick with that same intensity he always carried. He stood in the doorway, his broad frame casting a shadow across the floor. There was a fire in his eyes, one that hadn't been there when I'd first met him—so many years ago, back when we were both more naive, thinking the world had a way of settling into neat little boxes.

I didn't look up from the reports. "A whole lot of nothing," I muttered, my voice barely above a whisper. The weight of my own disappointment made the words feel heavier. "The original investigation was a joke. It's like they didn't even try to look into the people who could have really been behind it."

Rafe took a step closer, his footsteps deliberate, each one echoing off the hardwood floors like a warning. "You think someone close to you was involved?"

I straightened up, suddenly aware of the pounding of my heart. The thought of it made me feel dizzy, like the floor beneath me could give way at any moment. The house had been my sanctuary for as long as I could remember. It was more than just a home; it was the very heart of my family, a symbol of everything we'd built. The idea that someone from the inside, someone I knew, could have orchestrated such a thing was almost too much to bear.

"I don't know," I said, my voice shaking more than I cared to admit. "But... Wilder. Detective Wilder. He told me there were things he wasn't allowed to pursue back then. Powerful people who wanted the case closed. Things they didn't want anyone digging into." I leaned back in my chair, suddenly feeling the weight of a thousand years pressing down on me. "What if it was someone we both knew? What if it was someone from our own circle?"

Rafe's eyes darkened. His lips pressed into a thin line, his jaw tight with frustration. "Then we need to find out who. Now. Because if we don't, we might not just lose our footing—we might lose everything."

I nodded, the tension building between us like a live wire. I wanted to tell him that I wasn't ready, that I wasn't sure I could handle the truth, whatever it was. But there was something about his certainty, his determination, that made me feel like I didn't have a choice. If this was really as big as it seemed, if there was more to this than anyone realized, then we were already in deeper than we could have imagined. And there was no turning back.

"I've got a contact," Rafe said after a long pause, his voice low. "Someone who might know more about the people Wilder's talking about. They're not going to be easy to find, but they're tied to this. I can feel it."

I raised an eyebrow, trying to suppress the sudden surge of panic. "And you trust them?"

He didn't hesitate. "I trust them more than I trust most people. But that doesn't mean it's going to be safe. You need to be ready for whatever comes next."

I stood up, moving around the desk, the creak of the chair behind me a small reminder of how precariously balanced everything felt. I wasn't sure I was ready for whatever dark alley Rafe was about to lead us down, but I knew that if we were going to get to the truth, we had no other choice. We were in this together now, tangled in the mess of half-buried lies and secrets that had been left to fester.

The air between us crackled with something I couldn't quite name, something that made my skin feel too tight, like I was wearing someone else's clothes. The thought of the people we would have to face, the people we would have to uncover, made me want to retreat into the safety of ignorance. But then I remembered the fire, the devastation it had wrought. I couldn't let that be the end of it. Not when there was still a chance to uncover the truth.

I met Rafe's eyes, my gaze steady despite the storm of emotions swirling inside me. "Where do we start?" I asked, my voice firmer than I felt. "Let's finish this."

His smile was fleeting, almost ghostly, before he turned on his heel and headed for the door. "Let's go find some answers."

The next few hours felt like I was walking through a fog, the edges of reality blurred and indistinct. Rafe and I had spent the morning in my office, the air thick with tension, scouring through files that seemed to multiply as soon as you turned your back. The silence between us was not comfortable, but rather the kind of quiet that presses against your chest like a heavy weight. Each file, each document, each scrap of paper only deepened the mystery, the sense that we were so close, yet so far. We were close to the truth, I was certain of that. But closer meant that the world I thought I knew might crack wide open, and I wasn't sure I could handle it.

As we left my office, I glanced at Rafe, his jaw clenched, his movements sharp and purposeful. It wasn't the usual calm, collected persona he showed to the world. No, this was a man who had seen something, understood something, and was now steeling himself for a storm. I could see the storm in his eyes. There was no room for hesitation, not now.

He gave a sharp nod toward the back door, where the gravel driveway stretched out, the world outside as uncertain as the one we were about to step into. "We need to move quickly. The longer we wait, the more people will cover their tracks."

I followed his gaze, and for the first time, I understood the meaning behind his words. This wasn't just about finding a culprit anymore. This was about uncovering something that had been buried for far too long, something that was powerful enough to destroy us if we weren't careful. It was a game of survival now.

The day had turned colder, the wind picking up as we stepped outside. The scent of wet earth and pine needles clung to the air. Fall was settling in around us, a season of change, of things dying and being reborn. It felt appropriate, given the weight of what we were about to face. But as much as the landscape outside seemed to shift with the season, nothing about the tension between Rafe and me had changed. If anything, it had thickened, like the air before a storm, still but charged with unspoken words.

"Who are we meeting?" I asked, trying to keep my voice steady. I hated how it wavered, how it betrayed the unease I couldn't shake.

Rafe glanced over at me, his lips curling slightly in something that wasn't quite a smile but held a hint of amusement. "Someone who owes me a favor. And trust me, it's a favor I've been waiting to cash in for a while."

I raised an eyebrow, skeptical. "Someone who's not exactly on the up-and-up, I take it?"

"Is anyone?" He shot me a look. "You'll see."

The drive was short, but every mile felt like we were heading deeper into the unknown. The town had long since faded behind us, the familiar houses and streets replaced by dense trees and isolated cottages. The wind had picked up, a gust slapping against the windows with a force that made me instinctively grip the seat beneath me. I wasn't sure what I was bracing for—whether it was the meeting ahead or what we might find when we arrived.

Rafe's silence was heavy, pressing against my skin, and I couldn't help but wonder if he, too, was feeling the weight of what we were about to do. I had seen him face danger before, with the kind of cold resolve that only comes from experience. But this was different. This wasn't just about getting out alive. This was about exposing something that would unravel everything we knew, and I couldn't help but wonder if we were ready for it.

When we finally pulled up to a small, nondescript house on the outskirts of town, the air seemed to still. Even the trees seemed to hold their breath as we got out of the car, the crunch of gravel beneath our feet unnervingly loud. I glanced at Rafe, who was already heading up the front steps, his expression unreadable.

The door opened before we even reached it, a tall man in his mid-forties standing in the frame. His eyes were sharp, assessing, and there was a guardedness to him that made it clear he wasn't someone who gave his trust easily. He didn't offer his hand, didn't offer a smile, just stepped aside to let us in.

"Nice to see you again, Wilder," Rafe said, his voice even, controlled.

"Don't make it sound like a reunion," Wilder replied, his tone dry. He led us into a modest living room, the kind of place that didn't want to be noticed. If you had a choice between the rest of the world and this place, you'd pick the world, but there was a quiet kind of strength to it—like it had withstood more than its fair share of storms.

I took a seat, trying not to let the nervous energy I was feeling bleed into the room. "So," I began, trying to keep the tremor out of my voice, "what's so urgent that it couldn't wait?"

Wilder's gaze shifted between us before he spoke, his words slow and deliberate. "You two are digging in places most people have forgotten about. And someone wants to keep it that way."

Rafe leaned forward, his intensity flaring again, that familiar edge creeping back into his posture. "Who's involved? We know there are people with influence, but we need names, Wilder."

The detective paused, his fingers drumming lightly on the coffee table. "Names are tricky. Some people play their cards close. But I can tell you this: if you keep pushing, you're going to rattle a cage that's been locked for a very long time. And when you do, you might not like what comes out."

The room grew colder, the walls pressing in, suffocating in their quiet menace. My heart hammered against my chest, but I kept my focus on Wilder, forcing myself not to let the fear rise up in my throat.

"Tell us what you know," I said, my voice firmer than I felt.

Wilder's smile was thin, like he was enjoying the game, the chase. "You're already too far in. It's just a matter of how much you want to risk now."

The silence between us was thick, pregnant with implications. And as Wilder's words sank in, I realized something—this wasn't just about the fire anymore. This was about power. And whoever controlled it, controlled everything.

The tension in Wilder's living room hung thick, like smoke still curling around us from a fire that refused to die. His words weren't comforting. They weren't even cryptic in a playful way. They were a warning—a plea wrapped in a riddle. And though I hated it, I could feel myself being pulled deeper into the whirlpool of uncertainty. The truth, or whatever version of it Wilder was hinting at, was not a thing I could control, no matter how badly I wanted to.

Rafe shifted beside me, and the subtle clenching of his fists didn't escape me. He had his own demons gnawing at him, demons I was starting to suspect were more connected to this mess than either of us realized. His eyes were locked on Wilder, but I saw the slight tremor in his jaw, the way his body was taut, as if waiting for the storm to break. We'd already peeled back a few layers of this case, but the deeper we went, the more I wondered whether we were simply unearthing things better left buried.

"Who is this 'someone' you keep mentioning?" I asked, my voice more composed than I felt. I was getting too used to this feeling of walking a tightrope, but I wasn't about to tip over just yet.

Wilder's lips pressed together in a tight line, and I could see him weighing his next words like they carried more weight than he was ready to reveal. "There are some things in this town," he began slowly, "that nobody talks about. Things that have been swept under the rug for decades. The fire was just one of many incidents, but the real story is much older. Whoever set that fire wasn't acting alone, and they weren't just after your family. They were sending a message."

I leaned forward, suddenly aware of just how much was riding on what came next. "A message to whom?"

Wilder glanced between Rafe and me, his eyes dark with what I could only assume was regret. "To the people who thought they could control everything. The ones who are still pulling the strings from behind the scenes."

I exhaled sharply. "You're telling me this is about power, not just revenge."

"Exactly." Wilder's voice was heavy with resignation. "And the people behind this have a lot of power. More than you realize. They've been orchestrating things in this town for years, manipulating events to their advantage. They keep things quiet. They always have. And they'll do whatever it takes to keep it that way."

Rafe stood up suddenly, the chair scraping loudly against the hardwood. "We're not walking away from this, Wilder. You owe us more than this vague crap. Who are they? Who's involved?" His voice was raw, the controlled anger barely masked beneath the surface.

Wilder held up a hand, his expression unreadable. "You don't want to know," he said, his voice low. "I'm telling you now: you dig too deep, and you'll be playing with fire in ways you can't control."

"And if we don't dig?" I asked, trying to keep the desperation from creeping into my voice. "If we walk away now, what happens? Will they just... let us go?"

A grim smile tugged at the corner of Wilder's mouth, but it didn't reach his eyes. "Oh, they'll let you go. For a while. Long enough to make you think you're safe. But don't fool yourselves. They never forget. And they never forgive."

Rafe's eyes narrowed, a flicker of suspicion crossing his features. "And you? Why are you helping us? What's in this for you?"

Wilder hesitated, his gaze darting briefly toward the window before settling back on us. "Some debts are harder to pay off than others," he said, his voice low and steady. "I'm not doing this because I think you'll come out of it unscathed. I'm doing this because I owe someone a favor. And trust me, you don't want to be in my position."

The weight of his words sank into the room, pressing down like a physical force. I was starting to feel the tightness in my chest again, the growing realization that we were all in over our heads. Whatever happened next, we couldn't turn back. The clock was ticking, and I had a sinking feeling that we were already too far gone.

"Where do we go from here?" I asked, my voice barely a whisper.

Wilder stood up, his movements sharp. "There's a place," he said, almost to himself, as if considering whether to share it. "A place where they keep everything. The people in charge. The ones who think they own this town. They've hidden their dirty little secrets for a long time, but if you're brave enough, you might be able to find something useful."

"And you'll lead us there?" Rafe's voice was taut, the skepticism thick in his tone.

Wilder gave a slow, calculating nod. "I'll take you to the edge. But after that, you're on your own. Don't say I didn't warn you."

The words echoed in my mind, reverberating like a dull throb in my temples. We were on the brink of something, a precipice we couldn't even see the bottom of. And the worst part? I wasn't sure if I was ready to jump. But there was no going back now. The game had already begun.

Rafe turned to me, his eyes burning with something unspoken, something sharp and dangerous. "Are you ready for this?" he asked, his voice low, his words hanging in the air between us like a challenge.

I met his gaze, my own heart hammering in my chest, and for a brief moment, I was reminded of the fire that had torn through everything—how quickly things could be consumed, how fragile the line between survival and destruction really was.

"I don't have a choice," I said, swallowing against the knot in my throat.

With one last look at Wilder, we turned toward the door. The weight of the world pressed down on us as we stepped out into the cold night air. The journey ahead was uncertain, but one thing was clear: we weren't the only ones who had been playing this game for years. And now, it was our turn to see how far the fire would spread.

And just as we reached the car, my phone buzzed in my pocket. I glanced at the screen and froze.

It was a message.

You're getting too close.

Chapter 11: Flammable Bonds

The wind tugged at the hem of my jacket, its chill creeping in despite the warmth of the night. I leaned against the low stone wall that separated us from the sprawling view of the town below, watching the lights flicker like scattered stars, unaware of the darkness that clung to the air. Rafe stood beside me, his profile etched sharply against the endless stretch of sky. He had a way of being so quiet, so still, that it was easy to forget he was standing next to me at all.

But his presence—his constant, magnetic presence—was undeniable. It always was. There was a weight to him, something that pulled me in, no matter how hard I tried to resist. That night, the one that had started it all, was still too fresh, too jagged to touch. It haunted him like the remnants of smoke in the air after a fire. His eyes flickered in the dark, and for a moment, I thought I saw a shadow pass across them. But it was gone before I could reach for it, leaving me with only a vague sense of unease.

I tucked my hands into my pockets, suddenly aware of the way my heart was thudding too loudly in my chest. I had come to terms with the fact that I was drawn to him in ways that made no sense. But I didn't know if I could keep walking down this path—this unlit road we were both stumbling along, blinded by our own tangled emotions.

"What's on your mind?" I asked, the question coming out softer than I intended, my voice betraying the uncertainty that had taken root.

Rafe didn't answer immediately. His gaze stayed fixed on the town below, his jaw tight, his lips pressed into a thin line. For a moment, I wondered if he even heard me at all. But then, just as the silence between us began to feel unbearable, he shifted slightly, as if some invisible weight had lifted from his shoulders.

"I don't think I'm good for you," he said, his words low and unsteady, as if they were something he'd been meaning to say for a long time but hadn't found the courage.

I blinked, the words slamming into me like a punch to the gut. "What?" I couldn't hide the confusion that shot through me. It wasn't what I expected. Not in a million years.

Rafe didn't look at me. Instead, he stared out into the night, his voice tight, almost strangled. "I've got... things. Things that don't belong in someone else's world. And I—I'm not sure how to leave them behind. Or if I even can." His shoulders tensed again, the muscles in his back coiling like he was preparing to run, to flee.

The air between us felt suddenly too thick, and I wondered if he was talking about the fire—about that night—about the pieces of himself he thought had burned away. But there was something else there, something deeper, like a wound that had never healed.

"I don't need you to be perfect," I said, my voice quiet but firm. I stepped closer, the words spilling out of me before I could stop them. "I need you to be real. All of you. Flaws and all. I don't want you to carry that weight alone."

Rafe's eyes finally met mine, and for a moment, I saw something break behind them. His face hardened, like he was bracing for impact, but the softness in his gaze gave him away. I knew him well enough to see the cracks in the façade.

"I'm not asking for your forgiveness," he muttered, his words barely audible. "I'm asking you to walk away before you get dragged down with me."

I shook my head, not knowing if I was more frustrated with him or with myself. How could he be so blind? So determined to protect me from him when he couldn't even see what was right in front of him?

"I don't want to walk away," I said, my voice steady but strained. "And I don't think I could, even if I tried."

The silence stretched between us again, but this time it didn't feel like a gulf that separated us. It was more like a quiet understanding, a shared space where words had become unnecessary. The tension between us buzzed like a live wire, electric and dangerous. I could feel it—feel him—almost like I could taste it, that volatile mixture of longing and pain that had been simmering beneath the surface for so long.

Rafe's hand brushed mine then, just the lightest of touches, but it was enough to send a shock of heat through me. My pulse quickened, and I wondered if he could feel it too—the way the world tilted slightly off-center when our hands connected. He pulled back quickly, like it was an accident, like it had never happened. But I felt the echo of it lingering in the air.

"I can't promise you anything," he said, his voice ragged, but there was something raw and honest in it that I hadn't heard before. "But I won't walk away. Not unless you tell me to."

I swallowed hard, the words I had been holding onto for so long threatening to spill out. But I couldn't. Not yet. Not until I understood what this was between us, what it meant to him.

"I don't need you to promise me anything either," I said, my voice small, almost fragile. "I just need you to stay."

The breeze swirled around us, tugging at my hair, the chill of the night cutting through the warm cocoon of my thoughts. Rafe's silence settled heavy between us, like a blanket too thick to lift, and I could feel the weight of it pressing against my chest. His hand had brushed mine, a spark, a jolt of connection—then gone, as if he were afraid the touch would burn us both. I glanced at him out of the corner of my eye, studying the lines of his jaw, the stiff set of his shoulders, the unspoken history he wore like armor. He wasn't just keeping his distance—he was fighting something, something so deep it made my heart ache for him, even as it made my feet drag in the mud of my own hesitation.

"Why does it always feel like there's something I can't reach with you?" I asked, my voice barely above a whisper. The words tumbled out before I could stop them, but there they were—raw, open, vulnerable. The truth that had been creeping up on me for weeks now.

Rafe's eyes flickered toward me, sharp and guarded, like he hadn't expected me to speak the thought aloud. I didn't expect him to answer. Not really.

"You don't need to understand it," he said, the words curt, as though they were nothing more than a shield he was throwing up between us. His gaze drifted away from me, fixing once more on the city below, as though the answer was there, waiting to be found in the lights. But it wasn't there. Not for me. Not for him.

"I don't need to understand you?" I echoed, not bothering to hide the incredulity in my tone. My fingers curled into the stone of the wall beside me, grounding me, keeping me tethered to this strange moment where the world was still spinning, but everything felt different. "You can't be serious."

"I am," he muttered, voice tight, like he was choking on the words, unwilling to let them out fully.

I wanted to press him. I wanted to demand an answer, to dig into whatever lie he was telling himself about me or this situation. But there was something in the way he held himself, the tautness in his every movement, that made me hesitate.

"Rafe, we're not... strangers," I said, softer this time, almost as if I were soothing him. "You're not a mystery to me. Not like this."

He turned his head slowly, finally meeting my gaze with eyes that were too weary, too distant for comfort. "You don't know me. Not really."

I swallowed hard, the words cutting deeper than I had anticipated. "Don't do that," I said, my voice trembling slightly despite myself. "Don't push me away. Don't tell me I don't know you when I do. When I've been trying to understand you for months now." I shook my head, suddenly feeling the sharp sting of frustration rise up inside me. I didn't know how to hold onto him when every time I tried, he pulled back, like my fingers were fire.

Rafe's jaw clenched. His hand gripped the edge of the stone, as if he were holding on to something more than just a rooftop. "I'm not asking for your understanding. Or your forgiveness," he said, the words flat and almost accusatory, like they were something he was too tired to carry anymore. "I'm telling you that you don't want to be anywhere near this. Trust me, you don't."

I flinched, my pulse skipping in my chest. "And yet here I am."

Rafe didn't look at me. He stared straight ahead, his shoulders pulled taut under the weight of a burden that seemed too heavy to explain.

"I'm not good for you, Anna," he said, the words coming out like a confession—shame, regret, and something darker swirling in the air between us. He sighed, long and deep, as though he were carrying the weight of the entire town on his back. "I won't be the one to undo all the damage. You deserve better than that."

I stared at him, feeling the words bounce around in my chest, trying to make sense of them. They didn't make sense. Not to me. Not to the person who had watched him fight his demons day after day, never once asking for anything in return.

"Don't," I said, my voice shaking with a fury I hadn't known I was capable of. "Don't tell me what I deserve. I'm not some fragile thing you need to protect, Rafe. I'm right here." I stood taller, trying to steel myself against the emotion that rose like a wave threatening to crash over me. "I'm not going anywhere."

He stiffened at my words, his hands clenched into fists. "You should," he snapped, his voice harder than I had ever heard it. "You should walk away before you get hurt. Before this..." He trailed off, his eyes flickering toward me briefly, almost as if he regretted saying anything at all.

"You think I'm afraid of being hurt?" I countered, a laugh that wasn't really a laugh slipping from my lips. It was bitter, sharp, and I let it hang in the air between us. "You think this"—I gestured between us—"is some delicate little thing that can be broken by one wrong move? You're wrong. You're wrong about me."

Rafe's face softened, but there was a storm behind his eyes, one that threatened to break free if I pushed him too far. And I could see it, could almost taste the raw edge of everything he was holding in. But I didn't care. I couldn't care. Not when he was standing there, cutting himself off from everything that mattered—everything that we could be.

"I won't walk away from you, Rafe," I said, my voice steady this time. "Not unless you make me. But don't ask me to, because I'm not going anywhere."

He turned toward me then, his face a mask of conflicting emotions. His lips parted as if he had something to say, but the words never came. Instead, his gaze softened, just for a moment, before it hardened again.

"I'm sorry," he muttered, the words so quiet I almost didn't hear them. "I really am."

I didn't know what to say to that. So I didn't. Instead, I just reached out, my fingers brushing against his wrist, a silent promise, a gesture of something neither of us could put into words. Not yet. But maybe, someday, we'd get there.

The words hovered between us, heavy with something unsaid. I could feel the air thicken, like it was stretching, waiting for a release. The light of the town below flickered and danced, mocking the stillness between us. Rafe stood rigid beside me, his face impassive, but there was something in his eyes—something wild, desperate, as if he were on the verge of cracking wide open and I didn't know if I could handle the mess that might spill out.

For a long moment, neither of us spoke. The night settled around us, heavy with silence, the kind of silence that was filled with too much. I felt it deep in my bones, the unsaid things, the things we both tried to keep hidden. But there was no ignoring them. Not now. Not anymore.

I took a breath, steadying myself. "You can't keep pushing me away, Rafe. I'm not going anywhere."

He exhaled sharply, a sound like frustration, like a man at the end of his rope. His eyes darted to the horizon before meeting mine. "You don't understand. I've seen what happens when someone gets too close. I've lost enough already." His voice was raw, stripped of any pretense.

My heart ached. I knew it. I knew the weight he carried. I'd seen the marks of that fire in the way he moved, in the way his eyes would sometimes flicker to the shadows, as if expecting them to rise up and claim him again. But I also knew that running, hiding, wasn't going to save him. And it certainly wouldn't save me.

"I'm not afraid of your past," I said, my voice firm but gentle. I reached out then, hand trembling, not because I was scared, but because it felt like I was offering him a part of me that could be burned. "I'm not afraid of what you think might happen. I want to be here. With you. Through whatever this is."

Rafe's gaze softened, just the smallest fraction, but then his hand shot out, gripping mine, his fingers cool but firm. "Don't make me choose, Anna," he said, his voice low and thick with emotion. "I don't want to pull you down with me. You deserve better than this... better than me."

My pulse quickened, a flicker of something deep and unrelenting stirring inside me. "I'm not here to be saved. I'm here because I want to be. And maybe that's messy, maybe it doesn't make sense, but I'm here."

He searched my face, his expression caught between something like hope and something darker, like he feared this would all slip away as easily as it had come.

And maybe he was right to be afraid. The world was messy, unpredictable. But sometimes, there was beauty in the mess. I didn't expect him to heal overnight or to open up like a book just because I was standing there. But I did know this: if he ever stood a chance at healing, if I ever stood a chance at understanding what was left of him, we had to start somewhere. And that somewhere was here, in the quiet, on this rooftop, with the town sprawled below us, full of unknowns, full of possibilities.

"Don't you see?" I said, the words rushing out, as though they might vanish into the night air if I didn't say them now. "I'm not running. I'm staying."

There was a long pause. His grip tightened around my wrist, but the look in his eyes was different this time. I wasn't sure if it was relief or more fear, but it was something. I could feel the unspoken promise hanging between us, fragile but real.

"I'm not the man you think I am," he muttered, his voice tinged with bitterness. "I can't be the man you deserve. Not when there's so much darkness in me."

"Then we'll figure it out together," I said, meeting his gaze. "Because I don't need you to be perfect, Rafe. I just need you to be real."

His breath caught in his throat, his jaw tightening as though my words hit a nerve he wasn't ready to face. But before he could respond, a sharp noise cut through the air—a sound so out of place, so sudden, that my heart skipped in my chest. It was a low rumble, like distant thunder, but this wasn't weather.

Rafe whipped around, his eyes narrowing, his body stiffening with the kind of alertness I recognized from hours of watching him on edge. The sound came again, and this time I could hear it clearly: the unmistakable screech of tires, followed by a sharp, jolting crash.

Without thinking, I grabbed his arm. "What was that?"

Rafe's face hardened, his muscles tense under my touch. "Stay here," he said, but the order was already meaningless. I was already moving, already following him as he rushed to the stairs, his steps quick and sure.

But when we reached the ground, the scene waiting for us stopped us both dead in our tracks.

There, in the middle of the street, a car was smashed against the side of a building, its front end crumpled like paper. The headlights flickered weakly, illuminating the wreckage. And standing beside the car, silhouetted against the glow, was a figure I didn't recognize.

Before I could speak, Rafe was already moving toward the figure, his expression unreadable. I hesitated for a second—long enough to feel the tension coil in my chest—then followed him, trying to ignore the nagging feeling that something had just shifted, something had broken loose, and it wasn't just the wrecked car.

"Rafe," I called, but my voice was swallowed by the night, by the sound of the wind, the distant echo of the crash.

He stopped suddenly, his body going rigid as the figure turned, revealing a face I thought I'd never see again.

I froze.

It was him.

Chapter 12: Smoke Signals

I was used to the quiet hum of the town at night, the kind of stillness that settled in your bones, making the air feel thick and heavy with unspoken secrets. But the silence now felt different. It was the kind of quiet that had a sharp edge to it, like a knife wrapped in velvet. The kind that told you something dangerous was lurking just beneath the surface, waiting to snap. And in the heart of it all was Rafe.

I watched him from across the room as he leaned over the table, his eyes scanning the mess of papers and photographs we'd spread out in front of us like a map of a crime scene. The dim light from the desk lamp caught the angles of his face, throwing shadows that made him look even more like the man I couldn't stop thinking about. His jaw was tight, his brow furrowed in concentration. The soft buzz of the lamp overhead was the only sound in the room as I waited for him to speak.

"I think we're getting closer," he said, his voice low, almost like he didn't want to say the words out loud. He ran a hand through his hair, a frustrated sigh escaping his lips as he shifted the papers around.

I wasn't sure if he meant the investigation or us. But I didn't ask. Instead, I nodded, pretending like everything was fine, when in reality, everything felt like it was slowly slipping away. The police chief had made it clear—stop digging, or there would be consequences. But I couldn't. I couldn't walk away when I felt like the truth was right there, hidden behind locked doors and faded photographs. There was too much at stake.

"You're sure we should keep pushing?" I asked, my voice barely above a whisper. The question felt absurd, given the circumstances, but there was something in me that needed to hear it. Needed to hear him say we weren't wasting our time. "I mean, it's getting pretty dangerous, Rafe."

His eyes flicked to mine, a brief flash of something crossing his face—anger? Fear? I couldn't tell. "If we stop now, they win," he said, his words clipped. "And if they win..."

I didn't need him to finish the sentence. I already knew the stakes. If we stopped now, it wasn't just about us anymore. It was about everything we cared about, everything we'd worked for, all the things the town tried so hard to keep hidden. But there was more to it than just the investigation. There was a weight that hung between us, unspoken and yet undeniable.

I shifted my position, trying to get comfortable, but the chair beneath me creaked under my movements, reminding me how tired I was. It felt like we'd been at this for weeks, long nights spent in search of something that might not even exist, but we couldn't stop. Not now.

"Maybe," I said, my voice trailing off as I picked up a photo of the old mill. The one that kept showing up in every lead we'd followed. "Maybe it's not just about stopping them. Maybe it's about stopping what they're going to do next."

Rafe didn't say anything, but I saw the way his eyes softened when he looked at me. He knew what I meant. The town had been quiet for too long. It had been sitting on its own secrets, festering like an open wound, waiting for the right moment to bleed. And whatever we were uncovering, it was only the tip of the iceberg.

I dropped the photo back onto the table with a sigh, rubbing my temples as a headache began to take hold. The tension between us had been building, but it wasn't just the investigation that had me on edge. It was him. The way he had been holding back, the way his words sometimes felt like they were buried beneath something deeper, something he wasn't ready to share. And then, just when I thought I couldn't take it anymore, he did something unexpected.

"I never told you this," Rafe said suddenly, his voice barely audible as he looked at me, almost like he was testing the waters. "About my sister."

I froze, my heart skipping a beat. My mouth went dry as I met his gaze. He had never talked about his sister—not really. I knew she had died, but the details were always vague, like a fog hanging around the truth. And now, he was opening the door, and I wasn't sure if I was ready to walk through it.

"I don't know if I'm ready to hear it," I said, my voice trembling slightly despite my best efforts to keep it steady. But he was already leaning forward, his eyes locked on mine, his lips pressed together in a thin line.

"You need to know," he said, his voice low, raw with a kind of pain that made my chest tighten. "She was... she was the reason I came back here, the reason I didn't leave when everything fell apart. But I never told anyone why she died. Not even my parents."

The air around us seemed to shift, like the room had suddenly gotten smaller, the walls closing in. I could feel the weight of his words pressing down on me, the vulnerability in them raw and unfiltered. And for the first time since we'd started this, I wasn't sure what to say. What could I say? There was nothing to say. The truth was dangerous, like a match to a pile of dry leaves, and once it started burning, there would be no stopping it.

But then he spoke again, his voice barely above a whisper, as if he were confessing a sin he'd carried for years. "I think she knew something. Something about what happened to our father... to all of us."

And just like that, I was no longer sitting at the table with Rafe. I was somewhere else—lost in the story of his sister, in the quiet pain he wore like a second skin. My breath hitched in my throat, the mystery deepening with every word he spoke.

There was no going back now.

The night air outside was cool, crisp with the kind of bite that made your breath visible, like it could freeze and shatter if you weren't careful. But it wasn't the chill that was making my skin prickle. No, it was the weight of what Rafe had just said, the way his words had settled into the room, thick and unsettling. He hadn't just confessed something about his sister; he'd thrown a grenade into everything we thought we knew.

"I don't understand," I said, my voice coming out rougher than I intended. "What do you mean, she knew something?"

Rafe's gaze remained fixed on the table, though I could see his jaw working, like he was trying to chew through whatever it was that had been stuck in his throat for so long. The silence stretched between us, heavy and taut, until he finally spoke, his voice barely above a whisper.

"She'd been asking questions," he said. "Questions about Dad. About the way things were—before he... before everything happened." He looked at me then, his eyes dark, guarded. "She thought something wasn't right. She thought he wasn't being honest with us. She thought he was hiding something."

I leaned back in my chair, the creaking of the wood echoing too loudly in the room, almost as if the house itself was holding its breath. It was hard to wrap my head around what he was saying. Rafe's father—big, imposing, the kind of man who had a hand in everything that happened around here—was hiding something? The thought sent a cold shiver down my spine. I had grown up with the stories, the rumors that floated like smoke in the background, the whispered glances that people shot when they thought no one was looking. But this? This was different. This was personal.

"How do you know?" I asked, leaning forward, the words slipping out before I could stop them. "How do you know she wasn't just... wrong? How do you know she wasn't just paranoid?"

Rafe's laugh, low and bitter, cracked through the tension in the room. "Because she was never wrong," he said, his eyes narrowing. "Not about anything."

His words hit me harder than I expected. I had heard of Rafe's sister in passing, but it was always like she was a ghost—just a name, a shadow. She had died young, under mysterious circumstances, and the town had chalked it up to an accident. But hearing Rafe talk about her now, with such raw emotion, made the hair on the back of my neck stand up. There was so much more to the story, I could feel it in my bones.

"So what happened?" I asked, even though I wasn't sure I was ready for the answer.

Rafe's eyes flicked away, his hand brushing over his face, as if he were trying to erase the memory. When he spoke again, it was with a quiet intensity that made my stomach twist.

"She... she was found in the river," he said. "They said she drowned. But I don't believe that. I don't believe it for a second." He stood up suddenly, his chair scraping across the floor, and walked to the window, looking out into the night. "She was too smart for that. She knew too much. She was digging into things she shouldn't have been."

I stood up too, crossing the room to join him at the window. We both stared out at the town below, the lights from the streetlamps casting long, thin shadows across the buildings. It looked so peaceful, so ordinary. But I knew better. There was nothing ordinary about it. Not anymore.

"So you think..." I trailed off, unsure of how to phrase the question that had been lingering in the back of my mind since the moment he started talking. "You think someone killed her?"

Rafe didn't answer right away. Instead, he ran a hand through his hair, his eyes distant, as if he were seeing something far away.

Finally, he turned to face me, his expression hard, his jaw clenched tight.

"I don't think it was an accident," he said, his voice tight with conviction. "And I don't think she's the only one who's going to end up dead if we don't get to the bottom of this."

I felt a chill seep through my bones, not from the night air, but from his words. There it was again—the weight of the danger we were both in. The same danger that had been hanging over us ever since we started poking around in places we weren't supposed to. But now, with what Rafe had just said, it felt like it was closing in. There was something bigger at play, something that stretched far beyond just a few break-ins or petty thefts.

"What do we do now?" I asked, my voice barely audible in the heavy silence that filled the room.

Rafe didn't look at me. Instead, he stared out into the darkness, his eyes searching for something I couldn't see. "We keep going," he said, his voice cold and steady. "We find out what happened to her. And we make sure it doesn't happen to anyone else."

The resolve in his voice sent a shiver through me, but it wasn't fear—not exactly. It was something else, something deeper. There was no going back now, not for either of us. Not after what he had just shared.

I turned away from the window, moving back to the table where the evidence lay. The photographs, the notes, the tiny threads of information that we had been pulling together. They were all pieces of a puzzle, and I could feel it now, in my gut—the pieces were starting to fit together. But the picture they were forming was darker than I had ever imagined.

"Are you sure we're ready for this?" I asked, my hand hovering over a photograph of his sister, her bright smile frozen in time, her eyes filled with something I couldn't quite place.

Rafe didn't look up from the window. He didn't need to. "We don't have a choice."

And that was the truth, wasn't it? We didn't have a choice. Not anymore.

I felt the weight of Rafe's words like a stone lodged in my chest. There was a depth to his confession that hadn't just cracked the surface of a mystery—it had shattered everything I thought I knew about the town and its people. What he was saying wasn't just about his sister's death. It was about a series of hidden truths, buried beneath layers of silence and secrets that, if revealed, could tear the entire town apart.

I could still hear his voice, that quiet, bitter edge to it when he spoke about her death—about the way she had been digging into things no one else dared question. She hadn't just been a casualty of an accident. She had been an unintentional martyr, searching for something dangerous, something that had gotten her killed. And the worst part? I knew he wasn't lying. There was no mistaking the raw pain in his eyes, the same pain that had driven him back here, to the very heart of the town he tried to escape.

I stood up abruptly, unable to sit still any longer, my heart pounding in my chest. "We can't ignore this, Rafe," I said, turning to face him, my voice sharp with the urgency of it all. "If your sister was onto something—if she was really onto something—then we have to find out what. We have to know the truth."

Rafe didn't meet my gaze at first, and when he finally did, there was a weariness in his eyes that made me question whether he believed we could handle it. He had spent years running from this town, from his past, from whatever ghosts his sister had left behind. I could see it in his posture, the way his shoulders hunched, like he was already carrying more than anyone should.

"I know," he said quietly. "But that doesn't mean it's going to be easy. It never is."

His words hung in the air, but they didn't reach me. I was beyond caring whether it would be easy. I was already too far gone, drawn deeper into this web of lies and murder, unable to pull myself out. And I knew Rafe was right there with me, even if he wasn't ready to admit it yet.

I walked over to the table, grabbing the stack of evidence that we'd been combing through for days now. Photos of the break-ins, of the townspeople who'd seemed so normal on the outside but had been harboring so many dark secrets beneath their skin. There were notes scribbled in the margins of the photographs, half-formed theories that had led nowhere but in circles, back to the same dead ends. But there was something there—something more than just petty thefts. Something connected to the break-ins, to the pattern of strange behavior among the townspeople.

"Look at this," I said, turning one of the photographs to face Rafe. It was of an old warehouse near the edge of town, one that had been abandoned for years. But recently, it had been showing up on every list of leads. There were no clear explanations for why anyone would break into such a run-down place, but every clue we had seemed to point back there.

Rafe's eyes flicked over the photograph, his face unreadable, but I could tell he was thinking. Thinking about his sister, about the night she disappeared, about everything he had tried to push away. I could see him wrestling with it, like he was trying to decide whether he was ready to dive back into the past or keep running.

"You think this is it?" he asked, his voice quiet, though there was an edge to it that made my heart race. He knew—he had to know—that there was no turning back now. "You think this warehouse has something to do with what happened to my sister?"

"I don't know," I admitted. "But it's the only thing that keeps showing up over and over again. There's a connection, I can feel it."

Rafe nodded slowly, but there was a darkness in his gaze now, a kind of resignation I hadn't seen before. "I know what you're thinking. But it's not just a warehouse. It's a place people disappear to."

My breath caught in my throat. "What do you mean, people disappear to?"

He pushed himself away from the window and took a few steps closer to the table, leaning over the scattered photographs, his hand hovering above the one of the warehouse. "Before my sister... she was trying to get inside the warehouse. She'd seen something. She'd overheard something, and she was getting too close. That's why they took her."

My pulse quickened. The room seemed to shrink around me as the pieces of the puzzle started to fall into place. Rafe's sister hadn't just been a casualty. She had been targeted. And if we were digging into the same things she had been, we were walking the same path—one that led to something far darker than either of us had anticipated.

"We can't go in there, Rafe," I said, my voice tight, the weight of his words sinking in. "If people are disappearing into that warehouse, we're not just looking for answers. We're looking for a fight."

Rafe's eyes met mine then, and in that moment, I saw it—the same resolve that had driven him all these years to keep pushing forward, to keep searching for something, even when it meant risking everything.

"I didn't come back here to run," he said, his voice low but steady. "And neither did you."

I felt the ground shift beneath my feet, the danger of it suddenly too real to ignore. He was right. We hadn't come back here to run. We'd come to finish what we'd started.

But as I turned back to the photographs, the sound of tires crunching on gravel outside sent a jolt of fear through me. It wasn't just the town that was watching us. Someone—or something—was keeping track of every move we made. And just like that, the door creaked open.

Someone was here.

I looked at Rafe, his expression unreadable, but the tension in the air was thick enough to cut with a knife.

Chapter 13: Scorched Earth

The air smelled like smoke, but not the kind from a fire. This was the stale scent of old things burning—dust, broken dreams, and something far more sinister. The days had dragged on, each one heavier than the last, and it had begun to feel like I was suffocating under the weight of it all. But nothing compared to the feeling of being alone in a room full of fire. Alone with him.

Rafe stood by the window, arms crossed, his profile sharp against the dying light. His jaw was tense, his eyes narrowed, the muscles in his neck taut as if he was trying to force out some truth he wasn't ready to face. The room was too quiet, the kind of silence that makes you hear your own thoughts too loudly. I leaned against the doorframe, watching him, and I wasn't sure which was more dangerous: the fire he was chasing or the fire we were both playing with.

"I need to know," I said, breaking the silence like a knife cutting through fog. The words felt like they shouldn't leave my mouth, but they did. They had to. "What's your plan here, Rafe?"

He turned, his eyes dark, unreadable. "I'm going to stop this before it gets any worse," he said, voice low, rough. He sounded like someone who had been holding himself together for far too long. Like someone who had already lost so much, he couldn't bear to lose anything else.

I didn't move. "That's it? No grand plan? Just... stop it?"

His gaze flickered to me, the briefest moment of vulnerability flashing through him before it was buried again, deep and hidden. "You think I don't have a plan?"

I took a step forward, crossing the room with quiet determination. "I think you're using this case like a crutch, Rafe. You think if you solve it, if you catch the bastard who's been setting these fires, it'll fix something. Maybe it'll even fix you."

His lips tightened, the muscle in his jaw jumping as if I had struck him with something sharp. "Don't act like you know me," he snapped, voice low but the anger behind it undeniable.

"I don't," I replied, stepping closer until we were almost toe to toe. "But I know this case is eating you alive. And I know what it's doing to you."

For a long moment, neither of us spoke. He was studying me now, eyes flicking from my face to my hands, and back again. The silence between us had shifted from the weight of tension to something more... charged. I didn't know what to make of it. I didn't know if I wanted to.

Finally, he looked away, breaking the moment. "I'm not going to let him get away with it," he muttered, almost to himself. "I won't."

"Who?" I asked, barely breathing as I waited for his answer.

His gaze stayed fixed on the window, the faraway look in his eyes saying more than words ever could. "My sister," he said, the two words dropping from his lips like stones into a quiet pond, making ripples that spread out far beyond what I could see.

I didn't know what to say to that. I had heard the rumors—everyone in town had—but hearing it from him was different. It was raw, exposed, and I could almost feel the heat of it on my own skin. His sister, the one who had died in the fire two years ago, the one whose death no one had ever been able to explain.

And now, as if the universe had decided to mock him, the same flames that had taken her were back again, threatening to take even more.

I couldn't ignore it. I couldn't pretend it wasn't eating away at him, inch by inch. This wasn't just a case for him. This was a personal vendetta, a chance to settle the score with a ghost he couldn't let go of. But I couldn't let him burn himself up in the process. Not when I was starting to care far too much.

"You can't do this alone," I said softly, my voice barely above a whisper, but it was enough. The words were a plea and a warning all at once.

He didn't answer right away. Instead, he walked toward me, his boots heavy on the floor, the room seeming to shrink with every step. When he was close enough that I could almost feel the heat radiating off him, he stopped. We stood there, so close I could see the tiniest flecks of gold in his eyes.

"I'm not asking for help," he finally said, voice steady but still holding that undercurrent of something darker, something desperate. "But I'm telling you, if you're going to keep walking down this road with me, you need to understand something. This isn't just about catching a criminal. This is personal. And I won't stop until I find him."

I nodded slowly, trying to ignore the tremor in my chest. "I understand," I said, but even I wasn't sure I did. "But you don't have to do this alone."

His lips curled, a half-smile that didn't reach his eyes. "I think you might be wrong about that."

The door behind me creaked open, cutting through the tension between us. I turned to see my partner, Theo, standing in the doorway. His expression was neutral, but the tension in his shoulders told me everything I needed to know.

"We've got a lead," he said, voice sharp, but his eyes flicked from me to Rafe, clearly picking up on the unspoken words that had passed between us. "It's the Devereux family. They're somehow connected to the arsonist."

Rafe's eyes went cold, the resolve in them sharpening like the edge of a blade. "The Devereuxs," he repeated, his voice low, almost lethal. "I should've known."

The fire he was chasing had just gotten hotter. And so had we.

The tension between Rafe and me had stretched thin, like a wire pulled tight just before snapping. There was something in the way he moved now, something I hadn't seen before—an edge, sharp and dangerous. He didn't speak much, but when he did, it was always to the point, no room for pleasantries or filler. I had always known him to be driven, but this new urgency... it was different. It was personal.

I tried to focus on the investigation, to remind myself that this was about more than whatever strange connection we had started to build. This wasn't a romance. This was a fire, literally and metaphorically, and I was standing right in the middle of it, playing the role of the reluctant firefighter. But every time Rafe looked at me, his eyes a little darker, a little more intense, I felt that familiar spark. I couldn't ignore it, no matter how much I tried.

The Devereux family wasn't just some old money house in the middle of town. They were the family, the kind of people whose names were whispered in every corner of the county, whose influence stretched beyond the county line and whose fortune was as much a part of the land as the trees in the woods. They had a history here, one that ran deeper than anyone cared to admit. But with that history came secrets. And if there was one thing I'd learned in my years of digging through the muck, it was that secrets had a way of coming to the surface, no matter how hard you tried to bury them.

"We're going to need more than a hunch," I said, my fingers drumming on the edge of the table as I stared at the old family estate on the map, the red marker a glaring presence in the center of the page. "What do we know about them, Rafe? I mean, really know?"

He leaned back in his chair, his fingers rubbing his temples like he was trying to ward off a headache, but his eyes never left the map. His jaw clenched. "Not much, except that they've always been untouchable. They've got connections, money, power—more than any one family should have. And if they're involved, it means this whole thing's about to get a hell of a lot messier."

My stomach tightened. "Messier how?"

"The Devereuxs don't just ruin people's lives," Rafe said, his voice flat, emotionless. "They bury them."

I swallowed, suddenly aware of the weight of the room, the air thick with the promise of danger. This was no longer just about the arsonist. It was about something darker, something far more sinister, and Rafe was right in the middle of it.

I shifted in my chair, trying to shake off the chill creeping up my spine. "We need a plan," I said, my voice more forceful than I intended, but the urgency was there. "We can't just walk into their house and start asking questions. We need leverage. A way to get inside."

Rafe didn't respond right away, but the flicker of something in his eyes was enough. He was already thinking of a way in. And I knew whatever it was, it wouldn't be pretty. He had a way of doing things that was... unconventional, to put it lightly. I wasn't sure I wanted to know what kind of favors he was willing to call in for this one.

"I've got a few ideas," he said finally, a slow smile curling at the corners of his lips, though there was no warmth behind it. "But we'll need to be careful. The Devereuxs have eyes everywhere."

I gave him a pointed look. "And you think that's going to stop us?"

His smile faded, but there was something in his gaze—something that flickered between us, an unspoken understanding. It was an understanding I didn't want to acknowledge, but there it was, heavy and impossible to ignore. We were in this together. Whether we liked it or not, we were partners now, and nothing would change that.

Theo, ever the realist, walked into the room then, his expression grim. He had a way of looking like he was constantly fighting off the inevitable, and today was no different. "I've got some intel on the Devereuxs," he said, flipping through a stack of papers he carried with him. "But you're not going to like it."

I raised an eyebrow. "How bad are we talking?"

Theo handed me a file, and I opened it slowly, already dreading what I might find. The first page was a list of names, dates, and connections—a family tree, of sorts. The Devereuxs had their hands in everything: law enforcement, local government, construction, even the church. There were a dozen businesses with their name on it, most of them legitimate. Some not so much.

"Wait a minute," I said, my eyes skimming the page. "This person... James Devereux. He's listed as the owner of a warehouse down by the river. That's where we found the first fire. The one that started it all."

Theo nodded. "Exactly. And if that wasn't enough, I've got confirmation that James was at the scene of the last fire. The one just last week."

I felt my stomach drop. "He's tied to the fires?"

"Not just tied," Theo replied. "He's the one who set them."

Rafe's eyes were cold again, the fire in them burning bright. "This just got personal," he muttered, more to himself than to anyone else. "And I'm not letting him walk away from it."

My breath caught in my throat. "We need to be careful. If he's behind this, we don't know what lengths he'll go to. He won't hesitate to silence us."

Rafe's gaze met mine, a flicker of something dangerous flashing in the depth of his stare. "I don't care. He's going down."

I knew he wasn't talking about just the fires anymore. And that, more than anything, made the hairs on the back of my neck stand up.

The night had fallen heavy over the city, its shadows stretching longer with each passing minute. The streets were still, the kind of stillness that made you feel like you were walking through a dream—half awake, half suspended in time. But the stillness in the air wasn't calming. It was suffocating, pressing in on me, reminding me that we were all racing against something we couldn't control. And the closer we got to the truth, the more I could see the toll it was taking on Rafe. The man I was starting to see beyond the investigator's mask was unraveling, little by little, and I wasn't sure how much longer he could hold himself together.

He hadn't said much since Theo dropped the bombshell about James Devereux. Rafe had gone quiet, his mind clearly elsewhere, tangled in thoughts too dark for anyone to truly understand. And I couldn't help but feel myself slipping deeper into this mess with him, despite every instinct telling me to pull away. But how could I? Every time I thought about leaving, about stepping back, Rafe's eyes—those dark, intense eyes—pulled me in again. I didn't know how to escape him, or if I even wanted to anymore.

"I don't know how much longer I can do this, Rafe," I finally said, my voice quiet, unsure of what I was even trying to express. "This—this thing with Devereux. It's not just about catching him anymore, is it?"

His jaw tightened, and he finally looked at me, his gaze flickering with something I couldn't quite decipher. "No. It's never just been about that."

The admission hit me harder than I expected. It was raw, unguarded, and for a split second, I saw the man who was still grieving the loss of his sister, the man who had been holding a grudge for so long he couldn't tell where the anger ended and the need for justice began.

I stood there, waiting for him to say more, but he didn't. He didn't need to. There was something unspoken between us now, something heavier than the air we breathed. It wasn't just the case anymore. It was us.

"So what now?" I asked, crossing my arms in front of me. "We go after Devereux directly?"

He nodded slowly, but there was something in the set of his shoulders, the rigid tension that hadn't been there before. "I have a plan," he said, but it was a lie. I could see it. His plan wasn't about following the evidence anymore. It was about him. And that wasn't going to end well for anyone.

I shook my head, frustration bubbling up. "I don't think you do," I snapped, the words harsher than I intended. "You're not thinking clearly, Rafe. You're too... too close to this."

He turned away from me, pacing the length of the small room, the wooden floors creaking under his weight. His hand ran through his hair, the frustration in his movements mirroring my own. "I don't have the luxury of thinking clearly anymore. If Devereux is behind this, it's not just about the fires. It's about her. My sister."

I swallowed, the weight of his words hitting me square in the chest. I hadn't realized, not fully, just how deep his obsession ran. I'd known about his sister's death, of course. Everyone had. But now, standing in front of me, was the person who had never let go. The person who couldn't move on. And I wasn't sure I was strong enough to hold onto him if he kept spiraling like this.

"You're angry," I said quietly, stepping closer, my hand instinctively reaching out, though I wasn't sure if I was trying to calm him or myself. "And I get that. But this—this thing with

Devereux, with the fires—it's a trap. If we go in like this, we're going to get burned."

Rafe's eyes snapped to mine, dark and fierce. "I don't care if I burn," he said, voice low and raw, the edges of his control slipping with every word. "Not anymore."

The words hung in the air between us, and for a moment, neither of us moved. I wanted to tell him to stop, to walk away before it was too late. But I could see it in his eyes—he wasn't going to stop. And neither was I.

A knock on the door broke the moment, sharp and insistent. We both turned toward it, and before I could ask who it was, Theo stepped into the room, his face pale. He didn't look like someone who had just come from a break; he looked like someone who had seen something he wasn't supposed to.

"We need to go," Theo said, voice tight with urgency. "Now."

I didn't wait for any further explanation. I grabbed my jacket, the coldness of the evening air rushing in as we made our way out the door. The city was dark, the streetlights flickering above us like ghosts in the night. My mind raced as I followed Rafe and Theo down the street, adrenaline pumping through my veins, the uncertainty gnawing at me.

"What happened?" I asked, keeping my voice steady despite the unease settling in my stomach.

Theo glanced over his shoulder, his face grim. "We found something," he said. "Something big."

We turned the corner, and I saw what he meant. The glow of the firelight flickered on the horizon, the unmistakable red-orange hue that only came from something burning, something intentional. I felt the air grow thicker, the weight of it pressing on my chest as we neared the source of the blaze.

And then I saw it.

The Devereux estate, the grand mansion that had stood tall for generations, was burning.

But that wasn't the worst part.

Rafe stopped dead in his tracks, his breath catching in his throat. I followed his gaze to the front gates, where a figure stood watching, his face partially hidden by the smoke.

It was James Devereux.

And he was smiling.

Chapter 14: Backdraft of Betrayal

The old wooden floor creaked beneath my feet, a sound so familiar it almost felt like home—yet tonight, it only served to remind me that nothing was as it seemed. I stood there, in the dim glow of the kitchen light, the flickering flame from the stove casting shadows on the walls like old ghosts trying to find their way back. The scent of simmering soup filled the air, but it did nothing to calm the tightness in my chest.

"Dad," I started, my voice tentative, unsure of the words. He was sitting at the kitchen table, elbows resting on the surface, his fingers tapping a rhythmic warning that echoed in the silence between us. His eyes, once a mirror of mine, now seemed to be filled with a weight I hadn't noticed before, like some unspoken knowledge had settled there, leaving no room for anything else.

"Stay away from him," my father said, his voice low, each word carved from stone. "You don't know him like I do."

I wanted to argue. I wanted to shout that I did know him—that I'd seen more of Rafe than anyone else had. But those words stuck in my throat, tangled with the pieces of the puzzle that were slowly starting to make sense in my mind. Pieces that had never quite fit, like the jagged edges of a broken mirror.

"Dad," I repeated, more forcefully this time, my hands gripping the edge of the counter. "What's going on? What aren't you telling me?"

He looked away, his gaze drifting to the window as if the answers lay outside in the darkness, just out of reach. "You wouldn't understand."

His words were like a slap, the kind that stings long after it's over. I hated that phrase, the one that said so much without saying anything at all. But before I could muster a response, there was a knock at the door—a sharp, insistent sound that made the hairs on the back of my neck stand up. I froze. Dad stood up from the table, his movements stiff, as though the sound had woken something in him he wasn't ready to confront.

I didn't wait for him to answer. My feet moved on their own, carrying me to the door before I could stop them. And when I opened it, there he was. Rafe. Standing there in the soft glow of the porch light, his expression unreadable, his hands shoved deep into the pockets of his jacket. There was something dangerous about the way he looked at me, like he knew something I didn't—like he was the one holding all the cards.

"Can we talk?" His voice was quiet, but there was a tremor in it that sent a ripple through my chest.

I nodded, stepping aside to let him in. But as he crossed the threshold, I saw my father's gaze harden, the tension in the air thickening like smoke. Rafe didn't even acknowledge him, which only seemed to make Dad angrier. The door clicked shut behind me with a finality that felt like a judgment.

I turned to Rafe, trying to read him, trying to piece together the man who stood in front of me—who seemed to be a stranger despite the hours we'd spent together. "What's going on?" I asked, my voice barely above a whisper. "Why did my dad say—"

But before I could finish, my father's voice cut through the silence, as sharp as a knife. "I warned you."

Rafe didn't flinch, didn't even seem surprised. Instead, he glanced over at my dad, his lips pulling into a thin line, like he was trying to hold back a storm.

"You don't know everything," Rafe said, his voice steady, but there was something beneath the surface—a flicker of uncertainty that I couldn't quite place. "Your father's kept secrets from you, just like I have."

I took a step back, feeling the ground shift beneath me. Secrets? What kind of secrets? The questions piled up faster than I could process them. Was it possible that everything—everything—had been a lie?

My father stood rigid in the doorway, his jaw clenched tight, his hands still at his sides, as if he was trying to keep himself from doing something he'd regret. I saw the way his eyes flicked between us, like he was weighing whether to say more. The silence stretched between us, thick with the tension of all the words that weren't being said. Then, finally, he spoke.

"I did what I had to do to protect you," my father said, his voice softer now, but still carrying that weight of something unsaid. "Sometimes the truth isn't what it seems. And sometimes, protecting the people you love means keeping them in the dark."

I looked at him, my chest tightening with the realization that I had no idea who he really was—not the man who had raised me, not the man I thought I knew so well. My entire life, every choice I'd made, had been based on his version of the truth. But what if that truth wasn't real?

Rafe's eyes met mine, and I saw the flicker of something dangerous there—a promise, perhaps, or a warning. He wasn't going to back down. But neither was I. This wasn't just about him anymore; it was about me, about finding out who I really was in all of this. And if that meant unraveling the tangled mess of lies my father had woven around me, then so be it.

My heart pounded in my chest, the weight of the decision pressing down on me like a storm cloud. But the question lingered in the air, unanswered, between us all: How far were we willing to go to uncover the truth, knowing it might break us in the process?

I wasn't sure. But I knew one thing—I couldn't walk away. Not now.

Rafe didn't flinch when my father's voice cracked through the air like thunder. In fact, he seemed almost too calm, a man accustomed to storms that didn't faze him. But the way he looked at me—eyes dark and knowing—made something cold crawl up my spine. It wasn't pity, nor was it sympathy. It was... resignation. Like he knew I would find out, and the only question left was how long it would take me to piece it all together.

I shifted my weight, unwilling to break the silence. It was as though the words we were all avoiding were hovering just above our heads, waiting for the moment someone would reach up and pull them down. My heart drummed in my chest, too loud, too fast. I wanted to scream, to demand answers from my father, from Rafe, but somehow I knew it wouldn't help. No one was going to tell me what I wanted to hear—not yet, anyway. And deep down, I knew the answers I was chasing were only going to complicate things further.

"I'm not going to stay away from him," I said, more to myself than anyone else. My voice had lost its sharpness, reduced to a weary whisper, as if the weight of the evening was finally crashing down on me. "I need to understand. I need to know why you're both acting like I'm some kind of fool."

My father's shoulders stiffened at my words, his jaw clenching. But Rafe, ever the enigma, gave me a small nod, as though I'd passed some sort of test he'd been waiting for me to take. He leaned against the wall, arms crossed, his expression unreadable, but his eyes—those damn eyes—told a story that he wasn't ready to share, and I wasn't ready to hear. Not yet.

"If you want to know what's been going on," my father began, the words like stones being dragged across the floor, "you're going to have to stop thinking of things in black and white. There's a lot more to this than you realize."

I opened my mouth to argue, but my father held up a hand, silencing me before I could speak. "Not now," he said, his voice quieter, more dangerous. "You want answers? Fine. But you're not going to like what you hear."

A chill ran through me. I didn't know whether to feel relief or dread. My father was never one to be so forthcoming. He wasn't the type to offer up anything unless he had no other choice. That only made me more suspicious, more determined to know everything. But part of me—an annoying, stubborn part—wanted to shut it all out, to retreat into a world where none of this was real.

I glanced at Rafe again, wondering how he was handling the onslaught. If he was rattled, he wasn't showing it. He just stood there, watching us, as if he had all the time in the world.

I turned back to my father. "Tell me."

He exhaled slowly, as if gathering the strength to speak. The years of silence between us seemed to fill the room, pushing out everything else. "Rafe's not who you think he is. And neither am I."

I felt the floor shift beneath me, as though the ground had suddenly become unstable. "What does that mean?" I asked, my voice thin.

My father's gaze flicked to Rafe briefly, before he focused on me again. "There are things... things I've done, things I've kept from you. Not because I wanted to protect you, but because you weren't ready for the truth. I didn't want you to know how deep this ran."

Rafe's lips quirked upward, the barest hint of a smile, as if he found my father's admission amusing. "Funny," he said, his voice soft but with an edge, "I thought I was the one with the secrets. Turns out, we're all guilty here."

I couldn't tell whether his words were meant to provoke or whether they were just his way of coping with the tension in the room. Either way, the barb hit its mark. My father's nostrils flared, and for a split second, I thought the storm between them might finally break, might explode in a rush of accusations and anger.

But instead, my father just shook his head. "You still don't get it. You think you know what's going on, but you have no idea."

I folded my arms across my chest, the weight of the evening settling on me. "Then tell me, Dad. I'm done guessing."

There was a long pause, a pregnant silence that stretched so long it felt like it would swallow us whole. Finally, my father took a step forward, his voice low and tight, as though the words themselves had a weight he couldn't bear.

"There's more to Rafe than you know. More than I should have ever let you get involved with. But you're already too far in. And so am I."

I swallowed hard, the air thick with something unspoken. My father wasn't just talking about secrets. He was talking about danger. I could feel it, creeping into the corners of the room, curling around my ankles like a snake.

"Danger?" I whispered, barely daring to ask.

But my father didn't answer right away. Instead, his gaze flicked once more to Rafe, and that fleeting moment of understanding between them sent a cold shiver through my veins.

"I didn't want you to get hurt," my father finally said. "But now it's too late. You've already seen too much."

Rafe pushed off from the wall, his eyes locking onto mine. "He's right," he said softly. "It's too late for all of us."

I shook my head, the confusion swirling in my mind threatening to drown me. "What does that mean? What are you both involved in?"

"Things you don't want to know," Rafe said, his voice quieter now. "But you're going to have to face them. We all are."

I didn't have the strength to argue anymore. Whatever game they were playing, whatever lies they were caught in, I was already in too deep. And no matter how much I wished I could turn away, walk out of that door and pretend none of it had ever happened... I knew I couldn't. There was no going back.

The tension in the room grew heavier with every passing second. I stood frozen, unable to tear my eyes away from Rafe, from my father, from the tangled mess we were all caught in. The truth, like a shadow lurking just out of reach, was finally starting to take shape, but every time I thought I understood, it slipped through my fingers, elusive as smoke. I wasn't sure who I should be angry with—Rafe, for keeping secrets from me; my father, for lying all these years; or myself, for trusting them both despite the red flags I'd ignored.

"I never should've let you get involved," my father muttered, his voice tight with regret, but also something else, something darker. "I knew this day would come. I knew you'd start asking questions. But I thought I had more time."

Rafe's eyes darted to my father, the two of them locking in some silent exchange I couldn't begin to decode. It wasn't a look of betrayal or anger—no, it was something more complicated. A look that said they were both in over their heads. And I was caught in the middle of it, like some helpless bystander watching everything burn around me.

"Time?" I asked, a bitter laugh escaping my lips despite myself. "Time for what, exactly? To make sure I never found out the truth? To keep me in the dark?"

My father's face contorted in something close to pain. "Not like that. I never wanted to hurt you. But this... this isn't something you can just walk away from. It's too big for that."

"What is?" I pressed, my frustration boiling over. "What's too big, Dad? What's so dangerous that you couldn't trust me with the truth?"

Rafe stepped forward, finally breaking the silence that had hung between us like a heavy fog. "This is bigger than your father or me. You have no idea what we've been involved in, what we've been trying to keep from you. But you're not going to like it. No one does."

I shook my head, feeling the ground shift beneath me. "I'm already in the middle of it, Rafe. I've been in the middle of it from the start. So stop talking in circles and tell me what you're hiding. Tell me what you've all been hiding."

There was a hesitation in Rafe's eyes, a flicker of uncertainty, before he opened his mouth to speak. But before he could say a word, my father's voice cut through the tension like a knife.

"Enough, Rafe," my father barked. "You don't get to tell her anything. Not yet."

Rafe's jaw tightened, but he didn't argue. Instead, he crossed his arms, leaning against the wall with a quiet resignation. As if he already knew this wasn't his fight anymore.

My father turned back to me, his face weary, but there was a glint of something—anger? Guilt?—in his eyes. "You're not ready for the truth. And I don't want to drag you any deeper into this than you already are."

But it was too late for that. I could feel it deep in my gut—the gnawing certainty that I was already too far in to walk away now. I had already seen too much. Known too much. The question wasn't whether or not I should be involved anymore. It was what I was going to do with all the pieces I had—pieces that didn't seem to fit together, no matter how hard I tried.

I took a step forward, defiant, unwilling to back down. "I am ready. I deserve to know. If you've been lying to me all these years, then I deserve the whole story."

My father's eyes softened, but his expression didn't shift. "You think you want the truth, but you don't. It's going to change everything."

I wasn't sure whether I wanted to hear the rest or not. My heart was pounding in my chest, racing with fear and anticipation. The air in the room felt charged, like static before a storm.

"I'm not afraid," I said, my voice coming out sharper than I intended. "Just tell me."

There was another long pause, a beat of silence heavy with the weight of unspoken words. And then my father, as if finally giving in to some unseen force, opened his mouth to speak.

"Rafe isn't just some guy you've been getting to know," my father said, each word slow, deliberate. "He's been a part of something much bigger than anything you or I could ever have imagined. Something that's been unfolding for years, and it's only a matter of time before it all comes crashing down."

I felt the blood drain from my face as the implications of his words began to sink in. "What are you talking about?"

My father met my gaze, and for the first time in years, I saw a flicker of something in his eyes—fear, perhaps, or regret. It was gone so quickly I almost wondered if I'd imagined it. "You're tangled up in something much worse than you realize. And I've been trying to protect you from it. But you won't listen."

Rafe's expression hardened, the vulnerability I'd seen earlier disappearing behind a mask of stoicism. "He's right," he said, his voice gravelly. "We've all been trying to protect you. But it's too late for that now."

I shook my head, my pulse quickening. "Too late? What does that even mean?"

Before either of them could answer, the sound of footsteps echoed from the hallway outside, sharp and quick—too quick. My heart skipped a beat, a fresh wave of panic sweeping over me. I glanced toward the door, and just as the realization hit me, the door slammed open.

Detective Wilder stood in the doorway, his eyes locked on me, cold and hard. I barely had time to react before he spoke, his voice low, yet carrying a weight of finality.

"It's over."

Chapter 15: Kindling

The air smelled of damp earth and ash, a bitter reminder that the storm had passed but the weight of its aftermath still clung to everything. I leaned against the cool stone wall outside the firehouse, watching the flickering orange light cast long shadows across the ground. The fire that had devastated Rafe's life had left more than just physical scars on him. There was something about the way he carried himself—his broad shoulders hunched, his jaw locked as if he were holding in every secret he'd ever been forced to keep. It wasn't just the weight of responsibility that he wore like an ill-fitting coat; it was grief, unspoken and relentless, hanging over him like the scent of smoke that never quite washed away.

"Rafe," I said, my voice softer than I intended. He didn't look at me right away, instead staring out at the horizon, the moon casting a cold glow over his face. The same face that had once smiled at me with teasing ease, now rigid, unyielding. It was a face I had come to crave, even if it was guarded, closed off in a way I could never quite understand. "I need you to tell me what happened."

I saw his breath hitch, just for a second. That was all I needed. I wasn't sure what it was—maybe it was the desperation in my voice or the way I had asked him for the hundredth time—but something in him cracked, like the first soft layer of ice breaking beneath the weight of winter's thaw. He turned to face me, and for a moment, the world around us felt like it had paused, holding its breath. His eyes were darker than I remembered, tinged with something heavier than the shadows that surrounded us.

"You're right," he said, his voice low, almost hoarse. "You deserve to know. I owe you that much." The words came out haltingly, as though he was choosing them with careful precision. I wanted to reach for him, to smooth out the raw edges of his pain, but something told me that this wasn't the moment. Not yet. He needed to say it all, and I had to let him.

He stepped closer, the scrape of his boots against the gravel almost too loud in the stillness. "It was the fire," he continued, his eyes fixed on some distant point in the dark, as though the past still haunted him there. "It wasn't just the house. It was everything that came after. My sister—she..." His voice faltered, a crack slicing through it that made my heart ache in ways I didn't know how to name. He closed his eyes, rubbing a hand over his face. "She was my responsibility. Always had been. We didn't have much growing up. Our parents were gone long before I could remember, and it was just me and her, trying to make it work. I promised I'd always take care of her."

I stood still, barely breathing, as he spoke of his sister. There was a depth of love in his voice, the kind that only comes when you've known someone so intimately that you feel their heartbeat in your own chest. His pain was the kind that rippled out, touching everything he had ever touched in this world, and I knew then that he had carried it alone for too long.

"I couldn't save her," he said, the words coming out ragged, like they had been choking him for years. "The fire—everything happened so fast. I was too late. By the time I got to her, there was nothing left but smoke and... and the smell of burnt wood. I tried. I swear to God, I tried."

I could see it in his eyes—the torment, the guilt, the endless cycle of 'what ifs' that would never stop spinning. His sister's face, her laughter, the promise he had broken, all of it was alive in him. And I knew, deep down, that he blamed himself for everything.

Without thinking, I reached for his hand, my fingers brushing against his rough, calloused skin. It was a simple gesture, but the way his hand enveloped mine made me feel like I had offered him something he had been starving for without even realizing it. His grip tightened, not painfully, but with an urgency that spoke volumes.

"I'm sorry," he whispered, almost too quietly, as if the words weren't meant for me at all. "I didn't want you to know. I didn't want anyone to know. It's not something you share."

I shook my head, my thumb running gently over his knuckles. "You don't have to carry this alone," I said, my voice steady even though the storm inside me was starting to churn. I hadn't expected this—this rawness, this vulnerability from him. It was something I hadn't prepared for, but I couldn't look away. "I'm here, Rafe. Whatever this is, whatever you need."

His eyes met mine then, and for the first time in what felt like forever, they were open—honest, unguarded. "I don't know what to do with any of this," he admitted, his voice barely above a whisper. "I've been pretending for so long that I forgot what it feels like to let someone in."

I wanted to tell him that it was okay, that I understood, but the words felt inadequate. Instead, I stepped closer, standing on the edge of something I wasn't sure I could define, but I wasn't about to turn back. Something in me—a deep, instinctive pull—told me this was just the beginning. And maybe, just maybe, we could figure it out together.

"I don't expect you to have all the answers," I said, my voice soft but steady. "But I'm here. We can figure it out together."

I held my breath as Rafe's fingers curled around mine, his grip tight, as though he were afraid that if he let go, something fragile would slip through his fingers—something he wasn't quite ready to lose. And maybe that was the truth: he wasn't just holding on to me, but to a part of himself that had been buried so deep, it had taken a spark, something as small as the touch of my hand, to make it flicker back to life.

It was a feeling I couldn't quite place, not yet. It wasn't just pity, and it wasn't some grand, sweeping romance either. It was more like being tethered to a storm—a tempest that had been brewing inside him for years, and all I could do was hang on and hope I wouldn't get swept away.

"You don't have to do this," I said, my voice softer now, understanding the weight of his past wasn't something I could lift with a few comforting words. But I wanted him to know—no matter how tangled his memories were, no matter how much he carried—that he wasn't alone.

But he didn't seem to hear me. His eyes were focused on the ground, his knuckles white against my skin as though he were trying to anchor himself to something solid, something real. For a long time, we stood there, the cool night air swirling around us, until finally, he spoke again, the words coming out slowly, like they had to fight their way through a lifetime of silence.

"She died in my arms," he murmured, the weight of it sinking into the space between us, thick and suffocating. "It's the kind of thing you don't forget. Not ever. I kept telling myself if I had been faster, if I hadn't hesitated—she'd still be here. But she's not. And now... now I've got this hole in me that won't heal."

I wanted to reach for him, to pull him into something that could shield him from the pain that was all too evident in the way his chest rose and fell, in the jagged way he spoke, like every breath he took carried a shard of broken glass.

"Rafe," I said, my voice barely a whisper, but it felt like something more—like a plea. "It wasn't your fault. You're not the one who set the fire. You didn't cause the things that happened after."

His head jerked up, and his eyes—dark, intense, and full of something I couldn't quite name—locked onto mine. "Don't tell me that," he growled, the fire in his tone making me flinch. "You don't get to just brush this away like it's nothing. I failed her. I failed her in ways you can't even imagine. I had one job, and that was to protect her. And I couldn't do it."

The anger that rippled through him wasn't directed at me. I knew that. But it was still a tidal wave, one that threatened to drag me down into the same depths of guilt and regret that he seemed to be drowning in. I swallowed hard, trying to steady myself against the force of his pain. This wasn't just about a fire anymore. This was about everything that had come after—the loneliness, the darkness, the weight of responsibility he had carried for years, thinking he could somehow make up for something that couldn't be undone.

"I'm not brushing it away," I said, finally squeezing his hand tighter. "But you have to let go of it. You can't carry this with you forever. And you don't have to carry it alone."

The silence that followed was thick, like the air before a thunderstorm. I could see the muscles in his jaw clenching, the storm still raging behind his eyes. But then, something in him softened—just a little. The rage and guilt still simmered, but there was a vulnerability beneath it, the kind of rawness I wasn't sure I was ready to handle, but I knew I couldn't walk away from.

"Maybe you don't know what you're asking for," he said quietly, his voice more resigned than before. "Maybe you don't know what it's like to feel like the world's crumbling, and you're the only one who can keep it from falling apart."

I took a deep breath, trying to steady the pulse that was now thundering in my chest. "Maybe I don't. But I'm here anyway. You don't have to push me away."

For a long time, he didn't respond. He just stared at me, his gaze piercing, and I wondered for a moment if I had made a mistake—if I had gone too far, too fast. But then, something shifted. A small, barely noticeable change, like the first stirrings of spring after a brutal winter. His fingers loosened slightly, the tension leaving his body in a slow exhale.

"I don't know what to do with any of this," he muttered, his voice a rasp. "I don't know how to be the person you think I am."

I couldn't help but smile then, just a little. It wasn't a mocking smile, but one that was laced with something more—something tender, something that made my chest ache in ways I couldn't quite explain.

"Well, you're not the person I think you are," I said, my tone light and teasing, trying to crack through the hard shell he'd built around himself. "I think you're a stubborn, brooding firefighter with a giant chip on his shoulder. But I also think you're capable of more than you give yourself credit for. So let's take it one step at a time. I'm not asking you to figure everything out all at once. Just... let me in. A little bit."

He looked at me then, really looked at me, as though seeing me for the first time. The silence stretched between us, but it wasn't uncomfortable. It was something else—something that felt like the beginning of a new understanding.

And for the first time, I didn't feel like I was talking to a man broken beyond repair. I felt like I was talking to someone who was simply lost, searching for a way back to himself. And maybe, just maybe, I could be the one to help him find his way.

The weight of his confession still hung in the air between us, a fragile thread that tethered us together. His hand remained in mine, warm and solid, but there was an uncertainty in the way he held onto me—like he was afraid I might slip through his fingers if he let go too soon. And I didn't blame him. He had built walls around himself for so long, it must have felt like a lifetime since someone had cared enough to get this close. But what I couldn't understand was why he couldn't see the way I was drawn to him, the way my heart seemed to beat in time with his own.

"You can't keep doing this," I said, my voice steady now, even though the uncertainty clawed at my chest. I wasn't talking about the fire, not anymore. I was talking about the way he pulled away, the way he kept a part of himself hidden, locked up tight as if to protect me from whatever darkness he thought might be contagious. "You don't have to be the only one who carries this weight. Not anymore."

For a moment, Rafe didn't speak. He just stood there, his jaw clenched, eyes shadowed in a way that made me wonder if he even saw me standing right in front of him. Maybe he was afraid to. Afraid that if he really looked at me, he'd see something he wasn't ready for.

"I don't know how to do this," he muttered, barely audible. The words were so raw, so vulnerable, they made my heart ache in ways I hadn't anticipated. "I don't know how to let anyone in. Not again."

"I'm not asking you to," I said, my voice soft, but firm. I wasn't going to let him retreat this time. "I'm not asking you to forget your past or pretend it didn't happen. But you can't keep running from it either. And you don't have to carry it alone. I'm here, Rafe. I'm not going anywhere."

His eyes flickered to mine, and for a moment, I saw something there—something like hope, buried deep beneath the layers of pain. But it was gone as quickly as it appeared, leaving me wondering if it had ever really been there at all.

"I don't know if I can trust you," he said, his voice low, the words edged with doubt.

My heart sank, but I didn't back down. I had never been one to back away from a challenge, especially when it came to matters of the heart. "That's your choice. But trust isn't something that's handed to you on a silver platter. It's earned. And I'm willing to prove that I'm not going anywhere."

Rafe stood still, his eyes darkened with something unreadable, but there was a shift in him. I could feel it, like the first stirrings of a storm on the horizon. There was a moment of stillness between us, a space where all the unspoken things seemed to gather. Then, finally, he nodded once, a small, almost imperceptible movement. But it was enough.

"I can't promise I'll make it easy," he said, his voice rougher than before, but there was a flicker of something that made me believe, for the first time, that maybe—just maybe—he was ready to face whatever came next.

"You don't have to," I replied with a small smile, my fingers still intertwined with his. "I'm not expecting easy."

He looked down at our joined hands, his expression unreadable for a long moment. And for a moment, I wondered if he was going to pull away again. If he was going to retreat back into that dark place where nothing could touch him. But then he didn't. Instead, he squeezed my hand, just enough to let me know he wasn't letting go either.

We stood there in silence for a long time, the cool night air swirling around us, the faint hum of the firehouse in the distance. The world felt distant, far away, as though it had all paused just for us. But in that stillness, something shifted. It wasn't a grand gesture, but it was real—like a door cracking open just enough to let in a sliver of light.

I wanted to say something—anything—to break the quiet. But I didn't. Because in that moment, the silence between us felt like a promise. And maybe it was the kind of promise I had always been afraid to make, the kind that required more than just words. It required trust.

But as the moment lingered, something in the distance caught my eye—a flicker of movement, a shadow darting in the periphery of my vision. I turned, my pulse quickening, as I tried to make out what it was. It was too dark to be sure, but the hairs on the back of my neck stood up.

"Did you see that?" I asked, my voice tense, heart racing for a different reason now.

Rafe tensed beside me, his body going rigid. He glanced over his shoulder, his eyes scanning the shadows, his hand already moving toward his jacket, where his phone rested in the pocket. "Stay close," he said, his voice low and commanding, but there was a hint of something else in it—something that made my stomach tighten with unease.

"I'm not going anywhere," I replied, but I couldn't shake the feeling that something was off. The night seemed to stretch out before us, quiet and too still, like a breath held in anticipation.

The flickering light from the firehouse seemed to dim, casting long shadows over the pavement, and I could feel the hairs on the back of my neck prickle, a sharp sense of foreboding settling in my chest.

And then, without warning, the figure stepped forward, emerging from the darkness, a shape too familiar to be a coincidence.

I froze. Rafe's grip on my hand tightened, and I saw the tension in his body flare into something almost frantic.

"You," he muttered under his breath, his voice hardening with recognition. "What are you doing here?"

Chapter 16: Sparks That Smolder

The quarry was a place that had witnessed the weight of time. Long abandoned by the trucks and men who had once worked its depths, it sat now in quiet neglect, its jagged edges softened by the relentless passage of years. Moss crawled up the weathered stones, and ivy clung to the gnarled remains of what had once been a thriving industry. The wind whispered through the cracks of the crumbled walls, carrying with it the scent of damp earth and something sharper, almost metallic, that lingered in the air. It was a place of stillness, and yet, tonight, it thrummed with something else—something dangerous, as if the ghosts of the past were stirring, just out of reach, watching us.

Rafe stood at the edge of the quarry, his hands shoved into the pockets of his leather jacket, the worn cuffs peeking out from underneath the sleeves. The light from the distant street lamps barely reached this far, but he didn't seem to care about the darkness. There was something about the way he moved—about the way he was—that made the night feel less empty, less alone. He looked like a man who had learned to live in the shadows, and yet I felt drawn to him like a moth to a flame, unable to turn away even though I knew it was risky, even though the weight of our shared history loomed between us.

"This place always makes me uneasy," I said, more to fill the space between us than anything else. The silence had grown too heavy, too thick to bear, and I needed to hear his voice again, needed to feel connected to the world outside my own racing thoughts.

Rafe glanced at me, his mouth twitching into the ghost of a smile. "Uneasy is an understatement. This place... it's the kind of place you forget about, but it never forgets you." His voice had that rough quality to it, like gravel being ground underfoot, and for a moment, I wondered if he was talking about the quarry or something deeper. Something that had been buried long before either of us had arrived.

He turned away, taking a few steps toward the edge, where the cliff face dropped away into the shadowed abyss below. He motioned for me to follow, his gesture casual but somehow commanding. As I closed the distance between us, I couldn't help but notice the way the moonlight caught his features, illuminating the sharp angles of his jaw, the way his dark eyes seemed to absorb the light instead of reflecting it. There was a starkness to him, a rawness that pulled at something inside me I couldn't name.

"The fires," I said, my voice barely above a whisper, like speaking too loudly might shatter the fragile tension between us. "You said they're connected. You said someone's trying to erase the town's history."

Rafe turned back to face me, his eyes darkening as he leaned in a little closer, dropping his voice to match mine. "Yeah. It's deliberate. Every fire has a pattern, a mark of intention. Someone's trying to erase the past, like they want to bury it so deep no one remembers it. But there's a problem with that," he paused, letting the words hang in the air, heavy and thick with meaning. "You can't erase history. Not really."

I stepped a little closer, feeling the ground shift beneath me, both physically and emotionally. I could see it now, the tension in his posture, the way his hands clenched into fists by his sides. He was holding something back, something that made his jaw tighten and his eyes narrow with frustration. The air between us was charged, thick with an unspoken truth neither of us dared voice yet.

"What do you mean?" I asked, almost afraid of the answer, of what he was trying to say without actually saying it.

He hesitated, glancing away for a moment, his gaze searching the darkness around us. It was as though the words were sitting there, just beyond his reach, waiting to be dragged into the light. But when he spoke again, his voice was low, almost conspiratorial.

"I mean... whoever's doing this, they've got more to hide than just the fires. There's something here, something bigger than what we're seeing." He turned fully toward me now, his expression shifting, the lines of frustration softening into something else. "I think it's connected to your family."

I froze, the words hitting me like a punch to the stomach. My pulse raced, the blood in my veins turning cold as his gaze met mine, his eyes searching mine for any hint of understanding—or disbelief.

"My family?" I repeated, trying to keep my voice steady, but I knew I had failed when I heard the shakiness in the words.

Rafe didn't answer right away. Instead, he took a step back, his hands finding the edge of a rusted steel beam half-buried in the dirt. He leaned against it, crossing his arms over his chest like he was suddenly preparing for a fight. "There's more going on here than just arson, Anna. Whoever's behind this, they're trying to take something from you. And I don't think they're going to stop until they do."

My mind was spinning now, every word crashing against the walls I had carefully built around myself. The idea that this was personal, that it was connected to my family—my history—felt like a blow I wasn't ready for. I opened my mouth to respond, but the words got stuck somewhere deep inside me. Instead, I simply nodded, trying to process what he had said, trying to understand what it meant for us, for the town, for everything we thought we knew.

Then, without warning, Rafe stepped closer again, his gaze softer now, but still intense. And in that moment, the world around us seemed to fade, until all I could hear was the sound of my own breath and the rapid beating of my heart. Before I knew what was happening, he was right there in front of me, his eyes flicking between mine, as if searching for something.

I didn't have the chance to stop him. Didn't have the chance to think through what we were doing, what it meant. And in the space between one heartbeat and the next, he kissed me.

The kiss hit me with an intensity I wasn't prepared for, sweeping me up in a torrent of heat and raw emotion that felt as though it had been building for years. Rafe's lips were firm, insistent, yet somehow gentle, as if testing the waters of something we had both known, deep down, was inevitable. I hadn't thought this far ahead, hadn't anticipated the way my body would respond, or how I would lose myself in the simple, unexpected tenderness of it.

For a moment, the world outside of us disappeared—the quarry, the fires, the mysteries that had brought us here—all of it became irrelevant. There was only the feeling of him, so close, his warmth seeping into me like an unspoken promise. When I pulled away, breathless and wide-eyed, the silence between us felt so heavy, so full of meaning, that I didn't know where to start. My pulse raced, my mind scrambling for something—anything—to say, but the words were lost to the dizzying swirl of everything else.

Rafe, for his part, seemed just as shaken, his breath coming in short bursts, his eyes still locked on mine with a mix of wonder and wariness. He stepped back, slowly, like he was giving me room to breathe, or maybe giving himself a moment to process what had just happened. I wasn't sure which. I wasn't sure of anything anymore.

"That was..." I started, but I didn't know how to finish. How could I? How do you explain a moment that felt both electric and fragile, like a spark that could ignite a wildfire if you weren't careful?

"Yeah," Rafe replied, his voice hoarse, and for the first time, I saw something in his eyes I hadn't noticed before—a flicker of uncertainty, buried beneath the cool exterior he always wore. "It was."

We stood there, neither of us moving, both caught in the weight of what had just transpired. And then, as if on cue, the tension between us snapped. He raked a hand through his hair, looking away, as though the sudden closeness had caught him off guard, too. I wasn't sure what to do with my hands, with my thoughts, with the unfamiliar flutter in my chest that seemed to grow with every passing second.

"We should get back to work," Rafe said, the words coming out more like a command than a suggestion, and I felt a surge of annoyance bubble up in me. Why was it that every time something real happened, he always retreated into that pragmatic, emotionally distant version of himself?

"I don't know," I shot back, crossing my arms over my chest, suddenly defensive. "You just kissed me and now you want to pretend like nothing happened? Is that it?"

His gaze snapped back to mine, sharp and unfaltering. "No. But we're not solving this mystery by making out in the middle of an old quarry, are we?"

I wanted to argue, to tell him that there was more to this than just the investigation, that something had changed between us and he couldn't just ignore it. But the truth was, he was right. And the more I thought about it, the more I realized how dangerous this was. Everything about this situation—the investigation, the secrecy, the way he made my heart race—was a powder keg waiting for a spark.

I exhaled sharply, running a hand through my own tangled hair. "Fine," I muttered, frustration rising within me like a storm. "But we need to figure out what's going on. We're not getting anywhere standing around here all night."

Rafe nodded, his jaw tight. He looked at me for a moment longer than necessary, and for just a second, I saw the crack in his armor, the man underneath all the cool detachment. The man who, just a moment ago, had kissed me as if it was the only thing that made sense in a world that had suddenly turned upside down.

"Let's go then," he said, the sharpness in his voice smoothing out, but the tension was still there, just beneath the surface.

We turned and walked toward the worn-out vehicle Rafe had driven to the quarry, neither of us speaking for the first few minutes. The air between us was thick with unspoken words, but for once, I didn't feel the need to fill the silence. It was better this way, I thought—better to let the quiet settle around us until we figured out where to go next.

As we drove through the winding roads that led back into town, my mind raced. The kiss, the mystery, the strange connection between the two—it was all too much to untangle in a single moment. But one thing was clear: this wasn't just about the fires anymore. Whatever was happening, whatever had been set in motion, was far bigger than either of us had imagined.

And it wasn't just about the past of this town. It was about us. About whatever this was, whatever we were to each other. The closeness, the chemistry, the danger of it all—it was like a slow burn, one that could either destroy us or change everything.

"We need to get more information," Rafe said, breaking the silence, and I nodded in agreement, though my thoughts were a million miles away. "I'll dig into the town's archives tomorrow. See if I can find anything unusual. You should talk to your father again. Maybe he knows something we're missing."

I stiffened at the mention of my father, suddenly feeling the weight of his expectations press down on me like a stone. He had been adamant about staying away from the investigation, about keeping me safe and out of trouble. He didn't understand what this meant—not just for the town, but for me. I wasn't some innocent bystander anymore. I couldn't just walk away, not when I knew something was happening—something that might change everything I thought I knew.

"I don't think my father will be much help," I muttered under my breath, but Rafe, as always, heard every word.

"He might surprise you," he said quietly, his tone softer now, but the undertone of resolve was unmistakable. He was still committed to this, still determined to see it through. "We can't afford to leave any stone unturned."

I nodded, though the words felt heavy on my tongue. But there was something else, something in his voice that made me wonder if he was talking about more than just the investigation. Or maybe it was just me, wishing for something I wasn't sure I had the right to want.

Either way, the night felt colder now, as though the distance between us had suddenly grown wider, not smaller. And as we headed back toward the town, I couldn't help but wonder if this was the beginning of something far more complicated than either of us had expected.

The drive back into town felt different, like the world outside had shifted, and I was left trying to catch up. The streets, usually so familiar, seemed to stretch out before me like a strange labyrinth, full of corners I hadn't noticed before, and hidden doors I wasn't sure I wanted to open. Rafe's presence beside me was a strange sort of comfort, and yet, as we neared the town center, the tension that had started to feel almost natural between us crackled, alive and unpredictable.

Neither of us spoke for the entire ride, but I could feel his gaze flickering over to me in those quiet moments. It wasn't uncomfortable—more like a soft, unspoken agreement that we were both trying to figure out what came next. But every now and then, a look from him—half longing, half frustration—made my pulse quicken, like something unspoken was hanging between us, waiting to drop.

I focused on the road, trying to steady my breath. "We're going to have to talk to my father," I muttered finally, the words tasting like bitter salt in my mouth. I had no idea how to approach the conversation with him, or if I even wanted to. The last thing I needed was him breathing down my neck about safety, about keeping away from this mess. But deep down, I knew it wasn't a choice. We were already too far in, and I couldn't back out now.

Rafe shifted in the passenger seat, his voice low and steady as ever. "Yeah, we do. But you've got to be prepared for him to be pissed." He paused, his gaze turning distant as if the words were too difficult to say. "He won't want you involved. Hell, I don't blame him. This... it's getting dangerous."

I bristled at the implication, despite the truth of it. "I'm not a child, Rafe. I can handle it."

He glanced at me then, his expression hard to read, like he wasn't sure whether to argue or let me have this one. "I know you can. But that doesn't mean I'm okay with it."

I let his words hang in the air, not knowing how to respond, not sure if I wanted to. The silence in the car grew thicker, wrapping around us, and I finally pulled into the driveway of my childhood home. My father's truck was parked in its usual spot, and I felt my stomach twist, just a little.

I wasn't ready for this. But then, when was I ever truly ready for anything my father threw my way?

I parked the car and cut the engine, the sound of the world outside returning with a sudden rush of quiet. Rafe didn't move right away, and I didn't either. For a moment, we just sat there, the weight of everything pressing down on both of us. It wasn't just the fires anymore. It wasn't just the investigation. It was everything—the kiss, the feelings that had followed it, and the question of whether this was just another fleeting moment or something that could change everything.

"I'll go in first," I said, opening the door before he could respond. "It'll be easier if you wait here."

He didn't argue, but the look in his eyes spoke volumes. "I'll be here."

I stepped out of the car, feeling the cool night air cut through me like a blade. My father's house was a big one, sturdy and square with wide windows that looked out over the front yard. It had always felt like a fortress to me, a place of safety and security, even when I'd been restless to leave it behind. Now, standing in front of it again, I wasn't sure where the security ended and where the walls began. It felt like both a home and a cage, and I was caught somewhere in between.

I climbed the porch steps, my heart pounding in my chest. The door swung open before I even knocked, and there was my father, his broad frame filling the doorway, his expression unreadable.

"Well, look who's decided to come home," he said, a slight edge to his voice. His dark eyes scanned me briefly before shifting to the car parked in the driveway, where Rafe remained in the shadows. "And you brought company."

"I need to talk to you," I said, the words coming out more firm than I'd intended. My father had always been the kind of man who believed in getting straight to the point. There was no room for small talk, and that was something I'd grown up with. "It's about the fires. I'm involved. I'm not turning back."

His eyes darkened, and I saw the muscles in his jaw tighten, a sure sign that he was weighing his options. "I told you, Anna, this is dangerous. You're my daughter. You have no business getting wrapped up in this mess."

"I don't care what you told me," I snapped before I could stop myself. "I'm already in it. And I'm not backing out now."

For a long moment, neither of us said anything. The world around us seemed to hold its breath, the tension building like a storm about to break. My father's gaze was sharp as a blade, his silence thick with something—concern, frustration, maybe even fear. He didn't want me involved, but I could tell there was more to it than that. Something he wasn't telling me. Something he wasn't ready to admit.

I pushed past him into the house, feeling the familiar weight of the place around me. The smell of old leather and pipe smoke still lingered in the air, the dim light from the hallway casting long shadows on the walls.

"Anna," he began, his voice softer now, but there was a warning there, too. "This isn't just some town issue. You don't understand what you're dealing with. You can't—"

I turned to face him, cutting him off with a look. "I know exactly what I'm dealing with, Dad. And I'm not walking away."

The silence between us stretched long, too long, before my father let out a sigh. "You've always been stubborn," he muttered, like he was speaking to himself. Then, he nodded slowly, the decision settling into his shoulders like a weight. "Fine. But I won't be a part of this."

I didn't say anything else. I knew my father. I knew how he operated. But as I stepped back toward the door, I caught a glint of something in his eyes—a warning, perhaps, or a shadow of a secret too big to share.

And then, before I could leave the room, my phone buzzed in my pocket. My hand froze as I pulled it out, my gaze immediately snapping to the screen. It was a text from Rafe.

"Get out of the house now. They know you're here."

Chapter 17: Smoke in the Air

The smell of smoke was in the air, thick and acrid, settling in my lungs like an old, stubborn memory. It had been nearly two weeks since the first fire broke out in the eastern district, but the scent lingered as if the flames had never truly gone out. It stuck to my clothes, my hair, and no matter how many times I washed my skin, I could still taste it at the back of my throat. The fires were different this time, more targeted, more calculated. And every time I stood near the charred remains of a building, I felt the weight of something watching me, waiting. I wasn't sure if it was my father's eyes I felt on me, or something more sinister.

When I walked into the kitchen that afternoon, the familiar sound of my father's boots scraping across the floor made my heart skip. I didn't need to look up to know he was there, the air thickening with his presence. He had that way of filling a room, even when he wasn't speaking. He cleared his throat, a sound like gravel scraping against stone, and I braced myself.

"You've been spending a lot of time with him," he said, his voice sharp, the edges of it like knives being drawn slowly. "More time than you should."

I set the cup of tea down, the porcelain clinking softly against the table, and met his eyes. They were hard, like polished stone, and I could see the weight of the past in them. My father wasn't a man to show much emotion, but when he was worried—or angry—it was as though the years of his life had been boiled down to that one, unrelenting look.

"Rafe?" I asked, keeping my voice steady, though the twist in my gut betrayed me. I'd expected this confrontation, but not so soon. "You know we're working together on the investigation."

His eyes narrowed, his hands bracing on the back of the chair like he wanted to break something. The tension between us was suffocating. "I'm not blind. I see how you look at him. How he looks at you."

I exhaled slowly, trying to keep my voice even. "He's a good investigator, Dad. We're just... trying to figure things out."

"You're doing more than figuring things out." His voice dropped lower, an accusation curling around his words like a snake. "You're getting involved in something you don't understand."

The words hit harder than I expected. I hadn't realized until that moment how much my father's disapproval could wound. I could see it in his posture, the way his shoulders hunched with the weight of whatever he was carrying, the way his jaw clenched like he was holding back more than he wanted me to see.

"Don't make this about him," I said, my voice tight, though I could feel the heat creeping up my neck. "This isn't about Rafe. This is about the fires, about what's happening in this town. We can't ignore it any longer."

He shook his head, turning away. "You don't get it, do you? It's not just about fires. It's about our name, our legacy. We've been in this town for generations. You think Rafe cares about that?"

I didn't have an answer for that. I wanted to say something, something to make him understand that I wasn't just blindly following Rafe, that my actions weren't motivated by anything more than the need to uncover the truth. But there was a truth in my father's words I couldn't deny. Rafe was a stranger here, a loose thread in a web that I had spent my entire life trying to untangle.

"I'm not asking for your approval," I said finally, my voice quiet but firm. "But I need you to trust me. This isn't about legacy. This is about stopping whatever's going on before it gets worse."

The silence that followed felt like a lifetime. My father turned his back to me, his shoulders tense, as if he were holding something in, something I wasn't meant to know. I wanted to reach out to him, to tell him that I was still his daughter, that I hadn't forgotten everything he had taught me, but there was a wall between us now. A wall built from years of secrets and lies.

"I'll do what I need to do," I added, my voice softer now, not wanting to push him any further. "But I'm doing this my way."

He didn't respond, but I felt the weight of his stare as I walked out of the room. It was a look I knew all too well, a look that said he was already thinking ten steps ahead, preparing for something he wasn't telling me. The fire had ignited something deeper in him, something darker. And I couldn't shake the feeling that it had been smoldering for much longer than I'd realized.

Later that night, as the sun dipped below the horizon and the shadows grew long, I found myself standing at the edge of the burned-out warehouse with Rafe. The heat from the flames still clung to the ruins, though the fire had been put out hours ago. The air smelled of ash and charred wood, and the only sound was the distant murmur of the town settling into the night. We didn't speak at first; there was no need. The weight of the investigation hung between us like a thread, taut and fraying at the edges.

Rafe's voice broke the silence, low and steady. "He knows, doesn't he? About us."

I didn't answer immediately. I wasn't sure how to. My father's warning echoed in my mind, but there was something in Rafe's voice, something raw, that made it hard to lie.

"He's worried," I said finally, my voice catching. "But it's not just about us. He's afraid."

Rafe's eyes softened, the intensity of the investigation fading for a moment. "Afraid of what?"

"Of what we're about to find," I whispered, my stomach twisting with the weight of the truth I hadn't fully understood until that moment. There was more to the fires than anyone was willing to admit. And my father, the man I had trusted above all others, had been hiding something from me all along.

The days following the conversation with my father were heavy, like the oppressive weight of an impending storm. It seemed as though the town itself was holding its breath, waiting for something to shift. People moved more slowly, their eyes darting to the horizon, always watching the skyline, just in case the flames returned. The entire town smelled like burnt sugar, an unmistakable sweetness that clung to everything, from the walls of the bakery to the metal handrails on the bus stop. It was the scent of something lost, something never fully rebuilt.

I tried to bury myself in the investigation, throwing myself into every detail, every lead, and every small piece of evidence I could get my hands on. Rafe was an invaluable partner. He had an uncanny way of reading people, of peeling back layers that I hadn't even known existed. But lately, I'd started to notice the way his eyes lingered on me—just a second longer than necessary, a flash of something in his expression that wasn't just about the case. It was as if the heat between us had ignited a fire of its own, one that neither of us could fully control.

"I don't like this," Rafe muttered one afternoon, his eyes scanning the charred remains of an abandoned factory. His voice was tight, like the words themselves had been wrapped in barbed wire. "We're getting too close. Too many people are watching."

I glanced over at him, my stomach doing a little flip. The town had always been small, but now, it felt suffocating, as if every shadow hid someone waiting to pounce. "You mean your friends in high places?" I asked, my words sharper than I intended. It was the first time I'd voiced the suspicion that had been swirling in my head for weeks now—that maybe Rafe wasn't just a stranger who'd stumbled into this case, but someone with a deeper connection, a personal stake I didn't fully understand.

Rafe's expression hardened, his jaw tightening. "You think I'm hiding something?"

I didn't know if he was talking about the investigation or us, but I didn't have the heart to push it further. Not then. The air between us crackled with something both electric and dangerous, and the last thing I wanted was to make things more complicated than they already were. "I don't know what to think anymore," I admitted quietly, my voice almost drowned out by the soft wind that rustled the nearby trees.

He studied me for a long moment, his lips parting as if he were about to say something more. Instead, he exhaled, the sound heavy with frustration. "I wish I could make it easier for you," he muttered, half to himself, but I heard it all the same. The confession hung in the air, an unspoken promise that neither of us could ignore.

I knew I should have walked away then, let the silence settle like the dust, but instead, I found myself stepping closer. Something in me—a part of me that I'd been trying to ignore—pushed me forward. Rafe caught my movement, his eyes flashing with uncertainty. But he didn't step back, didn't pull away, and before either of us could stop it, the world seemed to pause as I reached out, my fingers grazing his arm.

For a heartbeat, everything else disappeared. The investigation, the fires, my father's warnings—they all vanished as if they'd never existed. There was just us, standing there in the ruins of something that could have been built, something that might have been.

But before I could say anything, the moment shattered. A low rumble of thunder echoed in the distance, and Rafe pulled back, his body stiffening. The brief flash of vulnerability I had seen in him was gone, replaced by the same guarded expression he always wore. "We need to focus," he said, his voice low, but there was something else in it now—a hint of regret, or maybe it was just fear. Fear that I was beginning to peel back the layers he'd worked so hard to conceal.

I took a step back, suddenly aware of how badly my heart was racing. "You're right. We can't afford distractions."

We spent the next few hours in tense silence, combing through the evidence with a precision neither of us had had before. But even as I studied the files in front of me, my mind kept drifting back to that moment. The heat of his skin beneath my touch, the way his eyes softened before he shut it all down. It wasn't just the investigation that was pulling me in—it was him. And I hated it.

When we finally called it a night, I didn't expect to see my father waiting for me at the doorstep of my house. His shadow stretched long across the porch, as if he were trying to stake a claim on the space, to remind me that I was still his daughter, despite whatever I was doing with Rafe.

"You've been gone all day," he said, his voice tight with something I couldn't place. "I hope you're not getting too close to that... man. You don't know what kind of things he's involved in."

I stiffened at the word "man." I had known my father all my life, but this, this was a different kind of anger. It wasn't just a father's concern for his daughter; it was the kind of fear I had seen before, when people were protecting something. Something they were terrified would be discovered.

"I'm not getting too close," I said, trying to keep my voice steady, but something in me felt as though I were lying, even as the words left my lips. "But I need to be involved in this. You can't protect me from the truth forever."

He took a step toward me, his eyes sharp, like knives. "Sometimes, the truth is worse than you can handle. And you're walking straight into something that could burn you alive."

The words hung between us like a declaration, as if he knew something I didn't. Something I needed to uncover. But he wasn't going to make it easy for me. And with that final warning, he turned and walked away, leaving me with the eerie feeling that whatever was happening, it was much bigger than I could ever imagine.

The house was quiet when I returned, the kind of silence that felt like it had been soaking in tension for hours. I pushed the door open slowly, careful not to make a sound. The last thing I wanted was for my father to have any reason to confront me again. He'd made it clear, in no uncertain terms, that I was walking a dangerous line with Rafe. And while I knew I couldn't simply walk away from this investigation, I also knew that the closer I got to the truth, the more it felt like I was losing my grip on everything else.

The faint glow of a lamp cast long shadows across the living room, and there, sitting in his usual spot by the window, was my father. His eyes were sharp, calculating, the way they always were when he was deep in thought. He hadn't heard me come in—probably too lost in his own mind to notice—but I didn't dare approach him. Not yet. I had learned early on that my father didn't like being interrupted when he was thinking.

I stood there, half-hidden in the doorway, unsure of whether to speak or just retreat upstairs and avoid the confrontation that seemed inevitable. But then, as though he had sensed my presence, he looked up. His eyes flickered with a mixture of concern and something else—something colder. He didn't speak at first, just studied me as if trying to figure out which version of me had just walked through that door. I wasn't sure which one I was, either.

"You're back late," he finally said, his voice low but controlled. "And where's Rafe?"

I winced. He'd never been subtle, but it didn't make his questions any easier to answer. "Rafe's not here," I said, stepping into the room and pulling the door closed behind me. The truth was, he hadn't been with me at all. I'd needed time alone to think, to process the weight of everything that had happened. But I wasn't about to tell my father that. Not with the look in his eyes.

"I've been thinking about what you said," I continued, keeping my voice steady. "About me and Rafe. And I'm not trying to disrespect the family, or—"

"You don't get it," he interrupted, his tone sharper now, cutting through my words like a blade. "This isn't just about respect, it's about survival. You're playing with fire, and you don't even see it. You think you're some kind of investigator now? That you're smarter than everyone else? You're not."

His words hit harder than I expected. A part of me wanted to yell, to lash out, but something in the way he looked at me made me hesitate. His fear was too real, too raw. This wasn't just about me being reckless—it was about something far more dangerous than I had realized.

"You're not telling me everything," I said, crossing the room to stand in front of him. I wasn't sure where the courage came from, but I was done being the daughter who didn't ask questions. "You know something about these fires, don't you? About why they're happening. What's going on here?"

My father didn't answer right away. Instead, he looked away, his gaze shifting to the darkened window, as if seeking some kind of refuge from the truth. The silence stretched between us, suffocating in its weight. I waited, my breath catching in my throat. I had never pushed him like this before. But this—whatever this was—was bigger than both of us.

Finally, he spoke, his voice quieter now but still tinged with that same underlying fear. "I've been trying to protect you. From what I know, from what I've seen. You don't want to get involved in this. I don't want you to get hurt."

I felt a chill spread down my spine. "What is it you're afraid of, Dad?"

For a long time, he didn't say anything. His eyes flickered to mine once more, but there was nothing in them now—no love, no regret, no comfort. Just emptiness. "I don't want you to make the same mistakes I did."

The words hung in the air between us, as heavy as the smoke that seemed to cling to everything around us. What mistakes? What had he done that he couldn't face? My mind raced, but I didn't know where to start, where to look, or even what question to ask. Everything felt out of reach, just beyond my grasp.

Suddenly, the sound of a door opening upstairs cut through the silence. I turned, startled. "Who's there?" I called out, already knowing the answer.

My father's face went white, his hand clenching around the arm of the chair like he was about to spring into action. "No," he murmured, more to himself than to me. But before I could ask what he meant, the shadow that had been lurking upstairs emerged into the hallway.

It was Rafe.

His face was pale, his eyes wide, and his expression—distraught, almost wild—sent a jolt of panic straight through me. I opened my mouth to ask him what had happened, but the words caught in my throat. There was something in his eyes, something I hadn't seen before. Something that made me take a step back.

"Rafe?" My voice came out too quiet, too fragile. "What are you doing here?"

He looked at my father, his jaw clenched, his fists tight at his sides. "I couldn't find you," he said, his voice low and strained. "I need to talk to you. Both of you."

Before either of us could respond, Rafe stepped into the room, and that's when I saw it. The blood. Dark, thick blood staining his shirt. My stomach lurched, my heart stalling as panic flooded my veins. The sight was enough to freeze the air in my lungs.

"What happened?" I managed to whisper, my mind spinning with a thousand questions.

Rafe's lips parted as though he was about to answer, but no words came out. And that's when I saw the shadow lurking behind him—the one I'd been running from all along. Something worse than fire, something far more dangerous.

And this time, it was coming for me.

Chapter 18: In the Line of Fire

The wind smelled like wet earth and burnt rubber when I stepped onto the street, my boots scraping against the cracked pavement as I glanced over my shoulder, half-expecting someone to be watching. The sun had sunk behind a thick veil of clouds, but the sky still hummed with that electric feeling of a storm. It made my stomach churn—like everything around us was about to change in ways we weren't prepared for.

Rafe walked beside me, his pace steady but unhurried, as if the world wasn't crumbling around us. He had that way about him—calm, like he was always in control. I envied it. If I could have a fraction of that control, maybe I wouldn't feel like I was drowning in a sea of secrets.

"I don't like this," I muttered under my breath, more to myself than to Rafe, though I knew he was listening. It wasn't the first time I'd said it, and it probably wouldn't be the last. "We've got something here, something big. It doesn't feel right."

His hand brushed against mine, a small gesture of reassurance, but there was a slight tension in his grip, the same kind of tension I was feeling. The kind that doesn't go away even when you try to shake it off. I wasn't sure what was worse—the fact that the evidence we'd found tied everything to a well-respected local developer or the fact that this developer had ties to my father. Ties I never imagined could exist.

Rafe turned his head just enough to catch my gaze. "We'll figure it out. One step at a time."

His voice was steady, but I could see the shadows in his eyes. He wasn't just saying those words to comfort me. He meant them. And somewhere deep down, I realized that I didn't want him to face whatever storm was brewing alone.

"That's what scares me," I said, my voice thick with the truth I hadn't wanted to admit. "I don't know if I can trust my own blood anymore."

Rafe didn't answer right away, and the silence between us stretched like a taut wire. In the distance, I could hear the hum of traffic, the occasional honk of a horn, and the low murmur of voices as people shuffled in and out of the local shops. It all seemed so normal, so mundane, like the world hadn't just flipped on its head.

But I knew better.

We made our way down to the old warehouse, the place where everything had started. Where the first fire had broken out. The building loomed ahead, its windows blacked out and its walls charred in places where the flames had left their mark. The smell of smoke still clung to the air, even after weeks of rain. As we got closer, I could feel the hairs on the back of my neck stand up. It wasn't just the charred remains of the fire—it was the weight of the lies that had been building for months.

"You sure you want to do this?" Rafe asked, his voice low, but I could tell he wasn't just asking about walking into the building. He was asking if I was ready for whatever the next layer of the puzzle would bring.

I nodded. "I don't have a choice. Not anymore."

We stepped through the broken doorway, the air thick with the smell of mildew and ash. My footfalls echoed in the vast, empty space. The shadows were long here, stretching across the room like dark fingers reaching for us. Rafe's flashlight flicked over the walls, casting an eerie glow over the blackened ruins of what had once been a thriving business.

I moved past him, my mind racing with the realization that everything I thought I knew about my father, about the people I'd trusted, was beginning to unravel like cheap thread.

"Rafe," I said, my voice tight. "You know, I never thought my dad would be involved in something like this."

"I don't think he's the type," Rafe replied, his tone cautious. "But he's mixed up with some dangerous people, and that can cloud anyone's judgment."

I wanted to believe him. I wanted to believe that my father wasn't involved in this mess, that he wasn't somehow complicit in the fires, the destruction, and the shady dealings that had been happening behind closed doors. But the more we uncovered, the harder it became to ignore the growing doubt gnawing at me.

I thought about the conversations I'd overheard as a kid, the whispered words between my father and his friends—the ones who always seemed to be too well-dressed, too polished, too important to be anything but trouble. But I never paid attention. I had always been a good daughter, always believing the best in him, even when I should have questioned things.

We reached the back of the warehouse, where the old office still stood, its door hanging crooked on its hinges. I pushed it open with a groan, the metal scraping against the floor, and stepped inside. The room was cold, the air stale. Papers were strewn across the desk, some of them burned, others untouched, their ink smudged and unreadable. But there, in the corner, was a small safe, its combination lock staring at us like a challenge.

"Think it's worth a try?" I asked, my fingers already itching to get to the heart of whatever secrets it held.

Rafe nodded, his eyes narrowing as he surveyed the room. "We've come this far. Might as well."

I could hear my heartbeat in my ears as Rafe knelt down and began working the lock. It was quiet in the room—too quiet. And for a moment, I couldn't shake the feeling that we weren't alone.

The safe clicked open, the sound almost deafening in the silence that followed. Rafe reached inside and pulled out a folder, its edges frayed, the paper yellowed with age. I didn't need to look at the contents to know we were on the verge of something that would change everything.

I wasn't ready for it. But I had no choice but to face it.

The folder in Rafe's hands felt heavier than it should have. It wasn't just paper and ink—it was everything I hadn't wanted to see, everything I feared. My father's name was stamped on the front of it, an innocuous little mark, but it might as well have been a scarlet letter. My fingers hovered over it for a second, unsure whether I wanted to know what lay inside or if ignorance might somehow be a safer place to dwell.

Rafe gave me a look that was equal parts comforting and urgent. He didn't need to say a word; the weight of everything that was unspoken passed between us in the silence. He opened the folder, and my stomach dropped.

Inside, the documents were a mess of contracts, plans, and notes scrawled in a hurried, almost frantic handwriting. Some of it was familiar—a few pages detailing the development of the properties on the outskirts of town, the ones that had been caught in the path of the firestorm. Those had been the target, it seemed, but the real bombshell was in the handwritten notes at the bottom of the last page. A set of instructions—complicit, detailed instructions—leading back to my father.

It was all right there. In black and white. My father's name, in ink I couldn't deny, associated with deals that couldn't be explained away. That last transaction... the one about selling properties for pennies on the dollar, the one that would hand control of the land to a developer with deep pockets and even deeper connections.

I could feel the blood drain from my face. My legs felt like they might give way beneath me. I braced myself against the edge of the desk, my knuckles white against the wood. I didn't want to look at Rafe—didn't want to see the judgment or pity in his eyes. But I couldn't avoid it.

"Is this..." I whispered, barely able to form the words, "Is this real?"

Rafe didn't answer right away, his eyes scanning the papers like they were some sort of map to a hidden treasure, except this treasure was a nightmare. Then, slowly, he placed the folder down on the desk, his hand lingering over it for just a moment longer than necessary.

"Seems like it," he said, his voice low, quiet. "Too clean. Too well-organized."

I nodded absently, not really hearing him. It was my father's signature, his hands in the mix of something I hadn't been able to see, hadn't been able to wrap my mind around. How long had this been going on? Was this the part of him I hadn't wanted to see? Or was this the part I never knew existed? Either way, the betrayal was sharp—like a knife twisting in my chest.

"He's involved," I said finally, more to myself than to Rafe. I had to hear it, even if it made me sick. "He's complicit."

Rafe's eyes softened, and he stepped closer, placing a hand on my shoulder, his touch light but grounding. "You don't know that for sure. It's a mess of papers, a lot of loose ends. We don't have the whole story yet."

"Don't we?" I said, a bitter laugh bubbling up in my throat. "This is enough to start with, isn't it? We're already down the rabbit hole, Rafe. And the more I look at this, the more I see a connection I wasn't ready for. My father's fingerprints are all over this. If we keep digging, I'm not sure I'll be able to find the man I thought I knew."

"You'll find him," Rafe said, his voice a quiet anchor in the storm that was slowly taking shape around us. "But maybe this isn't the time to make any final conclusions. Not yet."

I felt a knot tighten in my throat, my frustration bubbling up with nowhere to go. I wanted to scream. I wanted to rip the paper to shreds and pretend it didn't exist, pretend none of this had ever happened. But reality had already sunk in too deep for that. There was no escaping it. My father, the man who had raised me, taught me how to face the world with my head held high, was somehow entangled in something that smelled foul. I could feel the pieces of my life falling out of place, slipping through my fingers like water, and I couldn't stop it.

"I can't just ignore this, Rafe," I said, my voice shaking now. "This isn't a mistake. This is intentional."

I watched Rafe's jaw tighten as he stepped back, clearly struggling with his own thoughts. "I'm not asking you to ignore it. I'm asking you to think. You don't have to make any decisions right now. We need more. We can't go in blind, not when we don't know the full picture. If your father's mixed up in this—"

"He is," I cut him off, the words coming out faster than I could stop them. "You don't understand. I knew there was something wrong. I knew things didn't add up. But this? This is worse than I ever imagined."

"You're not alone in this," Rafe said, his hand slipping into mine, the warmth of his palm a strange comfort in the midst of all the confusion. "Whatever you decide, we're in it together."

I took a deep breath, the weight of his words settling over me like a blanket. We were in it together. And that meant I had someone who believed in me when everything around me seemed to be falling apart.

The papers, the clues, the connection to my father—they were all pieces of a puzzle I wasn't sure I wanted to finish, but now that we'd started, there was no going back. I looked at Rafe again, searching his face for any sign of doubt. There was none.

"We need to get to the bottom of this," I said, the words feeling heavier than they should have. "But I don't know how I can do that if I'm constantly wondering what my father knew. What he didn't tell me."

"You'll figure it out," Rafe said quietly, like he wasn't just speaking to me, but to himself too. "You always do."

And for the first time in a long while, I believed him.

I stood there, staring at the papers in front of me, feeling the weight of them like I had a hundred-pound rock in my chest. My hands were shaking slightly, but I didn't want to show it. I couldn't show it. Not now. Not when Rafe was so close, so steady, his presence the one thing in this mess that felt real. It felt like a betrayal, and the worst part was the lingering doubt. What if I had been wrong all along? What if my father wasn't the man I thought he was? The very thought made me sick.

"What's next?" Rafe's voice broke through my thoughts, soft but firm. His question wasn't just about the investigation; it was about me. About how I was going to move forward with this. I could hear the undercurrent of concern in his tone, though he tried to hide it. His hand found mine again, grounding me in the moment, like I needed his touch to keep from floating away into a sea of confusion.

I forced myself to breathe. "I don't know." The words felt foreign in my mouth. "I don't know how we fix this, Rafe. How do we even begin to undo this kind of damage?"

He didn't answer immediately, and for a moment, the only sound in the room was the faint hum of an old, dying air conditioner. The paper between us rustled, as if even it couldn't stand the silence. The kind of silence that makes you question everything.

"You start by trusting the people who've got your back." His voice was steady, but there was an edge to it that hinted he was holding something back, something he wasn't saying. "You're not alone in this."

I wanted to believe him. I really did. But trust was a currency that had run dry between my father and me. Every shred of evidence, every whisper in the dark made me question the foundation of everything I'd known.

"Do you believe him?" I blurted out, the question hanging in the air between us, sharp and desperate. "Do you believe my father could be... involved in this?"

Rafe didn't hesitate, but his answer wasn't immediate, either. His lips pressed together, and he gave a small shake of his head as if weighing every word. "I think there's more to this than we can see. But we're not in a position to make judgments without the facts. That's what we're here for, right? To uncover the truth, no matter how ugly it gets."

"And what if the truth is worse than I think? What if it's not just the fire, but everything?" My voice cracked, and I hated myself for it. I wasn't some fragile thing to be coddled. I didn't want to be fragile. I didn't know how to be anything else but strong, but the weight of all of this was pulling me under.

"Then we face it. Together."

The simplicity of his words struck me harder than any sharp truth ever could. Together. How long had I been trying to fight this battle alone? Too long. I had been circling around the truth, dancing around the facts, hoping I could pretend that everything was fine when it wasn't. But this—this—was something else entirely. This was bigger than my father, bigger than me. This was something that could change everything.

The door to the warehouse creaked, and we both froze. A cold chill ran down my spine. It was barely a sound, but it felt like the warning of something looming just outside our reach. I could feel Rafe tense beside me, his body a coil ready to spring into action.

"Did you hear that?" I whispered, though it wasn't necessary. Rafe had already moved into a position between me and the door, his hand shifting toward the gun that always stayed hidden in the waistband of his jeans.

"I heard it," he muttered, low and dangerous. "Stay close."

My pulse raced. I wasn't stupid—I knew when to be cautious. But this wasn't just fear for my safety; it was fear of what came next. The feeling in the pit of my stomach had shifted from dread to something colder. We weren't alone.

"Who is it?" I whispered, my breath catching in my throat.

Rafe's eyes narrowed as he strained to hear any movement beyond the door. "Don't know. But we're not taking chances."

He motioned for me to stay back as he moved closer to the edge of the room, his steps quiet, calculated. The room seemed to close in around me, the shadows pressing in like they knew exactly what we were up against. I didn't move—couldn't move. Part of me wanted to run, but I knew there was nowhere to go. Not with everything hanging in the balance.

The door creaked again, louder this time, followed by the unmistakable sound of footsteps shuffling just outside. Someone was trying to be discreet, but the shuffle of feet on the cracked concrete betrayed them. My heart pounded in my chest, every muscle in my body tensed in anticipation.

Then came the sound of a key turning in the lock.

"No." I didn't even realize I'd said it until the words spilled out, but they were already too late. Rafe spun around to face me, his expression hardening in a way that made me feel like we were both on the verge of something we didn't fully understand yet.

We had no choice but to wait, the minutes stretching into an eternity. And then the door opened, slow and deliberate.

A figure stood in the doorway, backlit by the fading light from outside. For a split second, all I saw was a silhouette, and I couldn't breathe. The figure took a step inside, and the shadows shifted.

"I thought I'd find you here." The voice was low, smooth, and too familiar. It made my stomach drop.

It wasn't just anyone standing there.

It was my father.

Chapter 19: Inferno of Secrets

The ballroom was alive with the clink of champagne glasses, the low murmur of polite conversation, and the rustling of silk gowns as the town's wealthiest mingled with the bravest. The chandelier overhead sparkled like a thousand tiny stars, casting soft light on the sea of expensive suits and flawless smiles. But all I could focus on was the heat—no, the heat—radiating from across the room.

Rafe stood by the bar, one arm casually draped over the counter as he laughed, deep and rich, with a group of firefighters, but his eyes never left me. The moment they found me, everything else seemed to blur. The noise, the laughter, the glittering crowd—they all faded into nothingness, and I felt it again, the same pull that had haunted me for years. The same pull that had nearly burned me alive the last time I let it consume me.

I had no business feeling this way. I was here with my father, at his insistence, of course, to mingle with the important people in town. His expectations weighed on me like an iron chain. But I couldn't help it. I was already sliding my hand to my side, hoping to mask the tremor that threatened to betray me. My father was close, always close, the quiet giant of disapproval he had always been. His piercing gaze swept over the room like a hawk, occasionally landing on Rafe and me, an unspoken command in his stare.

"Don't even think about it, Lily," he had whispered to me earlier, his voice low enough to ensure no one else heard. But the warning had no teeth—only the quiet conviction that he was right, that this—Rafe—was something to avoid. And yet, here I was, feeling every inch of the temptation.

Rafe's lips twitched into a smirk, as if he knew the effect he had on me, and with a fluid motion, he excused himself from the group and began walking toward me. His gaze was relentless, like a storm gathering on the horizon. His black suit fit him so perfectly it was as if it had been sewn into the shape of his body. Every step he took made the air feel hotter, thicker, as if the space between us couldn't hold the tension any longer.

I tried to turn away, to focus on the sparkling wine in my hand, but I couldn't. My fingers tightened around the delicate stem, my pulse quickening as he approached. The crowd parted just enough to let him through, like some invisible force making way for him. He was like a predator, but I wasn't sure if I was prey or willing accomplice.

"Lily," he said, his voice rough, the sound of it sending a shiver up my spine. It wasn't a greeting so much as a low, hungry acknowledgment of everything that lay between us.

"Rafe," I managed, keeping my voice steady, though I could feel my heart tripping over itself. He wasn't even trying to hide it anymore—there was no pretense, no games. His eyes were fixed on mine, daring me to look away.

He took a step closer, the space between us shrinking until all I could hear was the pounding of my own heart. "You look stunning tonight," he said, his voice warm with the kind of sincerity that made me want to melt into the floor beneath me. It was ridiculous, how good he made me feel in the simplest way. No one else could do that.

I blinked, caught off guard. "Thanks," I managed, feeling something like a flutter in my chest.

And then, because I couldn't stop myself, I added, "I don't suppose you're planning on leaving anytime soon, are you?"

Rafe's grin deepened, that infuriatingly charming smile that both made me want to slap him and kiss him all at once. "Would you care if I did?"

I couldn't help the laugh that bubbled up, though I quickly stifled it. "I suppose I'd just have to make do without you."

He reached out then, his fingers brushing mine in a light, casual touch that sent a spark of electricity up my arm. "I don't think you could make do without me, Lily," he said softly, his eyes never leaving mine.

A breath caught in my throat. I wanted to argue, to push him away, to claim that I was in control of this. But the truth was, I wasn't. Not anymore.

Before I could say anything else, I felt my father's presence behind me like a shadow. "Lily," he said sharply, his tone colder than the chill that suddenly seemed to fill the room. I turned, startled, to find him standing there with his usual stern expression, his lips pressed into a thin line.

"Father," I said, forcing a smile. He didn't return it.

"You know better than to entertain this sort of thing," he said, his voice low but full of authority. His eyes flickered to Rafe for just a moment, enough to convey his disapproval.

Rafe didn't flinch. He didn't even acknowledge my father's presence. Instead, his gaze remained locked on me, and for a moment, I was sure that everyone in the room could feel the storm raging between us.

"I'll be seeing you around, Lily," Rafe said, his voice a soft threat laced with promise as he took a small step back. He turned, his back to us, but not before I saw the slight smirk that tugged at the corner of his lips.

I didn't know whether I should be furious or relieved. But either way, the tension between Rafe and me wasn't going anywhere. And my father's warning, as much as it echoed in my head, only fueled the fire inside me.

The night didn't feel like a celebration anymore. It felt like a series of delicate traps, each step I took a potential misstep, each word I spoke a slip on the precipice of something dangerously close to unraveling. The air was thick with perfume and the faint, lingering scent of sweat and burning wood from the bonfire outside. A part of me, a foolish part, was drawn to it, to the heat, to the risk.

Rafe was still somewhere in the periphery, his presence like a subtle flame that I couldn't quite escape. My father's eyes followed me wherever I went, like a hawk circling its prey, his disapproval so palpable it might as well have been a physical weight pressing down on my chest. He was never one to show affection openly, and certainly not in front of people, but tonight, the lines of his face were sharper, his posture more rigid. It was like a warning, a constant reminder that no matter how far I tried to pull away, there were certain things—certain people—I was never supposed to touch.

I excused myself from the conversation with a group of locals, my laugh too loud, my smile too bright as I tried to dissolve the awkwardness that seemed to cling to my every movement. They didn't know, of course, what it was like to carry the weight of a family's expectations, the pressure to always be what they wanted me to be. To always be perfect.

Slipping into the hallway, I needed air, something to clear the fog in my head. My heels clicked sharply against the polished floors, the sound unnervingly loud in the empty space. I leaned against the cool wall, my breath shaky as I tried to slow the rapid beat of my heart.

"Running away already?"

The voice, deep and familiar, made my heart stutter in my chest. I didn't need to look up to know who it was. The way his words felt like a caress, like a hint of something dangerous and thrilling, gave him away.

Rafe was leaning against the doorframe, arms crossed, eyes tracing the curve of my body like he was memorizing every inch of me. There was no hesitation in his gaze, no apology for the way he made me feel seen in a way no one else could.

I closed my eyes for a moment, exhaling slowly as if I could somehow distance myself from the temptation in front of me. "I needed a minute," I said, keeping my voice steady. "My father—"

"Your father's not here," he cut in, his smile crooked, knowing exactly what that meant.

I met his gaze, my breath hitching slightly. "And that means what exactly?"

Rafe pushed himself off the doorframe and took a step closer, closing the gap between us in an instant. The air around us felt heavier, like the whole room had gone still. "It means you don't have to pretend. Not with me, not tonight."

A shiver ran down my spine, and I hated how much I wanted to believe him. To believe that for just this moment, I could be free of everything I was supposed to be.

"You think this is freedom?" I asked, raising an eyebrow. My voice sounded sharp, defensive, as though I could push him away with words. I wanted to believe I could, but it wasn't true.

Rafe's gaze softened slightly, the corner of his mouth twitching with something like regret. "No, but it's real. We're real, Lily. And for once, you don't have to hide from it."

I took a step back, forcing myself to steady myself, though my insides were anything but. "You don't understand," I said, the words coming out more forcefully than I meant. "You have no idea what it's like—"

"To be held to impossible standards?" he finished for me, his voice quiet but full of understanding. "I think I understand more than you realize."

I stared at him, searching his face for some sign of mockery, some hint that he didn't mean it, but there was nothing there. Just sincerity. It was almost too much to bear. His gaze was so intense, like he was looking right through me, seeing every layer I'd carefully built up around myself.

"Maybe you do," I whispered, my voice cracking. "But you don't get to pretend it's that easy. I can't just—"

His hand shot out, brushing a loose strand of hair behind my ear, the touch electric and tender in a way that made it impossible to breathe. "I'm not asking you to pretend," he said softly. "I'm asking you to stop pretending that you don't feel the same way I do."

I felt the heat of his fingers linger on my skin, and for a moment, I could hardly think. The world seemed to narrow down to just the two of us, the gentle rhythm of our breaths the only sound in the air.

"I hate that you make me feel this way," I said suddenly, my voice barely above a whisper. The words felt like they'd been waiting to escape for too long, and now that they were out, I could hardly bear the weight of them.

Rafe chuckled softly, and his eyes darkened with something almost dangerous. "Funny. I hate it too. But it doesn't change anything."

I didn't have a response to that. How could I? It didn't change anything. I was still here, still tied to a life I didn't want, still trapped by the rules that had been set out for me long before I'd ever known what it was like to feel something real. To feel this.

He took another step forward, his voice low and intimate. "You're not the only one who has a fight on their hands, Lily. But I'm not going anywhere. Not this time."

There was no way to ignore it anymore, not the way my heart raced, not the way the world seemed to spin when he was close. Maybe I had always known that this would happen. Maybe I had always known that there was no way out, no way to escape the storm that had been gathering between us since the very first moment we met. But I had never been ready to face it. Not until now.

I swallowed hard, my hands trembling slightly as I tried to steady myself. "You have no idea what you're asking," I said, though it sounded more like a plea than a statement.

Rafe's gaze softened, and for a moment, he almost looked like the man who had stolen my breath years ago. The man who had made me feel things I didn't want to feel. But that man was gone, and in his place, there was only a shadow. And me.

And the fire. Always the fire.

The music swirled around me, a soft melody that should have been comforting but instead felt like a backdrop to the chaos in my head. I could barely breathe, my chest tight from the unspoken tension that seemed to hang in the air. The crowd continued its slow dance, the laughter and polite chatter blending together in a sea of noise that didn't reach me. My focus was entirely on Rafe, who, despite the distance between us, seemed impossibly close. His presence hummed in my veins like static, electric and insistent.

"Are you planning to spend the entire evening hiding in here?" Rafe's voice broke through the haze, startling me. His figure emerged from the shadows, his silhouette framed by the doorway. His eyes gleamed with that mischievous light I knew too well, the one that always promised trouble.

I hadn't realized I had been standing there, leaning against the cool marble of the hallway wall, my fingers pressed against it for support. I had meant to escape for just a moment, but the quiet space, the solitude, felt like the calm before a storm.

"Can't a girl have a little peace and quiet?" I managed, forcing a smile. It didn't reach my eyes, though. Not when he stood there, every inch of him a temptation I had tried so hard to resist.

Rafe took a slow step toward me, his gaze never wavering. "Peace and quiet, huh?" he said, his voice low and teasing. "I thought you were running away from something."

I rolled my eyes, attempting to sound unaffected. "Not running. Just...taking a breather. My father's glare is starting to burn a hole through me."

"Ah, the father glare," he said with a half-smile. "Always a fun one. But we both know you're not hiding from him."

I shifted uncomfortably. "What are you talking about?"

Rafe stepped closer, now only a few feet away, his presence pulling at something deep inside me. "You're hiding from us, Lily. From this." His voice softened as if the words held weight, like the truth of them was something neither of us wanted to face.

The room felt smaller as I took a step back, trying to maintain some semblance of control. I had spent so long convincing myself this thing between us wasn't real—just a passing spark that would fizzle out. But standing here now, with Rafe inches away, I knew I was lying to myself. The fire between us wasn't something that could be snuffed out, not easily.

"I don't need a reminder of what this is," I snapped, more defensively than I intended. "It's not real. It's just—"

"Just what?" Rafe interrupted, his voice cutting through the air, sharper than I expected. "Just a mistake? Something to forget?"

I closed my eyes, gripping the edge of the hallway table for support, trying to force my racing heart to slow. "I'm trying to keep my life in order. My father..." I trailed off, my breath shaky. "He wants me to marry someone respectable. Someone with the right name and the right...future."

Rafe's expression softened, though his eyes remained intense, focused on me in a way that left no room for distraction. "And what about you? What do you want?"

His question hung in the air, and for a moment, I couldn't bring myself to answer. What did I want? My mind was a whirlpool of competing desires, and at the center of it all was Rafe—irresistible, infuriating, dangerous Rafe, who made me feel things I had no business feeling.

"I don't know," I whispered, the words slipping out before I could stop them. It was the truth, and it terrified me. "I don't know what I want. But I know what I don't want, and that's to be stuck in a life that feels like it was chosen for me. I can't—"

"You can't keep pretending to be someone you're not," he finished for me, his voice a mixture of frustration and something else—something tender, though I couldn't quite grasp it.

Before I could respond, I heard the unmistakable sound of footsteps echoing down the hallway—heavy, deliberate. I looked up, my heart sinking. It was my father.

Rafe seemed to sense the shift in the air, his body tensing in response. Without a word, he stepped back, distancing himself just enough to make it appear like nothing had passed between us. His gaze flicked to the corner, where the shadows deepened, and for a split second, it felt like time had frozen. We both stood there, caught between what was and what could never be.

"Lily," my father's voice called, sharp and commanding. I stiffened, my stomach turning with dread.

I glanced back at Rafe, who gave me a subtle nod, his face impassive, as though the conversation we were having didn't exist. "I'll see you later," he said quietly, though his eyes said much more.

I couldn't help but wonder if he really would.

I turned toward my father, who stood at the end of the hall, his arms crossed, his face a mask of displeasure. He had been watching, as always, from the edges of the room. He wasn't one to miss a single detail. Not one.

"I hope you haven't been standing out here alone," he said, his tone low but with an unmistakable edge. "It's not safe."

I swallowed, trying to steady my breathing. The last thing I needed was to face his wrath now. "I was just...stepping out for some air," I said, forcing a smile.

My father's gaze softened, just a touch, before he spoke again. "Your mother's looking for you. Come, let's join her."

I nodded, but as I turned away, I felt that familiar weight in my chest, the one that always followed when I was forced to choose between what I wanted and what I had been taught to expect. As we walked back toward the gala, I glanced over my shoulder one last time.

But Rafe was gone. And I couldn't shake the feeling that I had just made the biggest mistake of my life.

Chapter 20: Scorched Allegiances

The next morning, the air hung thick with a damp chill, a stark contrast to the warm glow of last night's gala. I'd barely slept, my mind replaying the conversation with my father in agonizing detail. Every word he spoke to me felt like another layer of betrayal. His justification had been as predictable as it was infuriating—he hadn't wanted to destroy the town's reputation. And I had to wonder, had that ever been the truth? Or was it just the perfect excuse to keep his hands clean, his secrets buried? His loyalty had never been to me, not really. It had always been to whatever version of the world he could manipulate into being.

I stood in the kitchen, hands wrapped tightly around a mug of lukewarm coffee, my gaze unfocused as I stared out the window. The sun barely peeked through the clouds, casting a muted glow over the small town that had both raised and trapped me. This town, its charming streets and sleepy corners, had become my prison, a gilded cage built by the very people who claimed to love me. And now, I wasn't sure where my loyalties lay.

A soft knock at the door snapped me from my thoughts.

"Come in," I said, though the words felt forced, like I was attempting to hold onto some semblance of civility in a world that had lost its meaning.

Rafe stepped inside, the familiar smell of his cologne mixing with the scent of fresh rain. He didn't say anything at first. He didn't need to. His eyes spoke volumes, his silent understanding filling the space between us. I could feel the weight of his presence as he crossed the room to where I stood, taking the mug from my hands and setting it aside.

"You okay?" His voice was low, rough in a way that made my pulse quicken, even in my sorrow.

I gave him a tight smile, a poor attempt to mask the storm swirling inside of me. "Define 'okay,'" I said, my voice trembling more than I cared to admit. I hated that he could read me so easily, hated that even in my pain, he was the one I turned to.

Rafe's lips twisted into a half-smile, his eyes softening as he tucked a loose strand of hair behind my ear. "You don't need to do that with me, you know. I can't help if you won't let me in."

I exhaled sharply, a mix of frustration and exhaustion flooding through me. "I don't know what to do anymore. I trusted him—my father—and now I feel like everything was a lie."

His hand found mine, his fingers gentle but firm. "You're not alone in this."

I wanted to believe him. But the truth was, I wasn't sure where my place was anymore. In this town, with my family, or even with Rafe. My world had been so neatly divided into roles—daughter, friend, confidante. But the edges of those roles were blurring, and I was finding it hard to stay within the lines.

"You know," I said, my words coming out in a soft laugh, "I used to think I had everything figured out. That this town, this life, was where I was meant to be."

Rafe raised an eyebrow, his thumb brushing over my knuckles. "And now?"

"Now I feel like I'm drowning in all the secrets," I whispered. "And it's not just my father's. It's... it's this town. It's the way people smile at you one minute and stab you in the back the next. It's everything."

The silence between us grew thick, the weight of our unspoken thoughts pressing in on me. I wanted to pull away, to retreat into the comfort of distance, but something in me refused. Maybe it was the way Rafe always managed to anchor me, always knew exactly what to say or what not to say. Or maybe it was because for once, I didn't feel like I had to hide.

"You think you can ever forgive him?" Rafe asked, his voice barely above a whisper.

I chewed on my bottom lip, avoiding his gaze. "I don't know. Part of me wants to, but the other part..." I trailed off, shaking my head. "He's not the man I thought he was. He's not even the man I needed him to be."

Rafe's hand tightened around mine. "Maybe you don't need him anymore."

I swallowed, my throat dry. His words hit me harder than I expected. Could I really let go of everything I'd known? Could I sever the last thread that tied me to a past I wasn't sure I even wanted anymore?

"You know, I used to think you were just a distraction," I said, my voice thick with emotion. "But now..." I swallowed again, my words faltering. "Now, I think I might need you more than I ever thought possible."

Rafe's expression softened, the storm in his eyes receding, replaced by a tenderness that made my heart ache. "I'm not going anywhere," he said, his voice steady, unwavering.

I nodded, though I wasn't sure I fully believed him. The town, my family, even Rafe—they all felt like fragile things in a world that seemed to be falling apart at the seams. But in that moment, in his arms, I was willing to let myself believe that maybe, just maybe, there was something worth holding onto.

A soft knock at the door interrupted our silence.

"Don't answer it," Rafe muttered, his voice darkening, but the moment had already passed. I could hear the distant murmur of voices outside, and I knew the call for truth was just beginning.

I stood, pulling away from him reluctantly. "I have to face this," I said, my voice hardening with resolve.

Rafe watched me for a moment, his jaw tightening. "Be careful."

I didn't have to look at him to feel the weight of his gaze, the unspoken warning. The town had its claws in me, and no matter how far I ran, it would always pull me back. But this time, I wasn't going back without answers.

The knock at the door came again, louder this time, as though it carried the weight of everything I hadn't yet processed. I could feel Rafe's tension coil at my side, but he didn't move, didn't make a sound. I wasn't ready to face anyone. Not after the conversation with my father. Not after everything that had started to unravel in ways I couldn't control. But the knock insisted, a rhythmic thudding that pulled me back to reality, and reality had a cruel way of forcing you to pay attention.

With a quick glance at Rafe, I turned away and walked to the door. It was only after I twisted the knob that I realized how shaky my hands were. I could still feel the press of Rafe's fingers around mine, grounding me, but the moment I opened the door, I knew I was stepping into a storm that had already begun.

Jenna stood in the doorway, her expression unreadable. Her dark hair was pulled back into a loose ponytail, strands falling around her face as if she'd been running. She looked nothing like the poised woman I remembered from high school—now, her eyes held a wariness I couldn't ignore. The kind of wariness you wear when you've seen something you can't unsee.

"You're the last person I expected to see here," I said, stepping aside to let her in. My voice came out sharper than I intended, but I wasn't sure I cared. Everyone in this town was either hiding something or lying through their teeth. And right now, Jenna looked like she was teetering on the edge of a truth too dangerous to keep buried.

She didn't respond right away, just stepped into the foyer, her boots clicking on the hardwood floor. The silence stretched long between us, until she finally looked up, meeting my gaze with a cool resolve.

"I think you know why I'm here."

I didn't, actually. Not entirely. But I could guess. There was only one reason she would show up on my doorstep, knowing everything that had been going on.

"Does it have to do with my father?" I asked, crossing my arms as the tension in the room thickened.

Jenna nodded slowly, her lips tight as if she was trying to keep herself from saying something she knew would be too much. She didn't need to say it, though; the weight of her presence here told me everything I needed to know.

"What do you know?" I asked, my voice suddenly low. The room seemed to shrink around us, the walls closing in as I waited for her answer.

Jenna hesitated, her eyes flicking to Rafe who had silently stepped into the doorway, his presence just as imposing as ever. He didn't move, but I could see the storm brewing in him, too. The same way he had stood by me when my father's words had nearly cracked my resolve, now he seemed to stand there as a silent protector. I wasn't sure how much longer either of us could keep pretending that we didn't know what was really going on.

"He's involved," she said, the words coming out in a clipped, almost angry tone. "Your father. In more ways than you're willing to accept."

I felt the ground beneath me shift. A sickening twist in my gut told me I wasn't going to like what came next.

"I don't understand," I said, though I was fairly sure I already did.

Jenna looked over at Rafe again before stepping further into the room, her gaze never leaving mine as she spoke. "I wasn't supposed to tell you. But I'm done pretending I don't know. I've kept quiet for too long, and now it's too late for that." She paused, taking a breath as if steeling herself. "He didn't just know about the arson cover-up. He was involved. He helped bury the evidence."

A chill ran down my spine, and for a moment, the world seemed to tilt on its axis. My breath caught in my throat, the room closing in on me. I tried to swallow, but my mouth had gone dry, the words I wanted to say clogging in my chest.

Rafe moved then, crossing the room to stand next to me, his hand slipping around my waist, steadying me. I didn't know whether I was grateful for the comfort or frustrated that everything was starting to collapse in front of me. I wanted to be angry, to shout, to demand explanations, but what could I say? What could I do when it felt like the ground was crumbling beneath my feet?

"You're saying my father set the fire?" I managed to ask, my voice barely above a whisper.

Jenna nodded slowly, her expression tightening with the weight of her words. "Not directly. But he did everything he could to make sure no one would find out the truth. The fire wasn't an accident, and it wasn't random. Your father knew exactly what he was doing when he made sure the investigation went cold."

I felt as though I'd been struck in the chest. It wasn't just the shock, though that was bad enough. It was the realization that everything I'd built my understanding of this place, this life on, was a lie. The ties that bound me to this town—my family, the people I'd grown up with—had all been soaked in the same fuel that had started the fire. I had no idea who I could trust anymore.

Rafe's grip on me tightened, his voice soft but firm. "What's the endgame, Jenna?" he asked, his gaze hard. "What's the point of bringing this to light now?"

Jenna met his gaze with a strange mixture of defiance and exhaustion. "Because it's already out there. People know. And if you don't do something about it, the town will tear itself apart."

I felt my heart racing. The danger was no longer hypothetical—it was real, and it was coming for all of us. I turned to Rafe, my mind spinning as I processed what Jenna was saying. She was right, in a way. The truth was already out there, and if we didn't act fast, everything I'd ever known would be buried in the ashes of this town's past.

For the first time, I felt like I might be fighting a battle I couldn't win.

The air in the room felt like it was closing in on me, suffocating. Jenna's words had landed like a brick in the pit of my stomach, and I could feel them sinking in deeper with every breath I took. My mind was racing, tangled in a mess of half-formed thoughts and unanswered questions. I looked at Rafe, his face grim as he held me steady, his grip unyielding. It was almost like he could sense the storm brewing inside me, and for a moment, I hated that he was right there—right next to me. I hated how much of my life had come down to this, to a choice between my family, the town, and... him.

Jenna wasn't finished, though. She stood across from us, her arms crossed tightly against her chest, her eyes flicking between the two of us like a silent spectator waiting for the next act to unfold.

"If your father is so sure no one will find out, why are you here?" I asked, my voice low and dangerous, like a warning. I was done with half-truths, with the cryptic whispers and carefully measured words. If she was going to play this game, then I was in it now, too.

"Because the longer I stay silent, the harder it gets," Jenna said, her eyes softening just slightly, though her resolve remained. "I don't want to be the one to destroy everything, but you need to know what's really going on. The fire wasn't the only thing he's hiding."

I could feel my pulse pounding in my temples. "What else is he hiding?"

Jenna looked at Rafe, her expression unreadable. She knew what kind of man my father was, and yet, she still felt compelled to drag us into this mess. She looked back at me, taking a slow breath before she spoke again, her voice quieter this time, like she was weighing her words carefully.

"Your father didn't just protect the arsonists. He was one of them."

I froze. Every muscle in my body locked up, my breath caught in my throat. It felt like the entire world had stopped spinning for a moment, and in the stillness, her words echoed in my ears, growing louder with each passing second. Your father was one of them.

Rafe was beside me in an instant, his hand gripping my arm with a sharpness that pulled me back to the present. I hadn't even realized I'd started to sway until he steadied me. I didn't know if I was angry or terrified—or if it was a twisted combination of both.

"I don't believe it," I said, my voice trembling despite myself. I wanted to believe her, wanted to scream in denial, but there was a cold, rational part of me that whispered the truth. It wasn't impossible. Nothing in this town had ever been truly innocent, not for long.

Rafe's hand tightened around mine, his eyes searching mine, trying to gauge how deep this wound went. "You don't have to believe it right now," he said, his voice low and steady. "We'll figure this out. Together."

I didn't know what I wanted from him, what I expected him to say, but his calmness only heightened the storm raging inside me. Together. How could we possibly tackle something this big? Something that could destroy everything?

"I'm not doing this alone," I whispered, mostly to myself, but Rafe heard it, of course he did. He always heard the things I didn't say. His gaze softened, and for a split second, it felt like maybe, just maybe, everything would be okay. But I knew better. This wasn't just about us. This was about the town, my family, my past—and the suffocating weight of the truth that had finally come crashing down.

Jenna spoke again, her voice cutting through the fragile silence. "I'm not asking you to believe me, but I need you to know what's at stake here. This goes way beyond your father's involvement in the fire. There are people in this town who've been covering for him for years, people you wouldn't expect. The fire was just the beginning."

I tried to process her words, but they felt like shards of glass being driven into my mind. My father, my family—everyone I'd known and trusted—had been tangled in this web of lies.

"What are you trying to say?" I asked, struggling to keep my voice even.

"I'm saying that if you want to bring the truth to light, you'll need more than just proof of the fire. You need to take down everything, or it won't matter," Jenna said, her eyes hardening. "Your father isn't the only one with secrets, and those people won't let go of them easily. They'll fight to keep it buried, even if it means burning down everything else in the process."

I felt a tight knot forming in my stomach as the implications of her words hit me like a freight train. Jenna wasn't just talking about the fire anymore. She was talking about something much bigger, something that stretched beyond the arson—beyond even my father. There were people in this town who would go to any lengths to protect their own dark histories, and now it was clear: I was one of the few people who knew. Who could expose them.

And they would stop at nothing to silence me.

I glanced over at Rafe, and his expression mirrored my own fear, a flicker of something darker in his eyes. He wasn't afraid of a fight—I wasn't afraid of a fight. But I could already feel the weight of the battle we were about to step into. It wasn't just about exposing the truth. It was about surviving long enough to tell it.

I felt a sudden heat rise in my chest, a rush of adrenaline pushing back the fear. I didn't know how to do this. I didn't know how to fight this war. But I did know one thing.

I couldn't back down.

I opened my mouth to say something, but before I could, the front door burst open with a force that made me jump. And there, standing in the threshold, was someone I never expected to see.

My father.

Chapter 21: Unmasked Flames

The air in Wilder's office was thick with the scent of stale coffee and something faintly metallic, like the remnants of a long-forgotten crime scene. It clung to the walls, lingering in the corners, and made the silence between us feel all the more suffocating. Rafe's presence beside me was the only thing that kept my thoughts from running wild. He stood there, tall and steady, his fingers brushing against mine in a way that suggested he didn't quite trust the air around us, either.

Detective Wilder leaned back in his chair, the leather creaking beneath his weight. He seemed smaller than I remembered—slightly hunched, his brow furrowed in a way that made him appear far older than his years. He was one of those men whose past had worn away at him, layer by layer, until there wasn't much left but a hardened core. But even that was cracking now, exposed under the pressure of something much larger than he seemed prepared to handle.

"So, you've been poking around in the fire files, huh?" Wilder's voice was low, like he was trying to swallow the words before they escaped. I wasn't sure if it was because he didn't want to admit the truth, or if he feared someone might be listening. Either way, it made me uneasy.

I met his gaze, the weight of everything pressing down on me. "You told us there was an investigation, but you never mentioned it got shut down."

Rafe's hand tightened around mine, a silent reassurance that I needed right now. I wasn't sure if it was for me or for himself, but I didn't mind. We were in this together, and I wasn't about to let go of that connection, no matter how deep the hole we were digging became.

Wilder sighed, rubbing a hand over his face like he was trying to wipe away the exhaustion that seemed to be permanently etched into him. "I didn't want to drag you both into this. The higher-ups—they don't like it when people dig into things they've buried. And trust me, this—" He gestured to the pile of fire investigation reports scattered across his desk, "—this goes deep. Too deep."

The air in the room seemed to freeze. It wasn't just the fires we were dealing with. It was something bigger, something darker. The truth lurked beneath the surface like a poison, and the more we uncovered, the more I felt it seeping into my skin.

"Who's shutting you down?" Rafe's voice was sharp, cutting through the tension like a knife. His eyes never left Wilder, but I knew he wasn't just talking to him—he was talking to me, too. We had to know what we were up against.

Wilder shifted uncomfortably in his seat, eyes flicking toward the door as if he feared someone would walk in at any moment. "It's not just one person. It's—well, it's a web. People in this town, in this county, in the whole damn state. I tried to connect the dots once, years ago, but they made it clear that some things were better left forgotten." He paused, his lips pressing into a thin line. "And people who don't forget... they disappear."

I could feel my heart hammering in my chest. The silence that followed his words was oppressive, like a thick fog rolling in, swallowing everything around us. I looked at Rafe, his jaw clenched, his expression hardening with each word. The man didn't scare easily, but even he seemed to feel the gravity of Wilder's confession.

"What are we dealing with?" I asked, my voice sounding smaller than I intended, but I couldn't help it. This wasn't a game anymore. It never had been. But now, it felt like we were standing on the edge of something much darker than I'd imagined when we first started looking into the fires.

Wilder hesitated, then stood abruptly, pacing the length of the small office. His shoes tapped against the hardwood floor, the rhythm unnerving in the otherwise still air. "It's not just about the fires. That's the bait. What they're hiding—it's something else. Something that goes back years, maybe decades." He paused, turning to face us. His eyes were wide, the weight of whatever he knew pressing on him like a physical burden. "You have no idea what you're walking into."

Rafe stepped forward, his presence solid and unyielding. "We're already in it, Detective. We've already seen things we can't ignore."

Wilder swallowed hard, his fingers twitching at his sides. "Then you're already in too deep," he muttered. "And you might want to think twice before you dig any further." He looked at us both, a flash of something like fear crossing his features. "You don't understand. The people behind this—they'll do anything to protect their secrets. And if you're not careful, you'll end up just like the others."

The words hung in the air, thick and suffocating. I could feel the chill in my bones, the sharp prickle of something terrible on the horizon. The detective's warning should have been enough to make me stop, but instead, it fueled the fire inside me. I wasn't going to turn back. Not now. Not when the truth was so close, it practically screamed at me.

I looked at Rafe, who gave me a small nod, his eyes steady. We were in this together. And nothing—nothing—was going to stop us from finding out the truth.

Wilder's gaze softened for a moment, almost as if he were about to offer some sort of warning, but he thought better of it. "Just—just be careful. This isn't a fight you want to pick."

But it was too late. The fight had already picked us.

The evening air was thick with tension as we left Detective Wilder's office, the door creaking shut behind us like a warning. I could feel the weight of everything pressing down on me, the questions swirling faster than I could catch them. The thought that someone—someone powerful—had been pulling the strings from the shadows had never crossed my mind. But now, it hung between us, heavy and undeniable, like an invisible weight pushing us forward.

Rafe didn't say anything at first. He didn't need to. His hand was still wrapped around mine, warm and steady, and that was enough. His silence was his way of grounding me, reminding me that we were in this together, no matter how deep it got. Still, I couldn't shake the feeling that we were standing on the edge of something we couldn't even begin to understand. And, for the first time in a long time, the fear wasn't just about what we might uncover—it was about what we might lose in the process.

"Are you okay?" Rafe asked, his voice soft but insistent. He didn't pull me closer, didn't try to force me into a false sense of comfort. He just wanted to know.

I nodded, though I wasn't entirely sure I was. "I'm fine," I said, but my voice was brittle, as if the words had to fight their way out.

We reached the car, and I slid into the passenger seat, still trying to make sense of what Wilder had said. The truth wasn't just buried—it had been actively hidden, sealed away by someone who had the power to make problems disappear with a single phone call. And that thought? That one thought made my skin crawl, because it meant the very thing I feared most: there was something bigger than us at play here. Something with its own agenda, and we were just pawns in its game.

Rafe started the engine, the sound of it rumbling beneath us almost comforting, like the steady beat of a heart. He didn't drive fast—he never did—but there was a determination in his movements, like he was navigating through invisible obstacles. I could see the wheels turning in his mind, the way his grip tightened on the steering wheel every time he thought of something new.

"You heard him, right?" I said, breaking the silence. "He's scared. I can see it in his eyes. Something bigger is going on. It's not just about the fires."

Rafe glanced at me, his eyes narrowed in concentration. "I know. And I think Wilder knows more than he's telling us. But I don't think he's ready to go up against whoever's behind all this." His voice was tight, controlled, and for a moment, I saw a flicker of something darker in his eyes—a kind of resolve that felt both comforting and dangerous. "We have to be smart about this. We can't just rush in. If we make one wrong move, it could be the end of it."

I exhaled slowly, the weight of his words sinking in. It wasn't just about uncovering the truth anymore—it was about surviving long enough to expose it. But I wasn't about to back down. I couldn't. Not when I knew, deep down, that this wasn't just about arson. It was about everything that had been hidden beneath the surface for so long.

The drive felt longer than it should have, each turn and each mile taking us farther from the safety of our known world and deeper into a place where nothing made sense. When Rafe finally pulled into the driveway of my place, I didn't get out immediately. I stayed in the car, staring out the window, my thoughts scattered, racing. The dark sky above us seemed to press in, swallowing the light, making the whole world feel like it was closing in around us.

Rafe sighed, his hand moving to the ignition, but then he paused, turning to me. "You're thinking about it too much," he said gently, though there was a seriousness behind his words. "Take a break. Get some sleep. You've been at this for days without stopping."

I shook my head, finally looking at him. "You think I can just sleep through this? After what we just found out?"

He didn't answer right away. Instead, he just stared at me, and for a moment, it felt like he was seeing through me. I could tell he understood, even if he didn't agree. Rafe had always been the calm one, the steady hand when everything else felt like it was falling apart. But this? This was different.

"You're not in this alone," he said, his voice soft but firm. "You don't have to carry this weight by yourself. I'm here, okay?"

I nodded, a lump forming in my throat. He wasn't just offering reassurance—he was offering partnership, a promise that we would face whatever was coming together. I squeezed his hand, a small gesture, but enough to remind both of us that we weren't backing down.

We stayed there for a moment, the hum of the engine the only sound between us. There was so much more to uncover, and the stakes were higher than I ever could have imagined. But with Rafe by my side, I felt something solid beneath my feet, something I could hold onto in the chaos.

The world outside the car seemed to hold its breath, waiting for us to make the next move. And when I finally stepped out, my feet hitting the gravel of the driveway, I knew there was no turning back. Whatever was lurking out there—whatever danger was creeping closer—we were going to face it. Together.

The rain started just as we stepped into my living room, soft at first, as if the sky was testing the weight of the moment, but it quickly grew heavier, beating against the windows with a kind of urgency. I sank onto the couch, wiping my hands over my face, trying to shake off the heaviness of everything Wilder had said. The truth felt like an iron door slamming shut, and the key to unlocking it was buried deeper than I ever imagined.

Rafe stood near the window, staring out into the night, his broad back rigid with thought. His silence, though heavy, was a comfort to me. It wasn't an avoidance of the problem; it was his way of wrapping his mind around it, knowing that words would only clutter the quiet. I could tell by the tight set of his shoulders that the same storm I felt in my chest was tearing through him too.

"I know you're angry," I said finally, breaking the silence that had stretched between us for too long. My voice felt small in the vast space, but it was the only thing that felt right at that moment. "But we have to be careful. Wilder wasn't exaggerating when he said we were in too deep."

He turned, his eyes meeting mine, and for the first time in hours, his expression softened. "I'm not angry," he said, and his voice had that same calm strength it always did, even when the world was falling apart. "I'm worried. You don't see it, but I do. You're diving headfirst into this, and I don't want you to drown in it. These fires, they're not just about a few lost buildings. They're about something much bigger, something we might not be able to stop."

I hated that he was right. I hated that the more we learned, the clearer it became that we were in over our heads. But my instincts weren't wrong. The fires weren't just random acts of destruction—they were a message, and we were too close to reading it.

I stood, moving toward him, my hand reaching for his. The touch was familiar, grounding, a reminder that we weren't completely alone in this. "I know what we're up against," I said, my voice gaining strength, "but we can't back down. There are people out there who think they can control everything, manipulate every little thing in their path. But we're not going to let them."

Rafe's grip tightened around my hand, his eyes flickering with something darker, a fire of his own. "And what if they're already too far ahead? What if, by the time we find the truth, it's already too late?"

His words stung, but there was a truth in them that made my stomach twist. What if we were too late? What if the people behind the fires weren't just arsonists but something far more dangerous—something that had been lurking in the shadows for years, waiting for the perfect moment to strike?

Before I could respond, my phone buzzed on the table, the sharp vibration cutting through the tension in the room. I glanced at the screen, my heart skipping a beat when I saw the name flashing across it. It was Wilder.

I didn't even hesitate before answering, my voice steady despite the knot in my stomach. "Wilder?"

There was a brief pause on the other end, and when he spoke, his voice was thick with something that sounded like fear. "You need to listen to me. You're not going to like this, but you need to hear it. I—" He stopped, the line crackling as if something was interfering with his words. "I've been trying to figure this out for years, but now... it's bigger than I thought. Someone—someone you don't know—is watching you. Watching both of you."

I froze, the blood draining from my face. "What are you talking about?"

"I don't have much time. Listen," he said, his voice a low hiss now. "You need to stop looking into the fires. Whatever you're planning to do next, forget it. I'm telling you, they'll make sure you don't get another step closer."

Before I could ask another question, the line went dead. The sudden silence felt deafening, and for a long moment, I couldn't move. I couldn't think. The world outside my window was spinning, but I was trapped in the stillness of Wilder's warning. I looked at Rafe, his face pale, his jaw tight. He must have heard it too, the cold edge in Wilder's voice, the urgency that made every warning feel too real.

"I don't believe it," I whispered, though I wasn't sure if I was convincing myself or him. "We've come this far. We can't stop now."

Rafe was already moving toward the door, grabbing his jacket off the chair. "We're not stopping. But we need to figure out what Wilder's talking about. If someone's watching us, we have to make sure we're not walking into a trap."

I nodded, the rush of adrenaline filling my veins, pushing out the doubt that had crept in. We didn't have the luxury of time. We couldn't let the fear of an invisible enemy dictate our next move.

We were stepping into dangerous territory, but there was no turning back now.

We had to know the truth. We had to stop them.

Rafe opened the door, his eyes scanning the street outside, but it was dark, silent, like nothing had changed. But something had changed. I could feel it, like a pulse beneath the ground. The air had shifted. And just as we were about to step outside, the unmistakable sound of a car engine started down the street.

A black sedan, its headlights cutting through the rain like a predator stalking its prey, rolled to a stop right in front of my house.

And that's when I knew we were no longer the hunters.

We had become the hunted.

Chapter 22: Crossfire

The air was thick with the stench of burning wood, acrid and suffocating, as Rafe and I stood in the ruined doorway of my father's office. The charred beams of the building groaned and cracked above us, a lament for everything that had been lost. The flames had been merciless, leaving little behind but blackened skeletons of desks and piles of ash. But in the midst of the devastation, my gaze was drawn to something that shouldn't have been there—something so out of place it nearly stopped my heart. A photograph, scorched at the edges but still intact, lay half-buried beneath a pile of smoldering debris.

I took a step forward, careful not to disturb the remains of the fire, my boots crunching on broken glass. The photograph was slightly curled at the corners, but there was no mistaking the faces staring back at me. My father—his strong jaw set, his eyes shadowed with something far darker than I was used to seeing—stood side by side with someone I didn't recognize at first.

The other man was tall, with a sharp, hawkish nose and a cruel glint in his eye. His expression was the same as my father's—grave, guarded, almost as if they were standing in front of a camera to pose for a portrait, but their thoughts were miles away, and far more dangerous. It wasn't until I reached down to carefully pick up the photograph, my fingers trembling, that I recognized him. I froze, my breath catching in my throat. The developer. The one whose name I had heard in passing, too many times to count, and dismissed as nothing more than a whisper on the wind. The man behind the luxury condos. The one whose projects seemed to spring up overnight, their construction tied to far too many rumors for anyone's comfort.

I turned to Rafe, the photograph clutched tightly in my hands. His eyes were already on me, scanning my face with a mixture of concern and something far more acute, like he was waiting for me to say something. But there were no words. Not yet. The realization had hit me harder than I was prepared for, my stomach twisting in knots as the pieces of the puzzle I hadn't wanted to acknowledge began to fall into place.

Rafe stepped closer, his hand resting on my shoulder. His grip was tight, warm, and somehow grounding. His voice was low, measured, but there was a hardness there—something I recognized all too well. "It's worse than we thought, isn't it?"

I didn't need to answer. The question hung between us, thick with the weight of what I'd just discovered. My father, the man I had trusted more than anyone in the world, had been tied to this developer. And now, as I looked at the burned remains of his office, the question of who had been behind the fire didn't feel like a distant worry anymore. It was a reality I couldn't ignore. My father's involvement with the man was no coincidence, and whatever this connection was, it was dark enough to burn everything to the ground.

I bit back the urge to vomit, the betrayal like a physical blow to my chest. The flames may have taken my father's office, but they had also taken away the last of the innocence I had clung to when it came to him.

"We need answers," Rafe said, his voice still calm, but his eyes were narrow, calculating. "Now."

I nodded, the photograph still clutched in my fingers. The fire had stolen so much, but it had also given us a clue. A thread to pull, one that would lead us deeper into a tangled web that I had no idea how to unravel. But I had no choice. Rafe was right. It was time to stop pretending we could keep avoiding the truth.

As we left the ruins of the office behind, the city's skyline in the distance felt more like a stranger than it ever had before. The lights glittered through the haze, almost mocking me. My whole life had been a series of carefully constructed illusions, each one built on trust, on loyalty. But now, with this photograph burning through my mind, I knew better than to believe anything was as simple as it appeared.

"I don't know what to do with this," I said quietly, holding up the photograph as if it might burn my fingers. "If my father was involved in something—if he's been hiding this for God knows how long—then what does that mean for me? What does that mean for us?"

Rafe didn't answer right away, and I didn't need him to. I could feel his determination in the way his hand tightened around my shoulder, his body close enough to mine that I could feel the heat of him, steady and strong. He didn't have the answers either, but I could see the fire in his eyes. He wasn't going to let this go. Not now. Not when the stakes had just gotten higher.

"We'll find out, one way or another," he said, his voice unwavering. "But we're in this together. You're not alone in this."

I wanted to believe him. I needed to. The idea of facing whatever lay ahead without him by my side was unbearable. But even as I nodded, a chill ran down my spine. Because deep down, I knew that the road ahead would be anything but simple. And no matter how much I wanted to trust Rafe—and to trust my father—it was becoming clear that everything I thought I knew was a lie waiting to be exposed.

The hours after the fire passed in a haze, each moment stretching into the next, drawn-out and suffocating. The photograph had left an imprint on my mind, so vivid and haunting that every time I closed my eyes, I saw my father's face—shrouded in secrecy and something far darker than I had ever expected. It wasn't just the grimness of the expression that disturbed me, though that alone was enough to make me shiver. It was the knowledge that whatever he'd been involved in, whatever deal had been struck with that developer, it was a betrayal not just of me, but of everything I thought I understood about him.

Rafe hadn't let me out of his sight since we'd found the photograph. It was as though he was holding me together by sheer will alone, and I hated how much I needed it. I hated the vulnerability that seemed to cling to me like a second skin. The man who had been a fixture in my life for as long as I could remember was suddenly as foreign to me as someone I'd never met.

We were standing in my apartment now, the late afternoon light filtering through the blinds in soft, muted stripes across the floor. Rafe had insisted I take a break from everything, but even the comfort of my own space couldn't shake the tension that had built up between us. He leaned against the kitchen counter, his arms crossed, eyes on me but never quite meeting mine.

"I'll say it once," Rafe began, his voice low, controlled, "and I won't say it again. You don't have to do this alone."

I shifted uneasily, letting my fingers trail over the edge of the countertop. "I know. But it's not just that. It's... It's everything."

The silence between us stretched again, more oppressive than the heat of the day. It was almost like I could hear the words hanging in the air, unsaid, too heavy to bear. Rafe finally moved, pushing off the counter and coming to stand beside me, his presence like an anchor in the chaos of my mind.

"You don't have to carry all of this weight on your shoulders," he said, his voice softer now. "There's no shame in leaning on someone. Not in this."

I shook my head, my eyes fixed on the floor. "I don't know how to separate what I feel from what I need to do," I confessed, the words slipping out before I could stop them. "I'm not sure I can even look at my father the same way anymore. The man I thought he was—"

"You're still trying to figure out who he really is," Rafe interrupted, his voice firm but not unkind. "And that's okay. But don't let this ruin the person you are. Don't lose yourself in all of this."

I looked up at him then, catching the intensity in his gaze, the quiet conviction that seemed to settle over him like a second skin. "And if I lose him?" The words felt raw as they left my mouth, like they hadn't quite been formed yet, and yet, they were the most honest thing I'd said in days.

Rafe's jaw tightened, and for a moment, I saw something flicker in his eyes—a flash of something deeply protective, almost possessive. He took a step forward, so close that I could feel the heat radiating from his body. "Then you'll find a way to make peace with that. No matter what it costs."

I didn't know what to say. The truth of his words settled deep into my chest, and for a moment, I felt something like relief—the idea that I didn't have to hold onto the ghost of the father I once knew, that I could find a way to move forward, no matter how painful it was. But the guilt that gnawed at me still lingered, curling around my insides like a poisonous vine.

"I'm scared, Rafe," I whispered, the admission tasting bitter on my tongue.

"I know." His voice softened, and he reached out to gently squeeze my shoulder. "But you're not alone. Not anymore."

We stood there in the quiet, the weight of what lay ahead pressing in from all sides. There was no simple answer, no easy way to fix what had been broken. The fire at my father's office had set more than just flames to the building; it had scorched the path ahead, leaving everything in shadows. I had to choose where I was going from here, and for the first time in a long while, I didn't know if I was ready for that kind of responsibility.

Rafe stepped away, his movements purposeful as he pulled a phone from his pocket. He glanced at me before dialing, and I watched as he spoke quietly, his voice serious but with a certain edge of authority I couldn't ignore.

"Yeah, we need to meet. Tonight," Rafe said into the phone, then paused, listening for a response. His eyes flicked to me, a flicker of something unreadable in his expression. "Get the information we need. It's time we dig a little deeper into who's pulling the strings here."

I couldn't help but feel a chill at his words. "Who are you calling?" I asked, trying to keep my voice steady.

Rafe's lips twitched into a small, knowing smile. "Someone who knows the truth. And someone who owes me a favor."

I didn't question it. Not right now. Because right now, I didn't have the luxury of asking questions. All I could do was hold onto the one thing that seemed certain—Rafe. And maybe, just maybe, he was the key to unraveling whatever dark secrets my father had buried so deeply.

The evening dragged on, the stillness of the apartment feeling oppressive. My mind raced, the quiet hum of city traffic below doing little to soothe my frayed nerves. The meeting Rafe had set up loomed on the horizon, and even though it wasn't going to be a pleasant one, I knew it was necessary.

It was time to dig into the past—to uncover whatever my father had been hiding all this time.

By the time the evening arrived, the city had shifted, its bustling pulse muted by the thick fog rolling in from the harbor. The light was dimming, but the tension inside my chest only grew heavier. I could feel it in every muscle, a tight knot that seemed to pull me in a thousand different directions, none of them anywhere near safe. The photograph, burned at the edges, still lingered in my mind like a curse. The image of my father standing beside that man—the developer—was a stain I couldn't scrub out. My hands itched with the need to do something, but what? What was I supposed to do when everything I thought I knew was falling apart in front of me?

Rafe had been quiet for the last few hours, his calm exterior now almost too much to bear. I wanted to shake him, demand answers. But I couldn't. Not yet.

We arrived at the bar just as the last rays of the sun dipped beneath the skyline, and already the place had the feel of a quiet haven, the clink of glasses mixing with the low hum of voices. The bartender gave us a nod as we slid into a booth in the corner, one of those hidden spots that could hold secrets as easily as it held drinks. I wasn't sure what I was expecting from this meeting, but I knew I wasn't going to like it.

Rafe didn't waste time. He slid the photograph across the table toward the man sitting across from us, his features sharp under the dim light. His eyes flicked from the photograph to Rafe, then to me. He was older than I expected—early fifties maybe—but his appearance had that sort of worn elegance to it, the kind you get after years of dodging trouble and taking favors. The kind of man who knew things, had seen too many things, and was very good at keeping his lips sealed.

"I don't deal in favors anymore, Rafe," the man muttered, not even glancing at me as he spoke. "Not for you. Not for anyone."

Rafe leaned forward, unphased by the man's sharp tone. "You'll want to make an exception," he said, his voice low and calculated. "We're not asking for your help. We're telling you it's time to talk."

The man didn't flinch. Instead, he took a slow sip of his drink, watching us both with that unsettling, unblinking gaze. His eyes flicked back to the photograph, the one with my father in it, and his face shifted, just slightly, but enough for me to catch it. A brief flash of recognition. Maybe fear. Hard to tell.

"You think that's gonna do it?" he asked, his voice growing darker. "You think this is the clue you need? You're playing with fire, kid."

I set my jaw, suddenly feeling like a stranger in my own life. "My father's involved in something, and I need to know what. If you've got answers, you better start giving them."

The man glanced at me then, his lips curling into something halfway between a sneer and a smile. "What do you think you're going to do with those answers? You really think you're ready to hear them?"

I didn't answer. What was there to say? No, I didn't think I was ready. I wasn't sure I could handle whatever truth this man was about to drop on us. But I had no choice. I needed to hear it.

The man set his drink down with deliberate slowness, the glass making a soft clink against the wood. He looked between Rafe and me, as if measuring us. Finally, he spoke, his words hanging heavy in the air.

"There's a lot you don't understand, kid. You think it's about the developer, but it's not. It's about the deal. Your father didn't just get involved for the money. It's deeper. Much deeper than that."

My pulse quickened. I wanted to press him further, but I didn't. Instead, I waited, leaning forward, my hands gripping the edge of the table.

"Your father," the man continued, his voice lowering, "wasn't just a businessman. He was a player in something far bigger. Something that reaches farther than you could imagine. And that photograph?" He let out a dry laugh, one that sounded like a warning. "That's just the beginning. You think you can untangle this mess? It'll eat you alive."

I felt a wave of nausea rise in my throat, but I swallowed it back, keeping my gaze fixed on him. "What mess? What deal?"

The man smiled then, the corners of his mouth curving up in a way that made my blood run cold. "If you really want to know, you're going to have to make a choice. Walk away. Forget this. Or dig deeper. But know this, kid—you won't like what you find."

Before I could respond, Rafe stood up abruptly, his chair scraping loudly against the floor. The movement was sudden, unexpected. He threw some cash on the table and turned toward the door without another word, not bothering to wait for me.

I hesitated, feeling the weight of the decision on my chest. Walk away. Forget it. Or dig deeper.

"Rafe, wait!" I called, but my voice was drowned out by the noise of the bar. He didn't stop, his broad back disappearing into the night, his footsteps fading into the distance.

I stood frozen for a moment, unsure what to do. I could walk away, pretend none of this had ever happened, pretend my father wasn't tangled in something dark and dangerous. But I knew, deep down, that I couldn't. I wouldn't.

I stepped out of the bar, following Rafe into the night. The air was cool against my skin, the city's lights flickering as we walked in silence. But the silence wasn't comfortable. It was charged with something more—something that made my heart race.

"What was that?" I asked, my voice quieter than I meant it to be. "What did he mean? What choice do I have?"

Rafe didn't answer at first. He kept walking, his strides long and purposeful, his expression unreadable.

"I'll tell you when we get there," he finally said, not looking at me. "But you have to know this: no matter what happens, you're in this now. And you won't get out."

His words hung in the air like a promise, a threat, and I wasn't sure which one I was supposed to fear more.

We rounded the corner, and I stopped dead in my tracks. A figure stood in the shadows ahead of us, and as it stepped into the light, my stomach dropped.

It was my father.

And in his hand, he held something that sent a jolt of panic straight to my chest.

The photograph.

Chapter 23: After the Blaze

The smell of smoke still clung to the air as I pushed open the door to my father's study, the hinges creaking in protest. The room felt suffocating, its warmth a strange contrast to the chill gnawing at my bones. I paused just inside the doorway, watching him. His back was to me, hunched, the weight of guilt visible in the curve of his shoulders. He was standing by the window, staring out at the burned remnants of the land that had once been our family's pride.

The silence between us stretched, thick with unspoken words, like the fog that rolled in from the bay each morning. I could almost hear my own breath echoing in the space between us, an uncomfortable reminder of everything unsaid.

"Do you want to explain yourself, or should I just leave it at that?" My voice cut through the stillness, sharper than I intended.

He didn't turn around, but I saw the muscles in his back tighten. His hands, which had once been so steady and sure, were now trembling slightly as they gripped the edge of the windowsill.

"I never meant for this to happen," he muttered, his voice hoarse. "You have to believe me."

I took a step closer, feeling the weight of the words he wasn't saying. My father had always been a man of action, quick to make decisions, even if they weren't always the right ones. But there was something in the way he stood now, something hesitant, as if the very ground beneath him had shifted, leaving him unsure of where to stand.

"You knew," I pressed, my voice quieter now, more deliberate. "You knew about the fires. For how long? And you didn't tell me?"

He finally turned, and I saw the haunted look in his eyes. It wasn't guilt alone that clouded his gaze. It was something deeper, something that made my stomach twist. "I tried to stop it," he said, his voice breaking. "Years ago, when the developer first came to us,

I tried to stop it. But you don't understand, honey. He... he made threats. I didn't want to drag you into it."

I blinked, taken aback. "Threats? What kind of threats?"

"Threats against the family. Against everything we've built," he said, his words tumbling out in a rush. "The developer was looking to buy up the land, you know that much. But it wasn't just business. He was playing a game, one that I wasn't ready for. And when I refused to sell, things took a darker turn. He said he'd make sure we'd regret it. That the fire would come for us, for everything we loved."

I froze, the gravity of his words settling like a heavy stone in my chest. "And you didn't tell me this before?"

He shook his head, his face pale. "I thought if I kept quiet, if I just stayed out of it, it would all go away. I thought I could protect you by keeping you safe from the truth. But I was wrong. I was so wrong."

The room felt smaller now, suffocating, as if the walls were closing in with every breath I took. My father had always been my protector, the man who had taught me how to stand tall in a world that wasn't always kind. But now, as he stood before me, I saw him for what he was: a man who had made a dangerous choice, one that had cost us everything.

"You think you were protecting me?" I whispered, the words tasting bitter on my tongue. "How is this protecting me? You let me walk blindly into danger, and now we're all paying for it."

His eyes flickered with pain, but I wasn't done. The anger that had been building inside me for days finally burst free, uncontrolled. "You think I can just forgive you? You think I can just forget that you kept this from me? That you let us burn without a word, without warning?"

He flinched at the venom in my words, but I couldn't stop. "All this time, I've been fighting for the family. I've been trying to save something that's already gone. And you knew. You knew, and you didn't say a damn thing."

I turned, walking away from him, the ache in my chest too much to bear. My heart was torn between the love I had for the man who had raised me and the betrayal I felt at his silence. As I reached the door, I heard him call my name, his voice a desperate plea.

"Please, don't walk away. I never wanted this. I didn't know what else to do."

I stopped, my hand on the doorframe, but I didn't turn around. "You should have trusted me," I said, the words heavy with all the years of unspoken truth. "But you didn't. And now, I don't know if I can ever trust you again."

The silence that followed was deafening, the kind of silence that settles between two people when everything has already been said, when the damage is done.

I left without another word, stepping into the night that felt colder than the flames that had ravaged our land. The wind howled through the trees, carrying with it the scent of smoke and ash. And as I walked away, I realized that nothing would ever be the same again. Not the land, not the family, and certainly not me.

The choices before me were clear now. I could remain loyal to the man who had raised me, the man who had tried to protect me in his own twisted way. Or I could follow the path of justice, the path that would take me into the heart of the darkness he had created. Either way, I knew one thing for certain: I would never be the same person I was before the fire.

I wandered through the silent streets, each step feeling heavier than the last, as though the weight of my father's confession had latched itself onto my bones. The night was thick with fog, the kind that curled around corners like a secret, suffocating any hope of clarity. I hated that the fire had become the measure of everything now, that every choice I'd made, every breath I'd taken since that moment, felt like it was all shifting on the brittle foundation of my father's lies.

It wasn't just the betrayal that stung. It was the regret, the cold realization that I'd been so naïve, so desperate to protect what was left of this family. I should have known something wasn't right when the air had thickened with tension, when his eyes had flickered with shadows that no amount of love could dispel. But I had let myself be wrapped in the illusion of his strength, his stoic silence.

I paused, leaning against a lamppost, feeling the slickness of the mist against my skin. The city was asleep, wrapped in a false sense of calm, but I couldn't shake the burning questions that rattled through me like loose change in a pocket. What had my father really been protecting? Had he been trying to shield me from the truth, or had he been covering up his own mistakes?

It didn't matter. I knew that now. The damage was done. What mattered was what came next, and for once, I had no idea.

I turned on my heel and headed toward the one place I could find some kind of solace, even if it was only temporary. The small café on Maple Street had always been a refuge for me. The worn chairs, the faint hum of conversation, and the thick smell of coffee had once made it feel like home. But tonight, as I pushed open the door, a sharp pang of nostalgia sliced through me. It felt hollow now, as though the world outside had seeped into its walls, leaving behind only traces of what it used to be.

Behind the counter, Henry was busy with his usual meticulousness, arranging pastries with the precision of a surgeon. He didn't look up when I walked in, but he didn't have to. He knew me well enough to sense when something was wrong.

"Long night?" he asked, his voice soft but not without its usual warmth.

"That's one way to put it," I muttered, sliding into the booth by the window. I wasn't sure what I was hoping for—perhaps just the comfort of a familiar face, the kind that didn't come with a side of guilt and betrayal.

Henry didn't press, but I saw the way his gaze flickered over me, as though he was weighing whether or not to offer his own kind of solace. In the past, I might have welcomed it, might have even sought it out. But tonight, I didn't want comfort. I wanted clarity, and there was no one who could give that to me but myself.

When he finally came over with a cup of coffee, I noticed the way his fingers lingered on the edge of the mug, as if offering it to me was some sort of silent offering, a gesture of understanding. I picked it up and took a sip, the bitter warmth flooding my senses, but it didn't bring any of the peace I was searching for.

"You know," he said, sitting down across from me, "I've known you long enough to see when something's eating at you." His eyes were steady, too steady, as though he could already guess the truth.

I sighed, setting the mug down with a soft clink. "I'm not sure I want to talk about it."

"I didn't ask you to," he said gently. "But I'm here if you need to."

I shook my head. What did he know about betrayal? About walking the fine line between family loyalty and the pull of justice? The kind of justice that felt more like a wrecking ball than a noble pursuit. I couldn't begin to explain to Henry what it felt like to discover that your whole life had been built on the sand of secrets.

"What if everything I've believed about my father is a lie?" I whispered, not expecting him to answer but needing to hear the words.

He didn't flinch, didn't offer empty words of consolation. Instead, he took a moment to let the question settle in the space between us before speaking.

"Then you decide what's worth keeping," he said simply. "But don't make it about the lies, or the past. Make it about what you want moving forward."

I wanted to be angry, to tell him that it wasn't that simple. But I couldn't. It was that simple. In the end, it always came down to one thing: the choices you made, and what you did with the mess you were handed.

I stared at my hands, the fingers curling around the edge of the mug, feeling the hot ceramic as if it could provide the answers I sought. The weight of my father's words lingered in my mind. "I never meant for this to happen," he'd said. "I was trying to protect you."

But protect me from what? From the truth? From the fire that had already come for us, leaving nothing but charred remnants of a life we could never return to?

I was done waiting for someone to fix it. If justice was going to be served, it would be up to me.

I pushed the mug away, standing up. Henry watched me silently, as though he knew the decision I was making even before I did.

"Thanks," I said, my voice a little rougher than I wanted it to be. "But I've got to go. There's something I have to do."

He didn't ask what, didn't offer advice. He just nodded, his expression soft with understanding.

As I walked out of the café, I felt the weight of the world shift beneath my feet. The fog had thickened, but I wasn't afraid. I had made my decision. It was time to face the truth, no matter how much it hurt. No matter who it would break.

The streets were quiet, as though the city itself had held its breath, waiting for something I wasn't sure I was ready to face. The air had that heavy, expectant quality, the kind that clings to your skin long after the sun has set. I had no destination in mind—no real plan—but I knew I couldn't stay where I had been. The weight of my father's admission hung around me like a cloud that refused to move. If I didn't get it out of my head, it would swallow me whole.

I walked without thinking, the rhythmic beat of my shoes on the pavement grounding me, reminding me that I was still moving forward, even if it was only because I had nowhere else to go. My mind was a tangle of thoughts, none of them particularly useful but all of them urgent. Every time I tried to untangle one thread, another two would appear, knotting up any clarity that might have been left.

My phone buzzed in my pocket, pulling me from my spiraling thoughts. I glanced down at the screen, half-expecting it to be a call from my father, pleading for my forgiveness or—more likely—offering another excuse. But instead, it was a message from Leo.

I need to see you. Now. It's about your father.

I stopped in my tracks. The words were a sharp jab, slicing through the haze that had settled over me. I wasn't sure what I'd expected from Leo, but this wasn't it. The last time we'd spoken, things had felt... unfinished. No, unspoken was a better word. There had been something in the way he'd looked at me—something that said we were standing on the edge of something, and neither of us was sure if it was worth stepping off of.

I hadn't expected him to reach out again, but here he was, a lifeline thrown from a distance I wasn't sure I was ready to cross.

I tapped out a quick response.

I'm not sure now is the best time.

The reply was instant. It's not a question. It's urgent.

I stared at the screen, feeling the weight of his words settle deep inside me. The timing was off. I knew that. But something about Leo's insistence, the sense of urgency in his message, made me hesitate.

With a frustrated sigh, I started walking again, the phone still clutched tightly in my hand. I wasn't sure where I was going or how I would feel once I got there. But the nagging pull of needing to hear what Leo had to say was stronger than the voice in my head telling me to run in the opposite direction.

The bar was quiet when I arrived, a low hum of conversation spilling from the door as I pushed it open. It was just the sort of place you could lose yourself in if you wanted to—dimly lit, filled with the scent of bourbon and wood. It had become a kind of neutral ground for me and Leo, a place where we could talk without the weight of the world pressing down on us.

Leo was seated at the back, his back to the wall as usual. I could see the sharp outline of his shoulders even in the low light. He was waiting for me, but there was none of the ease I had come to expect from him. His posture was rigid, tense.

"Got your message," I said, sliding into the chair across from him. "What's this about my father?"

Leo didn't speak right away. Instead, he gave me a long, unreadable look. There was something different in his eyes now, something sharper, like he was seeing through the walls I'd built between us. I wondered what had happened in the time since we'd last spoken. Had he uncovered something? Had he figured out what I had only begun to understand?

"I need you to trust me," he said, his voice low, more serious than I had ever heard it.

I raised an eyebrow, caught off guard by the intensity in his tone. Trust? After everything? Trust was a currency I'd been running low on for a while now, and I wasn't sure I had any left to give.

"Trust you?" I repeated, my voice flat, trying to disguise the bitterness creeping into my words. "After everything, you want me to trust you?"

Leo didn't flinch. He just leaned forward slightly, the weight of his gaze locking onto mine. "I don't expect you to forgive me, but I do need you to hear me out." His hand reached for a napkin, crumpling it in his fingers before letting it fall to the table. "I've been looking into your father."

My breath caught in my throat. "What do you mean, looking into him?"

Leo leaned back, his jaw tight. "Not what you think. I didn't go digging for family secrets. But what I found isn't something I can ignore."

I stared at him, trying to make sense of the pieces in front of me. There were so many questions, so many pieces of the puzzle that still didn't fit. But if Leo was involved, it wasn't something I could just walk away from. Not now.

"What did you find?" I asked, the words slipping out before I could stop them.

Leo hesitated for a moment, his eyes darkening. "The fire wasn't an accident," he said, his voice barely above a whisper. "Someone set it. And your father knew about it."

I froze, every muscle in my body locking into place. The world around me seemed to stop moving, the weight of his words crashing over me like a wave I wasn't prepared for. I opened my mouth to speak, but no sound came out. Leo was watching me, waiting for me to process it, but I couldn't.

And just as quickly as the words had left his mouth, I felt the shift—the sense that I was no longer in control of the narrative, that the threads I'd been holding on to were unraveling faster than I could follow.

I stood up abruptly, my chair scraping across the floor. "You're telling me my father was involved in setting the fire?" I asked, my voice shaking.

Leo didn't move. He just nodded, his expression unreadable.

"That's not possible," I muttered, the disbelief flooding my veins. "He would never—"

But before I could finish, the door to the bar swung open, the sound of it slamming against the wall cutting through the conversation like a knife.

And then I saw him.

My father.

Chapter 24: Trial by Fire

The air in the office was thick with the smell of stale coffee and the hum of computers, all of us trapped in this never-ending loop of searching for the one piece of evidence that could bring it all crashing down. It wasn't glamorous work. No one would write a novel about what we were doing in that dingy, windowless room. But if you had to ask me, I'd tell you this was where the real story was being written. We weren't chasing glory or recognition, and it certainly wasn't for the paycheck. We were chasing something far more elusive: justice.

Rafe sat across from me, his fingers tapping on the table, his face a mask of concentration as he reviewed the latest batch of documents. The kind of documents that could have, if not for this investigation, been shuffled away into some dusty file cabinet, where no one would ever find them. The thought of those files disappearing made my stomach tighten. In a town like ours, where backroom deals were the currency and trust was in short supply, what we were doing felt dangerous. But it also felt inevitable. Like a storm that couldn't be stopped.

The constant buzz of my phone broke my reverie. I glanced at it, but there was no name, just an anonymous number. I let it ring out. The last thing I needed was another cryptic message. Ever since we'd started digging into the developer's shady dealings, I'd become a target for unwanted attention. Whispers in the streets. Eyes that followed me as I walked to the corner store. A car that always seemed to park just down the block from my apartment. Someone was watching us.

"Hey," Rafe said, his voice soft but urgent. "You okay?"

I blinked, pulling my gaze away from the phone. Rafe's dark eyes were focused on me now, the lines around his mouth deepening. I nodded, not trusting myself to say anything just yet.

The weight of everything—of what we had uncovered and what we still had to uncover—pressed heavily on me. Rafe knew me well enough to sense when I wasn't being honest, but even he couldn't force me to talk about the creeping sense of dread I couldn't shake. The danger wasn't just theoretical anymore. It was real, and it was closing in.

He didn't press. He never did, which was one of the things I appreciated most about him. Instead, he pushed a file toward me, the edges of it crinkled from overuse. "This came through," he said. "You might want to take a look."

I reached for it, feeling the paper beneath my fingertips. Inside, there was a chain of emails. A thread that seemed to be leading to something bigger, something much more dangerous. I skimmed through the messages, my eyes narrowing as I took in the names, the dates, the coded language that only someone entrenched in the web of corruption could truly understand. It was starting to click into place. The developer wasn't just stealing from local businesses. No, it was bigger than that. He was involved in laundering money. And not just a little. Enough to shake the foundations of the entire town.

"We're getting close," I whispered, more to myself than to Rafe. The words tasted both sweet and bitter. Sweet because the end of this nightmare was in sight, but bitter because I knew we were about to expose things that no one was ready to see.

"Too close," Rafe muttered. His eyes flickered to the door, as if he expected someone to walk in at any moment. "We need to be careful, Eliza. They won't go down without a fight."

I didn't need him to remind me of that. I'd seen the way people looked at us in town now. The way the friendly faces I used to see every day had grown colder. More guarded. Every time I stepped into the local diner, the chatter stopped. The polite smiles felt like masks, and the air was thick with unspoken words. There were people in this town who would do anything to keep the status quo, even if it meant destroying anyone who dared to challenge it.

A soft knock on the door broke through my thoughts. My heart skipped a beat as I looked up, half-expecting someone to burst in with a gun or a warning, or worse, a bribe. But when the door opened, it was just Anna. She stood in the doorway, her face pale but determined.

"You need to come with me," she said, her voice low, almost frantic. "It's about your father."

My breath caught in my throat. "What about him?"

"I don't know, but I've seen the signs. He's been talking to people. People you don't want to know about." Her eyes flicked to Rafe. "It's bad, Eliza. Really bad."

I stood, my chair scraping across the floor. "Where is he?"

"I don't know. He's not at home. But I think they've found him." Her words were rushed, laced with a panic that I hadn't seen from her in years. Anna, the calm one, the one who always knew what to do. And now she was scared. I couldn't remember the last time I had felt this afraid, but whatever it was, it was coming straight for us. And it wasn't going to stop until it had destroyed everything in its path.

Rafe rose to his feet, a grim look on his face. "We'll go together," he said, his hand resting on my shoulder in a gesture that was both protective and reassuring. I didn't ask how he knew my father's name was tied up in this mess. We didn't have time for that.

Anna led the way out of the office, her pace quickening as we moved through the narrow hallways. I could feel my pulse hammering in my chest, the panic threatening to overtake me. Every instinct screamed that this was it. This was where everything unraveled.

The sun had dipped low by the time we reached my father's house, a pale orange that spread across the sky like spilled paint.

The quiet street was too quiet, almost suspiciously so. The kind of silence that makes you feel like you're walking through a dream you don't fully understand. My heart pounded in my chest, each beat echoing in my ears, and I wondered, not for the first time, if this was a mistake. If walking into whatever mess my father had gotten himself into would be the end of something—maybe even us.

Anna was ahead of me, her steps frantic now, as though she were trying to outrun her own fear. Rafe matched her pace, his long legs carrying him effortlessly. I couldn't decide if his calmness reassured me or made me feel even more frantic. He never seemed to be in a hurry, like he had all the time in the world, and I hated how much that made me wish I could bottle that composure and drink it all down. I'd been running on adrenaline for days, and it wasn't making anything clearer, least of all my father's involvement in all this mess.

We reached the front door. It stood ajar. Not wide open, but enough to make the hairs on the back of my neck stand at attention. Anna hesitated before pushing it all the way open, her breath shallow, like she was expecting someone—or something—on the other side. I stepped in first, Rafe close behind. The smell of my father's house hit me instantly. It was a familiar mixture of old wood, something faintly like garlic, and a hint of something floral that I had never quite been able to place. But it wasn't the scent that unsettled me now; it was the stillness. The kind of stillness that settled deep in your bones and made you think that the world had simply stopped moving.

I reached for the light switch by the door, but before my hand could touch it, I heard it—footsteps above us. Heavy, purposeful. My heart leapt into my throat. "Dad?" I called out, my voice trembling before I could stop it.

The footsteps stopped. Then, slowly, they resumed. Whoever it was didn't answer, and the thud of shoes against the floorboards grew fainter, heading toward the back of the house. I motioned for Anna and Rafe to follow, and we moved silently, our steps careful, the kind of careful that means you know the situation is already out of your hands.

We crept toward the back, the tension building with each step. There were no more sounds from above now, just the muffled noises of the house settling, the rustle of curtains in a breeze that didn't feel as warm as it should have. The back door, which led to the yard, stood open, and the cold night air rushed in, tangling with the smell of freshly cut grass.

"I don't like this," Anna muttered under her breath, her eyes flicking between Rafe and me.

"Neither do I," I whispered back, my words feeling too loud in the hush of the house. "Stay close."

We stepped outside, the gravel crunching beneath our feet. I squinted into the darkness, my pulse quickening. My father's garden, which he used to take such pride in, was overgrown now. Weeds had taken root in the flower beds, and the plants he'd carefully tended to were withering. It felt wrong. The garden had always been his escape, his way of making sense of the world, and now, it looked like a graveyard for his misplaced hopes.

A figure moved at the far end of the yard, and I froze. It was him. My father. His broad shoulders were slumped, his head bowed as if weighed down by a heavy burden. He was standing near the small shed at the back of the property, the one where he kept his tools and the old wooden chairs he'd once made with his own hands. I had no idea what he was doing out here, but it wasn't good. The air felt charged, thick with the promise of something awful.

"Dad?" I called again, louder this time, unable to keep the worry from creeping into my voice.

He didn't turn, but I saw his hand move to the shed door, pausing just before he pulled it open. He glanced over his shoulder, but the look he gave me was more vacant than surprised, more empty than I could ever recall.

"Eliza," he said, his voice rough, like it hadn't been used in days. "You shouldn't be here."

"Why?" I took a step toward him, but Anna caught my arm, her grip tight.

"Don't," she warned softly. Her voice shook, and for the first time, I saw real fear in her eyes. "Something's wrong. I don't think we're alone."

I knew she was right before the sound reached us—low, a hum, like an engine idling in the distance. The hairs on the back of my neck stood up as the sound grew louder, closer. I turned, my heart sinking as a black car appeared from the darkness of the street, its headlights cutting through the night like a blade.

I felt a cold sweat break out across my skin. The world around us seemed to freeze for a moment, everything caught in the space between breaths. Rafe stepped forward, his posture shifting, alert now, ready for whatever came next.

"Get inside," he ordered, his voice suddenly sharp, commanding. "Now."

Anna grabbed my arm, pulling me toward the door as I glanced back at my father. He wasn't looking at us anymore. His attention was fixed on the car, and I knew, deep down, that whatever was about to happen was going to change everything.

I wanted to ask my father why—why he hadn't told me. Why he'd let this happen. But the words got stuck in my throat, tangled in the web of everything I'd already learned and everything I still didn't understand.

The door slammed behind us just as the car rolled to a stop in front of the house, and I felt the familiar sensation of being trapped, cornered, with nowhere to go.

The sound of the car engine shutting off echoed in the quiet, the rumble of the vehicle's finality settling over us like a dark cloud. My heart thudded against my ribs, each beat another reminder that there was no turning back now. The shadows stretched long on the lawn, their fingers creeping closer, pulling us deeper into a web I didn't fully understand. I moved back instinctively, away from the door, as if the solid wood could protect me from whatever was coming next. Anna's grip on my arm tightened, but I didn't look at her. I couldn't. My eyes were locked on the window where the headlights bathed everything in a pale, ghostly light.

"I don't like this," Anna muttered again, her voice barely above a whisper. "They're here."

Rafe, standing just behind us, didn't respond. He didn't need to. His presence was like an unspoken promise—he wasn't going anywhere, and neither was I. But as the silence stretched on, the weight of the moment bore down harder. He'd always been the kind of person who kept his cool in the chaos, but I could feel the tension in the way his body was coiled, waiting. Like a predator, ready to pounce.

A sharp knock on the front door snapped me from my thoughts. It wasn't loud or demanding—more like a polite request. Too polite for what was surely about to happen. I shot a glance toward my father's study at the back of the house. The door was still open, but I couldn't see him anymore. The fact that he'd retreated into his sanctuary only made the situation more uncertain. If he was hiding from something, or someone, then what had he gotten himself into?

Rafe was already moving toward the door before I could speak. He didn't ask who it was, and frankly, neither did I. There were only a handful of people who would come to the house like this—none of them good news.

The knock sounded again, sharper this time. My stomach twisted as Rafe paused, his hand on the doorknob. I couldn't see his face, but I knew the question was there: should we open the door? Should we trust whoever was standing on the other side?

The decision was taken out of our hands when the door swung open with the faintest creak, revealing two figures silhouetted in the dim light of the porch. The taller one was all sharp angles—dark coat, dark hair, a presence that felt like it belonged in the shadows. The other was shorter, but his eyes were the first thing I noticed. Cold. Empty. Like a man who had already made up his mind about what needed to be done.

The taller one stepped forward first, his gaze sweeping over us before resting on Rafe. "You're the one they've been talking about," he said, his voice a smooth baritone. "The investigator. The one looking into things that don't concern you." His words held a bite, but it was his eyes that made me shiver. Calculating. Deadly.

Rafe didn't flinch. "And you're the one who's been lurking around," he shot back, his voice low, steady. "What do you want?"

"Not much," the man said, a small, humorless smile tugging at his lips. "Just for you to leave things alone."

There it was—the threat, hanging in the air between us. It wasn't a suggestion. It wasn't even a warning. It was an order. The kind of order people like him gave to people like us. To people like me.

I stepped forward before I could stop myself, instinctively wanting to stand between Rafe and this man. "You don't get to make those decisions," I said, my voice coming out sharper than I intended. The words were out before I could think through them, but I didn't care. The arrogance in the man's posture, the way he spoke as if the very air around him bent to his will, made my blood boil.

For a split second, the man's eyes flicked to me, then back to Rafe. He tilted his head, his smile widening just slightly, like I was some interesting puzzle he hadn't figured out yet. "You're the daughter. I should've known."

I felt a sudden chill, and it wasn't the cold night air. "What do you mean by that?" I asked, my voice tight, even though every fiber of my being was screaming to back down.

But the man didn't answer. Instead, he turned to his companion, who had remained silent up until now, his posture just as rigid. A barely perceptible nod passed between them, and before I could react, the shorter man stepped forward, hand raised as though he were preparing to grab me. I couldn't breathe. My mind raced for an escape, a way out of this, but there was no time.

And then, just as quickly as the tension had escalated, there was a loud noise—something crashing from inside the house. A chair scraping against the floor, followed by muffled shouting. It was my father. I could tell from the urgency in his voice. My heart skipped.

Before anyone could move, the man with the cold eyes glanced behind him, then back at me, his expression hardening. "Get inside," he commanded, as if he were the one in charge of all of us. "This isn't over."

I didn't move immediately, and for a second, the air between us thickened with something dark and foreboding. But Rafe's hand on my arm, a subtle but firm pressure, made me take a step back, then another. He was pushing me inside, not aggressively, but with purpose. I could feel his pulse, steady and sure, even though mine felt like it was about to burst from my chest.

We moved quickly, and I barely registered the door closing behind us until I heard the faintest click, signaling that we were locked inside.

But even then, I didn't feel safe.

Because in that moment, I realized something. Whoever these men were, they knew more about my father than they were letting on. They had plans for him, and they had plans for me too.

Chapter 25: Fanning the Flames

The heat was relentless, even in the late hours of the evening. The town was still smoldering from the most recent fire—the one that had nearly consumed half of the old library. I had driven past the charred remnants earlier that day, feeling a sick pang in my gut as I thought about how many memories had gone up in smoke. It wasn't just bricks and mortar burning; it was the heart of the town, everything that made it feel like home. The whispered promises of developers and their shiny plans for progress had always been a distant hum in the background of our lives. But now, the sound was louder, more insistent, and I knew I couldn't ignore it any longer.

Rafe had been right all along, but I hadn't been ready to hear it. The fire wasn't just about revenge or anger; it was about money and land—land that wasn't supposed to be sold. A plot of ground that had been part of the town for generations was being targeted, and the arsonist, whoever he was, had been doing his best to burn everything in sight to clear the way. It was like watching someone erase the soul of the place, one blaze at a time, and I couldn't just stand by.

"Stop, Ellie," my father had begged me earlier that evening, his hand gripping my arm with a force that made my bones ache. His face was pale, his eyes lined with too many years of worry. "You don't know what you're getting into. People have died over less than what you're digging into."

I could feel the weight of his words press against my chest, but there was something in my heart now that was stronger than fear—something sharper, more determined. I wasn't fighting for the past anymore; I was fighting for a future. One where I wasn't hiding in the shadows with Rafe, one where we didn't have to be afraid of being together because of some shadowy threat that had haunted both our families for decades.

I wasn't just fighting for the town, or for Rafe, or even for myself. I was fighting for all of us. For a life where we could live freely, without looking over our shoulders or hiding in dark corners. The more I thought about it, the clearer it became that everything I had been told about the fires was a lie. This wasn't just about someone taking revenge on the town. It was about land, power, and control—things I'd never thought I'd have to worry about, much less face head-on.

"Why are you pushing this so hard?" my father had asked me. "It's dangerous, Ellie. People like you, people with good intentions, they get hurt in situations like this. It's not worth it."

But I knew something he didn't. I had heard the whispers—the rumors that curled like smoke in the back alleys, the ones about the developer who had promised the town an influx of jobs, revitalization, and prosperity. He'd smiled in all the right places, shaken the right hands, but I could see through it now. His hands weren't clean. And the truth, buried beneath layers of politics and greed, was far darker than anyone could have imagined.

I thought about Rafe as I walked through the streets later that night, the wind biting against my skin like a reprimand. I couldn't remember the last time I'd truly felt afraid. Maybe it was before I realized what was really happening, before I saw the connections, the little pieces of a much larger puzzle falling into place. Rafe had always been a part of that puzzle, even if we'd never acknowledged it. His loyalty to his family, his strength, the way he carried himself with quiet authority—it was all part of a bigger story that wasn't over yet.

But then there were the stakes. Every piece of evidence I uncovered led to something bigger, something I wasn't sure I was ready to face. There were people in this town who had been complicit in the fires, people who would do anything to protect their investments. And I was starting to realize just how far they would go.

Rafe and I had met under the most unlikely of circumstances—two people from different worlds, trying to find our way in a town that had been shaped by secrets for so long. But we had found each other, and that meant something. The more I pieced together the tangled threads of the investigation, the more I realized I wasn't just uncovering the truth for the town's sake. I was doing it for us. For the future I wanted, one where we could finally be together without hiding, without fear. I couldn't let the past dictate our choices.

As I made my way down the empty streets, I found myself caught between the weight of my father's warnings and the fierce, stubborn pull of my heart. I wasn't sure where this would all end up, but I knew one thing for certain: I wasn't backing down. I had already crossed a line, and there was no going back now. The only question was whether I'd be able to expose the truth before the flames burned everything else to the ground.

The air smelled of ash and something more primal—fear, maybe, or the sharp scent of secrets too long buried. It clung to my skin as I paced through the dimly lit streets, the weight of what I knew pressing down on me like an invisible hand. The developer, the fires, the twisted politics that wound through the town like barbed wire—it was all connected, and I was tangled in it now. I could feel it, every step I took pulling me deeper into something I wasn't sure I could get out of.

Rafe hadn't called, but I knew he'd be waiting for me. He always did, like he had a sixth sense for when I needed him most. I had asked him, once, what made him so sure we could make it, that we could be anything other than two lost souls clinging to each other because it was all we had left. His response had been a simple shrug, a slow smile. "Because, Ellie, this town's been on fire for years. You're just the first one brave enough to hold the hose."

I had laughed at the time, thinking it was just a bit of Rafe charm, but now... Now, it felt like a prophecy.

I reached the bar, the neon sign flickering in the window casting long shadows on the cracked pavement. Inside, the usual clatter of glasses and murmurs filled the air, but there was an edge to it tonight. People were whispering, watching the door like something was about to happen. Maybe they knew. Maybe they didn't. But I could feel it. The tension was palpable, and I had the sinking suspicion that the next few hours would change everything.

Rafe was sitting in his usual spot at the far end of the bar, nursing a glass of something amber and strong. He didn't look up when I walked in, but I saw the slight twitch of his jaw, a little muscle flexing. The room was noisy, but there was a silence between us, thick and heavy, like we were the only two people in the world. I took a seat beside him, not bothering to order. I just needed to be near him, to feel the pull of the familiar, like it could keep me grounded in a world that was slowly unraveling.

He turned his head, his eyes dark and unreadable. "You're not going to stop, are you?"

I didn't have an answer for him—not the one he wanted, anyway. Because the truth was, I couldn't stop. Not now. Not when I had a choice between running away or standing my ground, even if it meant losing everything I thought I knew.

"Rafe," I started, my voice low, "you don't get it. I can't just walk away. Not now. Not with everything at stake. People are already dying—real people, Rafe. People who didn't deserve any of this."

He took a long drag from his drink, his eyes flickering to the side, watching the crowd. There was a deep-set weariness in him, one that matched my own, like we were both trying to carry the weight of something we weren't sure we could bear. "You think

I don't know that?" His voice was quiet but cutting, like a knife made of ice. "But you have to understand something, Ellie. There's a line. And once you cross it, there's no going back. You start digging too deep, and it won't just be the fires you have to worry about. You'll be fighting the whole damn town. And people... people like you don't win that fight."

I wasn't sure why it stung so much to hear him say it. Maybe it was because he wasn't wrong, or maybe because I knew he was only saying it out of love. Or maybe it was just the growing realization that I had never been good at taking orders. Not even from the man who loved me.

"I don't have a choice," I whispered, more to myself than to him. "I can't watch this town burn, not for their profit. Not when it's my home. My future."

Rafe's expression softened, just a fraction. "And you think that future's still out there? You think you can just walk out of this with your hands clean?"

I didn't answer him right away, because the truth was—no, I didn't think I could. But that didn't stop me. It never had before.

The bartender slid another drink in front of me, but I pushed it away. "I have to do this. For everyone who's been ignored. For the people who've been silenced by money and power. For you. For us."

His hand brushed mine across the counter, a brief touch, but one that said more than words could. I wasn't sure if it was a warning or an unspoken promise, but I felt it. The danger, the raw edge of something that could break between us at any moment.

"You know what this means, right?" Rafe's voice was softer now, more like a confession. "If you go through with this, we're both going to have targets on our backs. And there's no running away from that. The people who don't want the truth exposed, they'll do anything to make sure it stays buried. And I... I can't protect you if you keep pushing."

The truth of it hit me like a brick wall, and I found myself choking back a breath. He was right, I knew he was. But the fear of what might happen—what would happen if I just sat back and let it all unfold without doing a damn thing—it was worse.

"I don't need protecting," I said, though my voice was a little shakier than I'd intended. "I just need to see this through."

Rafe stared at me for a long moment, as if he were trying to read the very essence of my soul. Then, with a slow nod, he slid his chair back and stood. "Then let's get to work."

And just like that, the world shifted again. The lines we'd once drawn in the sand had blurred, and the path ahead felt more uncertain than ever. But for the first time in weeks, I felt like I had a chance at something real. Something worth fighting for.

The night had grown colder, and the wind had begun to bite at my skin with a ferocity that matched the storm brewing inside me. It had always been this way—life in this town, a delicate balance of fire and ice. And tonight, the flames were threatening to consume everything I held dear, including the fragile future I was trying to carve out with Rafe. We had crossed a point of no return, and there was no untying the knot we had both tied so willingly.

The walk to Rafe's truck felt like a thousand miles. My feet barely skimmed the ground, each step heavy with the weight of what we were about to do. I had never imagined it would come to this—staking everything on the hope that exposing the truth would be enough to stop the flames from spreading further, to stop the town from being sold piece by piece like some misplaced relic to the highest bidder.

"You sure about this?" Rafe asked as we reached his truck, his voice low, laced with concern. His hand hovered near the door handle but didn't touch it. He was waiting for me to decide if I was in, really in, or if I was still half in the world of denial.

I glanced at him, seeing the quiet worry etched into his features. It was almost as if I could read his thoughts in the lines of his face—he was scared, but not for himself. He was scared for me. And honestly, I didn't blame him. The deeper we dug, the more the town turned its back on us. The whispers from the people who once knew us as neighbors had shifted into cold stares and murmurs behind closed doors. But it wasn't the judgment of others that worried me. It was the escalating danger, the sense that we were now the targets in a game where the rules had already been written by people with too much to lose.

"I don't have a choice," I said, my voice steady, even though my heart was a little less certain. I could feel the thrum of adrenaline rushing through my veins as I spoke, but there was a tinge of doubt buried in the back of my mind. Rafe was right. This wasn't some amateur investigation anymore. We were no longer dealing with the small-town petty criminals or teenage pranks that had shaped our past. The stakes were larger now, more dangerous. And when you started looking into the pockets of the people who controlled everything, you didn't just risk exposing them. You risked becoming the target.

He gave a curt nod and slid into the driver's seat, starting the engine with a low rumble that seemed to vibrate through the metal frame. The truck jolted forward, pulling us into the night. The town slipped away in the rearview mirror, but the oppressive feeling of being watched followed us like a shadow. I didn't know what we were walking into, but I was past the point of turning back.

The silence between us stretched, thick and heavy, and I could feel the weight of the moment pressing against both of us. He was watching me, I knew it, but I didn't dare meet his eyes. Not now. If I did, I might lose the last thread of resolve that was keeping me anchored.

Finally, Rafe broke the silence, his voice low and guarded. "There's something I didn't tell you before. Something about the developer. It's bigger than you think, Ellie. Much bigger."

I turned my head sharply, my breath catching in my throat. "What do you mean?"

He hesitated, then cursed under his breath. "I was trying to protect you, okay? But you've got to know the truth. The developer... he's tied to more than just land deals. There's money laundering, a string of questionable transactions, and people—important people—who stand to lose everything if the truth comes out."

I blinked, trying to process what he was saying. "So, the fires aren't just about clearing land for a development project? They're a cover-up?"

"Exactly. And the fires? They're meant to drive out the last of the holdouts—the people who refuse to sell, who won't leave. They think if they burn enough, they'll break the town's spirit. But they're wrong." His grip on the wheel tightened, his knuckles white under the dim glow of the dashboard lights. "And if you keep digging, Ellie, they're going to come for you. We both know that."

The weight of his words crashed over me. It wasn't just about saving the town anymore. It was about exposing a system built on corruption, a system that was willing to sacrifice anything to maintain its grip on power. And now, it was my life on the line, not just the town's.

"I'm not running, Rafe. Not from this," I said, my voice barely a whisper, yet it felt like a vow. "I won't let them win."

He was silent for a long time, and the only sound in the truck was the low hum of the tires against the road. It wasn't just determination in his eyes when he finally turned to look at me. It was something darker. Something I didn't recognize. "You don't know what you're walking into," he muttered, as if the words hurt him.

"I know enough," I said, meeting his gaze for the first time since we started driving. "I know that if we don't do something now, we'll lose everything. We'll lose each other."

The truck lurched as Rafe slammed on the brakes, and my heart skipped a beat. We were parked outside a small, unmarked building that looked abandoned in the shadows of the night. There were no signs, no indication of what it was or who was inside, but I could feel the buzz in the air. Something was waiting for us in that building, something neither of us was prepared for.

Rafe reached for the door handle, but before he could open it, a figure stepped into the headlights of the truck, blocking our path.

I froze. The figure moved closer, slowly, deliberately, until I could make out the shape of a familiar face.

My breath caught in my throat. It was my father. But this time, he wasn't here to protect me.

Chapter 26: Beneath the Ashes

The ledger felt cold in my hands, the weight of its secrets pressing against my skin like a confession. My fingers grazed the edges of the pages, each turn revealing another layer of the scheme we had been chasing for months. The dim light of Rafe's flashlight flickered across the text, casting shadows that seemed to dance on the walls of the firehouse, whispering of things long buried. The faint scent of smoke still clung to the air, a reminder of the fires that had consumed so much—both the buildings and the lives within them. But now, we had the truth, hidden away in this small, unassuming book.

Rafe's breath came in short, controlled bursts beside me, his thumb absently rubbing the top of my hand as we both stared down at the page. The pages weren't just ink on paper; they were history, a carefully curated record of payoffs and promises. The arsons—each one orchestrated with such precision, so deliberate—had been funded by people who thought they were untouchable. But this ledger, this damned piece of paper, had found its way to us, and it wasn't letting go.

"Is it real?" he whispered, his voice tight, as if he was afraid the truth would slip through his fingers like sand.

I couldn't answer right away. I was still absorbing it, the realization sinking in slowly, turning my gut into a tight knot of uncertainty. The truth was right in front of me, written in black ink, but the consequences of exposing it weren't as simple as I wanted them to be. The men we were up against weren't just criminals—they were a network, a well-oiled machine that had been operating for years, and now we were about to put a wrench in it. They would retaliate. They always did.

"I'm not sure if this is the victory we were hoping for," I said, the words escaping before I could catch them.

Rafe looked at me, his eyes steady, but I saw the flicker of doubt there. He squeezed my hand, as if reminding me that we were in this together. "It's the only victory we've got left."

His words hit harder than I expected, and a strange surge of fear mixed with defiance bubbled up in my chest. He was right. This was the only proof we had that tied everything together—the fires, the money, the manipulation. If we took this to the authorities, it would be the end of the line. But it would also be the start of a much more dangerous game.

A soft knock echoed from the door behind us, pulling my attention away from the ledger and toward the sound. I froze, my hand instinctively tightening around the paper, my pulse quickening. No one ever came by the firehouse at this hour unless they were looking for trouble.

Rafe reached for the holster at his side, his movements swift and practiced. I leaned forward, peering around the corner of the desk. The dim light spilled over the silhouette of a man in the doorway, his face obscured by the shadows. His presence felt like a warning, his very existence a ripple in the quiet that had settled around us.

"Rafe," the man's voice broke the silence, low and gruff. "You've got company."

I recognized the voice instantly. It was Callahan, the one person I hadn't expected to see tonight. Callahan was a wild card—loyal when it suited him, dangerous when it didn't. I hadn't seen him since the last time we crossed paths with the arsonists, and even then, it had been a fleeting interaction, a brief nod of acknowledgment. But tonight? Tonight, he seemed different—tense, like a thread stretched too thin.

"Why don't you come inside, Callahan?" Rafe's voice was calm, but there was a sharp edge to it that made my spine stiffen.

Callahan stepped into the room slowly, his eyes flicking over to me before he took a seat across from us without waiting for an invitation. His gaze locked on the ledger, and I could see the moment he realized what we were holding. His jaw tightened, and a flicker of something—fear or perhaps recognition—flashed in his eyes.

"You don't want to go down this road," Callahan said, his voice carrying the weight of someone who had seen things they couldn't unsee. "You don't know what you're dealing with."

I could feel my breath catch, the tension in the room thickening. This wasn't just about proving something anymore. This was about survival, and Callahan knew it.

"I think we've made our choice," Rafe replied, his voice steady but resolute.

I didn't look at him then—I couldn't. I was still focused on Callahan, studying him closely, trying to read the flicker of hesitation in his expression. But it was no use. Whatever had been there moments ago was gone, replaced by something darker, something more guarded.

"You think you've got the upper hand," Callahan continued, leaning forward. "But you're wrong. The people behind this—they don't play fair. And when they come for you, there won't be a place left to hide."

I swallowed hard, the weight of his words sinking in. Rafe's hand still held mine, his grip firm but offering no real comfort. We were at the edge of something, and the ground below us felt shaky. No one could ever prepare you for the moment when the truth became too much to bear. But there it was, laid out in front of us, waiting for the push that would send it all crashing down.

"We're already in," I said, my voice firmer than I felt. "You think we don't know what's coming? We've been waiting for this."

Callahan didn't respond right away. Instead, he leaned back in his chair, his eyes narrowing as if he was calculating something in his head. For a moment, the room was dead silent, the only sound the soft rustling of paper as the ledger lay between us, like a ticking bomb counting down to its inevitable detonation.

"I just wanted to make sure you knew what you were getting yourselves into," he said, his voice low and almost apologetic, but there was an undercurrent of something else—something far more dangerous. "You won't be able to undo this once you take that step."

I met his gaze and held it, my heart pounding. This was it—the moment we could either back down or plunge headfirst into the unknown. And for the first time in a long while, I felt ready to burn everything down.

Callahan's words hung in the air between us, a thin veil of doubt settling over the room like a storm cloud. I could almost hear the crackling of the tension as Rafe and I exchanged a look, the kind of look you only share with someone who's been through the trenches beside you, someone who knows the cost of every decision, every breath. But still, there was a hesitation in his eyes, a momentary flicker that made my pulse quicken with the familiar sense of dread creeping in. Callahan was right about one thing: We were in too deep, and once we crossed that line, there would be no going back. But wasn't that the point?

"We've always known there was no turning back, Callahan," I said, my voice steady but edged with a challenge I hadn't meant to unleash. The words were out before I could pull them back, but it didn't matter. "So why are you warning us now? You know what they're capable of, and yet you're still here, playing both sides of the fence. Which side are you on?"

He didn't flinch, but I saw the tightening of his jaw. The muscles in his neck shifted, betraying his calm exterior. For a moment, I thought he might leave, or worse, walk out the door and never look back. But instead, he sat there, watching us with those sharp, calculating eyes. There was more to Callahan than met the eye, more to this tangled mess we were in. I knew it, and maybe, just maybe, he knew that I knew.

"I've never been on anyone's side but my own," he said, his voice almost too smooth. "And right now, that's the only side that matters."

Rafe stood up slowly, his movements deliberate, and the floor creaked beneath him. He towered over the desk, his presence filling the room in a way that left little space for doubt or indecision. "You've got a choice to make, Callahan. You can either walk out of here and disappear, or you can help us bring this down."

I could feel my heart pounding in my chest, the weight of the moment pressing down on me. This wasn't just a matter of evidence anymore; it was a battle of wills. Rafe's words weren't a plea—they were a demand, a challenge. He wasn't asking for help. He was telling Callahan that the clock was ticking, and there would be no room for playing games.

For a long moment, Callahan didn't speak. His eyes flicked over the ledger again, scanning the pages, the glint of something dangerous in his expression. He seemed to weigh the options, his mind working through a thousand calculations in the span of a few breaths.

"I'm not interested in playing hero," he muttered finally, rubbing his hand over his face as if erasing the weight of his own decision. "But I owe you both one. And maybe it's time I paid that debt."

There it was, that rare moment of vulnerability, hidden beneath his usual bravado. Callahan wasn't just some hired gun. He wasn't just some cold figure in the shadows. He had a history with Rafe, with me, with the mess we were now wading through. We had saved him once, in ways we never talked about, and now it seemed like he was returning the favor, in his own twisted way.

I let out a breath I hadn't realized I was holding. "You don't have to do this, Callahan," I said quietly, my voice softening just a little. "But if you do, you need to know there's no going back for you either."

He gave me a look that was too unreadable, too hard to crack, but the slight nod of his head told me he understood. Maybe it was just that damn ledger. Maybe it was the realization that we were all tied to this mess in ways we couldn't untangle. Either way, he had made his choice.

"Let's get to work," he said, a finality in his voice.

I turned back to Rafe, my eyes meeting his, and for a brief moment, the world outside seemed to pause, leaving us suspended in this uncertain space between decisions. The ledger sat between us, its pages glowing with the faint light of the flashlight, a map to destruction. This wasn't just about burning down a corrupt network. This was about burning down everything that had ever held us back from the truth, from the lives we'd tried to live under false pretenses.

I knew this would change everything—how could it not? The people behind this operation were powerful, ruthless, and they didn't take kindly to being exposed. The risks were too high, the consequences too great. But there was no other option. The ledger was the key, the evidence we needed to end this once and for all. The world would burn, and maybe it was time to watch it go up in flames.

"I'll gather the rest of the team," Rafe said, his voice low, almost as if speaking to himself. "We'll need everyone for what's coming next."

I nodded, feeling a strange calm wash over me despite the chaos building in the pit of my stomach. There was no turning back now, no safe place to hide from the storm that was coming. It wasn't just the fires that would burn this time—it was everything.

The room felt smaller now, as if the walls were closing in around us, tightening with every passing second. I could hear my heartbeat thundering in my ears, drowning out the rest of the world. But still, I didn't feel fear. Not anymore. Maybe it was the adrenaline. Maybe it was the strange peace that came with knowing this was the endgame. Whatever it was, it was enough to steady my hands as I slid the ledger into my bag, securing it for the inevitable fight.

"You sure about this?" Rafe asked, looking over at me with that familiar mixture of care and concern.

"More than ever," I replied, a wry smile tugging at the corner of my mouth. "Let's burn this down."

The air between us hummed with an unspoken tension, something thicker than the smoke that clung to our clothes. Rafe's eyes lingered on me for just a moment longer than necessary, the weight of the decision heavy in his gaze. His fingers flexed around my hand, the pressure a quiet anchor to the chaos swirling in my chest. The ledger was the key, yes, but what did that really mean? Could we really take this step, knowing that once the truth was out there, we'd be targets too?

We didn't have much time to waste. I could already hear the hum of the outside world creeping in—engines roaring in the distance, sirens echoing like a promise of impending chaos. This was the cusp of everything changing, the edge of a cliff we couldn't back away from. Yet, here we were, standing in the firehouse, the final piece of the puzzle between us.

"Rafe," I murmured, my voice lower than usual, the weight of the word carrying a finality that felt like it was etched into my very bones. "What happens when we give this to them? To the authorities?"

He exhaled slowly, the sound rasping in his chest, and I could tell the question had been echoing in his mind for days now. "We don't just give it to them," he said, his voice calm but sharp as glass. "We make sure they know it's us behind the whole thing. We make them see who they've been dealing with."

The thought of exposure, of stepping into the open with this truth, sent a fresh wave of unease flooding my veins. The people behind the arson ring were not just criminals; they were the kind of men who never left loose ends. Their connections ran deep, tangled like roots beneath the ground. If we weren't careful, we'd be another forgotten name, another casualty in a game where the rules were made by those in power.

I leaned forward, my fingers brushing against the edge of the ledger again, the coldness of it sending a chill through me. This wasn't just about burning down their operation—it was about setting the entire structure alight, watching it crumble to ash, and hoping we didn't get caught in the blaze.

"We're really doing this, aren't we?" I said softly, mostly to myself, feeling the gravity of the decision crush me in one swift moment.

Rafe didn't answer at first. He just stood there, as still as a statue, his brow furrowed as if he were fighting a battle inside himself. The silence between us stretched out like the miles of road we still had to travel. It was the kind of silence that hung heavy, filled with everything that hadn't been said, with every possibility both terrifying and exhilarating.

Then, his voice broke through, low and steady. "We've been doing this for months, Jessie. We've come this far. We don't stop now."

I looked up at him, our eyes locking in a rare moment of unity. For once, there was no fear. There was only a shared understanding.

This wasn't just about vengeance or justice anymore. It was about taking control, about doing something that mattered.

And then, in the distance, I heard it—a screech of tires. I stiffened, my hand gripping the ledger as though it could protect me from the rush of panic that began to surge through my chest. The sound was unmistakable: an engine roaring too loud, too fast.

Rafe was already moving, his hand reaching for his gun with practiced ease. "Stay behind me," he ordered, his voice calm but sharp.

I didn't argue. I knew better. The firehouse was quiet, too quiet, as if the entire world had frozen just long enough to give us a moment of false peace before everything went to hell.

The door rattled on its hinges, then slammed open. A figure stood there, silhouetted against the dim light outside, a shadow that shifted as it crossed the threshold. I couldn't make out the details of the person's face—only the gleam of something metal in their hand.

"Don't shoot," the voice called out, gravelly, strained. "It's me."

My pulse slowed just enough for recognition to settle in. I stepped forward, half-relieved, half-terrified, because I knew who this was. It was Callahan. But why was he here, looking like he had just stepped out of a war zone? His clothes were torn, dirt streaked across his face, and there was a wildness in his eyes that made the hairs on the back of my neck stand on end.

"What happened?" I asked, my voice tight with concern.

Callahan didn't answer immediately. Instead, he glanced over his shoulder, the tension in his posture betraying the fact that he wasn't alone. His eyes flicked toward Rafe, and for a moment, the three of us just stood there, waiting for the inevitable to happen. The air felt too thick, the room too small.

"I need you to listen to me," Callahan said, taking a step inside and shutting the door with a loud bang. "We don't have much time."

They're coming for you, Jessie. And they're not going to stop until they have you both."

A chill ran through me. "Who?"

His eyes darted around the room, his voice dropping to a whisper. "The ones you think you're bringing down... they already know. And they've got people in the force. People who are watching every move you make. This wasn't just a ledger you found, Jessie. It's bait."

I felt my stomach drop, a cold sweat breaking out along the back of my neck. "What do you mean?"

"They're setting you up," Callahan said, his voice rough, barely above a whisper. "And you've just walked right into their trap."

Before I could process his words, the sound of footsteps echoed down the hallway. Rapid, urgent, like the beat of a drum, signaling the end of whatever fragile peace we had left.

Rafe stepped forward, blocking me from view, but I could see the tension in his shoulders. "How much time do we have?"

"Less than five minutes," Callahan muttered, his eyes wide with fear. "They're already here."

And just as he spoke, the door behind us slammed open once more, and I felt the world shift beneath my feet.

Chapter 27: Flames of Retribution

The town was quieter than it had ever been. I could feel it in my bones, a hum in the air that seemed to pulse with the weight of secrets, of things not yet spoken but always there, lurking in the corners. It wasn't the usual comforting quiet of early morning or the lazy hum of late afternoon; no, this felt like something darker, something waiting. People had stopped saying hello, or even acknowledging us with the usual nods of politeness. Once, the cobbled streets would have echoed with the sounds of a dozen different conversations, laughter drifting from the cafes or the butcher's shop. Now, only the soft scrape of Rafe's boots against the stones and my own hesitant steps broke the silence.

He kept his hand firmly clasped around mine, a solid, unspoken reassurance, though I could feel the tension in his muscles. He was good at hiding it—his jaw set, eyes forward—but I knew him too well now. The last few days had been nothing but a blur of late-night research, phone calls, and emails. The ledger had been a key. A damning key. Each page had brought us closer to the twisted web that had ensnared this town, and with every word we'd uncovered, I felt more and more the weight of the people we were about to betray.

We had our proof. The developer, the one who'd promised to 'revitalize' the town, had been siphoning money from the local businesses, using false accounts and shady contracts to line his pockets. Rafe had known something was off from the beginning, but I hadn't believed him—couldn't believe that something so corrupt could take root here, in a place I'd grown up, where everyone knew everyone else's business. I should've known better.

The problem was, it wasn't just him. It was the people who'd enabled him—the ones who had turned a blind eye, or worse, taken their cut. The quiet complicity of the town weighed on me now, heavier than the ledger in my bag. I glanced at Rafe, his expression unreadable, and felt my stomach tighten. We hadn't planned on this. We'd thought we could expose the truth, shake things up, and somehow still walk away without leaving too many scars. But now, as we moved through the town square, it felt like we were already outcasts, the whispers already starting.

Rafe stopped at the edge of the square, near the fountain, where the water had once shimmered in the sun like a promise. Now it looked dull, the stones around it worn with age, the birds avoiding the area as if they sensed the shift in the air. He turned to me, his dark eyes searching mine, his thumb gently brushing against my wrist. "Are you ready for this?" he asked, his voice steady, but I could hear the question beneath it. Not just about the ledger, but about everything that was coming.

I hesitated. Of course, I wasn't ready. But who was ever truly ready to tear apart their own life, to burn it all down in the hopes of something better rising from the ashes? "We don't have a choice," I said, my voice stronger than I felt. "If we don't do this now, it'll just keep happening. To someone else. And we'll be complicit."

Rafe nodded, but there was a sharp edge to his smile, something resigned. "And we don't want that, do we?"

"No," I said, the word tasting like steel on my tongue. "We don't."

We walked past the baker's shop, where Mrs. Falwell had once handed me a loaf of bread with a smile so wide it seemed to stretch across the entire town. Her shop was still there, still open, but now there was a distance in her gaze as she peeked over the counter, watching us like we were strangers rather than the children she'd watched grow up. I tried not to let it hurt. But it did. It all hurt, this rift that had opened between us and the people we'd known all our lives.

It wasn't until we reached the town hall steps that the first voice broke the silence. It was old Mr. Harper, a man who'd once been as much a fixture of this place as the oak tree in the center of the park. He had a thin, weathered face and eyes that had always seemed to see too much. He leaned on his cane, a look of suspicion clouding his features, and his voice cracked the tension in the air.

"You don't want to go up there," he warned, his gaze flickering from me to Rafe.

I stopped. "What do you mean?"

"There's more at play than you think," he said, a grim smile tugging at the corners of his lips. "You think the developer's the only problem? Think again. People don't just get away with things like that here. Not unless they're covered."

I swallowed, suddenly cold. "Covered by who?"

Mr. Harper's eyes flickered, his face tightening with something almost like fear. "The same ones who've been keeping things quiet for years."

Rafe's grip on my hand tightened, his posture stiffening. "Are you saying there's more to this than we know?"

Mr. Harper didn't answer right away. His eyes darted across the street, scanning the empty square like he expected someone to jump out at any moment. He gave a low, frustrated sigh and hobbled back a step. "All I'm saying is... be careful. Not everyone's as friendly as they seem. And sometimes, the people you trust are the ones who will sell you out the quickest."

The words lingered in the air, cold and sharp. I wanted to ask more, to press him for answers, but I could already see that it wasn't going to be that simple. Whatever was happening here, whatever was going on behind closed doors, was far more complicated than we'd anticipated. And now, standing there with Rafe, with the ledger in my bag and the town around us holding its breath, I couldn't help but wonder if we were already too deep in to pull back.

"You hear that?" Rafe asked, his voice low and tense, his eyes scanning the square.

I nodded. "I hear it."

But the sound I heard wasn't just the quiet, the tension—it was something else, something darker. And for the first time in all this, I wasn't sure if we were the ones bringing the truth to light, or if we were just feeding the flames.

It wasn't long before the whispers began. The kind that you can almost hear without needing to see the mouths moving, the ones that slither like smoke through the cracks in the walls. We made our way through the streets, the sound of our footsteps becoming the loudest thing in the otherwise empty town. Rafe's hand still clung to mine, but I could feel the slight tremor in his fingers, betraying the calm front he wore so well.

"You ever think we might've made a mistake?" I asked him, the words slipping out before I could stop them. My voice felt too loud in the silence, too sharp. But the question had been hanging in my mind for hours now, like a weight I couldn't shake off.

He didn't answer right away. His gaze flickered toward the old brick buildings that lined the street, the shop fronts dark and closed despite it being midday. It was like the life had been sucked out of the place, the energy that had once filled every corner now a distant memory.

"Not for a second," he finally said, his voice low and steady, but with a quiet edge to it that I hadn't expected. "The people who've been keeping secrets—covering things up—they need to be held accountable. No one gets to live in the shadows forever."

I nodded, though it didn't make me feel any better. Rafe was right, of course. There was no turning back now. The truth was out, and it was our responsibility to make sure it didn't get buried again.

But as we passed the café on the corner, I caught sight of a figure standing in the window—someone I hadn't expected to see. Emily, the town's longtime librarian, her hands pressed to the glass, her eyes wide and alarmed as they followed us down the street. She was always so composed, so serene in her perfectly buttoned-up cardigans and her soft-spoken ways. Seeing her like that—panicked, unsettled—was like a slap to the face.

I stopped, squeezing Rafe's hand just slightly. "Do you think she knows?"

Rafe glanced at the café and then back at me, his expression unreadable. "She knows something. Everyone does. We're not the first to catch on, just the first to have the proof."

That didn't make me feel better either. The idea that people had known, or at least suspected, and done nothing about it, stung. How could they live with that? How could they sit idly by while everything they cared about was being used as a pawn in someone else's game?

We continued walking, the weight of it all pressing down on us more with every step. I could see the flickering of movement in some of the houses as we passed—eyes peering out from behind curtains, the soft scrape of a door latch as someone quietly shut themselves inside. It was like the town was closing in on us, its once-friendly streets now a maze of suspicion and fear. And it wasn't just the developer we were up against anymore. It was everyone who had something to lose if the truth came to light. The town had its own code, one that didn't care much for right or wrong, only for survival.

When we reached the courthouse steps, I was almost relieved. It felt like the first step toward something solid, something unmovable. But as soon as I looked up, I saw the figure waiting for us on the steps, arms crossed, standing with an air of authority that made my stomach flip.

"Jenna." The voice was familiar, like a thorn stuck in the back of my mind. Too calm. Too controlled.

I had expected this moment, of course. But that didn't mean I was ready for it.

"Brian," I said, my voice coming out far colder than I intended. I hadn't seen him in months, not since the day he'd walked away from the case he'd promised to help with, leaving us to deal with the fallout. Now, here he was, standing in front of us, as though he hadn't just abandoned us when it mattered most.

He was dressed in a suit that looked too polished for the small-town setting, his shoes gleaming in the dull light. He looked the same as he had all those years ago when he'd been the golden boy of our class—handsome, composed, a little too perfect.

"What are you doing here?" I asked, crossing my arms in defiance, the frustration bubbling inside me.

"I was hoping we could talk," Brian said, stepping down the steps slowly, his eyes locked onto mine. "I've been hearing rumors, and well, I think we need to clear the air."

"Clear the air?" I let out a short, bitter laugh. "There's nothing to clear. You walked away from this, Brian. You made your choice."

"I didn't walk away," he said, a sharpness in his voice now. "I had my reasons."

I raised an eyebrow. "Reasons? You mean the ones where you sold your soul to the highest bidder? The ones that led you to shut down the investigation, to let him walk away without consequence?"

Brian's jaw tightened, his eyes narrowing. "You don't understand—"

"No, I think I understand just fine." I took a step forward, my frustration turning into something more dangerous, a fire that was impossible to ignore. "You think I don't know what's been going on here? You think you can just sweep it under the rug and move on like nothing happened?"

For a moment, Brian didn't speak. He just looked at me, the silence between us heavy with things unsaid. I could see the tension in his shoulders, the way his hands flexed at his sides, like he was trying to hold back something. But then, his face softened, just a little, and he took a deep breath.

"I never meant for things to go this far," he said quietly. "I thought... I thought I could protect everyone, keep things from getting ugly. But now, I see what a mistake that was."

"Protect everyone?" I echoed, incredulous. "By keeping us all in the dark? By letting him get away with it?"

"I didn't have a choice!" His voice rose, and for a split second, I saw the cracks in his perfect exterior. "You think I didn't care? You think I didn't want to stop it? But you don't know what it's like when the people who hold all the cards are the ones you rely on. The ones who control everything."

The air between us was thick with the unsaid. The town, the developer, the secrets—everything had been tangled together for too long, and now, with each word we spoke, we were unraveling it all. But I couldn't shake the feeling that there was more to this story, something he wasn't telling me. And as he stood there, looking at me like he had the answers I needed, I realized that trusting him had never been more dangerous.

Brian's words hung in the air, sharp and brittle. I didn't want to hear him. I didn't want to listen to any of his explanations or excuses. His reasons were the same ones everyone else had used—"protecting" the town, "keeping things quiet," as if it was their right to decide what we were allowed to know. It was all a mess of pretenses, and I was done with it.

"You didn't protect anyone," I said, my voice a little louder than I intended. "You covered your own back, Brian. And you let the rest of us hang out to dry."

His face faltered, a flicker of something almost like regret crossing his features before he pushed it away. "I didn't know how deep it went," he muttered, his voice rough, as if the words themselves were foreign. "I never thought it would get this bad."

I laughed, a sharp, bitter sound that bounced off the cold stone of the courthouse. "You're just as guilty as the rest of them, Brian. You knew what he was doing. You saw the signs."

"I didn't have a choice," he repeated, more forcefully this time, his fists clenching at his sides. "The stakes were too high. I thought I could control it. Keep things from spiraling out of control."

"You mean you thought you could ride it out. Play both sides, pretend like everything was fine, and then walk away when it all came crashing down."

His eyes narrowed. "You don't understand what it's like to be in my position. To have everything you've worked for hanging by a thread."

I shook my head, the weight of everything we'd uncovered making my mind spin. "No, Brian. You don't understand what it's like to be betrayed. To find out the people you trusted were nothing but liars in disguise."

"Is that what you think?" he asked, stepping closer now, his voice soft but insistent. "That I betrayed you?"

"You betrayed all of us," I snapped, not backing down. "And now you want to act like you're the one who's been wronged? You're pathetic."

For a moment, his face went blank, as if my words had struck a chord deep inside him. He opened his mouth to speak, but the sound of approaching footsteps interrupted us. We both turned toward the sound, a shift in the air that I couldn't ignore. I could feel the change, the sudden surge of tension in the space between us. And I knew, instinctively, that something was about to break.

Rafe's hand tightened around mine, his body stiffening. "We're not alone," he murmured, barely audible.

I didn't have to look to know he was right. The hairs on the back of my neck prickled as if some unseen force was closing in. I didn't know who, but I could feel the weight of their presence, pressing down on us from all directions. I was already regretting standing here, facing Brian like I could still trust him.

The footsteps came closer, the sound growing more defined. My heart began to race as I turned to face the direction of the sound. But before I could react, I heard the unmistakable click of a gun being cocked.

The chill that washed over me was instantaneous, the blood draining from my face. Brian's expression morphed into something I couldn't quite place—guilt, fear, maybe even anger. But before I could ask him what the hell was going on, I saw him move. Not to protect me, but to step aside.

A tall figure emerged from the shadows, stepping into the dim light with the kind of confidence that immediately sent a shiver down my spine. Dressed in black, the figure's face was hidden behind a mask, but the posture was all too familiar—too purposeful. I didn't need to see the eyes to know who it was. I could feel it in my gut.

"Thought you'd get away with it, didn't you, Jenna?" The voice was deep and smooth, too controlled, like a predator toying with its prey. It was him—Lukas, the one I had been trying to avoid. The one I had no idea was this close, this involved.

My stomach twisted into knots, nausea creeping up the back of my throat. Rafe shifted beside me, pulling me closer. His grip on my hand was firm, but I could feel the uncertainty in his movements now. This was different from anything we'd faced before.

"You should've stayed quiet," Lukas continued, his tone almost conversational, as if we were discussing the weather instead of a potentially life-threatening situation. "You've stirred up too much trouble for yourself. And for what? A few pieces of paper that don't mean anything to people who matter?"

I didn't answer him immediately. I wasn't sure I could trust my voice at the moment. Fear had a way of swallowing up your words, drowning you in the terror of the unknown. But I wasn't going to let him see that. Not now. Not when it felt like everything I had fought for was about to be ripped from my hands.

Instead, I lifted my chin, meeting his gaze, feeling the weight of his eyes on me. "What do you want, Lukas?" I asked, my voice steadier than I expected.

"What do I want?" He chuckled, a dark, humorless sound. "You really don't get it, do you? You think you're going to walk away from this with the truth in your hands and nothing else? The truth doesn't save anyone. Especially not you."

Rafe stepped in front of me, his body tense, blocking Lukas's view of me. "Leave her out of this," he growled, his voice low and dangerous. "This is between you and me."

Lukas tilted his head, considering the offer for a moment. His hand, still holding the gun, shifted slightly, but his eyes never left me. "You think I'm going to let you threaten me? You're not in a position to negotiate, Rafe. And neither is she."

The gun in his hand gleamed ominously in the dim light. My breath caught in my throat as I realized we were at the mercy of a man who had no qualms about making us disappear. He had the power, the leverage. But that didn't mean we couldn't fight back.

I wasn't sure how, but as I looked between Lukas and Rafe, something sparked in me—a wild, reckless surge of defiance. We weren't going down without a fight. Not now, not when we had so much to lose.

The moment hung there, stretched tight between us. I could almost taste the tension in the air, thick and heavy. And then, Lukas made his move.

The sound that followed was like a thunderclap, so loud it almost deafened me. But it wasn't the gunshot I expected. It was the sound of shuffling footsteps—too many to count, all around us. And before I could fully process what was happening, a new voice broke the silence.

"Freeze!"

Chapter 28: Blazing Betrayals

The air in the police station was thick, like an uninvited guest at a dinner party. The fluorescent lights buzzed overhead, casting a sickly glow on everything they touched—making the polished floors look like they hadn't seen a mop in years, and the cold, sterile walls felt like they were closing in around me. The smell of stale coffee mingled with the metallic tang of the bars, which stood like a constant reminder that I was stuck. For a moment, I almost forgot how I got here. The confusion, the urgency, and the heat of adrenaline had all blurred into one chaotic mess. It wasn't until I heard the unmistakable sound of my father's boots echoing through the hall that everything hit me with full force.

He came into view, the broad-shouldered silhouette of the man who had always towered over me, both figuratively and literally. His face was a landscape of harsh lines, each one telling a different story, a different regret. He had aged in ways I hadn't noticed before—his hair graying at the temples, the fine wrinkles around his eyes deepening as if someone had drawn them in with a pencil. The power that once radiated from him now felt like a thin veneer, ready to crack at any moment. But it was the tension in his jaw that gave me pause.

"Dad," I said, even though I wasn't sure how to say it. How to bridge the gap between us that had been widening for years.

He didn't answer immediately. His eyes scanned the room, making sure the world knew he wasn't some hapless fool, dragged into a situation beyond his control. The officer who had been sitting at the desk watched him, her gaze neutral but not unfriendly. She'd seen it all, I imagined. Rich man's daughter caught in a scandal—nothing new under the sun. But as she handed over the papers, she caught sight of me, and for a split second, her expression softened.

"Thank you, Officer," my father said gruffly, his words clipped as if he were doing me a favor just by being here. His eyes flicked to me, scanning my face, looking for signs of... I don't know what. Maybe guilt? Defiance? Or worse—fear.

I had never been afraid of him, at least not in the way you might think. It wasn't the kind of fear that comes from physical threats, but the deeper, quieter kind. The kind of fear that makes you wonder whether the person who raised you truly sees you, or whether you're just another pawn in their game. I could tell he wasn't angry, at least not at first. The anger would come later. This was something else. Something quieter. I knew it well enough to recognize the fear in his eyes—the kind of fear that makes a person reckless, desperate.

"You've made a mess of things," he muttered, though his tone didn't carry the full force of the words. He sighed, rubbing the back of his neck as though the weight of the world had settled there in one heavy, burdensome heap. "What were you thinking, really?"

I opened my mouth, ready to defend myself, but stopped short. What could I say? That I had been trying to protect the family's legacy? That I'd been trying to fix a problem that had been festering for years? That I didn't care about the ledger, but everything that it meant? It would have sounded too much like an excuse.

"I wasn't thinking, I guess," I said, forcing the words out. "Not in the way you want me to. But I had to do something."

He looked at me for a long moment, his brow furrowing as though he were struggling to find the right words. His lips pressed together, hard, and then he finally spoke, the words coming out like a whip crack.

"You put everything at risk. Everything we've built. You've jeopardized the reputation of this family, our name. For what? Some damn ledger?"

I winced, as though he'd slapped me across the face. He wasn't wrong, of course. The ledger was a dangerous thing, something better left untouched. But it wasn't the thing I was trying to protect. It wasn't the family's name, either. What I was trying to protect—what I had always been trying to protect—was the truth. The truth that had been buried for years, tucked away in shadows where no one could find it, not even me.

"Is that all you care about?" I demanded, the words coming out sharper than I intended. My voice echoed in the small room, bouncing off the walls like an unwanted guest. "The name? The reputation? Do you even care about what's really happening here? About what's been happening all along?"

The words hung between us, like a dangerous thread on the verge of snapping. I could see his knuckles whiten as he gripped the edge of the desk, and for a moment, I thought he might yell, might lose his temper in the way he always had when we disagreed. But instead, he exhaled, long and slow, and his shoulders sagged.

"You think this is easy for me?" His voice softened, the harshness slipping away. "You think I don't want to protect you? To keep you safe? This... this isn't just about us. It's about everything we've worked for. Everything that's been handed down through generations. Our legacy."

He stepped closer, his gaze meeting mine with something like desperation. "I'm doing this because I'm afraid for you. I'm afraid of what will happen if you don't stop. What they'll do to you."

I could see it now—the cracks in his armor. The fear that wasn't just about the business or the family name, but about me. About losing me.

"Maybe you should be afraid," I whispered. "Maybe you should be afraid of everything we've been pretending isn't there."

I could feel the weight of his gaze on me, heavy like a stone lodged in my chest. It wasn't just disappointment; it was something more, something jagged and raw, the kind of look only a parent can give when they've seen their child make a mistake that can't be undone. His hands gripped the edge of the desk as though he could somehow steady himself by holding onto the small, lifeless object. I wasn't sure if he was trying to steady his emotions or the overwhelming rush of anger that threatened to spill over.

"I didn't do it for the family, you know," I muttered, a bitter laugh escaping my lips. I hated the sound of it. "I didn't do it to preserve the name. I didn't even care about the ledger that much." The words felt like nails in my throat, the truth of them sharp and bitter.

My father's expression darkened, the muscle in his jaw twitching as he struggled to understand what I was saying. His eyes flickered with confusion, and for a brief moment, I wondered if he had ever truly known me. He had always thought he understood my every move, every decision, but maybe he had only been seeing the version of me he wanted to see—perfect, polished, in line with what he had hoped I would be. The daughter who carried the family banner without question. The obedient, docile woman who would never dare to upset the order of things.

"Well, then, why?" His voice cracked, the vulnerability in it sharp enough to cut through the tense silence. "Why go through all of this, throw away everything we've worked for, for what? To prove a point?"

The truth slipped out before I could stop it. "To find the truth," I said, barely a whisper. "I've been digging through lies my whole life. What's a little more dirt?"

His face went pale, and for the first time, I saw the truth of his own torment reflected in the way he held his body—tense, like a coiled spring, ready to snap. The words he had been holding back seemed to struggle against his lips. I knew them already, knew them in the marrow of my bones. The unspoken accusations, the quiet disappointment that was slowly turning into rage.

"You think this is about truth? About some noble cause?" he spat, his voice growing low and dangerous. "You've been playing a game, and you've dragged us all into it. You've cost us everything. This isn't some harmless pursuit. It's the end."

The venom in his voice stung, but I wasn't about to back down now. Not when I had already sacrificed so much. The ledger wasn't the only thing I was holding onto anymore; I had my own rage, my own hunger for answers. And I wasn't going to let him—or anyone—stop me.

"I didn't drag anyone into anything," I snapped, my voice rising. "You did that. You built this empire on lies, and I'm the one who's supposed to clean up the mess? Well, guess what, Dad? I'm done pretending I don't see what's really going on."

The words hung in the air between us, thick and heavy. His face turned an unsettling shade of crimson, and I could almost hear the breath he sucked in before he let it out in a slow, measured hiss. "Don't you dare, Olivia. You don't know what you're talking about."

I stepped closer to him, my heart hammering in my chest, daring him to push me further. "I think I do," I said quietly, the challenge in my voice making it clear that I was no longer afraid. "I think you've been hiding behind your reputation for so long that you can't see the truth anymore. And maybe that's why you're so scared—because you know what I'll find if I keep digging."

His hand shot out, grabbing my wrist with surprising strength. The force of it caught me off guard, and I flinched, but I didn't pull away. His grip tightened, the pulse in his fingers pressing into my skin.

"Do not threaten me," he growled through clenched teeth. His eyes burned with a fury that was as familiar to me as the scent of his cologne, as familiar as the grip of his hand, the roughness of his voice. It was the same rage I had seen before, when he had lost control, when the pressure of his world had become too much to bear. But this time, something was different. This time, I saw a flicker of something else in his eyes. Something that terrified me more than any of his anger ever could.

"I'm not afraid of you," I said, barely a whisper. "But I'm afraid of what you'll do to stop me from finding out what's really happening."

His hand fell away from me as though it had been burned. For a long moment, neither of us spoke. The silence between us was suffocating, and the weight of the air in the room made it feel as though we were both trapped in a space too small for our emotions to breathe.

Finally, he broke the silence. "You think you're the only one who's been fooled?" he asked, his voice low and strained. His eyes flicked to the door, to the world beyond this small room. "You think I haven't seen the way things are falling apart? That I don't know exactly what's happening?"

I swallowed hard. "Then why haven't you done anything?"

He ran a hand through his hair, and for the first time, I saw him—really saw him—as a man, not just the pillar of authority I had always assumed he was. There was no ease in his face anymore, no certainty in the lines of his posture. He was a man whose world was crumbling, and I was the one he had dragged into the rubble.

"Because I couldn't protect you," he said, his voice breaking in a way that made my stomach twist. "And now, it's too late."

The words hit me like a blow. And for the first time in a long time, I felt my anger falter. The edge that had been so sharp and sure now felt brittle, like it might shatter under the weight of his admission. It wasn't what I had expected to hear. It wasn't even what I had wanted to hear. But somehow, it felt like the first real truth in a long time.

The silence between us grew heavier with every passing second. The air in the small, stark room seemed to thicken, suffocating any attempts at reconciliation. I stared at my father, the man who had spent my entire life teaching me how to walk in the shadow of his legacy, only to find that it was built on something I could no longer respect. For years, I had been told that family came first. Reputation, loyalty, trust—all the things that were supposed to matter above all else. But now, in the pit of my stomach, all I could feel was the suffocating weight of the truth I had uncovered.

"I've been protecting you," my father said, his voice no longer a harsh bark but a quiet confession, his gaze unfocused, lost in thoughts that were not mine to understand. "I didn't want you to know. I didn't want you to carry the burden of it all. And now... now, I'm afraid you're too deep to turn back. I can't save you from this anymore."

The words hit me like a slap to the face. It was as though he had finally let his guard down, revealing the crumbling foundation of his control. His pride. His carefully constructed world. His admission stung, but more than that, it rattled me—because for the first time, I saw the cracks in the armor that he had worn so confidently for so many years.

"What are you talking about?" I managed to croak, my throat tight with a mix of confusion and rising fury. "What do you mean, you can't save me? You never tried to save me. You just tried to control everything, to keep me in the dark. I was never allowed to see what was really happening, to know what was at stake."

He finally met my eyes, his expression more vulnerable than I had ever seen it. "I didn't want you to hate me," he said simply, his voice rough, cracking under the weight of the admission. "I didn't want you to resent me the way I... the way I resented my own father.

You don't understand the things I've had to do to keep this family afloat. The sacrifices, the choices... You're not the only one who's been living in the dark."

His words hit harder than any accusation could have. They were no longer just about the ledger or the secrets I had uncovered. They were about the unspoken history that we both carried. The weight of legacies, both his and mine. For the first time, I realized that maybe we weren't so different, after all.

"Maybe I would have understood," I whispered, my voice thick with the sting of tears I wasn't ready to shed. "Maybe I could have been part of this if you hadn't shut me out. But now... Now I don't know what's real anymore."

There it was—the truth of it all. The raw, unfiltered reality that had been hidden beneath layers of carefully constructed facades. It wasn't just the family legacy that was at stake; it was everything we had built, everything we had believed. My father had been trying to protect me, but all he had really done was create a maze that I couldn't navigate without losing myself in the process.

Before he could respond, the door to the station swung open with a sharp bang, cutting through the fragile moment we had created. Both of us turned, startled, but the figure standing in the doorway froze me in place. I didn't recognize the officer at first—tall, dark hair, a face that looked like it belonged in a crime drama. But it wasn't his face that caught my attention. It was the gun in his hand.

The tension in the room shifted in an instant, morphing into something darker, something far more dangerous. The officer stepped inside, his eyes scanning us with the cold precision of a trained professional. He didn't look like someone who had just walked in to take a statement or deliver a message. No, this man was here for a different reason altogether.

"Who are you?" my father demanded, his voice low and dangerous.

The officer didn't flinch. "I'm afraid I'm the one who's going to have to take you both into custody."

The words were like a punch to the gut. For a second, I couldn't process them, couldn't understand what was happening. My heart raced in my chest, the blood pounding in my ears. I opened my mouth to protest, but the officer's gaze locked on mine, and I felt a chill run down my spine.

"You've been under investigation for a while now," the officer continued, his voice smooth and emotionless. "But this goes beyond the ledger. This goes straight to the heart of your family's business. There are things you're not privy to yet, things that could put you in a far worse situation than you realize."

"What is this?" My father's voice cracked, disbelief in every word. "What do you mean, 'worse situation'? You're saying this is about the business? The company?"

The officer's gaze flickered for just a second, but in that moment, I saw something—a glimmer of hesitation, a spark of something that told me this wasn't just a routine arrest. This was bigger than either of us. Something had shifted, and it was no longer just about the legacy we had been trying to protect. It was about survival.

"I'm not here to explain everything," the officer said, taking a step closer. "But I am here to make sure you don't destroy what's left of it. Whatever you think you know, it's nothing compared to what's coming. You're tangled in something much darker than you can imagine."

My heart skipped a beat, the weight of his words sinking in. I could feel the gravity of the situation tightening around us, like a vice squeezing the air from my lungs. For a moment, everything went silent. And in that silence, something unspoken passed between my father and me—an understanding, a realization that we were both in far deeper than we could have ever predicted.

I took a step back, my body trembling with the sudden realization of how quickly everything had changed. The walls of the station, the coldness of the metal bars, all felt like a distant memory now. Something darker was coming, and it was coming for us.

"Get up," the officer said, his voice now a command. "It's time to go."

Before either of us could react, the door slammed shut behind him, sealing our fate.

Chapter 29: Forged in Fire

The air in the town had grown thick with an unspoken hostility, as though the very atmosphere conspired against us. Walking down the cracked pavement, I could feel every eye on us, though I couldn't see the faces behind the drawn curtains or the shadows in doorways. It wasn't so much the town's betrayal that cut the deepest; it was the silence that followed. The sharp, unblinking silence that spoke louder than any accusation. A silent refusal to acknowledge that we had ever belonged, and a quiet judgment that now clung to our every step.

Rafe, walking beside me with his hands shoved deep into his jacket pockets, had become a ghost of the man I once knew. His posture had changed, tense, guarded, like someone expecting a punch from behind at any moment. His usual easy confidence had been replaced with something darker—something that felt like resignation. He didn't say much these days, and when he did, his words were weighed down with a heaviness I couldn't quite lift. The carefree jokes that once flowed between us were gone, and in their place was a silence that stretched long into the hours we spent alone together. A silence punctuated only by the ticking of clocks, the scraping of chairs, the occasional sigh.

It wasn't that I wasn't worried about the plan we had laid out. I was. But more than that, I was worried about him. For the first time, Rafe seemed... fragile. As though, if you took a good look at him, you'd see the cracks in his armor, the weariness etched into his face, the dark circles under his eyes. I used to joke about his arrogance, the way he wore his stubbornness like a second skin. But I never realized just how thin that skin could be, how quickly it could tear.

"Are you sure this is the right move?" I asked one evening, our voices echoing in the empty kitchen. The house, once a warm refuge from the world's chaos, had taken on the same cold, neglected feel as the rest of the town. "I mean, confronting him at the town meeting... it feels like we're walking into the lion's den with no weapons."

Rafe didn't look up from the cup of coffee in his hands, staring down into it like the answer was hidden in the swirling brown liquid. His jaw tightened, the muscles flickering with the tension that ran through him.

"We don't have a choice, Zoey," he said, the words rough, like he was trying to convince both of us. "If we don't do this now, everything we've been working for, everything we've uncovered, will go to waste. We can't let them get away with this. Not again."

I wanted to believe him, wanted to hold onto the conviction in his voice, but something in my gut twisted with unease. I knew what kind of man the developer was. Cold, calculated, and willing to destroy everything in his path for profit. But Rafe's certainty made my skin crawl. There was a quiet desperation in him now, an edge to his determination that made me afraid for us both. He didn't care if he won or lost anymore—he only cared that he did something. Anything to make the town see the truth.

"I just don't want you getting hurt," I said, my voice softer than I intended. There was no real softness in Rafe, not when it came to the fight we were in, and yet I knew he would carry the weight of it all. Always had. Always would.

Rafe finally looked at me, the weight of his gaze making my chest tighten. There was no mask now. No bravado. Just raw emotion, the kind that made everything else feel insignificant in comparison. "You think I don't know that?" he asked, his voice thick with a rough edge of emotion. "But this isn't just about us anymore, Zoey. We're in this together. And if something happens, then... damn it, I'd rather be with you than face it alone."

I wasn't sure what to say to that, so I didn't say anything at all. I just let the words sit between us, heavy and unspoken, as though acknowledging them would change everything.

In the days that followed, we continued our preparations, moving like shadows in the night, with only Wilder as our ally. He was our lone contact with the outside world, the only one who hadn't turned their back on us, and he had a way of making me believe that maybe—just maybe—we could still win. But each plan we made, every move we anticipated, felt like we were stacking dominoes in a game where the rules kept changing. It didn't help that the town's whispers were growing louder. The hostility was no longer subtle; it was in their eyes, in the way they turned their backs when we walked into a room.

I couldn't tell if they were afraid of us or if they were afraid of what we knew, but it didn't matter. We were trapped in a town that had already made its judgment, and there was no way out. No easy answers. Just the looming weight of what came next, and a growing fear that maybe we were too late to stop it.

And as the day of the meeting loomed closer, I realized something else. The plans, the stakes, the risks—they were nothing compared to the battle raging inside Rafe. The battle he wasn't letting me fight with him.

I couldn't help but notice how differently Rafe's worry now manifested. Before, there was always an air of certainty about him—his confidence contagious, his every move decisive, as if he had the answers to everything the world threw at him. Now, it was like he was wading through a fog of doubts, unable to find his way back to the familiar ground he once stood on. And I couldn't decide if it made him more real or more terrifying.

"I've been thinking," Rafe muttered one morning, his eyes focused on the horizon as if the answers to all his questions could be written in the rising sun. "About what we're really up against. It's not just the developer anymore. It's the entire damn town."

I bit back a laugh, though it was more out of habit than humor. "Well, welcome to the club," I teased lightly, though my words didn't have their usual bite. The weight of the situation was too much for me to be glib about it anymore. "But seriously, if you want to back out, now's your chance. You can't say I didn't warn you."

He flashed me a half-hearted smile, the edges of it strained. "Funny. But I think we're in this too deep now."

A part of me wanted to scream at him, tell him to stop. Tell him that maybe—just maybe—we hadn't made the right choices. That there was a way to fix everything before we lost ourselves to this insane race we were running, hurtling towards something none of us could control. But I didn't. Instead, I nodded, the silence between us hanging thick and heavy. The road ahead was clear, yet obscured by everything we didn't know.

It wasn't that I had any grand illusions that we could fix it all. The town was far too ingrained in its corrupt ways for a few outsiders to make a dent. No, what bothered me was the toll it was taking on Rafe, the quiet unraveling of the man I had come to know. He was stretched so thin I feared he might break under the pressure. Yet, he wouldn't let me in. Not completely.

"Rafe," I said, my voice softer now, as I reached out to touch his arm. He flinched ever so slightly, but didn't pull away. "We don't have to do this alone. Not this. Whatever happens, we're in it together. Don't shut me out."

His gaze hardened, and I could see the inner conflict playing out behind his eyes. It was clear he didn't want to drag me down with him, but it was also clear that he didn't know how to ask for help without feeling like he was giving up. He had always been the one who took charge, the one who made things happen. But now, even the slightest suggestion of failure seemed to push him further away from me.

"You've never been afraid, Zoey," he said, almost as if talking to himself, but loud enough for me to hear. "And maybe that's what scares me the most."

I swallowed the lump in my throat, my pulse quickening with the gravity of his words. "You think I'm not scared?" I asked, a sharpness to my voice that I didn't fully intend. "You think I'm not terrified that one wrong move could shatter everything we've worked for?"

He exhaled sharply, rubbing a hand across his face. "I didn't mean it like that." His voice softened, though the hesitation was still there. "You're too... damn strong. I'm not sure I can keep up with you."

I couldn't decide whether to laugh or to cry. So, I did neither. Instead, I reached for him, my hand resting gently on his arm, grounding both of us in the chaos that swirled just beneath the surface.

"You've never been alone, Rafe," I said, my words quiet but firm. "And I'm not going anywhere."

That was when he finally let out a breath—long and slow, as if he had been holding it in for too long. The wall he had built around himself cracked just enough for me to see a glimpse of the man who was still there. The man who needed me just as much as I needed him.

The town meeting was only two days away. There was no turning back. No more last-minute revisions to our plan. The ledger was our ace, and Detective Wilder had promised to make sure the evidence would be waiting for us when we made our move. I had to trust him, just as I had to trust Rafe, even if that trust was slipping through my fingers like sand.

We spent the hours before the meeting in silence, each of us lost in our thoughts, each of us mentally preparing for the confrontation ahead. Wilder had arranged for us to have a front-row seat, though I wasn't sure if it was a privilege or a death sentence. The developer, standing at the head of the room, would try to paint us as traitors. The town council would be so blinded by the developer's influence that they wouldn't care about the truth.

I wasn't worried about the developer. I wasn't even worried about the town. What kept me up at night was the thought that whatever happened in that room might tear us apart. That Rafe and I would find ourselves standing on opposite sides of a battle we didn't know how to win. That the silence between us would become permanent.

I hadn't realized how much I had come to rely on him, how much I needed his presence to steady me in the storm. And now, in the final hours before the meeting, I found myself wondering if we had any chance at all of coming out of this intact.

The night before the town meeting, I found myself standing at the edge of the small, weathered porch of Rafe's house, staring at the horizon as if I could somehow predict what would happen the next day. The cool breeze was a welcome relief from the heat that had clung to the town all day, but the quiet only amplified the chaos brewing inside me. I had never felt more uncertain in my life. The ledger, the evidence, the confrontation—all of it felt like the beginning of the end, yet I couldn't see the end clearly. What came after the storm? Would we walk away victorious, or would this town grind us into dust?

Rafe was inside, his back to me, his silhouette framed by the faint light from the kitchen. He wasn't talking much, his usual need for action replaced with a quiet, consuming tension. The man who once faced everything head-on with a smile now moved with a deliberateness that made him feel like a stranger to me. And yet, I couldn't find it in me to pull away. His vulnerability, raw and unspoken, was enough to bind me to him, even though every instinct told me to run.

When he finally came outside, the door creaked behind him, and I didn't turn to face him. I just let him stand there in the silence, not needing to ask, because we both knew what was coming. He stepped up beside me, his shoulder brushing mine, and the proximity sent a jolt through me—a jolt that was both comforting and unnerving. We hadn't talked about the meeting. We hadn't even talked about the things that were starting to feel more important than the plan itself—the things that might outlast whatever happened with the developer.

"I keep thinking about the first time I walked into this town," he said, his voice low, as if the words carried more weight than they should have. "How simple it felt back then, you know? It wasn't a fight. It wasn't a war. I just... I just thought we were here to live, to make something of ourselves."

I didn't say anything. The truth was, I didn't know what to say. I didn't know how to respond to a man who had built a life from the ground up, only to watch it crumble beneath the weight of corruption and greed. But then he surprised me.

"You think we can make it out of this?" he asked, his voice so quiet, I almost missed it. "I'm not talking about the developer or the town. I'm talking about us."

I turned to him then, meeting his gaze, searching for the man I knew beneath all the doubt and fear that had clouded his eyes. The man who believed in us. Who believed in something more than just survival.

"You want the truth?" I asked, the words tumbling out before I could stop them. "I don't know. I don't know if we're going to make it out of this or if we're going to lose everything. But I do know this.

Whatever happens, we're in this together. You and me. And that counts for something."

He didn't respond right away. He just stood there, looking at me, as if trying to decipher my words, my heart. Then, finally, he gave a short, humorless laugh and shook his head.

"You're too damn optimistic," he muttered, but there was no bitterness in his voice. Only an aching resignation, like he was trying to shield himself from whatever feelings had suddenly come to the surface.

And then, as quickly as the moment had arrived, it was gone. He turned, pulling me gently along with him into the house, and the conversation shifted back to the logistics of the meeting the next day. Plans, movements, strategies. The things we could control.

But deep inside, I knew nothing would prepare me for the moment when everything finally came to a head.

The next day, as we made our way toward the town hall, my hands were clammy, and my mind raced through a thousand scenarios, each one darker than the last. We arrived early, just as Wilder had instructed, and sat in the back row of the room, our eyes scanning the crowd. Most of the council members had already gathered, all in their usual spots, pretending that nothing was amiss. The developer hadn't yet arrived, but I could feel his presence hanging over us, like a shadow too large to ignore.

Rafe sat beside me, his eyes fixed forward, his body tense. I reached for his hand without thinking, needing to feel the warmth of his skin, needing to ground myself in something real. He squeezed my fingers once, briefly, before letting go, his attention never wavering from the front of the room. His lips were pressed into a thin line, and I couldn't tell if it was fear or fury that had taken root inside him. Maybe both. Maybe a hundred other things I couldn't name.

The door to the room creaked open, and in walked the developer. Tall, confident, his smile as polished as his expensive suit. He was everything I had come to despise in a single, neatly pressed package. He swept his eyes across the room, and the subtle nods of approval from the council members were enough to send a spike of disgust through me. They were already bought and paid for, and they knew it. They just didn't care.

Wilder appeared soon after, slipping in quietly through a side door, his eyes darting around the room before they settled on us. His expression was unreadable, but I could tell he was just as ready for this confrontation as we were. We had everything we needed to expose him. The ledger. The evidence. All the pieces of the puzzle laid out in front of us.

But there was one thing we hadn't counted on.

As the developer began speaking, I noticed something out of the corner of my eye. A movement. A flicker of motion from the back of the room, where the shadows were thickest.

I couldn't quite place it at first, but then I saw him. A figure I never expected to see again. A man whose name had been lost in the shuffle of everything that had come before. And his presence, here, now, sent a ripple of panic through me.

The room felt suddenly too small. Too suffocating.

Rafe turned to me, his expression hardening as he saw the same thing I did. The same person I had hoped was long gone. The question hung between us, unspoken but undeniable.

What was he doing here?

Chapter 30: The Infernal Truth

The air in the town hall was thick with the scent of stale coffee and the murmur of dozens of voices simmering just below a boil. It was the kind of tension you could slice with a knife—no one really wanted to be here, but no one dared to leave, either. The walls, which had once echoed with the cheer of a community that stood together, now felt like a cage. A hundred years of history weighed heavily on the old wood beams overhead, groaning with the strain of all that had been hidden beneath the surface for so long.

I could feel the ledger burning a hole in my hands, heavy with the truth it contained, yet somehow impossibly light in comparison to what I knew it would destroy. Rafe stood beside me, his jaw clenched, his eyes fixed straight ahead as if he were staring through the stone wall to the secrets on the other side. He was calm, but there was a quiver to his breath I could almost hear—a tremor beneath the carefully composed mask he wore. It had taken everything in him to bring this to light, to drag the town's rot out from under the rug where it had been swept for generations. And yet, as I glanced over at him, I could see it—the quiet resignation that this was more than just a fight for justice. It was a battle for his own place in the town he'd spent so long trying to belong to.

The murmurs grew louder as I opened the ledger, the pages crackling under my fingertips. I looked at the faces of the people before us—friends, neighbors, some I'd known since childhood. Their eyes flicked nervously from the page to me, from me to Rafe, the question hanging in the air like smoke. It wasn't just about the document in front of us anymore. It was about everything we'd built together and everything we'd been lied to about.

With each name I read aloud, each damning link between the developer and the series of arsons that had plagued our town over the past few years, the weight in the room grew heavier. The crowd stiffened, faces flushing, jaws tightening as they processed the undeniable connection between the men they trusted and the devastation that had torn through their homes and businesses.

But then, as if on cue, the developer—Rodney Carrington, smooth as ever—rose from his seat in the front row. His suit, too expensive for this town, hung like a shadow on him, all sharp angles and precise lines. He wasn't sweating, not even a hint of nervousness creased his forehead as he adjusted his tie with deliberate slowness. When he spoke, his voice was a cool river, flowing with practiced ease.

"I find it rather... charming," he said, his gaze flicking over to Rafe with a sardonic smile, "that our friend Mr. Rafe, so clearly still haunted by the tragic loss of his sister, has decided to bring this... personal vendetta to the public stage."

The air seemed to thicken as his words settled over the crowd, the weight of them pressing down like an iron blanket. I could feel the people around me shift, their eyes flicking nervously between us, as if unsure who to believe. But I knew what they were hearing. They weren't hearing the truth. They were hearing the story Rodney had crafted for them—a story where Rafe was an angry man, bent on revenge, and the rest of us were merely collateral damage.

Rafe didn't flinch, though I saw the way his fingers curled around the edge of the podium. The subtle tremor of restraint was there, but his voice, when it came, was steel.

"You don't get to rewrite the story, Rodney," he said, his voice low but edged with something dangerous. "You don't get to stand here and pretend you didn't set this fire, just like you've set all the others. And you don't get to use my sister's death as your scapegoat."

There was a ripple of disbelief in the crowd, followed by a sudden, uncomfortable silence. I could see the doubt creeping in.

Rafe had told me once that people were more likely to believe the lie they wanted to hear than the truth that might make them question everything they'd built their lives on. And here it was—the seeds of that doubt sprouting in real-time.

Rodney smiled then, but it wasn't a smile of victory. It was the smile of a man who knew he had already won.

"Ah, the drama of it all," he said, shaking his head with a mock sorrow. "But we all know what happens to people who lose control. Their minds tend to slip. They start to see enemies where none exist, start to accuse good men of things they haven't done."

My heart squeezed as I watched Rafe's eyes tighten, his jaw working in silence. The words struck him like a blow, though he didn't show it—not outwardly. But I knew. I could see it in the way his shoulders slumped, the subtle shift of his weight as if the world had just tilted against him.

"Do you believe him?" Rodney asked, his gaze sweeping over the crowd now. "Do you believe this man who's so clearly obsessed with his own tragedy that he's willing to drag us all into it?"

The crowd's murmurs were louder now, like a storm rolling in from the horizon, but still, I couldn't tell which way the tide was going to break.

I reached out, my hand brushing lightly against Rafe's arm. It wasn't much—just a touch, a reminder that I was still here, still fighting alongside him—but it was enough to keep him steady, to keep him from breaking. And that's when I realized something: this wasn't just about exposing the truth. This was about making sure the people we cared about didn't lose themselves in the lies. Because in a town like this, where the past and present intertwined like vines, the truth could easily be buried again if no one stood to protect it. And for better or worse, that responsibility fell to us.

The crowd had shifted, as though the air had thickened and become a tangible thing, suffocating the space between us. People who had once been close neighbors, who had exchanged greetings at the market and shared coffee at the diner, now eyed one another like strangers. Rodney's words had hit their mark, even if the sting wasn't immediate. Doubt, that most insidious of emotions, had found fertile soil in the minds of those who had never dared to question the developer before. I could see the seeds of it taking root, settling into the quiet pockets of the room, where suspicion grew in silence.

Rafe stood still beside me, his eyes fixed on the floor, his shoulders tense beneath the weight of the accusation. I wanted to reach out, to wrap my arms around him and tell him it would be okay. But I couldn't, not now—not when I could feel the eyes of the town burning through us, waiting for something more, something to make this all go away.

A bead of sweat formed at the edge of his temple, catching the low light of the room, and for a brief moment, I wondered if that was how the truth worked. It wasn't some great revelation, some thunderous, world-changing moment. It wasn't meant to be a spectacle. The truth was ugly. It was quiet. And it bled in small, painful ways—just like the sweat on Rafe's brow, or the way his hands curled into fists at his sides.

Rodney's smile never wavered as he returned to his seat, his eyes flicking over the crowd as though he were reading a script only he knew. His calculated charm was a dangerous thing—smooth as velvet, soft as cashmere—but underneath it was steel. The kind of steel that could cut through a man's reputation, slice through a town's history, and leave nothing but a mess of jagged edges in its wake.

I took a step forward, drawing the attention back to the ledger in my hands. The pages were still warm from where I'd held them, the ink still dark and fresh against the grain of the paper. It was an old ledger, stained and battered by years of misuse, but there was power in it. In the careful, deliberate lines of the names, the dates, the cryptic notes that hinted at deals made in dark rooms. The truth was in those pages. It always had been.

"I think it's time we all took a good, hard look at what's really happening here," I said, my voice cutting through the murmur of the room. "These aren't just names. These are people who've profited from our misery. People who've burned this town to the ground, literally and figuratively, all for the sake of money and power."

The crowd stilled, the air vibrating with the weight of my words. It was quiet, like everyone was holding their breath, waiting for something to break—something that would either shatter the lie they'd lived with for so long or force them to face the truth they weren't ready for. I could feel the tension, the unspoken resistance from those who didn't want to believe that the people they'd trusted could ever be capable of such things.

I looked at Rafe, who was still standing, his expression unreadable. But I knew him. I knew the way he held himself when he was fighting a battle that didn't have an easy answer. This wasn't just about exposing the developer. It wasn't about revenge. This was about saving the town, saving everything they'd built—everything that had been lost. And that, more than anything, was what made Rafe so damned stubborn. He wasn't doing this for glory or for some hollow sense of justice. He was doing this because, despite everything that had happened, he still loved this place.

"You're all smart enough to know that there's more going on here than what meets the eye," I continued, feeling the pressure of their gaze, but pushing forward anyway. "The question is, are you willing to face it?"

There was a long pause, as though the town itself was holding its breath, teetering on the edge of something monumental. Then, one of the older women in the front row, a long-time supporter of the developer, stood up. Her eyes were red-rimmed, her face pinched with years of worry and disappointment.

"I... I can't believe it," she said, her voice wavering. "Rodney's been a good man to this town. He's built things. He's helped us."

"And how much of that was built on lies?" Rafe cut in, his voice tight but controlled. "How many times did he build at the expense of the people who actually live here? How many times did he set fire to something just to watch it burn, just to turn a profit?"

The woman's face flushed, her hands trembling as she clutched the back of her chair. "You don't understand—he's been good to us. All of us."

Rafe's eyes softened, but only for a moment. "And he's been good to you, because you've been useful to him," he said, his words careful, but they stung. "The moment you stop being useful, he'll burn you just like he's burned everyone else."

The room was quiet, the tension like a taut string ready to snap. I could feel the weight of it pressing against my chest, making it hard to breathe. The truth was inescapable. But how many people were ready to accept it? How many people could turn their back on the man they thought they knew?

And that was when I saw it—one of the younger men in the back of the room, a quiet figure who had always kept to himself, standing up. His eyes were clear, his face pale but determined as he stepped toward the front.

"I've seen the fires," he said, his voice ringing out with an unexpected certainty. "I've seen the damage up close. And I've never said anything because I was scared. But if what you're saying is true—if what's in that ledger is true—then I can't stay silent anymore."

The room went still as a deathly silence took hold, every eye now fixed on him. There was no turning back now.

The room was alive with an uneasy hum, the kind of silence that always follows a revelation too big to ignore, but too shocking to fully digest. I watched as the young man, the one who had broken the silence with his confession, stood at the front of the room, shoulders tense, his eyes still focused on the ledger. The entire room had shifted its gaze toward him, as if expecting him to continue, to clarify what he meant. His voice, raw with the weight of his own hidden guilt, had cracked the façade of comfort everyone else had been clinging to.

"I've seen the fires. I've seen them," he repeated, his voice trembling with something between fear and resolve. "And I've never said anything before, but it's not just the property that's been burned. It's everything—everything we've worked for. We've all known what's been happening, even if we've pretended not to see it." His gaze swept over the crowd, the older faces full of shame, the younger ones uncertain, as if waiting for someone else to make the first move.

Rafe took a step forward, his voice steady but edged with something dark. "We've all seen it, haven't we?" His words cut through the growing tension like a knife through butter. "The only difference is that some of us were brave enough to speak up."

There it was again—the hesitation, the tension that bound the town together. It was as though everyone had agreed, either consciously or by some silent collective contract, to pretend that everything was fine. As if by closing their eyes to the truth, they could keep the ugly things at bay, tucked in the corners of their minds where no one had to look.

The man who had spoken first—Jared, I remembered him now—shifted uncomfortably, his gaze darting from face to face. He wasn't sure where he belonged anymore, whether he'd just crossed an irrevocable line or whether this was his moment of redemption.

"I didn't—didn't know who else to tell, I guess. But we all know the developer's been behind all of it. The fires. The deals. The pressure."

A ripple of discomfort spread through the crowd, whispers traveling like wildfire. The older residents seemed paralyzed by the accusation. They had long since learned to distrust change, but this—this was a betrayal they hadn't seen coming. The developer, Rodney, had been a fixture in their lives for so long. Too long. He was part of their landscape now, as much a part of the town as the old oaks lining Main Street or the chipped paint on the clock tower.

Rodney's fingers drummed lightly on the back of his chair, the only sign of strain he allowed himself, and his lips twisted into the most polite smile anyone could manage under pressure. "Isn't it interesting," he said, raising his voice with the practiced elegance of a man who knew how to manipulate a room, "how the truth always comes with such… dramatic flair? Jared, dear boy, I'm sorry to say, but your memory seems to be playing tricks on you. We've all suffered loss here, but we're not in the business of dragging each other through mud over imagined slights."

Jared flinched at the smoothness of Rodney's words, but I noticed the way his hands clenched into fists at his sides. The storm was brewing inside him now, and there was no way he could hold it back. He wasn't done. "I'm not imagining anything!" he shot back, his voice rising, trembling with the pressure of years of unspoken truths. "It's all been right there, in front of us, the whole time. The property deals, the fires that—"

Rodney's voice cut him off like a razor. "Enough." His tone was unyielding, but there was something in his eyes that flickered—a brief glimpse of a man whose mask was cracking.

"I'm afraid this is a waste of time. These accusations are wild, baseless, and frankly—" he paused, his eyes narrowing as he looked directly at Rafe, "—the result of a mind unhinged by grief. You've all seen the pain he's carried. I don't blame him for his need to strike out, to find a villain when the real villain is... is life itself."

The crowd shifted uneasily. I felt a pang of sympathy for them, for everyone who had ever believed that life was just a string of coincidences, that people couldn't be this cruel, this calculating. But they had been wrong. And now, they had to decide how to face it.

"Rodney," I said, my voice hard as I stepped into the circle of tension, "you're the one twisting the truth. You're the one turning this town into a battlefield, and for what? A few extra zeros in your bank account?"

Rodney's smile never faltered, but I could see the veins in his neck tightening, the pressure mounting beneath his cool exterior. "I've built this town. Everything you see—the roads, the infrastructure, the businesses—they wouldn't exist without me." He looked around, sweeping his gaze over the crowd, daring them to disagree. "I'm the one who's given this place life. And I'm the one who'll bring it back from the brink when the time comes."

But the time had already come. And everyone in that room knew it.

Jared stepped forward, his fists clenched, but his eyes were unblinking, a fire of resolve behind them. "You've taken too much. We're not going to be silent anymore. Not after everything."

The air hummed with a dangerous energy. The crowd was waiting, holding its collective breath as the truth hung between us like a sword poised to fall. And then, without warning, the door at the back of the room flew open, and a figure stepped inside—someone I hadn't expected to see. Someone I hadn't even thought about in days.

And just like that, the floor beneath our feet shifted.

Chapter 31: Smoldering Hearts

The house stood like a forgotten relic, its weathered stone walls barely holding back the relentless march of time. Rafe had always called it a family home, though it had been years since anyone truly lived there. The scent of dust and aged wood mingled with the faintest trace of cedarwood—his father's choice for the beams. I had always imagined a different sort of house when I thought of a place that held memories, but this one, with its muted charm and neglected corners, felt more like a shrine than a home.

Rafe led me inside, his presence both a comfort and a mystery. His steps were heavy, the floorboards creaking beneath him, but it was his silence that spoke the loudest. It wasn't the kind of quiet that invited conversation; it was the kind that demanded respect, that told you there were ghosts in the room—ones you weren't allowed to ask about, no matter how much you might want to.

The house seemed alive, the air thick with secrets, and I couldn't help but think that Rafe had spent more nights here than he'd ever let on, pacing the rooms, waiting for something that never came. I followed him through the narrow hall, my footsteps quick and light against his heavy tread, as if to fill the space that seemed too vast for just the two of us. The place had a history, one that clung to the walls like the ivy crawling up the cracked exterior. I wanted to ask about it, to know every little detail, but I didn't. Not yet. Tonight wasn't about stories. Tonight was about him.

We ended up in what used to be the kitchen, though the scent of cooked meals had long since evaporated. The wooden countertops were scarred with years of wear, and a lone chair sat at the small table in the center of the room. He motioned for me to sit, his fingers brushing against mine in a fleeting touch, grounding me when I thought I might float away. I sank into the chair, watching him as he lingered by the window, staring out into the darkening world outside.

The fire, he'd said earlier, was an accident. But I knew better. Rafe was a man who kept his cards close to his chest, revealing only the necessary truths. And tonight, he had promised to tell me everything. As he turned to face me, his eyes shadowed with something I couldn't quite place, I realized he was no longer the confident, collected man I had come to know. This was the raw version of him—the one that was still picking up the pieces after everything fell apart.

He sighed, the weight of the world seemingly pressed into his chest. "I never wanted to tell you this," he began, his voice low, thick with emotion, "but it's time. I owe you that much." He ran a hand through his hair, a nervous tic that always surfaced when he was about to say something that mattered. His gaze met mine, the vulnerability in his eyes something I'd never seen before. "You know about my sister, but not the whole story. I've never told anyone, not really."

I nodded, my heart suddenly pounding in my chest. This was the moment—the one that would change everything.

Rafe paced, the silence between us as heavy as the air in that forgotten kitchen. The dim light from the single bulb overhead cast shadows across his face, but I could see the tension in his jaw, the tightening of his fists. He seemed a million miles away, lost in a memory I wasn't sure I was ready to hear.

"It wasn't just a fire, you know," he continued, his words barely above a whisper. "It was… it was more than that. It was her. It was all her fault."

The bitterness in his voice cut through me like a shard of glass. I wanted to reach out, to stop him, but something in his eyes told me I needed to let him speak.

"She was always reckless. Always pushing the limits," he said, the words escaping him as though they had been building up for years. "I tried to stop her. I begged her to be careful, to leave it alone, but she never listened. Not to me. Not to anyone." His voice faltered, and for the briefest moment, I saw the young man he used to be—the one who had tried to protect her, to keep her safe from the very thing that had destroyed her.

He clenched his jaw, his fists trembling. "We were supposed to be safe. We were supposed to be in the cabin, far from everything. But she decided to go back. To check on something. And that was it. I... I didn't go with her." His voice cracked, and I could see it now—the regret that had twisted him into something unrecognizable. "I should have been there. I should've stopped her. Maybe if I had—"

"Rafe," I interrupted gently, rising to my feet. I could see him spiraling, and I knew if I didn't stop him now, he would break in front of me, and I couldn't let that happen. Not here, not now.

He shook his head, his gaze refusing to meet mine. "I should have been the one to save her," he whispered, the words barely audible.

I crossed the room, my hands trembling as I reached out to him. When my fingers brushed against his arm, he flinched, but I didn't pull away. I wouldn't. "You can't carry this alone, Rafe," I said softly, my voice steady despite the storm brewing inside of me. "You're not the one who failed her. Not this way. It was an accident. And accidents... accidents happen."

He finally looked at me then, his eyes dark, filled with years of grief and guilt. And just for a moment, I saw it—the man he could have been, the one he was trying so desperately to protect from the world. I stepped closer, lifting my hand to his cheek, gently pressing against his skin, feeling the heat of him, the tension of his emotions pouring through every inch of him.

"You're not alone," I whispered again, the weight of my words carrying more than just comfort. I meant it. I would stand by him.

Rafe closed his eyes, letting out a shaky breath. And in that moment, I knew that whatever came next, whatever lay in the darkness of his past, we would face it together.

The room felt smaller now, the silence heavier, as though everything in the house had paused to listen to Rafe's confession. He didn't move much after I spoke; his body still, but the tension in his shoulders was palpable, a tightness that had nothing to do with the walls around him and everything to do with the storm he was weathering inside. The quiet lingered between us like a wound, open and raw.

I didn't know how to fix this—how to fix him—but I knew I had to try. I reached out again, my fingers brushing the back of his hand, the touch gentle but insistent. "You're not alone in this, Rafe. Whatever you need, I'm here."

He turned to face me slowly, his eyes still dark with grief but something else lingering beneath it. Something softer, like a thread of hope, though it was buried beneath a sea of pain. His voice was thick when he spoke again. "I didn't want to bring you into this. Not like this. But you deserve to know."

I nodded, even though the tightness in my chest made it hard to breathe. I wasn't sure how I felt about knowing all of this, but it didn't matter. What mattered was that he needed to say it, and I would be here, listening, no matter how much it broke my heart.

His gaze flicked to the window, his eyes distant again, as if he were searching for something in the darkness outside. "You ever feel like... like there's a part of you that just doesn't fit anymore?" His voice was barely a whisper. "Like you've lost a part of yourself and you can't find your way back?"

I wanted to say yes. I wanted to tell him that I understood—that I, too, felt like I was a puzzle with missing pieces.

But the words stuck in my throat, because the truth was, I didn't understand. Not entirely. I couldn't. And that made me feel helpless, in a way I wasn't used to.

But I could try. I could try to be the piece he needed, the one that helped him see the picture in full again.

"I think you're more than just the parts you've lost," I said softly, watching him. "You're also the ones that remain. The pieces you still carry with you."

He looked at me then, his expression unreadable. But for a moment, I thought I saw something—something like a smile, though it was fleeting, as if he wasn't sure it belonged there. And that was enough.

"I don't know how to do this," he admitted, his voice strained, as though the confession took all his strength. "I don't know how to be... this person, with all this weight. I've been running from it for so long, I don't know how to stop."

I stepped closer to him then, close enough to feel the heat of his body, close enough that I could see the small tremors in his hands. "You don't have to do it alone anymore. I'm here. And I'm not going anywhere."

He exhaled, his breath shaking, and for a moment, I thought he was going to pull away again. But instead, he leaned into me, just slightly, as though testing the waters. My heart thudded in my chest, the urge to hold him, to reassure him, overwhelming.

"I'm scared," he said, the words coming out rough. "I'm scared that if I let go of all this... if I stop carrying it, I won't know who I am anymore."

"You're still you," I replied, my hand finding his. "You're still Rafe. And I can't promise you it won't hurt to let go, but I promise I'll be here while you figure out what comes next."

He didn't say anything for a while, and for once, the silence between us didn't feel heavy. It felt safe. Like we had built something in that space, something delicate but real, that neither of us was ready to break.

The weight of the moment settled over us again, but this time, it wasn't suffocating. It wasn't overwhelming. It was just there, a quiet, steady presence that I could almost breathe around. I squeezed his hand, just once, then let go, stepping back a little to give him space.

"So," I said, trying to shift the atmosphere, my voice light. "Do you want to talk about something else? Anything else?"

He chuckled, but the sound was hollow, not quite there. "Like what? The weather?"

I grinned. "I don't know. Anything. You can't seriously expect me to sit in a room full of secrets and guilt and not change the subject."

His lips twitched, and I saw the hint of the old Rafe, the one who wasn't burdened with so much history, so much hurt. "You're a hard woman to read," he said, his eyes narrowing in a teasing way. "But I think I'll take my chances with you."

"Good." I straightened up, standing a little taller than I had a moment ago. "Because if I have to spend another second in here listening to your brooding, I might just have to start asking you to sing show tunes or something."

His expression shifted, the corner of his mouth lifting as he leaned back against the worn table. "Oh, you would, wouldn't you?"

"Of course I would. I'm full of surprises."

The smallest laugh escaped him, and it was enough to pull at something deep inside me, something I didn't even know I'd been holding back. I didn't want him to feel alone in his grief, but I knew that it wasn't just his past that needed healing—it was us, too. And somehow, in this quiet moment, I could feel the bond between us strengthening, even if we didn't have all the answers yet.

I could feel it. And that was enough. For now.

I wanted to say more, but the air between us was full, heavy with the things left unspoken. So instead, I held on to him, the comfort of his warmth steadying me in ways I didn't even know I needed. His hands were cold, his skin a little too tight, and I wondered if he was fighting something just beneath the surface. Whatever it was, I wasn't sure if I could help him, but I would stay and try.

A few minutes passed before he moved, pulling away from the table with a sigh that seemed to settle in his bones. "I think I need a drink." His words were casual, but the sharp edge of them—the way his voice cracked at the edges—told me something else. It wasn't the drink he needed, it was the silence, the space to breathe.

"Is there any whiskey left in this haunted house?" I asked, my voice light, but there was no mistaking the undercurrent of concern. It wasn't the drink I was after, either. It was him.

He glanced over his shoulder at me, eyes shadowed in the dim light, a half-smile tugging at his lips. "I thought you didn't drink."

I gave him a playful raise of my eyebrows. "You're right. But desperate times, Rafe."

A small chuckle escaped him, but it was strained, as if the laughter were a thing too far from his reach to be truly real. Still, it was a sound I wanted to hear more of, a reminder that, despite everything, there was a flicker of life left in him. "I'll see what I can do," he muttered, turning toward the kitchen.

I stood there for a moment, just watching him—this man who seemed so strong, so resolute in his determination to protect, yet broken in ways he didn't quite know how to fix. How could I ever fix that? How could I stand by his side and not feel as if I were standing in the shadow of his grief? I didn't have any answers, but that wasn't going to stop me from trying.

The sound of clinking bottles broke me from my thoughts, and I turned to find Rafe at the counter, rifling through a dusty cabinet. His movements were jerky, as though he had forgotten the rhythm of being in this place. Maybe he had. It had been years since he'd lived here, after all. It made sense that the house, just like the man, had changed in ways I couldn't even begin to imagine.

He turned back to me with a bottle of whiskey in one hand and two glasses in the other. His lips curled in a half-smile. "You sure you're up for this?"

"Hey, you're the one trying to turn a haunted house into a bar," I replied, holding out my hand for the glass. "I'm just following your lead."

Rafe set the glasses down on the counter and poured the whiskey, the amber liquid catching the faint light of the room. As he slid a glass across the table toward me, his fingers brushed mine again, just enough to send a shock of electricity through my veins.

But before I could say anything, a noise came from outside—a sound that cut through the stillness like a razor. The unmistakable squeal of tires on gravel. A car, or maybe two, pulling up sharply in the driveway.

Rafe froze, his grip tightening around his glass. "Who the hell—?" he started, but the words trailed off as he moved toward the window, his face hardening.

I felt the tension in the air shift, the comfortable hum of our conversation suddenly turning brittle. "Do you recognize that sound?"

"No." He was already moving, heading toward the door. "But I'll find out."

I didn't wait for him to open the door. I grabbed my jacket from the back of the chair and hurried after him, my heart hammering in my chest. Something was wrong. I could feel it in my bones, that sharp, cold twist of dread that had been following us since the meeting earlier, since the moment Rafe opened up about his sister.

The porch creaked under my feet as I caught up to him, and I noticed that his jaw was clenched tight, his whole body coiled like a spring ready to snap. Rafe's hand hovered near the door handle, his back to me, and I wondered if he was hoping I wouldn't notice how his shoulders trembled slightly.

"Don't do this alone," I said, my voice low but firm, stepping closer.

He hesitated, and for a heartbeat, I thought he might shut me out. But then, with a quick glance over his shoulder, he sighed and gave a brief nod. "Stay close."

I followed him into the night, the cool air biting at my skin, my breath misting in front of me as we stepped into the yard. The headlights from the car cut through the dark, illuminating the overgrown path and casting long, sharp shadows. There were two vehicles now, both parked haphazardly at the edge of the driveway, and I saw figures moving in the shadows, too many to be a coincidence.

Rafe stiffened next to me, his hand curling into a fist at his side. "What the hell is going on?" he muttered, his voice barely audible.

One of the figures stepped forward, tall and broad, his face half-lit by the car's headlights. I didn't recognize him, but I knew the look in his eyes—too familiar, too full of intent.

"Rafe," the man said, his voice cold and deliberate. "We need to talk."

I took a half-step back, instinctively placing a hand on Rafe's arm. The air between us crackled with uncertainty, and the hair on the back of my neck stood up. Something was coming, something Rafe wasn't ready for, and neither of us were prepared for the chaos that would follow.

Rafe's eyes narrowed. "What do you want?" he asked, his tone low and dangerous.

The man smiled, a slow, calculating curl of his lips. "I think you know."

Chapter 32: Embers of Resilience

The night air was thick with anticipation, carrying the scent of wet asphalt and the faint smell of diesel from a truck that had passed through an hour ago. Rafe and I stood outside the dingy little office, watching the streetlights flicker like tired fireflies. The city, so far from home, seemed colder, more indifferent. I could feel my heart pounding in my chest, the weight of the decision pressing on me with every shallow breath. I knew there was no going back from this. No turning back.

I watched Rafe for a moment, his profile hard against the glow of the streetlight. He was pacing, hands shoved deep into the pockets of his jacket, the kind of movement that said he was trying to outrun something, but I wasn't sure if it was the cold or the anxiety or the guilt that had started to chip away at him. When I'd first met him, his sharp eyes had been full of confidence, a quiet but steady certainty. But now? Now, there was something else lurking behind those eyes. Something I couldn't quite name, but it didn't matter. What mattered was that we were in this together. For better or worse.

"You think we're doing the right thing?" His voice broke through the silence, rough with uncertainty.

I shifted my weight from one foot to the other, trying to keep the chill from seeping into my bones. I wanted to say yes, wanted to reassure him, to tell him that everything would be fine. But the truth was, I didn't know.

"I don't know. But I know this... We're out of options. If we don't take this shot, then we've already lost." The words felt hollow, but I hoped the conviction behind them would hold.

Rafe stopped pacing and looked at me, his gaze softening. "You're right," he said, but his voice was thick with something I couldn't place. "I just... I keep thinking about how we got here. All this time, all this fight, and for what?"

I swallowed hard, the bitter taste of failure rising in my throat. "For the truth."

I could see the skepticism in his eyes, the way his jaw tightened as if he wanted to argue but didn't have the strength left to do it. He'd been the one to dig deeper when everyone else had stopped looking. He'd been the one to push when the town seemed to fall silent under the weight of its own secrets. But now, standing here, at the precipice of something far bigger than either of us had ever anticipated, I could feel his resolve cracking, just a little.

"I hope that's enough," he muttered.

"I hope so too," I said, more to myself than to him.

The door of the journalist's office creaked open, and a woman stepped out, her heels clicking against the pavement. She was older than I'd imagined, her silver hair pulled back into a no-nonsense bun, her posture straight as a ruler. I couldn't help but feel a flicker of relief—she didn't look like someone who would be intimidated by a little corruption. In fact, she looked like someone who had seen it all before and was only mildly surprised by it now.

"Mr. Wilder, Miss?" Her voice was crisp, professional, but there was a warmth beneath it. The kind of warmth you could only find in someone who'd seen enough of the world's ugly truths to not be phased by much anymore.

"We've got something for you," Rafe said, his voice low and steady, but his eyes darted nervously to me, as if asking for permission.

I nodded, though I wasn't sure if I was nodding for him or for myself.

"Let's talk inside," she said, stepping aside to let us through.

The office smelled faintly of paper and ink, the kind of smell that made you feel like you were about to be buried under a pile of old news articles. But the walls were lined with shelves of books, not stacks of forgotten papers like I had expected. It was strange, this quiet, unassuming place that seemed so at odds with the firestorm it was about to ignite.

"Take a seat." She gestured to the two chairs in front of her desk.

Rafe handed her the file, his hand trembling slightly. I could feel the weight of it in my chest—the evidence, the ledger that could bring it all crashing down. It was a gamble, a dangerous one, but it was all we had left.

"You understand the gravity of what you're holding?" she asked, eyeing the file carefully before opening it. Her hands were steady, practiced, as though she had done this a hundred times before.

"We know," I replied, my voice tight. "This... this isn't just about us. It's about the town, about everyone who's been hurt. If you expose this—" I stopped myself, unsure if I should finish the sentence. Unsure if we were even ready to face what would come next.

Her eyes flicked up to mine, sharp, assessing. "I know what this is," she said. "I've dealt with enough backroom deals and backstabbing politicians to know exactly how these things go. You're asking me to trust you. But I don't know you."

"I get it," Rafe said, his voice low. "But we have to take the risk. There's no other choice."

For a long moment, she didn't say anything. She just stared at the file, her fingers resting lightly on the pages. Then, with a slow exhale, she pushed the file aside and met our eyes.

"You're right," she said finally. "There's no other choice. But I'm not doing this for you. I'm doing this for the people who deserve better."

A shiver ran down my spine, though it wasn't from the cold. It was something else—something electric, something that hummed through the air, heavy and charged. I wanted to believe that we were on the verge of something good, something that would make everything we'd sacrificed worth it. But as she reached for her phone, dialing a number with a practiced hand, I couldn't shake the feeling that the worst was yet to come.

The room seemed to shrink as the journalist dialed her phone, the faint buzz of the line connecting stretching out like an eternity. I couldn't help but notice the way her fingers gripped the receiver, the tension in her jawline betraying how much she, too, understood the stakes of what we were asking her to do. Every second felt like a quiet countdown, each one edging closer to something irreversible. I glanced at Rafe, his face drawn tight, lips pressed in a line that spoke volumes more than his silence ever could. His gaze flickered nervously between the journalist and the door, like he was just waiting for someone—or something—to come crashing through.

"Yeah, it's me." The journalist's voice cut through the stillness like a blade. "I need you to come in. It's big. No, you won't believe it. Just get here." She ended the call and met our eyes again, this time with a glint of something that wasn't quite hope, but maybe the closest thing to it.

"We've got an hour," she said, pushing back from the desk and standing. "You should both go get something to eat, sit tight. This could go in any direction. And if it goes sideways... you don't want to be around here."

"You think it'll go sideways?" I asked, a bitter laugh escaping before I could stop it.

Her eyes were steady as she shrugged, the weight of experience in her movements. "I don't know. But it always does when you poke a bear this big."

We didn't need to discuss it. Without a word, we both stood and made our way out the door. The cool air outside hit me like a slap, but it was a relief—an edge to shake off the fog of uncertainty that clung to me. We hadn't really spoken since the file had left our hands. I wanted to say something, wanted to fill the silence with anything that might make this whole thing feel less like we were walking into a lion's den with our arms tied behind our backs, but I couldn't.

"I don't know if I can do this," Rafe said suddenly, his voice low, but his words so heavy they almost seemed to reverberate in the space between us. "I don't know if I can stand by and watch everything we've worked for come apart. It's not just about us anymore, is it?"

I didn't answer right away. It wasn't just about us. It hadn't been for a long time. The weight of the town's past, the corruption that had seeped into its bones—none of that had been something Rafe or I had bargained for. But here we were, stuck in the mess, tangled in something bigger than we could have imagined. My throat tightened, and I turned my gaze out to the street, watching the headlights of passing cars slice through the dark.

"You think we're doing the right thing?" he asked again, quieter this time.

"I don't know," I said, my voice barely more than a whisper. "I just know we don't have any other choice. Do we?"

There was a long pause, the kind of pause that made you feel like you were standing in the eye of a storm, with chaos swirling around the edges but somehow suspended in time. I wasn't sure what Rafe was thinking—whether he was silently cursing me for dragging him into this, or whether, like me, he was holding onto the faintest thread of belief that maybe, just maybe, this would work.

"I didn't think it would come to this," he muttered.

I wanted to tell him I hadn't either. But the truth was, I'd seen it coming for a long time. Every corner we turned, every move we made, the ground underneath us had been shifting. The signs had been there, clear as day, but I'd ignored them. Too afraid of what it would mean to face the truth.

We stopped at a diner on the edge of town. It was one of those places where the neon sign flickered in the window, casting a soft, almost apologetic glow over the rain-slicked pavement. The kind of place where time seemed to slow down, like it was trapped in some forgotten decade. We sat in a booth, the vinyl squeaking under us as we slid into the seats. The waitress, a woman with tired eyes and a voice like melted honey, brought over coffee without asking, just sliding the cups onto the table as if she had done it a thousand times before.

Neither of us spoke as we stared at the steaming mugs in front of us, the coffee so black it looked like the night itself had been poured into the cups.

"Do you think she'll print it?" Rafe finally asked, his voice thick with doubt.

"I don't know," I said, staring into the coffee, watching the way the steam curled up from the cup. "I hope so. But I don't think it's going to be easy for her. She's got a lot more to lose than we do."

"Yeah, well, we're in it now." He took a long gulp of coffee, then winced, the bitter taste clearly biting. "You ever wonder how we ended up here? How we got stuck in all this?"

The question hung in the air between us, heavy with the weight of everything we'd both seen and done in the past few months. The twisted, tangled mess of it all—the developer, the town's shady dealings, the lies that had held it all together. But it wasn't just the mess that had pulled us in. It was something else. Something deeper. Something that made us both feel like we had to see this through, no matter how it tore at us.

"I don't know," I said finally, exhaling slowly. "I think we were always meant to end up here. Whether we wanted to or not."

Rafe didn't reply, but I saw the slight shift in his posture, the way his shoulders seemed to relax just a little. Maybe he understood, maybe he didn't, but for the first time in a while, I felt like we were on the same page.

The waitress came back with the check, and I could see the glance she gave us before she set it down—subtle, but knowing. We'd been in this town long enough for people to have an opinion about us, whether they wanted to or not. But we weren't the ones who needed to be worried about opinions now.

As we left the diner, the rain started falling again, light at first, but soon it would be a downpour. The kind that made everything feel like it was slipping away. The streetlights blurred in the distance, halos of orange and yellow against the wet pavement. Rafe and I walked side by side, both of us silent, but both of us knowing that the game was no longer just about us. It had become something else entirely. Something bigger. Something that could change everything.

The rain had picked up by the time we left the diner, a steady patter that seemed to match the rhythm of my nerves, pounding in the back of my skull. The sky had darkened, the clouds thick and low, pressing down on everything like the weight of a secret that couldn't quite be buried. Rafe walked beside me, his shoulders hunched, his eyes scanning the street with a kind of wariness that didn't seem to fit the quiet town we had grown up in. But I knew better than to think that place had ever been truly safe. We'd just been blind to it.

We didn't speak as we made our way back to the journalist's office. Words felt like the wrong currency now. What could we say? How could we explain the mess we'd gotten ourselves into without sounding like we were trying to justify it? The truth, as much as we'd tried to hold onto it, had started to shift beneath our feet, and the ground felt unsteady now, like it could swallow us whole without a moment's warning.

The office loomed ahead, a dimly lit building on a street that should have felt familiar. But tonight, it didn't. Tonight, it felt like a fortress. One we had stormed, and now all we could do was wait to see if the gates would close behind us.

When we reached the door, I hesitated. Rafe bumped into me, his arm brushing mine, and I felt the tension in his body, tight and coiled. He didn't say anything, but I could tell he was feeling it too—the knot of uncertainty tightening in my stomach.

"Let's just get it over with," he muttered.

I nodded, pushing the door open.

The journalist was waiting for us inside, her expression unreadable. The office was quieter than I expected. The hum of the fluorescent lights above us made the silence seem heavier than it should have been. I could feel my heart beating faster, my breath shallow as I scanned the room. It felt like a hundred little secrets were stuffed into this tiny space, and I was standing right in the middle of them, waiting to see which one would come tumbling out first.

"Good. You're back," she said, without looking up from the papers spread out in front of her. Her voice was steady, but there was an edge to it now—something sharp that hadn't been there when we first met. "The guy I called is here. He's ready to take the story."

My stomach churned at the thought. The story. The truth, so carefully tucked away, now primed to burst out of its cage and go running wild through the streets. But we weren't the only ones who'd been playing this dangerous game. The developer, the town's elite, they were all out there, and I had no doubt that they'd be watching. I wasn't sure how they'd react, but I knew it wouldn't be with open arms.

"Where is he?" I asked, my voice a little too high-pitched, even for me.

"Behind that door." She jerked her head toward a door at the far end of the office, the faintest hint of a smile tugging at the corner of her mouth. "He'll want to speak with you before he writes anything. You sure you're ready for that?"

I glanced at Rafe, whose jaw was clenched so tight I was sure his teeth were going to crack. He gave a short nod, then turned to me, his eyes meeting mine in a way that made everything feel too real. Too final.

"We've come this far," he said quietly, as if trying to reassure both of us. "Let's finish it."

So we did.

I walked toward the door, my legs feeling like they were made of lead. When I pushed it open, the figure behind the desk looked up. For a moment, I couldn't place him. His features were sharp, his eyes cold—calculating. He reminded me of a wolf in the way he sized me up, as if I were prey, but there was a layer of professionalism beneath it that made me pause.

"Miss…" he glanced at the file in his hands, his eyes flicking to me, then back to the papers. "Miss Kleszcz, I presume?"

"Yeah." I tried to steady my breath, but it felt impossible. I was standing there, on the precipice of everything, and the ground beneath me felt like it was made of glass. "That's me."

He motioned for us to sit, and we did, our knees almost brushing beneath the table. I could feel the heat from Rafe's body next to mine, the tension humming in the air between us. The journalist stood at the doorway, arms crossed, watching intently, as if waiting for the moment she would step back and let someone else take over. The man in front of us flipped open the ledger, the papers inside crinkling as he scanned them with quick, practiced eyes.

"This is..." He paused, looking up at us, a small frown pulling at his lips. "This is a lot more than I thought it would be. I need to ask you a few things before I can go any further. Just so we're clear."

I nodded. "Go ahead."

He leaned back in his chair, folding his hands in front of him, the motion almost casual, but there was an edge to his gaze. "You understand the implications of this, right? The people you're implicating—this could shake things up, big time. It's not just the developer, it's a whole network. The kind of network that doesn't like to be exposed. Are you prepared for that?"

"I wouldn't be here if I wasn't," I shot back, my voice firm, but my pulse quickening in response.

He nodded slowly, tapping the papers lightly. "This could be dangerous for you. For both of you."

Rafe leaned forward. "What are you saying? Are you backing out?"

The man studied us both for a long moment, and just when I thought he was going to speak, the door slammed open behind us. The journalist stepped back, a look of surprise flashing across her face.

Before any of us could react, a voice cut through the air.

"I think we need to have a conversation, don't you?"

Chapter 33: A City Ablaze

The morning the exposé hit, the city seemed to crack open like an overripe peach, its contents spilling out for everyone to see. The front pages gleamed with accusatory headlines, the kind of news that feels dangerous to touch, the ink practically sizzling with scandal. Every corner of the city buzzed, from the crooked coffee shops that smelled like burnt beans and burnt hopes, to the gleaming skyscrapers where suits slid by in their perfect patterns of power. But that's the thing about power—it's not so perfect when the cracks start to show. And show they did.

The developer's name was everywhere. On the lips of mothers in grocery stores, on the screens of commuters who had grown used to the hum of their morning routines, only to be jarred awake by the reality of betrayal. It was like waking up to discover the air you breathed was tainted, that the ground beneath your feet was crumbling away without your permission. People were angry, livid, howling for justice and for the heads of those who had orchestrated it all.

But I wasn't sure whether I felt relief or grief. Relief for the world seeing the truth, grief for the world that had allowed it to happen in the first place. Justice wasn't always as clean as the newspapers made it look. The truth stung, and it stung harder when it came from places you hadn't expected.

That afternoon, my phone buzzed with an unfamiliar number. I had been staring at the screen, the words of the exposé swimming in my head like a toxic cloud. The developer's empire was crumbling, the spotlight on every dark corner of the construction industry. But when I swiped the screen, a name I'd long avoided appeared, and my heart skipped a beat. It was my father.

He hadn't called in months. We had always been distant, but never like this. His voice was thick with something I couldn't place, a tremor in it that I hadn't heard since my mother's death. And yet, there was no warm greeting, no pleasantries to soften the blow.

"Darling, I... I don't know how to say this." His words were heavy, laden with an unbearable weight, like a stone sinking to the bottom of the ocean.

My throat tightened. I should have been prepared for this moment. I should have expected it, but the truth is, you can't prepare for betrayal—not the kind you don't see coming.

"Dad, what's going on?" My voice was hoarse, raw from the weight of what I'd uncovered. I had spent years questioning him, wondering where he stood on the things that mattered. But this? This was beyond any of my imaginings.

He exhaled sharply, like the air itself was a burden. "I... I knew. I knew about the corruption. I knew about the deals, the underhanded things. But I didn't have the guts to speak up. I didn't think anyone would listen, and... and I was afraid."

The words crashed over me, each one a blow, each one a piece of him I didn't recognize. This was the man who had always prided himself on his integrity, the man who had raised me to believe that right and wrong weren't so complicated. The man who had told me, time and time again, that loyalty mattered above all else. And now, loyalty to what? To a system he had watched crumble from the inside out, knowing he had the power to do something and choosing to do nothing instead.

"You knew," I repeated, the words tasting bitter on my tongue, and yet, I couldn't stop saying them. It was a need to make sense of something that would never make sense.

"I'm so sorry, sweetheart. I should have—"

I cut him off. "Should have what, Dad? Should have spoken up when you had the chance? When it might have actually meant something?" My voice trembled, despite my best efforts to keep it steady.

There was a long pause. It stretched between us, thick with the things that weren't being said. Finally, he spoke again, his voice small, defeated. "I was afraid, you understand? They control everything. The people with the money, the connections. I didn't think we could win against them."

And that was the moment everything shifted. The man I had known, the man who had stood tall through every storm, seemed to shrink on the other end of the line. His confession wasn't one of weakness—it was one of fear. And I could taste it, heavy and sour, sliding down my throat like a bitter pill I couldn't swallow.

I had spent my entire life trying to get him to see things differently, to step into the light instead of hiding in the shadows. But now? Now I saw him for what he really was—a man who had been complicit in his own silence, who had chosen to let the darkness flourish because it was easier. It was easier than fighting. Easier than risking everything he had.

"I can't forgive you, Dad." The words tasted like acid, burning on my tongue as I said them. "I can't. Not now. Not after everything. You had a choice, and you made it. Don't ask for my forgiveness when it's too late."

I hung up before he could respond, before he could say anything more to break me.

The city was still burning on the outside, but the fire in my chest was colder than anything I'd ever felt.

I sat in the silence that followed, the air thick with things unsaid and too heavy to lift. The phone lay on the table in front of me, a silent witness to the broken pieces of my father's confession, pieces I didn't know how to gather. I had thought I'd be ready for this moment. I'd thought I'd have all the words, the ones that would either cut him or heal him. But all I had was this weight in my chest, a feeling that settled deep, as if it had always been there and I'd just never been forced to acknowledge it.

It wasn't the betrayal that stung most, though. I'd learned long ago not to expect honesty from people who had mastered the art of deceit. It was the fact that I had spent so many years holding him to a standard he'd long abandoned, believing in a version of him that existed only in my mind. My father, the man I had wanted him to be, the man I thought I could rely on, had evaporated under the weight of his own fear. I had never been prepared for that.

The city outside my window had its own kind of chaos, but inside, my apartment was eerily still. The sun was setting, casting long shadows across the room, the glow of the evening light filtering through the blinds in delicate ribbons. I stared at the faint pattern they created on the floor, and for a moment, I wondered if everything would just stop. If I could make it all go away. But of course, life doesn't stop just because you want it to. The world keeps moving, and people keep talking, and the story keeps growing.

I stood up, walking over to the kitchen, half-focused on making myself something to eat, half-focused on the mess in my mind. The city was on fire, metaphorically and literally. News anchors blared updates as the story developed, detailing the developer's ties, his shady connections, the property deals, the money laundering. It was everything people had suspected but never dared to confirm. And yet, as the truth emerged, there was no celebration. Just this gnawing sense that no one was innocent anymore.

When I moved to the fridge, I found myself staring blankly at the half-empty shelves, unsure of what I even wanted. It felt like the world had imploded, and I had to find a way to rebuild, brick by brick, as though nothing had happened, as though I could simply sweep the ashes under the rug. I grabbed a bottle of wine, uncorked it with more force than necessary, and poured myself a glass. The cool, sharp tang was a welcome distraction from my thoughts, and for a brief moment, I felt the tiniest flicker of normalcy. I wasn't sure why I needed that feeling so much, but it felt necessary, as if I could keep the brokenness from taking over completely if I held on to it long enough.

I'd barely taken a sip when the doorbell rang, shattering the stillness like an unexpected clap of thunder. My heart skipped a beat, and I set the glass down, suddenly aware of how much I'd been dreading this moment. I hadn't been expecting company. I rarely did.

I opened the door to find Matt standing there, his expression tense, but his eyes softened with something that could only be described as sympathy—or maybe it was concern. I couldn't tell, not yet.

"Can we talk?" he asked, his voice low.

I stepped aside without saying anything, motioning for him to come in, but I didn't know what I was expecting. More of the same? More apologies? More problems I didn't know how to solve? He followed me into the living room, standing there for a moment as though deciding where to sit, before choosing the chair across from me.

"Has it hit you yet?" he asked quietly, settling into the seat.

I knew exactly what he meant, but I didn't want to say it out loud. Not yet. The truth felt like something I had to come to terms with on my own, even if I had been running from it for years.

"I'm not sure what you mean," I said, trying to keep my voice steady.

He leaned forward, his elbows on his knees, looking at me with that sharp, knowing gaze that always made me feel like he could see through my defenses. "You know what's going on. You know how deep this goes. How far-reaching it is. It's not just about your father. This thing is bigger than that, and you know it."

I stared at him, trying to read his expression. He was always so sure of himself, so confident in his ability to navigate the murky waters of our world. But today, there was something different about him—something that didn't quite fit.

"I don't know what to say, Matt," I confessed, the words slipping out before I could stop them. I had spent years convincing myself I could handle everything, that I could fix anything. But I had no idea how to fix this.

"I know." He leaned back, his eyes softening for a moment. "But you're not alone in this. You never have been."

I wanted to believe him. I really did. But there was a part of me—maybe a larger part than I cared to admit—that wasn't sure anyone could understand what it felt like to have the ground pulled out from under you, to realize that everything you thought was solid was made of sand.

"I don't know what comes next," I said finally, my voice barely above a whisper. The truth was, I was terrified. Terrified of losing everything. Terrified of facing my father, of facing the world, of facing myself.

He nodded, as though he understood more than he let on. "No one ever does. But I'm here for you, whatever you decide."

His words should have comforted me. They should have been the balm to my raw nerves. But instead, they felt like more pressure, more weight pressing down on me. Because how could I move forward, how could I keep going when everything around me seemed to be falling apart?

The air in the room felt thick, as though every word spoken in the past hour had piled on top of me, turning the space into something suffocating, like a fog that wouldn't lift. I could still hear Matt's words echoing in the back of my mind—You're not alone in this. The problem was, I didn't know how to believe him anymore. Not after everything. Not after what had happened with my father. The truth wasn't just a thing you could hold in your hand; it was messy, and raw, and it had a way of turning your world upside down when you least expected it.

I set my glass of wine down with a deliberate click, suddenly feeling its weight in my hand, its sharpness not quite as comforting as it had been a moment ago. I stood there for a moment, just staring at it, watching the red liquid swirl, like a reminder of everything that had been and everything I was still trying to make sense of. My father's betrayal, the developer's empire crumbling, Matt's offer of support—it all swirled together into something I couldn't untangle.

"I need to go," Matt said, breaking the silence. I hadn't realized I'd been standing there, lost in my thoughts, until he shifted in his chair, standing to his feet. His voice wasn't as soft now, the concern replaced with something more firm. He was right to leave. There wasn't anything left to say, not yet. Not when I was still fighting with my own emotions.

"I'll figure it out," I said, though I wasn't sure if I was reassuring him or myself. My words sounded hollow in the quiet room, like they were just bouncing off the walls without ever really landing.

Matt didn't argue. He gave me a single, pointed look, as though weighing something, but didn't press. Instead, he walked to the door, his footsteps slow, deliberate. I followed him, my own feet feeling heavy as if the weight of my thoughts was pressing down on me with every step.

"You'll come to a decision," he said, stopping just before the door, his hand on the handle. "When you're ready."

I nodded, not trusting myself to say anything more. He was right about that much. I would figure it out when I was ready. But that didn't make it any easier.

With the door closing behind him, the silence in the apartment felt almost louder than it had been before. The city outside had quieted as well, the usual hum of traffic dampened by the rain that had begun to fall, a steady patter against the windows like the world trying to wash away the sins of the day. I wasn't sure if it was the rain or the weight of everything else, but the room seemed to grow darker as the minutes passed, the light from the streetlamps flickering faintly through the blinds.

I sat back down at the table, my fingers tracing the rim of the wine glass absentmindedly, the coldness of the glass grounding me in a way that my thoughts refused to. I needed a plan. I needed to do something, anything, to push forward. But the weight of the question loomed over me—What now?

The phone buzzed on the table, dragging me out of my reverie. I glanced at the screen and saw an unknown number, but something about it made my stomach tighten, a sudden sense of dread creeping up my spine. I'd been avoiding the outside world for a while now, but the universe wasn't giving me much of a choice.

I hesitated for a moment, unsure whether to answer or let it go to voicemail. But the anxiety in my chest was louder than my common sense, and I swiped the screen, bringing the phone to my ear. "Hello?"

The voice on the other end was muffled at first, the sound of a shuffle and a cough before it cleared. "Is this Grace Jennings?"

My pulse quickened. "Yes," I said, trying to keep my voice steady.

The pause that followed felt deliberate, like the person on the other end was choosing their words carefully. "This is Detective Collins. I need you to come down to the precinct. We've got some questions for you."

The blood in my veins turned to ice. "Questions?" I repeated, unable to keep the edge of panic from creeping into my voice. "What kind of questions?"

"It's regarding the developer's case," the detective said, his voice smooth, but with an undercurrent I couldn't quite place. "We have reason to believe you might be more involved than we initially thought. Can you come down to the station? It's important."

I felt the phone slipping from my hand, my thoughts a blur as they scattered like leaves in the wind. My knees nearly buckled beneath me, but I steadied myself against the table. "I don't understand. I haven't done anything."

"That's what we need to figure out," he replied. "We'll see you soon, Miss Jennings."

Before I could respond, the line went dead.

I stood there for a moment, my breath caught in my throat, my heart racing. The detective's words rattled around in my mind like a ticking clock—more involved than we initially thought. What did that mean? Had my father somehow dragged me into this? Was there something I had missed?

I grabbed my jacket without thinking, my mind running through the possibilities faster than my legs could carry me. The rain had picked up outside, the world outside the window now a blur of gray as I hurried toward the door. I needed answers. And the police, whether I liked it or not, were about to give them to me.

But the question now was: What would I find when I got there?

I slammed the door shut behind me, my breath catching in the cold, and the world seemed to freeze just for a second. It wasn't just the city that was on fire anymore. It was my life.

Chapter 34: The Final Spark

The storm had been brewing for days, but it broke in one swift, vicious wave. I stood at the edge of the courthouse steps, watching as the media swarmed, their cameras flashing like a relentless thunderstorm. Reporters jostled one another, eager to catch a glimpse of the scandal we had unwittingly ignited, and the noise, the hum of buzzing voices, swirled around me, a constant reminder that there was no retreat from this. Some of the faces in the crowd were familiar, others were strangers, their eyes sharp with judgment, eager for the drama. It was a spectacle, a circus—one I wished I could flee from, but knew I couldn't.

Rafe was beside me, as steady as a mountain, though I knew the cracks in his resolve were widening. He didn't let it show outwardly, but I could feel the tension in his shoulders, the way he clenched his jaw whenever a new accusation was thrown at us. Every step forward felt heavier than the last, as if the weight of their words might bury us both. I wasn't sure how much longer we could stand under the scrutiny, but we stood. And that was something, wasn't it? In a town where silence was currency, where people preferred to let the scandal settle like dust on an old shelf, our refusal to back down made us either heroes or fools, depending on who was asked.

"I never thought I'd be on the wrong side of this town's history," Rafe muttered, his voice barely above a whisper, as we passed the throng of reporters.

"Since when did history have a side?" I shot back, my tone light, though my chest felt as if it had been filled with lead. "It's all about perspective, Rafe. You know that. They've got their story, we've got ours."

But even as I said the words, I couldn't help but feel the weight of what he was going through. His sister, Emily—the one person he had always fought to protect, the one who had held him together after everything else had fallen apart—had become a casualty of this war. The developer, desperate to salvage his reputation after the public backlash, had weaponized the memory of her death, twisting it into a grotesque narrative that painted Rafe as some kind of villain. They said he had been too focused on his own ambitions to notice her struggles. That his fight for justice had come at the cost of her peace.

I could see the shift in Rafe. The muscles in his jaw tightened, his eyes clouding over with a grief so deep I didn't know how it hadn't consumed him entirely. The loss had always been there, just beneath the surface, but now, with the public using her death against him, it was as if the wound had been torn open again. I wanted to tell him it wasn't true. I wanted to scream that he wasn't to blame, that he hadn't been responsible for her pain, but I knew that would never be enough. He carried that guilt with him, whether it was justified or not, and no amount of reassurance from me would erase the years of doubt he'd fought against.

We made our way through the crowd, avoiding the barrage of questions and intrusive microphones. But when we finally reached the quieter, more secluded corner of the courthouse, I could feel his eyes on me, searching for something—anything—to hold onto. And I knew, in that moment, there was nothing I could say to make it better. But I could be there. I could always be there.

"Rafe," I whispered, my hand brushing against his arm, feeling the tension like a live wire beneath the surface. "You don't have to carry this alone."

His gaze flickered to mine, and for a split second, I saw the raw, unguarded hurt. But it was gone as quickly as it had appeared, replaced by the familiar mask of stoicism. He shook his head, a faint, rueful smile tugging at the corner of his lips.

"I never wanted you to see this part of me," he admitted, his voice rough.

"You don't get to choose, do you?" I said softly, stepping closer to him, letting my touch linger just a moment longer than necessary. "But it's not about what you wanted. It's about what we can handle together."

He didn't respond right away, his eyes still haunted by something I couldn't name. But I could feel the shift, the way his breath seemed to steady, just slightly. It wasn't much, but it was something. And sometimes, something was enough.

The world outside kept spinning, the noise and accusations ever-present, but in that quiet corner, it was just him and me. The reality of what we faced didn't vanish, of course, but in the silence between us, I could almost forget it for a second. And that was the thing, wasn't it? We couldn't outrun the truth, but we could damn well face it together. There was no way to undo what had happened, no magic words to erase the pain, but we had each other—and that, at least, was something worth fighting for.

"Whatever happens," I said, my voice firm, steady now, "we'll get through it. You've fought worse battles, Rafe. This is just one more fight, and we're not backing down."

He didn't answer right away, but when he looked at me again, his gaze was clearer, his shoulders a little less tense. And for the first time in a long while, I could see the man I had come to know—the one who had fought for justice, for truth, for what he believed in—standing before me, ready to face whatever came next.

"We fight," he said, the words coming easier now, like the sound of an old, familiar song. "Together."

The days blurred together, each one folding into the next like a crumpled page that couldn't be straightened. The town was a pressure cooker, the heat building with every passing moment, and the whistle of it all was the constant rush of whispers. I could feel the tension crackling in the air, a gnawing anticipation that something big was about to happen. Whether that something was going to tear us down or raise us up, I wasn't sure—but I knew it was coming, and so did Rafe.

We had our share of visits from the town's biggest mouths, the ones who made it their business to know everyone's business. I'd always hated the way people were so eager to weigh in on things they couldn't possibly understand, but now, it seemed like every time I opened the door, someone was there, either trying to offer comfort or deliver the latest scandal. Most of them meant well, but it felt like each word they spoke only chipped away at what little peace we had left. Their sympathy, their opinions—it was all just noise. And I couldn't stand it anymore.

Rafe, on the other hand, took it in stride, as he always did. If he felt the weight of every side-eye, every judgment, he hid it well. He was a master of the poker face, and I had long since learned to stop guessing what was going on behind those cool, guarded eyes of his. But there were moments, little cracks in the armor, where I could see it—the toll the whole mess was taking on him. It was in the way his shoulders sagged after a long day, the way he'd rub his temples after every conversation with his lawyer. He was a man at war with himself, torn between doing what was right and keeping the people he loved safe from the fallout. And yet, through it all, he refused to let anyone else see the cracks.

We were walking back to the house after one such day. The air had cooled slightly, the kind of crisp evening breeze that promised a fleeting respite before the warmth of summer returned. The streetlights flickered on, casting pools of light across the pavement as we walked in silence, our footsteps muffled by the thickening dusk. I wanted to say something—anything—to fill the space between us, but I didn't know what. How do you reassure someone when you feel just as lost? How do you comfort someone when you know there's no quick fix, no easy way out?

"How long until they stop making it about her?" Rafe asked, breaking the silence as we turned the corner toward our street.

I glanced at him, surprised by the question. His voice was low, tight, as though it physically hurt to speak it. "I don't know," I said honestly. "I'm not sure they'll ever stop."

He gave a hollow laugh, the sound devoid of humor. "I didn't ask for any of this. I didn't ask for her to be taken from me. I didn't ask for her death to become the fuel they needed to burn me down."

"I know," I said, my voice softer now, as we reached the steps of the porch. I hesitated for a moment before adding, "But that's not what this is about, Rafe. It's not about her. It's about them. They want to make it about her because they don't know how to deal with the mess they created."

He didn't respond right away, instead taking a deep breath, as though trying to clear the weight of it all from his chest. The silence stretched on, but I wasn't ready to walk away. Not yet.

"You've done everything you could for her," I continued, stepping closer to him. "Everything you could for her, for your family, and for this town. And they'll never see that, because it doesn't fit the story they want to tell. But that doesn't make it any less true."

He turned to face me then, his expression guarded, but his eyes—his eyes—betrayed the exhaustion, the vulnerability he tried so hard to bury. I reached out, brushing my fingers lightly against his arm, offering him that quiet support that we both needed but never quite asked for.

"I'm tired, Kat," he murmured, his voice barely audible in the stillness of the evening. "Tired of fighting. Tired of being the one they throw their stones at."

I could feel the rawness in his words, a vulnerability I wasn't used to seeing from him. And it hit me, in that moment, how much he had carried—how much he still carried—and I knew that if we were ever going to get through this, it wasn't just about surviving the storm. It was about letting go of the weight of all those expectations. Letting go of the ghosts that haunted him.

"You don't have to carry it all alone," I said, my voice stronger now, steady, like I was trying to convince myself as much as him. "We're in this together, remember?"

He gave me a sharp look, a flicker of something in his eyes—surprise, maybe, or disbelief—but then he let it go, like a breath he'd been holding too long. "I don't know if I'm strong enough to keep fighting."

"You are," I said firmly, stepping into his space, closing the gap between us. "You don't have to do it alone. And you're stronger than you give yourself credit for."

Rafe's gaze softened, just a fraction, and he nodded slowly, as though the weight of my words had anchored something inside him. But there was still that doubt in his eyes, that lingering uncertainty. I couldn't promise him that everything would be okay, because I didn't know. I couldn't promise him that the town's opinion would shift or that the truth would ever fully come to light.

But I could promise him this: we would fight together.

We didn't talk much in the days that followed. The pressure of everything swirling around us—the media, the accusations, the townspeople either praising or condemning us—was enough to silence anyone, even someone like Rafe. It wasn't that he didn't have things to say; it was more that there was nothing left to say that would make any of this easier. His sister's memory was a wound the town kept reopening, and the more they picked at it, the deeper it seemed to go.

I'd wake up in the mornings, hoping for some semblance of normal, but the weight of the world pressed down the moment I stepped outside. We could no longer ignore the fact that this was a battle not just for justice but for survival. The developer, with his lawyers and his lies, was pushing harder than anyone had anticipated. He wasn't just fighting for his reputation anymore; he was fighting for control of the narrative, and he was willing to drag everyone down with him if it meant winning.

I remember one evening, as the sun sank beneath the horizon, painting the sky in streaks of red and purple, Rafe finally spoke, his voice quieter than usual, as though the words took everything out of him. "They keep twisting it, Kat. They keep making it about me. About my family. But it's not about that, is it? It never was."

I turned toward him, standing at the window, his silhouette framed against the fading light. His posture was rigid, but I knew better than to think he was fine. Not today. Not now.

"What is it about, then?" I asked, keeping my voice calm, though inside I was bracing for whatever storm was coming next.

He turned to face me, his gaze heavy, but there was something softer in it now. "It's about them," he said simply. "It's always been about them. They don't care about my sister. They don't care about any of us. They care about winning, about being untouchable. And as long as they keep people like us fighting each other, they stay in control."

There was a quiet intensity to his words, a frustration that seemed to hang in the air like smoke. I could see the wheels turning in his head, a plan taking shape behind the storm of emotions. But it wasn't just the developer at the center of this anymore. It was everything—the system, the power structures that enabled people like him to thrive while others were crushed beneath their weight. And Rafe, for all his faults, wasn't about to let that system break him.

I moved toward him, standing close but not touching him—he needed space, I could feel it—but I couldn't ignore the fact that we were caught in something much bigger than either of us. "So, what do we do now?"

His eyes flickered toward the door, as though the answer was waiting for him just outside. "We fight. Not just for us—for everyone who's been caught up in this mess. We've been handed the wrong story, Kat. And it's time we rewrite it."

Before I could respond, the sound of the phone ringing shattered the moment, cutting through the tension like a knife. I could see the sudden shift in Rafe's expression—his brow furrowed, his hand twitching at his side, instinctively reaching for the device. I watched as he picked it up, his voice low, controlled, but there was something sharp in it, a thread of something darker that ran beneath his words.

I couldn't make out the conversation—he was too far away, his back turned slightly—but I could tell from the way he gripped the phone that it was something important. His jaw tightened, his eyes narrowing in concentration. He muttered a few words into the receiver, his voice barely audible as the silence stretched between us, and I knew it was something bad.

"Who is it?" I asked, my voice tentative, knowing it was a question I might regret.

Rafe hung up the phone with an abruptness that startled me. His entire body stiffened, his eyes hardening as if a switch had been flipped, and I could feel the change in the room, like the air had just thickened.

"It's not over," he said, his voice grim. "The developer has one more trick up his sleeve. And he's bringing out the big guns now."

I couldn't suppress the shiver that ran down my spine. "What does that mean?"

Rafe took a slow breath, then met my gaze. "It means they've got someone on the inside. Someone who knows everything about us—everything we've tried to keep hidden. Someone who can make this worse for us than we ever thought possible."

I felt the ground shift beneath my feet. "Who is it?"

He shook his head. "I don't know yet. But we need to find out before they do. Before they turn this town into something we can't recognize."

The weight of his words hit me, and I realized that we had been playing on the edge of something much more dangerous than we'd ever imagined. The town wasn't just divided; it was at war with itself, and now we were right in the middle of it.

Rafe turned away from me then, walking toward the door, his steps heavy, purposeful. I wanted to follow him, wanted to tell him to slow down, to give himself a moment to breathe, but I knew better. He was a man on a mission now, and once he locked onto something, nothing could stop him.

I hesitated for a heartbeat, then made my decision. I wasn't about to let him face whatever was coming alone. With a deep breath, I followed him outside into the night, the sound of the wind picking up around us, the rustle of leaves whispering secrets we couldn't yet hear. We didn't know who was pulling the strings, or what the next move would be, but I knew one thing for sure: this wasn't just a fight for the truth anymore. It was a fight for everything we had left.

And as the first drops of rain began to fall, I realized that the storm wasn't just outside—it was inside, too.

Chapter 35: Firestorm of Redemption

The room buzzed with frustration, a thick, volatile air hanging over the crowd like a storm waiting to break. The town hall was packed, the dim fluorescent lights flickering every so often, as if even the building itself wasn't quite sure how to handle the weight of what was about to unfold. The hum of voices melded together, an indistinguishable sea of opinions, accusations, and the smell of old coffee and too many body sprays.

I sat beside Rafe, his hand warm against mine. The tension in his grip was impossible to ignore, a reminder of how precarious everything had become. The townspeople sat in rows, eyes narrowed, hands clenched. They were desperate for answers, but the truth? The truth felt like a dark cloud on the horizon, one that might shatter everything they thought they knew about the town, and about themselves.

The developer, a man I had come to know far too well in recent weeks, sat at the front, his tailored suit and expensive shoes betraying the small-town simplicity of his environment. He looked uncomfortable, shifting in his seat as the mayor called the meeting to order, his eyes darting nervously from person to person, as if searching for an escape route that didn't exist.

It didn't matter. The walls had closed in on him. But for me, sitting there with my heart pounding in my chest, it wasn't the developer I was focused on. It was the man beside me, the man who had been a fixture in my life since birth, the man I never truly understood.

My father. Andy Kleszcz. The giant of a man, stoic and unmoving in every corner of his life. The man who had taught me to keep my head down, to never show weakness, to stand tall no matter what the world threw at you. And now, he was about to reveal a truth that none of us had been prepared for.

The meeting rumbled forward, people voicing their anger and disappointment, some raising their voices to accusations, some asking questions they already knew the answers to. I could feel the burn of their eyes, the weight of their judgments, all aimed at the man whose name was synonymous with quiet strength in this town. It was all too much. I needed to look away. But then, his voice cut through the chaos, calm and measured, the kind of voice that commanded attention without demanding it.

"I know what you've all come here to hear," my father said, his deep, gravelly voice filling the room. There was no hint of hesitation, no pause to collect his thoughts. Just the raw, unfiltered truth spilling out like a torrent. "And I'll give it to you. The fires... the ones that have been tearing this town apart... they were no accident. I knew what was going on, and I chose to stay quiet."

The room fell dead silent. The air felt too thick, like it had stopped moving entirely, suffocating under the weight of his confession. I could feel Rafe tense beside me, his jaw clenched tight as if trying to hold himself together. But me? I couldn't breathe. My body went cold, a wave of disbelief crashing over me, dizzying in its intensity. I wanted to scream, to run, to tear my eyes away from my father's face, but I was frozen. This wasn't happening. It couldn't be.

"I was loyal to this town," my father continued, his gaze sweeping over the room, avoiding the eyes of the people who had once called him a hero. "But loyalty doesn't mean much when it costs the lives of others. I should have spoken up, should have stopped it before it ever began. But I didn't. And I'm sorry."

His words hung in the air, a bitter confession that settled like dust over the room. There was no anger in his tone, no defense. Just a quiet admission of guilt that shook the very foundation of everything I had believed about him. I wanted to cry. I wanted to feel something. But instead, all I could do was sit there, numb and stunned.

"Why?" The question came from the back of the room, an elderly woman with a trembling hand raised, her voice shaking as she demanded answers. "Why did you stay silent?"

My father took a long breath, his shoulders rising and falling as if the weight of his sins was pushing him deeper into the ground. "I was protecting the town, the people I've known my whole life. I thought that silence would keep us safe. I thought if I ignored it, if I turned a blind eye, it would all go away. But it didn't. And now, I have to live with that."

The room was still. People whispered to each other, their faces a mix of shock, disbelief, and, beneath it all, a flicker of understanding. They had known the man I thought I knew, the one who was always right, always steadfast, but they hadn't known him as I had. They hadn't seen the cracks in his armor, the fear in his eyes when he thought no one was watching. And maybe that was the hardest part. Realizing that the man I had spent my whole life trying to understand had been carrying a burden too heavy for him to bear.

I turned my head slightly, meeting Rafe's gaze. His eyes were soft, sad, but there was no judgment there. Only an understanding that mirrored my own. He didn't need to say anything. His presence, his steady hand holding mine, was enough.

The mayor finally spoke, his voice breaking the silence. "And what happens now, Mr. Kleszcz?" he asked, his tone more professional than personal, but the question was one everyone was dying to know.

My father's eyes met mine for the first time since he'd started speaking, and in them, I saw something I hadn't expected. Not regret. Not shame. But a kind of peace. "Now?" He let the question linger, as if savoring the weight of it. "Now, we move forward. Together. We face what comes, as a town, as a family. And we rebuild what was broken."

The murmur of voices grew louder as my father's words sank into the room, settling uneasily in the air. It was as though the fabric of the town had torn, the threads unraveling one by one. I could hear the disbelieving gasps from the people around us, the shocked exhalations of those who had spent decades revering him, trusting him, perhaps even building their own lives around his silent strength. The truth, now laid bare, was like a fresh wound that had just been ripped open—raw and bleeding, its edges jagged, the sting of it still sharp.

Yet, in the midst of it all, there was something else. A strange, almost imperceptible shift. The room, which had been tense with the energy of accusation, now held a quiet that felt like a breath, like the space between heartbeats. I'd expected rage. I'd prepared for outrage, for people to scream and hurl their anger like stones at my father's feet. But what I saw instead were faces that seemed to be processing, trying to reconcile this new version of him, this fragile man who wasn't the titan they had built him up to be, but just a man.

My own feelings were a mess, tangled in a knot I didn't know how to untie. My father had been my compass, the one who steered me through the darkest of days. He'd never flinched, never shown weakness. And yet, there it was—the undeniable truth that he had been complicit in the arson, in the devastation that had scarred the town. His quiet protection of the developer, his silence, had been his way of shielding the place he loved, even if it meant hiding a truth that would tear it apart.

"I should have told you sooner," my father's voice broke through the haze of my thoughts, rawer now, as if the weight of the confession had cracked him open. His eyes flicked around the room, finally landing on me, and for the first time in ages, I saw something I hadn't noticed before: a flicker of vulnerability.

I wasn't sure what to do with it. I wasn't sure if I should rush to his side, wrap my arms around him, tell him it was okay. It wasn't okay. It wasn't anywhere near okay. But that didn't mean I didn't understand. I understood more than I ever had. The depth of his loyalty had blinded him, yes, but I could see how hard it had been to live with that silence. How it had eaten at him over the years, until it finally bubbled to the surface like an overdue confession.

"You thought you were protecting us," the mayor said, his voice firm but not unkind. "But you weren't. You were protecting a lie."

My father nodded slowly, taking the words in like a punch to the gut. He wasn't defending himself, and for some reason, that made everything feel more real. More solid. The tension in the room shifted again, and the eyes that had been burning holes into my father's back seemed to soften just slightly. The desire for retribution still lingered, but now it was tempered with the kind of understanding that only comes when you've seen someone as human as you are, flaws and all.

There was a beat of silence before someone in the crowd called out, "What happens now?" The question hung heavy, and I could see the uncertainty in their eyes. This town had always been built on a foundation of pride, on a belief that it was something more than just a group of houses strung together by cracked roads and forgotten dreams. But now that foundation felt shaky, like it could collapse with the next tremor. What could come after a truth like this?

I looked at Rafe, his face unreadable, but his hand still steady in mine. I didn't need to ask if he was angry. He was, and yet, there was something else beneath that anger, something deeper that I couldn't put my finger on. Maybe it was the same thing I was feeling—an understanding that we weren't here for vengeance. We were here for something else, something quieter but no less necessary: redemption. The kind of redemption that starts with the most uncomfortable truths and ends with forgiveness.

The developer shifted uncomfortably in his chair, his expensive suit now seeming absurdly out of place in this room full of raw, ordinary people. He opened his mouth, but for once, the words didn't come. His eyes darted to the crowd, then to my father, and then he just... stopped. It was almost comical how out of his element he was. The quiet strength that had once commanded the room from behind the scenes was suddenly missing from his corner, leaving him floundering in front of a group of people who had seen through his polished veneer.

"Maybe you've got nothing to say now, Mr. Carmichael," a man from the back called out, his voice bitter, but also just a little amused. The crowd chuckled—an uncomfortable, nervous sound—but it was a small shift nonetheless. A bit of air finally getting into the room, a moment of levity in the midst of a storm.

The developer opened his mouth again, but it was just to mutter something unintelligible. It didn't matter. The damage had already been done. We all knew it. And for better or worse, we were all in this together now, bound by truths none of us had asked for but had to face head-on.

I looked back at my father, still standing, his face etched with exhaustion, his shoulders slumped in defeat. But there was something else there too. A quiet strength, a weight lifted that I hadn't realized he'd been carrying. He wasn't the man I'd always thought him to be, and in a way, that hurt. But in another way, it didn't. It was as if we'd both peeled back a layer of skin, exposing the truth, no matter how ugly or painful, and in that moment, I felt like I could breathe again.

For the first time, I wasn't just his daughter, trying to live up to a legacy that wasn't mine. I was just another person in the room, standing shoulder to shoulder with everyone else, asking the same question: What now?

The silence that followed my father's confession was suffocating. It wasn't the stunned quiet of shock; it was the kind of stillness that comes when everyone is holding their breath, waiting for the next move, as though the entire room were one precarious step away from catastrophe. I could almost hear the weight of the questions hanging in the air, the "What now?" that everyone was thinking but no one dared to speak aloud.

Rafe's fingers tightened around mine, and I didn't need to look at him to know that he was holding back—holding back the words that burned on the tip of his tongue, the anger that had been simmering ever since we'd uncovered the truth. But instead of the storm I'd expected, he stayed quiet, his gaze fixed on the ground, shoulders tense but unmoving.

My father's face had changed. He looked older now, a little more fragile, but there was a certain peace to him, too—like he had finally shed the armor he'd worn for so many years. I'd seen that look before, at times when he was alone with his thoughts, but I had never seen it so public. It was the face of a man who knew that whatever happened next, it couldn't possibly be worse than carrying the weight of silence any longer.

"Do you honestly expect us to forgive you for this?" someone shouted from the back of the room, their voice raw with emotion. The words sliced through the tension, and for a moment, I thought I might see my father break. His jaw tightened, his broad frame bracing against the onslaught, but he didn't flinch.

"I don't expect anything," my father said, his voice unyielding despite the tremor in his words. "What I did... what I failed to do... it can't be fixed. But I will make it right. I will do whatever it takes to undo the damage I've caused. All I can offer is that. My word."

There was a collective shift in the room. Not everyone was buying what he was selling, but there was a strange shift nonetheless—a flicker of recognition in the eyes of a few, a begrudging understanding that at least he was standing here, taking the heat. And there was something else, too. A quiet voice in the back of my mind telling me that this was the beginning of something—something that would reshape the town, reshape everything. And I wasn't sure if I was ready for it.

The developer, Carmichael, still hadn't spoken. In fact, he looked like he was about to crawl under his chair and disappear entirely. His eyes darted to the exits like he was calculating the quickest escape route. But the room was no longer looking at him. The focus was entirely on my father, on the one man who had the power to either destroy the town with his silence or rebuild it with his honesty. It was as if Carmichael had become a footnote in a much larger story.

"I think," someone else called out, a woman with dark hair and a sharp gaze, "that the question we should all be asking is—what happens next?"

There it was, the question that everyone had been dancing around. What happened next?

My heart hammered in my chest, and I couldn't help the shiver that ran down my spine. I knew, deep down, that the answer wasn't going to be easy. In a way, it was too simple. It was about redemption, about trying to piece together the fragments of a town that had been cracked apart by secrets and lies. But the cost of that redemption—of the truth—was too high to comprehend.

I glanced at Rafe again, only this time, I didn't find the anger I had expected. Instead, his eyes were dark, distant, as though he had already made a decision that I hadn't yet grasped. The storm was still there, simmering beneath the surface. But this time, it wasn't directed at my father. It was something else. Something much larger, much more dangerous.

"The developer isn't the only one with blood on his hands," Rafe muttered under his breath, his words a low hiss that I barely caught.

My stomach dropped. I turned to him, but his face was unreadable, his expression closed off.

"What do you mean?" I asked quietly, my voice betraying a tremor I couldn't suppress.

Rafe didn't answer immediately. Instead, he turned his gaze toward the front of the room, where the mayor stood, now awkwardly holding the gavel as if unsure what to do with it. There was a strange flicker in his eyes, and for a moment, I wondered if I had imagined the shift in his posture.

"What is it?" I pressed, a knot forming in my throat. The last thing I wanted was more secrets, more revelations that would shatter whatever fragile calm had settled over me.

He finally looked at me, his expression taut, like he was weighing whether to say more, whether it was wise to open up the floodgates any further. His voice was barely audible, but the words hit me with the force of a blow.

"I think there's more to this than just your father," Rafe said, his eyes narrowing as they flicked to the back of the room. "I think the man we should be questioning now is the mayor."

I stared at him, unable to comprehend what he was implying. The mayor? But why? What did he have to do with any of this?

Before I could ask, Rafe's eyes flashed with something—recognition, perhaps—something in the way he was looking at the mayor, and I followed his gaze. My stomach lurched.

The mayor was looking directly at us. And there was no mistaking the cold glint in his eyes.

Chapter 36: Rekindling Hope

I stood by the edge of the square, where the murmurs of a town that had been shattered were beginning to settle into something unrecognizable yet profoundly comforting. There was something about the way the sun cast its golden hue over the sidewalks, catching on the fresh paint and newly repaired storefronts, that made it feel like we were all waking from a long, stubborn sleep. The old gas station, with its rusted pumps and faded sign, had been torn down to make way for something better. The hollow spaces in our lives—the ones we didn't know we'd been carrying for years—were filling up again, slowly, but steadily.

I didn't think it was possible to feel this kind of relief. You always hear about people experiencing closure, about the healing that's supposed to come with time and justice, but until now, I'd only believed it was something that happened to other people. Something that came in the form of answers you didn't know you needed, or a hand to hold when the world was just a little too heavy.

Rafe's presence next to me grounded everything, as steady as the asphalt beneath our feet. His broad shoulder brushed against mine, a simple contact, but one that had more meaning than anything I could've said out loud. His hand, rough and calloused from years of hard work, rested on the small of my back, the heat of his touch both a reassurance and a reminder of how far we'd come. I could still feel the warmth of his hand from that day at the diner, when all I wanted was a simple, uncomplicated life and he'd asked, with such calm sincerity, whether I was ready to trust again. Ready to fight for something that was worth saving.

We'd both been scarred, one way or another. There was no getting around that. But with each passing day, with every brick laid in the revitalization of the town, the cracks in our past seemed to seal themselves up. It wasn't perfect, not by a long shot, but it was progress. I'd come to understand that perfection was an illusion—something we all chase, but rarely find. What really mattered was moving forward, no matter how many missteps or stumbles happened along the way.

"They're really doing it," Rafe said quietly, his gaze fixed on the steps of the courthouse where the developers, now in handcuffs, were being led away. The officials who had once seemed untouchable were walking with their heads down, their shoulders hunched in a way that spoke volumes about the power of exposure. No one could pretend anymore.

I nodded, the weight of his words sinking in. "Yeah. They are."

There was something in his voice, a note of disbelief mixed with admiration, as if he couldn't quite reconcile the truth that had been revealed with the man he'd once trusted to uphold the town's prosperity. I knew the feeling. It was hard to believe something so profound had come from a place so dark, but in the end, that was what made the light shine brighter. Rafe had been scarred by his own trust, but now, he was learning to trust again—not just in me, but in the people around us, in the way things could change when enough voices rallied together.

I glanced up at him, my heart twisting with a mixture of affection and something else I couldn't quite place. His eyes were softer than usual, the lines around his mouth not just those of someone who had lived a difficult life, but someone who had learned to find humor and beauty in spite of it. He wasn't just the man who had stood at my side through all of this, he was becoming someone I could imagine building a future with.

"Do you think it'll ever feel... normal again?" I asked, more to myself than to him. The question was full of all the uncertainty I couldn't put into words.

Rafe's thumb brushed across my skin, the simple touch sending a quiet shiver through me. He didn't have to speak right away. I knew what he was thinking. It had never been about the town or the scandals. It was always about the people. And as long as we kept showing up for each other, as long as we kept fighting, things would eventually find their way back to something worth celebrating.

"I think normal is overrated," he said, with that wry, almost-smile I was getting so used to. "Besides, I'd rather have this—what we have—than anything that was before."

His words settled over me like a blanket, warm and protective. But they didn't just reassure me; they sparked something inside, a quiet fire that had been smoldering for weeks, if not months. There had been times when we'd fought—oh, had we fought—and times when we'd stood in silence, too tired to argue anymore. But now, with the threat of our past behind us, there was room for something new to bloom between us. And I wasn't about to let it slip away.

I reached out, my fingers threading through his, the world around us narrowing into a single, defining moment. It was then that I realized what we'd both been dancing around for so long—what was between us wasn't just shared history or convenience. It was something far stronger, something that had weathered its own storm, just like this town.

As his hand tightened around mine, his voice low and sincere, he asked, "You still want to stick around for that future?"

I turned my head slightly, meeting his gaze. There was no hesitation. There couldn't be. "More than anything."

And in that moment, I knew I wasn't just talking about the town. Or the justice we'd fought for. I was talking about him. About us. And for the first time in what felt like a lifetime, I truly believed that the future we'd been building together would stand the test of time.

The tension that had once wrapped itself around my chest like an iron vise slowly began to loosen. I felt lighter, almost untethered, as if the weight of all those years of suspicion and betrayal had been shifted from my shoulders onto something far more deserving of it. The town felt like a different place now—somewhere between the innocence of its past and the sharp clarity of its present. It wasn't perfect, not yet, but it was alive in a way that made every breath feel like it was shared by all of us.

Rafe stood beside me, quiet now, his eyes tracing the people moving through the square with more purpose than I could remember seeing in years. They had their backs straight, their heads up. The arrests hadn't just removed corruption; they'd sparked something else entirely—a kind of collective pride that I hadn't realized had been dormant all this time. They were finding their footing again, even as the remnants of our past mistakes began to fall away.

I felt a familiar surge of affection for the man beside me, the way his presence seemed to steady the air around us. He wasn't a hero in the typical sense—not the kind you read about in books, with capes and dramatic rescues. No, Rafe had always been more subtle than that. He was a quiet force, steady as the heartbeat of the town itself. And I realized, with a deep, unexpected certainty, that we were a perfect match. Two pieces of a puzzle that had fought their way back into place. The kind of love that wasn't born from fireworks but from shared survival, from walking through fire and coming out the other side, knowing you wouldn't want to be anywhere else.

"You know, I think the town's gonna be okay," I said, my voice almost surprised by how hopeful it sounded.

Rafe gave a small laugh, the kind that was more exhale than sound, and nudged me with his elbow. "You just figuring that out?"

I looked at him, arching an eyebrow. "You're not exactly the sentimental type, are you?"

His gaze softened for a moment before he looked away, his jaw tight with some old, worn-out memory. "Sentiment doesn't pay the bills. But it doesn't hurt either, if you know where to find it."

There was a weight to his words, a history I knew I'd never completely understand. Rafe didn't talk much about the years before I came back to town, the years when he'd been trying to patch together a life that seemed just a little out of reach. But there were moments, little flashes in the way his shoulders tensed, or the way his hands would tighten when he thought no one was watching, that told me the truth. He had seen things. Things that didn't make a man trust so easily.

But I also saw how he wanted to trust. And how he was learning to. With me. With this town.

"You're right," I said, leaning my head against his arm, letting the quiet settle in. "It is a little easier to breathe these days."

The corners of his mouth twitched, and he glanced down at me with that look—the one that made my heart flutter like a bird caught in a storm. "We're not out of the woods yet," he said, his tone as dry as the wind sweeping through the streets. "But we're getting there."

I was about to reply, something witty and sharp about how "getting there" was the only kind of progress I'd ever really believed in, when the sudden clamor of voices broke through the calm. The square was filling up now, more people than I had expected. I hadn't even noticed them gathering—hadn't realized that, amidst the hush of our town's small victory, something else was happening. Something I hadn't anticipated.

A tall, wiry figure appeared at the far end of the square, his face lined with both age and something sharper, something colder. I recognized him immediately. Detective Markell. He had been a fixture in our town for years, though he'd never been quite as involved in the undercurrents of local drama as his reputation suggested. He was the kind of man who preferred to observe rather than act. But today, there was no mistaking the way he walked toward us, his eyes narrowed, lips pressed into a thin line.

"Something wrong?" I asked, before Rafe could respond. I didn't know what had changed, but the air between us had thickened with that familiar tension. Markell's presence had always been like that—a silent storm cloud that hung just overhead, waiting for something to spark it into action.

Markell stopped a few paces away, his hands tucked into the pockets of his coat, his gaze shifting between us with a knowing look that made the hair on the back of my neck stand up. "You two always seem to be in the thick of things, don't you?"

Rafe's stance shifted ever so slightly, his expression unreadable. "What do you want, Markell?"

The detective's lips curved into something close to a smile, but there was nothing friendly about it. "I'm just here to see how things shake out. You know, see if the pieces of the puzzle fit the way everyone expects them to."

It was a statement, not a question. A warning.

I crossed my arms, leaning forward a fraction, trying to keep my voice steady. "What's that supposed to mean?"

He stepped closer, his eyes never leaving mine. "Don't be so quick to assume that everything you think you've fixed is truly put back together. The real trouble always comes later. The cracks in the foundation, they don't always show up at first. Sometimes, they're hidden under layers you can't see."

The words hung between us, sharp and cutting, and for a moment, the world felt like it was spinning a little faster than I could follow. I had always known there were more layers to this town, but suddenly, they felt like they were threatening to close in. I looked at Rafe, whose expression had hardened, and knew that whatever Markell was implying wasn't something we could just brush off.

The game had just changed again. And this time, I wasn't sure we were ready for what was coming next.

The silence between Rafe and me stretched for just a beat too long, long enough for the weight of Markell's words to settle. He didn't move. Neither did I. I knew that look. The one that said we were on the verge of something, but exactly what, I couldn't yet name. Markell wasn't here to offer congratulations. He wasn't here to share in our relief. No, this was something else, something that tasted more like a threat than a warning.

"You've got a point, detective," I said, my voice coming out smoother than I felt. "But we've been putting up with your insinuations long enough. If you've got something to say, now's the time."

Rafe shot me a sideways glance, his lips tightening as he took a step closer to Markell. The detective wasn't one to back down, not without a fight, and Rafe wasn't exactly one to let things slide either. For a brief second, the tension crackled, an electric current between the three of us.

Markell's smile flickered—almost imperceptibly—and he took another step forward. "You're right about one thing, though," he said, voice low, almost conversational. "Things always look clearer after the dust settles. But the dust isn't done settling. Not by a long shot."

"Cut the cryptic nonsense," Rafe growled. "Spit it out."

"I'm just saying, you might want to keep an eye on that father of yours," Markell replied, his voice dangerously calm. "The confession he made? Well, there's a whole lot more where that came from."

I blinked, the sudden coldness of his words catching me off guard. My father. What more? My pulse quickened, blood rushing to my ears. Everything had felt so right, so final with his confession. The town was healing, the guilty were being held accountable, and yet here was Markell, making it sound like none of it mattered. Like it was all smoke and mirrors.

Rafe's jaw clenched, the muscle in his neck tightening with barely contained frustration. "What's that supposed to mean?"

Markell let out a long breath, like he was savoring the moment. "You'll find out soon enough. Just don't say I didn't warn you." And with that, he turned on his heel and disappeared into the growing crowd.

I stood there, frozen for a moment, my mind racing to catch up with the shift in the air. He couldn't possibly mean— could he? But there was something about the way he'd said it, so matter-of-fact, that made me think this wasn't just an idle threat. It felt calculated, like he knew something I didn't.

"You heard him, right?" I asked, my voice barely more than a whisper. "He's not just talking about my father. He's talking about... everything."

Rafe nodded, his gaze now distant, his hand absently massaging the back of his neck as if trying to work out some unseen tension. "I don't like the way he said that. Not one bit."

"I don't like it either." My voice was firmer now, though my insides felt like a swirling mess of confusion and disbelief. What was Markell trying to tell us? What did my father have to do with it?

I pulled my thoughts together, trying to focus. "Rafe, we can't let this slide. Not this time. Not when it's about my dad. We need to find out what he's really implying."

"Agreed," Rafe muttered, his eyes scanning the crowd as if waiting for something else to jump out at us. His mind, always sharp, was already moving. "We'll get to the bottom of it. But first, we need to be careful. We don't know what kind of game Markell's playing."

I nodded, but my stomach was in knots. Rafe was right—we had to be careful. The last thing I needed was to let my emotions get the best of me, especially when it came to my father. But this... this felt different. This felt like the beginning of a new storm, and I wasn't sure I was ready for it.

We both turned toward the small café across the square, the place where we'd shared so many quiet moments, before everything had spiraled out of control. But today, it wasn't the place of peace it used to be. Not with Markell's cryptic warning hanging in the air.

Rafe held open the door for me, and I stepped inside, the familiar scent of coffee and pastries greeting me like an old friend. But I couldn't shake the feeling that something was waiting just beyond the threshold, something I couldn't see but could feel creeping closer.

I ordered a coffee, my hand shaking ever so slightly as I fumbled with the change in my pocket. Rafe stood beside me, his presence a constant reminder that I wasn't in this alone, even if the weight of the world seemed to be on my shoulders at that moment.

As we sat down, the momentary peace of the café settled around us, but my mind was a whirlwind. I tried to focus on the now, on the smell of freshly brewed coffee and the faint chatter of the townspeople in the background. But my thoughts kept drifting back to Markell's words, his ominous prediction hanging over us like a storm cloud that refused to move on.

"What do you think he knows?" I finally asked, my voice a mixture of frustration and dread. "He can't just make a statement like that and leave it hanging in the air."

Rafe exhaled slowly, staring into his coffee as if the answer might be written there. "I don't know. But I've been around long enough to know when someone's trying to rattle us. Markell's always been about power, about control. If he knows something about your father, it's something he's not sharing."

I didn't like the way his words hung between us, as if we were both dancing around the inevitable. The inevitable what? The truth? The secrets that had been buried? I wasn't sure, but I knew one thing: I was done waiting.

My heart pounded in my chest as I leaned forward, the decision forming in my mind with sudden clarity. "Then we find out what it is. Now."

Rafe's eyes met mine, the understanding passing between us in a flash. But before he could say another word, the door to the café slammed open with a force that made everyone inside jump. A man rushed in, breathless, his eyes wide with panic.

"It's your father," he gasped, looking directly at me. "Something's happened."

The air seemed to freeze, and for the first time in years, I couldn't breathe.

Chapter 37: Ashes to Ashes

The air was heavy, thick with the scent of earth and the faint trace of something sweet, like the wildflowers that bloomed along the edges of the cemetery. I could hear the distant murmur of a crow cawing in the trees, its call jagged and intrusive, cutting through the stillness. But here, by Rafe's side, in the shade of old oaks whose roots sank deep into the soil, I felt a fragile peace settle over me, as though the very ground we stood on had absorbed our grief and offered up a quiet reprieve.

I squeezed Rafe's hand, feeling the roughness of his skin against mine, a tangible reminder of all that we had shared—fights, frustrations, but also love. His jaw was clenched, his eyes focused on the small gravestone in front of us, but I knew better than to ask what he was thinking. Some things weren't for words. Some things were too sacred, too raw, to be pulled out into the light.

The headstone was simple, unadorned except for a few delicate wildflowers laid at the base. Rafe didn't speak as he crouched, setting a single red rose gently on top. His movements were slow, deliberate, as though he was giving the moment the respect it deserved. His fingers lingered on the stone for a beat too long, as if he was tracing the outline of his sister's face, though he hadn't seen her in years.

"She would've loved this," I said softly, unsure whether I was speaking about the flowers or the quiet, the stillness. Maybe both. It wasn't a platitude, not really, just a simple truth.

Rafe didn't respond at first, and I didn't push. There were times when silence was more comforting than anything else. He stood up after a moment, his back straight, eyes still on the grave. When he turned to me, there was a softness there, a flicker of vulnerability that I didn't often see. It was strange how grief could make you feel raw and exposed, but also strangely whole, as though the jagged edges of your heart were being slowly smoothed over by time and shared experience.

"I should've done more," he said quietly, his voice barely a whisper, lost in the wind. "For her. For all of them."

I could feel the weight of those words hanging between us. Rafe had always been a protector—of his family, of me, of anyone who needed him. But sometimes, even the strongest hands couldn't hold everything together. And he had learned that the hard way, just as I had.

"You did what you could," I replied, my voice steady even though I could feel the tendrils of sorrow creeping into my own chest. "You're here now. That counts for something, doesn't it?"

He met my gaze then, his eyes dark with the remnants of pain, but something else too—something lighter, like a flicker of hope trying to push its way through the cracks. I wondered if he even realized how much strength it took to face the past head-on, to stand in the face of what you couldn't change, and still keep moving forward.

"I suppose," he said, his lips tugging into something that was almost a smile. "But I still feel like I left it all too late."

His words hit me with a quiet force, and I found myself caught between wanting to pull him close and give him the comfort he craved, and the knowledge that some things couldn't be fixed with a hug. This was one of those moments where the only thing I could offer him was my presence—solid, unshifting.

I reached up and touched his arm lightly, just a soft brush of my fingers against his sleeve. "You're here now," I repeated, more firmly this time, as though the words themselves had some kind of magic. "You're here."

He nodded, though I wasn't sure he was convinced. Still, he let out a breath, long and slow, like he was exhaling everything that had held him captive for so long. Maybe it was just the quiet of the moment, or the weight of his sister's memory, but in that breath, in the subtle shift of his shoulders, I felt something change in him. Something heavy lifting. It wasn't forgiveness—at least, not entirely—but it was the beginning of it.

"You know," I said, breaking the silence, "I think she'd be proud of you. Of how far you've come." I hesitated before adding, "Of us."

He glanced at me then, and for a moment, his eyes softened, no longer weighed down by the ghosts of what could have been. He stepped closer, so close I could feel the warmth of his body, the steady rhythm of his heartbeat. His hand reached for mine again, fingers sliding between mine in that familiar, grounding way he had.

"You're right," he said, the faintest trace of a smile curving his lips. "She would've liked you. I think you would've gotten along."

I laughed lightly, the sound strange in the quiet, but I couldn't help it. "Well, I'm not sure I'm up for living up to that expectation, but I'll try."

Rafe's smile deepened, and in that small, shared moment, the past seemed just a little less oppressive, the future a little brighter. And though we didn't speak further, we both understood the same thing: we were no longer prisoners to what had come before. We had each other, and that, for now, was enough.

The moment stretched, tender and almost suffocating in its quietude, like a piece of silk held too long in the palm. I could sense Rafe's reluctance to leave, his fingers still wrapped around mine, as though he was holding onto something far heavier than just my hand. But there was something else there now, something I could almost taste on the air—a flicker of resolution, a subtle shift in the way his shoulders set, as if the weight of it all had found a place to rest.

"I'm not sure I ever really let go," he said, voice low and rough, like gravel scraping over glass. "I don't think I knew how."

I turned to him, offering a quiet smile that I hoped he could take as reassurance. "Sometimes, it's not about letting go. It's about finding a way to carry it with you, in a way that doesn't weigh you down."

He looked at me then, like I had just handed him the most precious thing in the world, and in a way, I had. I wasn't offering him empty words, but a truth I had come to understand myself over the years. You don't just shed the pain; you learn how to live with it, how to let it exist without consuming everything you are.

His fingers tightened for a moment, then relaxed. The air between us grew lighter, as if the weight of his grief had finally eased, even if only by a fraction. "I think I can do that," he said, his eyes searching mine for a sign that I truly meant it.

I nodded slowly, watching as his gaze softened. We stood there for a long while, the cool breeze whispering through the trees, the light dimming as dusk fell around us. The sound of a rustling leaf seemed impossibly loud in the stillness, and for a moment, I felt as though the entire world had paused, just for us.

Finally, Rafe pulled me into his arms, the comfort of him familiar and grounding. His chin rested on the top of my head, and I could feel the tension in his body slowly melting away, like a river flowing from a jagged mountain, finally finding its way to the sea. There was something deeply intimate about this moment—about standing on the edge of the world, with nothing but the two of us and the whispered memory of a life lost.

"I don't want to go back," he murmured against my hair, the words thick with more than just the ache of the past. "Not yet. Not when it feels like we've finally... started again."

I tilted my head back slightly, meeting his eyes, finding that same vulnerability there—raw, open, and unguarded. "We don't have to. We can stay here as long as you need." The words slipped out before I could second-guess them, but somehow, they felt right. They felt like the answer to a question we hadn't yet asked.

Rafe smiled, the weight in his eyes lifting a little more. "You always know what to say." He gave me a wry, almost amused look. "That's your secret, isn't it? Knowing exactly what people need to hear."

I chuckled softly, stepping away from his embrace just enough to catch a glimpse of his face fully. "I don't know about secret. But I've learned a few things along the way. Like how to talk people down from ledges—both metaphorical and literal."

He grinned, that familiar spark of mischief returning to his gaze. "I'd say you've done a good job with me, but don't let it go to your head."

"Too late," I teased, raising an eyebrow. "I've already decided I'm the reason you're still sane."

His laughter bubbled up, genuine and full, and I felt something in my chest loosen in response. It wasn't just the moment of shared humor, but the reminder that we could still laugh—despite everything. That life, in all its messiness, could still surprise us with something beautiful.

The breeze picked up again, tousling my hair, and I caught a fleeting scent of something musky and wild, like the earth itself had sighed and shifted. The sky, which had been painted in shades of rose and lavender, was now darkening into the velvet tones of night. The stars were starting to peek through, faint pinpricks of light in the inky blackness.

"It's strange, isn't it?" I said, half to myself. "How a place can be so full of loss, yet so peaceful at the same time?"

Rafe didn't answer immediately. Instead, he turned to the horizon, his gaze lost in the distant stars, and for a moment, I thought he might be speaking to them, rather than to me. "Yeah.

It's like the land knows when to let go. But it also knows when to hold on."

I took a step closer, letting the quiet wash over me. "I think that's what you're learning too. How to hold on, without drowning in it."

He looked at me then, the barest hint of surprise flickering in his eyes, and I could see the weight of those words sinking in. Maybe it wasn't just about the grave, or his sister, or the pain that had shaped him. Maybe it was about the two of us, learning to exist in the space between what we had been and what we could be.

"I'm trying," he said softly, his voice steady despite the vulnerability there. "Trying to figure out how to carry it all and still be... us."

The honesty of it caught me off guard, and for a brief second, I wasn't sure how to respond. But when I met his gaze again, I found nothing but sincerity. There was a quiet strength in those words—a promise that no matter what had come before, we would face whatever was next together.

"You don't have to have all the answers," I said, stepping back slightly to meet his eyes, my tone light but firm. "Just be here. With me."

His lips curled into a soft, contented smile. "I can do that." And for the first time in a long while, I believed it.

The night deepened around us, pulling us into its quiet embrace, and I found myself grateful for the darkness. There was something sacred about it—something that kept the world at bay, allowing space for everything that had passed and everything yet to come. Rafe and I stood at the edge of the cemetery, the gravel paths beneath our feet crunching softly as we began to walk back toward the car, the glow of the headlights casting long shadows across the grass.

His hand was still firmly in mine, but there was something different now. The tension between us had shifted, no longer clinging to the jagged edges of our past, but woven into the quiet strength of our connection. It was subtle, but unmistakable—a change that felt like both a relief and a challenge.

"I can't believe we're leaving," Rafe said, his voice a mix of disbelief and something I couldn't quite place. He didn't seem to be talking to me so much as to the night itself, like he was still trying to make sense of everything that had unfolded.

I tilted my head, trying to catch his expression in the dim light. "What do you mean? We're not leaving. We're just... moving on."

He let out a low, bitter laugh, running a hand through his hair. "I wish it were that simple. But you can't just walk away from all of this. From the guilt. The... the emptiness."

I felt a pang in my chest, my grip tightening on his hand instinctively. It was as if the distance between us had suddenly felt too wide, too infinite. "Rafe," I began, my voice quiet but steady, "you don't have to carry all of it. You never have to carry it alone."

His eyes met mine then, dark and intense, searching my face for something—something like reassurance, or maybe something more.

"I don't know how to let it go," he admitted, the words jagged, like shards of glass. "I don't know how to stop feeling like I failed her."

"Rafe," I said again, my voice breaking through the weight of his confession, "you didn't fail anyone." I swallowed, feeling the enormity of his pain but also something else. A quiet, stubborn spark inside me that refused to let him sink under the weight of it. "You're here, now. And that matters. More than you think."

We stopped walking, standing there in the dark, the air thick with his grief and my determination. I didn't know what the future held for us, or for him, but I knew this: I couldn't watch him disappear under the weight of a past he couldn't change. Not when there was still so much life left in him. Not when there was so much to build, together.

"How do you know?" he asked, his voice thick with emotion. "How do you know I can't just be... broken?"

I took a breath, the words bubbling up from somewhere deep inside, unbidden and unprepared. "Because you're not. You're not broken, Rafe. You're just... wounded. And wounds heal. Eventually. But they take time."

His eyes softened then, and for the first time in a long time, I saw the man he used to be—the one who could stand tall in the face of anything, who had built his life out of pieces of the world that had tried to break him. I wasn't sure how much of that man was left, but I knew enough to believe in him. To believe in us.

"You're right," he said softly, almost to himself, like he was letting the words settle over him for the first time. "I don't want to be the guy who lets all of this destroy me."

"You won't be," I promised, my voice steady, unwavering. "Not with me here."

We stood there for a moment longer, the tension between us now a quiet hum, like the first stirrings of something new. Rafe took a deep breath, his shoulders relaxing just a little, and for the first time in a while, I saw the smallest flicker of hope in his eyes.

"Thank you," he murmured, his voice low and sincere. "For not giving up on me."

"Never," I whispered back, the word carrying more weight than I could have anticipated.

We walked back to the car, the quiet between us comfortable now, as though we had finally found our rhythm in the midst of everything that had come before. As we drove away from the cemetery, the last vestiges of daylight slipping away into the horizon, I found myself wondering where this new beginning would take us.

But the moment didn't last long.

We were halfway down the winding road when I saw it—a figure standing at the edge of the trees, just at the edge of the headlights' reach. For a split second, I thought my mind was playing tricks on me, that the shadows were playing their usual game of misdirection. But then the figure stepped forward, its silhouette becoming clearer. A man, tall and broad-shouldered, dressed in dark clothing that blended into the night.

I felt a chill creep up my spine.

"Who the hell is that?" Rafe muttered under his breath, his grip tightening on the wheel.

I couldn't take my eyes off the figure. Something about him felt... wrong. Like a disruption in the natural order of things. My heart picked up its pace as the car slowed, instinctively pulling over to the side of the road.

Rafe turned to me, his face hardening with concern. "Do you know him?"

I shook my head, my breath caught in my throat. "No. But I think we need to leave. Now."

Before Rafe could respond, the man stepped closer, his pace quickening, and for the first time since this entire nightmare began, I felt real fear slip through the cracks of my resolve.

I had a feeling this wasn't just a chance encounter. Something was coming. Something I couldn't see yet.

But I knew, without a doubt, it was going to change everything.

Chapter 38: Rising from the Embers

The dust had barely settled from the town's recovery, but the weight of the future felt heavier with every passing day. We were supposed to be celebrating, enjoying the end of the chaos. Instead, there was only silence, a quiet that stretched between us like a tightrope, fragile and unwelcome. Rafe stood by the window, watching the garden come to life again. It had been a year since the fire, a year since everything burned down and, in the process, became something else entirely. But the garden? It never stopped growing, never gave up.

"Do you think we could have saved more?" Rafe's voice was soft, barely a murmur over the hum of the wind against the house. He didn't turn around, but I saw the sharp line of his jaw tighten. His hands were shoved into his pockets, his posture tense with something unsaid. Maybe it was guilt. Maybe it was the weight of the house we were about to rebuild—or the one we had already rebuilt within each other's hearts.

I wasn't sure what to say. What could I say? That the house had been an inferno of memories, ashes that turned into the foundation of something new, something better? That wouldn't be fair to him. But in truth, sometimes, the past was meant to burn, wasn't it? Sometimes you had to let it all go, to watch it turn to smoke and fall apart before it could ever be reborn.

"I don't think we could have saved more," I finally said. "But we saved what mattered." I let the words hang in the air between us, hoping he'd understand.

He sighed, shoulders sagging slightly. "I know."

We were standing at the precipice, looking down at what had once been—at what we'd each lost, separately and together. And as much as I hated to admit it, I didn't have the answers, just the quiet certainty that things would never be the same. And somehow, that was okay.

I walked over to him and placed a hand on his shoulder. He turned to face me, his deep brown eyes reflecting something I couldn't quite name—maybe fear, or the remnants of grief. But there was something else there too, something deeper, as if he had come to terms with what we had and what we didn't.

"We can rebuild it," I said, surprising myself with the force of my own words. "You and me. One room at a time. We don't need a perfect house, Rafe. We just need this one."

He met my gaze, and for a brief moment, the tension between us vanished. He smiled, but it was a smile of understanding. We weren't just talking about the house. We were talking about us—what we could become, what we already were. We were rebuilding ourselves, each cracked and broken piece, with every step we took forward.

That's how it began, in the crumbling remnants of a house neither of us had any idea how to fix. We didn't have the expertise to repair a mansion, not really. What we had were hands that were willing to work, hearts that refused to break, and enough stubbornness to keep going no matter how many walls crumbled or windows shattered.

It was harder than I thought it would be. It wasn't just about scraping the soot from the walls or replacing the rotting wood. It was about uncovering memories that had been buried under layers of paint and dust, memories I hadn't realized I'd buried, too. Each room we tackled became a confession, an unspoken truth waiting to be unearthed.

The kitchen was the worst. The fire had started there, and the smell of smoke still lingered in the corners, trapped in the old cabinets. We tore them down first, the sound of nails pulling from wood louder than I'd expected. But with every cabinet ripped from the walls, a new sense of freedom took hold. I could almost hear the house breathing again, waking up from its long, suffocating slumber.

"I think I might actually love this place," I said one evening, sitting on the dusty floor, surrounded by piles of debris. "Despite the smoke stains and the shattered windows, I think I might be falling for it."

Rafe paused, looking at me with a playful glint in his eye. "Well, don't get too attached. We're just getting started."

I shot him a look. "Don't be so cynical."

He grinned. "You can't restore a house without a little cynicism."

That became our mantra. We fought, argued, and laughed more than I ever expected. Every nail we hammered into place felt like a promise, every wall we repaired like a new chapter. Sometimes, it felt like we were forging a new beginning, something pure and untarnished. Other times, it felt like we were dismantling the past, tearing it apart, and reassembling it in a way that would make it bearable, even beautiful.

It wasn't all work. Some nights, after hours of scraping paint or fixing the wiring, we'd sit on the porch with the setting sun casting a warm glow over the fields, and simply breathe. Those moments were enough.

"Do you think it will ever feel normal again?" I asked one evening, my feet bare against the cool wood of the porch, the evening air thick with the scent of earth and growing things.

Rafe's gaze softened, his hand finding mine. "Maybe not 'normal.' But something close to it."

I squeezed his hand, feeling the steady beat of his pulse against my skin. Maybe that was all I needed—something close to it. Something we could build, together.

The summer heat had a way of sneaking up on you in this part of the world, and it felt like it settled into the bones rather than just the air. It wasn't the dry, suffocating heat of the desert but the thick, weighty kind that made your skin feel like it was pressed against a hot stone. The kind of heat that makes you feel as if you're moving underwater, each breath a little slower than the last. And yet, it never felt quite as oppressive as it should have. Not while we worked together.

I could see Rafe in the yard from where I stood in the kitchen, his back to me as he wrestled with a stubborn old tree stump that had survived the fire. He grunted with exertion, sweat darkening the fabric of his shirt, but it wasn't frustration that knotted his brow. It was something else, something I couldn't quite put my finger on. The way he clenched his jaw when the stump resisted—there was something personal in it, something that told me this project was as much about him as it was about us.

I wiped my hands on the dish towel and stepped outside, the screen door creaking as I pushed it open. The sun was starting to dip lower, casting a golden light that made everything look like it had been dipped in honey. Rafe didn't hear me approach, his focus entirely on the task at hand. His broad shoulders tensed, muscles rippling under the strain of the work, and for a moment, I caught myself simply watching him. There was something about his stillness in those moments of concentration that was captivating, as if the world itself paused just to give him the space he needed.

"You need a hand?" I asked, a little quieter than I'd intended.

His head snapped up, and I caught the flash of surprise in his eyes before his lips curved into a half-smile. "What, you think I can't handle this myself?"

"Not at all," I said, crossing my arms and leaning against the porch railing. "Just thought you might appreciate someone else digging in the dirt for a change."

His eyes narrowed, but the grin on his face told me that despite the playful challenge, he appreciated my offer. "You sure you want to get your hands dirty?" he teased. "This stump isn't exactly the best kind of work."

I shrugged, a slow smile curling on my lips. "I've got the gloves. And besides, I think I can handle dirt just fine."

Rafe let out a low laugh and dropped the shovel, dusting his hands off on his pants. "Alright, then. Let's see what you've got."

I had no idea what I was getting into, but there was something about Rafe's presence, the way his energy filled the space, that made it impossible to back down from a challenge. So, I grabbed a second shovel and knelt beside him, pushing the dirt around the stump with all the grace of a child playing in a sandbox. The roots were thick and gnarled, twisting in every direction as if they were stubbornly holding onto something I couldn't see. It was hard work, the kind of work that made you feel like every muscle was made of fire, but with every inch of dirt we moved, something shifted inside of me too.

We worked in silence for a while, the sound of our shovels slicing through the earth a steady rhythm between us. But it wasn't uncomfortable. It felt… grounding, somehow, like this was exactly where we were supposed to be. And yet, in the midst of this simple labor, I could sense Rafe wrestling with something that had nothing to do with the stump.

"Rafe," I said, breaking the silence, "is everything alright?"

He paused mid-shovel, looking at me as if I'd just pulled him out of a fog. He stared at me for a beat too long before he cleared his throat and dropped his gaze to the dirt. "Yeah. Just… thinking about things."

"Like what?" I asked, my voice light but with an undercurrent of concern.

He hesitated, and for a moment, I thought he might brush it off. But instead, he set his shovel down and sat back on his heels, wiping his forehead with the back of his hand. "About the house. About all of this. About what comes next." He looked out over the yard, his eyes distant. "Sometimes I wonder if I'm doing the right thing. If I should just... sell it, let someone else take on the mess."

I nodded, taking in his words. The weight of it all was heavier than I thought. This house was his legacy, and that carried a pressure all its own. It wasn't just the foundation of brick and mortar we were repairing—it was the weight of history, of family, of everything that had come before us. But it was also the future we were trying to build. A future that didn't quite feel like it belonged to either of us yet, not entirely.

"You're not alone in this," I said quietly. "I'm here. We're in this together, remember?"

He looked at me then, his gaze softer, almost vulnerable, as if he were afraid I might not be strong enough to carry the load with him. But in his eyes, I saw the same thing I had seen from the very beginning: a man who, despite his doubts, wanted to build something lasting. Something real.

"I know," he said after a moment, his voice steady. "I just... I need to be sure it's worth it."

I smiled, brushing the dirt off my hands and offering him a hand up. "It's worth it," I said firmly. "Every bit of it. You'll see."

He took my hand without a second thought, his grip firm and sure. As we stood together, looking out over the yard we had both begun to shape, I knew we were creating something more than just a house. We were creating a place for us—something strong, something that could withstand whatever storms came next. And for the first time in a long while, I believed that maybe we had the strength to make it work, together.

The days blended together in a rhythm we both had learned to depend on. We'd wake up early, breakfast eaten in the quiet hum of the kitchen, and then we'd dive into the work. There were mornings when the house felt less like a place we were repairing and more like a living thing—a creature that demanded to be fed, cajoled, and coaxed back into the shape it once had. The walls, the floors, the peeling window frames—they all seemed to groan and stretch as if awakening from a long, unnatural sleep.

We'd spend hours pulling nails from crooked boards, replacing shingles that had long since lost their strength, and scrubbing away the remnants of the fire. And all the while, something shifted between us. Not that the work was easy—no, it was the kind of labor that wore at you until you didn't know where the fatigue ended and where the resolve began. But there was something grounding about it, something steady. We'd been through the fire, together, and now we were rebuilding. Piece by piece, moment by moment.

"How do you do it?" Rafe asked one afternoon, his voice low as he adjusted the weight of a beam we were both struggling to lift into place. "I don't understand how you can look at this house and still see what it could be. I can't even imagine it anymore."

I paused, letting the weight of the beam rest against my shoulder as I considered his words. The question had been gnawing at me too, only I hadn't been brave enough to ask it aloud. Rafe wasn't just struggling with the house—he was struggling with the idea of it. The past it carried. The legacy.

"You're looking at the house like it's a list of everything that went wrong," I said, adjusting my grip as we lifted the beam together. "But I'm looking at it like it's a blank slate. We're not just fixing what was broken—we're creating something new. Something ours."

He glanced over at me, his expression a little softer, a little less guarded. "Maybe you're right. But the past doesn't just go away, does it?"

"No," I agreed, my breath catching in my throat as I took in the full weight of what he was saying. "The past doesn't go away. But we don't have to be trapped by it. We've got the power to shape it into something we choose."

It wasn't a perfect answer. It wasn't the kind of definitive truth I thought he needed to hear. But it was enough. And that's when I realized that maybe, for all our work, we hadn't just been rebuilding a house. We were rebuilding us. Our relationship, our trust, our future. The house had become a mirror, reflecting everything we had fought for and everything we were still fighting for.

Later that evening, after another day of hard labor, we sat on the porch as the sun dipped below the horizon, the sky painted in shades of deep orange and purple. The air had cooled, but the day's sweat still clung to our skin, and the quiet was almost sacred. The wind rustled the trees, the faintest of whispers, and we didn't speak for a long time.

"I think we've done something good here," I said, breaking the silence at last. "Not just with the house, but with us. We've come a long way, haven't we?"

Rafe nodded, his eyes warm but unreadable. "We have. I don't know if I'd have made it without you."

There it was. The vulnerability I hadn't expected, the crack in his walls. But before I could respond, before I could offer some comforting words, the unmistakable sound of tires on gravel reached our ears.

I looked over at Rafe, raising an eyebrow. He was already on his feet, a tense stillness in his posture. "Who the hell is that?" I muttered, standing up as well.

The car came into view—a sleek black sedan that didn't belong. It wasn't the type of car you'd find in our sleepy little town. The tires crunched over the gravel of the driveway, and my heart skipped a beat. I could tell Rafe was bracing himself for something, though I wasn't sure what. He was staring at the approaching vehicle like he recognized it, but at the same time, like he wished he didn't.

The car stopped at the edge of the yard, and the engine cut out. There was a beat of silence before the driver's side door opened, and a tall figure stepped out.

My stomach tightened. The man was older, his features sharp, with an air of authority that made him seem like he belonged in some other world entirely. A world far removed from the dusty roads and worn barns of our town. He walked toward us with a purposeful stride, his eyes locked on Rafe with an intensity that made the air feel thick. I couldn't help but notice the way Rafe's posture changed, his jaw tightening, his hand instinctively moving to his side as if looking for something to grasp.

"I thought I might find you here," the man said, his voice smooth, clipped. "Rafe."

Rafe's lips tightened into a thin line. "What are you doing here, Sam?"

The name hit me like a cold wind. Sam. The last name wasn't spoken, but it didn't need to be. The way Rafe stiffened at the sound of it told me everything I needed to know. This wasn't a casual visit. This was something more.

Sam's eyes flicked over to me, but he didn't offer a greeting. His gaze was colder than I expected, as if I were a mere inconvenience in whatever business he'd come to address. "I see you're still playing house," he said, his words cutting through the evening air like a blade.

Rafe's jaw clenched, but he didn't say anything. Not yet.

I didn't know what to make of this sudden intrusion. Who was this man? What did he want with Rafe? And why did it feel like everything we had been building was suddenly on the verge of being torn down?

The tension between them was palpable, and it only grew thicker as Sam took another step forward, his presence commanding. "We need to talk, Rafe."

The words hung in the air like a heavy fog, suffocating any hope of peace.

And in that moment, I realized that everything—our house, our relationship, the life we had started to build—might just unravel with whatever came next.

Chapter 39: Rebuilt Foundations

The sun had barely set that evening, casting long shadows across the garden as I stood at the edge of the newly built deck, my hands resting on the smooth wooden railing. The scent of fresh timber still lingered in the air, mingling with the earthy aroma of damp soil. The house, though still in progress, was starting to take shape in a way that felt more like it belonged to us than to the ghosts of the past. Every nail, every board, was a declaration that we were moving forward, one piece at a time.

It was hard to say when it happened—the moment we stopped feeling like intruders in this town. It was as though the land had finally accepted us, wrapping us in its arms like a comforting quilt. The porch steps creaked under my feet as I took a step back, letting my gaze sweep over the horizon. There was something endlessly soothing about the way the sky bled into the hills. The town wasn't large, but it was sprawling enough that you could find moments of peace if you knew where to look. The houses were tucked into the landscape like old friends catching up over coffee, and I couldn't help but feel a strange sense of belonging that I hadn't expected.

My phone buzzed in my pocket, jarring me from my reverie. It was a message from Rafe.

"Dad's here. He brought photos."

I smiled to myself, fingers lightly brushing against the wood. My father, despite everything, had always been the kind of man who carried history with him like a badge. His love for nostalgia—those quiet moments of looking back—had often been a point of tension between us. And yet, there was something undeniably humbling about his need to reconnect. Maybe it was his way of finally seeing me as more than just the daughter who left for bigger things. I wasn't sure, but I was willing to find out.

I tucked my phone away and turned toward the house. Inside, the air was warm with the hum of conversation. My father had a booming voice that could fill any room, but today it was softer, more measured. It seemed that even after all these years of distance, he was learning how to navigate the fragile terrain of what had once been a fractured relationship. There was a time when I would've doubted that we could ever bridge that gap, but now, in the wake of everything that had shifted and changed, I was beginning to believe that we could.

The door to the living room creaked open, and I found them both seated on the couch. Rafe, as usual, was the picture of quiet strength, his expression unreadable, but his eyes soft when they met mine. And my father—sitting on the edge of the seat like he was still waiting for something—held out a weathered shoebox full of old photographs. His hands were steady, but his eyes darted nervously between us, as though unsure of how to proceed.

I joined them, sitting on the armrest of the couch, my knees drawn up to my chest. Rafe's arm brushed against mine in a quiet reminder that I wasn't alone in this moment. And for once, I wasn't.

"I thought you'd like to see these," my father said, voice low, his gaze avoiding mine. His fingers shook slightly as he sifted through the photographs, laying them out before us. There were black-and-white pictures of me as a child—my pigtails always lopsided, my face streaked with dirt from too much running through the fields. I recognized the house in the background, the small one-story home where I had spent most of my childhood, before everything had changed.

I leaned in, my fingers brushing against one of the pictures. It was a snapshot of my mother and father, smiling in front of the old house. They looked so young—so hopeful. The image felt distant, like a dream that had slipped just out of reach.

"I remember this," I said softly, my voice thick with nostalgia. "You two always looked so happy in this picture."

My father exhaled slowly, a long, almost imperceptible sigh. "We were, for a time." His eyes lifted then, meeting mine for the first time since I'd entered the room. There was an honesty in his gaze that I hadn't expected, and it took me off guard.

"I'm sorry, Anna," he added, the words slow but deliberate. "For everything. For not being the father you needed. For the times I wasn't there. And for the times I was too proud to see what was right in front of me."

The weight of his apology settled between us, filling the space that had once been full of silence and tension. I opened my mouth to speak, but the words tangled in my throat. What was there to say to that? The past had been ugly, and we had both carried it around like a heavy stone. But here, in this moment, I realized that it didn't have to define us anymore.

Rafe shifted beside me, his fingers brushing mine, a quiet reassurance. "It's okay," I said, my voice steady now, though it trembled just at the edges. "It's okay." The words were fragile, but they felt like the beginning of something new. A new chapter, maybe, where we could finally be honest with each other, without fear of what would come next.

My father's lips curled slightly, a reluctant smile tugging at the corners of his mouth. It wasn't much, but it was enough to make my heart tighten in a way I hadn't expected. This wasn't the grand reconciliation I had imagined, but it was real. It was enough.

We sat there for a while longer, flipping through the photographs, the tension in the room slowly dissolving, replaced by something quieter, more tentative. But in that moment, I felt the possibility of forgiveness, not just for my father, but for myself as well. The house we were rebuilding was more than just walls and wood—it was a symbol of everything we had lost and everything we were now trying to find again. And maybe, just maybe, it would hold us together long enough to let us heal.

The evening air had grown cool, a welcome relief after the suffocating heat of the day. I stood in the kitchen, the sharp scent of garlic and rosemary hanging in the air as I stirred the contents of the pot on the stove. The house was quieter now, the only sound the occasional scrape of Rafe's boots against the wooden floors as he moved about, fixing things, making his mark in every corner. His presence was a constant hum of energy, but it wasn't the frantic kind that made you feel tense. No, it was a slow, steady rhythm, like the comforting tick of a clock you didn't realize you were listening to until the silence settled in around you.

He came up behind me, his hands settling on the counter, close enough that I could feel the warmth of his body. "It smells good in here," he murmured, his voice low, that undertone of something private I was still getting used to. It was strange, this way he could speak without saying anything at all.

I glanced at him over my shoulder, a smile tugging at the corner of my lips. "You're just here for the food," I teased, stirring a little more vigorously, trying to ignore the way my heart did that little flip when he was close.

He grinned, a slow, lazy smile that made something tighten in my chest. "Maybe," he said, a gleam in his eye, but there was no mistaking the sincerity in his gaze. "But also... maybe not."

I turned to face him fully, resting the spoon against the edge of the pot. "What's that supposed to mean?" I asked, quirking an eyebrow.

Rafe leaned against the counter, crossing his arms, his eyes narrowing as if weighing something in his mind. "It means," he started, his voice dragging out the words just a little longer than necessary, "I've been thinking."

"Uh-oh," I said with a laugh. "That's usually the precursor to something either really good or really bad."

"You'll have to trust me on this one." His voice dropped even lower, a mock-seriousness replacing the teasing tone.

I leaned against the counter across from him, folding my arms, mimicking his stance. "Alright, I'm listening."

There was a brief, almost imperceptible pause before he spoke again. "Do you think we're doing this right? I mean, rebuilding this... whatever it is that's happening between us?"

I blinked, caught off guard. For a moment, I didn't know how to respond. The question hung there, floating in the space between us, so charged I could practically feel it vibrating in the air. We had been building, yes, but I hadn't stopped to consider what we were actually building. A house? Sure. A relationship? Maybe. Something in between? Definitely.

"I don't know," I admitted, surprising myself. "But I think it's the first time I've felt like it might be."

His eyes softened at that, and for a second, the air seemed to settle, the tension dissipating like fog in the morning light. But then he shifted, pushing away from the counter as if the conversation had taken a turn he hadn't expected. "I don't want to screw this up. Not this time," he said, the words heavy, laden with something I hadn't anticipated. There was vulnerability in them, an openness that unsettled me in the best way.

I blinked again, realizing that, in some strange twist of fate, we had both reached a place where honesty had become our only option. Maybe that was the difference now: we had both decided to stop pretending we could hold everything in. The cracks had already formed, the facade long gone. All we had left were the raw pieces, and somehow, those were enough to hold us together.

"You're not going to screw it up," I said, trying to inject some confidence into my voice. "I'm not going anywhere, Rafe. If we're doing this, we're doing it together. Even if it's a little messy."

He smiled then, and the weight of the moment lifted, just a little. It was a smile that made me believe him, even if I wasn't sure I believed in everything else we were still figuring out.

"Well, that's a relief," he said, turning back toward the stove, as if to pretend that his little confession hadn't just sent my heart into overdrive.

I watched him for a moment, my mind racing, before I cleared my throat. "Do you think we should, you know, tell people about us? I mean, it's not like we're hiding it or anything, but..." I trailed off, unsure of how to phrase it.

Rafe didn't turn around immediately, but I could feel his consideration. "We could," he said after a moment. "But maybe not today. Let's just keep doing what we're doing for a little while longer, yeah?"

I nodded, understanding what he meant. We were still building, still getting comfortable in the space we'd carved out for ourselves. And maybe that was enough, for now.

The doorbell rang then, cutting through the moment like a bolt of lightning. I froze, my pulse quickening as I exchanged a quick look with Rafe. Who on earth would be here at this hour?

Rafe wiped his hands on a dish towel before answering the door. The moment it swung open, I could hear the muffled sound of a familiar voice outside, the words too soft for me to catch. Then, just as quickly, Rafe stepped back into the kitchen, his expression unreadable.

"It's your dad," he said, his voice unusually tight.

I nodded, my stomach twisting with the sudden weight of his presence. I had expected the photos, the small gestures, but the real test, I realized, was still to come.

The doorbell rang again, this time louder, more insistent. I paused, hands still wrapped around the warm mug in my hands. Rafe was already halfway to the door, his footsteps quick and purposeful. I couldn't shake the sudden tightness in my chest, the unease that prickled my skin as if the air itself had thickened.

I set the mug down, my fingers lingering on the ceramic, cool against the heat of my palm. I could hear the murmur of voices outside—the deep, gravelly tone of my father's voice and Rafe's softer, more reserved response. It was only when the door creaked open that I allowed myself to move, crossing the room in three slow strides, my heart in my throat.

My father stood on the doorstep, his broad frame casting a long shadow across the porch. The harsh light from the streetlamp behind him illuminated his profile, making the deep lines on his face even more pronounced. For a moment, I wondered how many years had passed since I had truly looked at him—not just as my father, but as a person who had lived a life outside of our fractured relationship.

"Anna," he said, his voice tight but steady. "Can we talk?"

I didn't trust my own voice, so I simply nodded, stepping back to let him in. The heavy boots on the porch creaked under his weight as he crossed the threshold, the air in the house thick with unspoken words. I could feel the moment shifting, the familiar tension of old wounds starting to surface again.

Rafe followed us into the living room, giving my father a slight nod of acknowledgment before retreating to the other side of the room, his presence an unspoken anchor. I appreciated it, more than he would ever know. My father and I had never been great at navigating this space, the one between us that was always filled with too much history and too many unsaid things. But today, I wasn't sure what was worse—the silence or the feeling that something new was about to break.

"Sit," I said, gesturing to the worn leather armchairs that had once been a fixture of my childhood, but now seemed to belong more to this house we were creating together. My father sank into one of them, his large hands fidgeting at his knees.

"I brought something," he muttered, pulling a small envelope from the inside pocket of his jacket. His fingers were trembling, and for a moment, I almost couldn't bear it. But then he opened it, and the scent of old paper wafted into the room, familiar and oddly comforting.

It was a letter—one I had forgotten existed. One I had never expected to see again.

"I should've given this to you a long time ago," my father said, his voice breaking slightly. "But I... I was wrong. I didn't know how to be the father you needed, and I never took the time to understand what you were going through. I should have, Anna. I should have seen you. Really seen you."

The weight of his words pressed against my chest, suffocating in a way I hadn't anticipated. My father had never been good with words, never had the knack for making things sound right. His emotions were always buried beneath layers of pride and stubbornness, but this? This was different.

I stared at the envelope, unsure of what to do. My heart waged a war between the years of resentment and anger that had built up like stone walls between us and the strange, fragile hope that his apology could somehow heal it all. But could it? Could I believe him?

The letter trembled in his hands, and I took it from him, careful not to let my own trembling fingers betray me. It was old—yellowed with age, the ink slightly smudged, but the words were still legible, the handwriting unmistakable. It was a letter my mother had written to me years ago, before the end. Before everything had fallen apart.

I didn't know whether to laugh or cry.

"Why do you have this?" I asked, the words slipping out before I could stop them.

My father didn't meet my eyes. Instead, he stared at the floor, his shoulders hunched as though waiting for some inevitable strike. "I was going to give it to you on your wedding day. It was never the right time, though. I couldn't bring myself to do it, Anna. I thought it was too late, that the damage was already done."

I was silent for a long moment, turning the letter over in my hands. I didn't know what to say. I wasn't sure I was ready to let him in, to forgive the years of neglect and the choices that had hurt me. But I couldn't deny that part of me wanted to believe in the possibility of healing, of a future where we could rebuild not just the house, but our relationship.

"Anna, please," my father's voice cracked as he looked at me, pleading for something he couldn't quite name. "I've carried this guilt with me every day. I can't undo the past, but I'm here now. I want to make things right."

I took a breath, steadying myself. "I don't know if it's enough, Dad."

Before he could respond, Rafe stepped forward, his presence interrupting the heavy silence that hung between us. His eyes were steady, but there was something in the way he looked at my father—something sharp, protective, like a quiet storm brewing.

"It's not about fixing everything in one go," Rafe said, his voice calm but filled with an unspoken force. "It's about taking it one step at a time. If you're willing to try, then maybe that's a start."

My father nodded, slowly, as though taking in Rafe's words. But I could see the hesitation in his eyes, the fear that perhaps he was too far gone to repair the damage. For a moment, the room seemed to hold its breath, the only sound the faint crackle of the fire in the hearth.

And then, as if the universe had decided it had enough of our quiet drama, there was a loud, unmistakable crash from outside.

We all turned toward the window, the sound of breaking glass cutting through the tension like a knife. My father's eyes widened in alarm.

"What the hell was that?" he muttered under his breath, rising from his chair.

Rafe moved swiftly toward the door, his hand on the doorknob before I could say a word. He paused just long enough to catch my eye, his face hardening with a mixture of concern and resolve. "Stay inside," he said quietly.

Before I could protest, he stepped outside, disappearing into the night.

And then, all at once, the silence broke.

Chapter 40: The Heart of the Fire

The laughter of our guests filled the space, a sound that was once foreign to these walls but now seemed to echo from every corner. I had always been one for quiet moments, for the stillness of a solitary cup of tea in the early morning hours, but this—this energy—was something else entirely. It was a symphony of life, of community, and most of all, of resilience. The house was still alive with the scent of fresh paint and the faint, reassuring aroma of wood that had been scrubbed and polished to perfection. As I stood in the middle of the room, between the hearth we had spent hours crafting and the open windows that let the evening air dance through, it felt as though every corner was a testament to something larger than the fire that had once consumed it.

Rafe stood beside me, his fingers intertwined with mine, our hands joined as if the simple act of contact might hold the world together. His presence was both a quiet strength and a gentle reassurance, as though with him at my side, I could face anything. The weight of the past few months hung between us like a heavy tapestry, one that neither of us could fully explain to the others, but we didn't need to. Some things—too much, perhaps—were simply understood.

"I didn't think this day would come," Rafe murmured into my ear, his voice thick with emotion, a rough whisper only I could hear over the noise.

I squeezed his hand, and his thumb brushed over my knuckles, his touch as grounding as the earth beneath us. The house wasn't just a structure, not anymore. It was a story—a testament to both our love and our resilience.

"You didn't think we could do it?" I teased, the lightness in my voice betraying the depth of the sentiment I couldn't voice out loud. It wasn't just about the house, was it? It was about us. All the obstacles we'd survived, the endless days of uncertainty, the sweat and the doubts. And now, here we were. Not just surviving but thriving, in this home we had built—together.

He let out a low chuckle, a soft, private sound that only I could catch. "I meant the house, mostly," he replied, his words brushing against the shell of my ear. "But yeah, maybe that too."

It wasn't the first time I had caught him on the edge of a joke, but I knew the depths of his gratitude, just as he knew mine. Both of us had come to this place from different paths, and yet, the path had always led us back to each other. I looked around the room again, and for the first time in months, I felt something akin to peace settle in my chest, the kind that made every inch of my body relax in ways I hadn't known were possible.

The town was here. The people who had once cast sideways glances or raised eyebrows at the idea of us had now crowded into our home. They were here, laughing, celebrating, and in their own ways, embracing the life we had chosen to build. I spotted Sarah, her face flushed with joy, her arm wrapped around her husband's waist as they spoke in hushed tones, sharing their own quiet joke. The Harrises were across the room, their children darting about, filling the space with the kind of chaotic happiness only children could provide. They had once questioned us, wondered if we would make it. I wondered if they still doubted us, though I couldn't find it in me to care anymore. Not now, not here.

But my eyes kept finding Rafe, watching him as he caught the way the light flickered against his face, the glint in his eyes telling me that he, too, was feeling the weight of it all—the fire, the building, the struggle—and how, against all odds, we were still standing. We had built this home with the kind of sweat and love that makes a house something more than bricks and mortar. It had absorbed our pain, our hope, our laughter, and our tears. There was magic here, in these walls, in every piece of wood and stone, in every brushstroke that adorned the surface.

A tap on my shoulder broke my reverie, and I turned to find Ellie, one of my oldest friends, standing with a glass of champagne in her hand. Her eyes sparkled, her wide smile one of pure delight.

"You've outdone yourselves, you know that, right?" she said, her voice warm, but with that edge of mischief I'd come to expect from her. "I mean, I've seen this place evolve over the past few months, and you two—well, you've set the bar high for everyone."

I raised an eyebrow, leaning in slightly. "High enough that no one will ever be able to outdo us?"

She gave a dramatic sigh. "Of course. You always know how to make the rest of us look bad."

I laughed softly, nudging her with my elbow. "You're welcome. You'll just have to settle for being jealous."

Ellie's gaze drifted over the room before landing back on me. "This is more than just a party, isn't it?"

I hesitated for a moment, her question striking a chord deep within me. More than a party. It was the embodiment of everything we had fought for. This home was more than a structure; it was the heart of our fire, the one we had survived, the one we had learned from, and the one we had rebuilt.

"Yeah," I said softly, the weight of the moment finally settling in. "This is everything we've worked for."

And as the evening wore on, with conversations flowing like the wine, and the laughter rising and falling like the waves, I found myself still standing beside Rafe, our hands still linked, but our hearts now completely and irrevocably intertwined. This—this moment, this house, this life—was ours. The fire might have threatened to take it all, but it had only made us stronger. And as I looked around at the faces of those who had shared this journey with us, I knew that there was no force in the world that could ever burn us down again.

The sound of the evening seemed to grow louder, like the thick, sweet buzz of a honeybee's wings in summer. It was more than just chatter; it was a melody of togetherness, the kind that lingers long after the music fades. I caught snippets of conversation—people talking about their lives, their worries, their little victories. Even the ones who had never spoken a kind word to me in the past seemed to find a place at our table. It was funny, in a bittersweet way. The same folks who had once shaken their heads, muttering about how impractical it all was, now held glasses of wine in their hands, marveling at what we'd done.

I smiled, nodding politely to Mrs. Gallagher, who leaned in to compliment the new windows as if she were giving me a secret. "You know, dear, when I first heard about what you two were doing, I thought you were a bit mad," she said, her words carefully measured, though there was no malice in them. "But I have to admit, this place is something."

I could hear the unspoken "something" hanging between us, but I chose to ignore it. "Well, we've had our fair share of madness," I replied, a grin tugging at my lips. "But it's all part of the charm, don't you think?"

She studied me for a moment, her sharp eyes gleaming with curiosity, but I didn't let her read too much into it. After a long, awkward pause, she finally offered a hesitant nod, and I took that as a win.

Across the room, I saw Rafe slip into conversation with Rick, the local mechanic who had been one of the first to question our sanity. They were laughing now, the camaraderie between them unmistakable. It was a strange thing, watching Rafe with his friends. On the surface, he appeared so stoic—tall, dark, and a little too reserved for his own good—but in moments like this, when he let his guard down, it was easy to see why I had fallen for him. He had a dry wit and a laugh that could sneak up on you, quick and easy like a summer rainstorm.

And it was in these moments, when the room was filled with the warm murmur of voices and the clinking of glasses, that I realized how much had shifted, how much we'd all changed. Our pasts, once full of suspicion and doubt, had now become nothing more than whispers, drowned out by the present.

"Are you sure about this?" Ellie's voice broke through my thoughts, and I turned to find her at my side again, her fingers drumming absent-mindedly on the rim of her glass. Her gaze flickered nervously to the crowd, as though she expected someone to show up and disrupt the peaceful air. "I mean, this—this celebration. All these people. It's a lot."

I tilted my head, watching the laughter around me. There were moments when I wasn't entirely sure myself. "I think I'm sure. I mean, I know it's overwhelming. But it feels... right. All of this feels right."

She raised an eyebrow, looking skeptically at the group. "Even with people like Rick?" she asked, a hint of her usual playfulness returning.

I let out a short laugh, shaking my head. "Especially with people like Rick. I think that's the most surprising part of it all."

Ellie considered that for a moment, her eyes narrowing in thought, before she sighed in resignation. "Fair enough. I guess it's not the worst thing to surprise people. But if we're being honest here, I'd have never predicted this from you."

I grinned, lifting my glass to take a sip of my wine. "That's because you think you know me," I teased. "But I've always been full of surprises."

"Well, you sure surprised the whole town with this one." Ellie's smirk was playful, but there was something deeper in her voice, a note of unspoken understanding.

Before I could respond, I felt a tap on my shoulder. I turned to find Rick standing behind me, his grin wide and more genuine than I had ever seen it.

"Alright, I'll admit it," he said, his deep voice cutting through the buzz of the party. "You two know how to put on a show." He raised his glass, almost toasting us. "Didn't think I'd see the day."

I laughed, the sound rich with the satisfaction of having proved him wrong. "You and me both, Rick," I replied. "But we got here, didn't we?"

Ellie nudged me, her eyes bright with mischief. "What's next, huh? A local charity auction? Maybe we can sell your secret recipes, too. You've got plenty of surprises up your sleeve, don't you?"

Rick leaned in closer, lowering his voice so only I could hear. "If you're serious, I've got a few ideas for next year's fundraiser."

I arched an eyebrow, intrigued despite myself. "You're actually serious?"

He nodded, his expression far less combative than I was used to. "I mean, I wouldn't have believed it, but after tonight, I think this town owes you both. The house, the effort, the whole thing." He paused, his expression almost shy, which was a rarity for him. "It's impressive. And I can admit when I'm wrong."

My heart skipped in that moment. The idea that we could change a whole town's perception of us, that we could bring people together with something as simple as a house—it hit me like a punch to the gut, and for a second, I was uncertain whether to laugh or cry. We had done it. Against all odds, we had done it.

Ellie, ever the cynic, leaned in and whispered, "Now, if only you could teach me how to make this happen in my own life. Maybe then I'd stop getting kicked out of so many dinner parties."

I laughed, nudging her with my elbow. "That's the secret," I whispered back. "You've got to build the house first."

The crowd was beginning to settle into a comfortable rhythm now, their conversations flowing more easily, their shoulders relaxed. The atmosphere was lighter, freer, as if the weight of all those years of doubt had been lifted. And as I watched, I realized that this house—this stubborn, impossible dream—was more than just a place for us. It was a symbol of what we could accomplish when we didn't back down, when we didn't listen to the doubts of others.

I found myself leaning against the doorframe, feeling the cool evening breeze lift my hair from my shoulders, and I knew without a doubt: this was home. We had built it from the ground up, piece by piece, and now, with the people we cared about most around us, it was everything.

The night stretched on, a slow-moving river of voices and laughter, winding its way around the house like a story too good to ever end. Outside, the stars had begun to spill across the sky, silver threads weaving a tapestry that felt, for once, almost within reach. I could hear the soft rustling of the trees in the distance, a lullaby that whispered of quiet nights and the promise of more moments like this.

Rafe hadn't let go of my hand all evening, and I found myself clinging to the comfort of his steady presence. I was aware of the way the crowd swirled around us, the way they would look to him for leadership, for reassurance. There was something about him—his unspoken command that drew people in without effort. I envied that in him, how easy it was for him to stand tall and still in the midst of it all, while I felt the weight of every glance and every expectation pressing down on me.

It wasn't as though I wasn't proud of what we had built, of course. That much was beyond dispute. But I couldn't help the gnawing tension in my stomach, the feeling that something was still left undone. Something unsaid. Maybe it was just the night wearing on me, the hum of so many voices blending into a sea of faces I'd once considered strangers. Or maybe it was that old fear, that fear that had never quite left, the one that whispered that no matter how much you tried, no matter how hard you worked, it could all fall apart again.

"Can I steal you for a moment?" Rafe's voice broke through my thoughts, a soothing balm to my scattered mind. He tugged gently on my hand, his eyes dark and unreadable as always, but with an edge to them that told me he was as restless as I was.

"Of course," I replied, my voice quieter than I intended. Without hesitation, I followed him through the crowd, weaving between conversations and half-empty glasses, until we reached the back porch.

He led me to a quiet corner, hidden from the prying eyes of our guests. The night air was cool against my skin, and for a moment, I let myself lean against the railing, taking in the sound of the crickets and the soft rustle of the trees once more.

"Everything's perfect," I said, my voice steady even as my pulse quickened. "The house, the party... it's exactly what we wanted, isn't it?"

He didn't answer immediately, and I felt the shift between us before he spoke. "I think it's perfect, too. But there's something else."

I turned to face him, confusion creasing my brow. "What do you mean?"

He stepped closer, his proximity sending a ripple of heat through me, and I could see the weight in his eyes. "I've been thinking, Lila. About how much we've changed. About the path we're on now, and the path we were on before."

My stomach tightened. The air seemed to thicken around us, pulling the words from the space between us like an invisible thread. "And?"

Rafe took a deep breath, his hand moving to rest on the back of my neck, his thumb brushing lightly over the skin there, grounding me in the moment. "And I think it's time for us to take the next step. Together."

The words hung between us, pregnant with meaning, but I wasn't sure how to respond. We'd already come so far, hadn't we? We'd survived the fire, built this house from the ground up, and now—now, we were here, surrounded by the people who had once doubted us, finally seeing what we could do.

But Rafe wasn't looking for just the next step in the house. No. This was about something bigger, something I wasn't sure I was ready for. Not yet. My chest tightened at the thought.

"What are you talking about?" I finally managed, my voice barely more than a whisper.

He hesitated, his eyes flickering toward the horizon, where the night was just beginning to take on the faintest glow of the coming dawn. "I'm talking about us, Lila. About the future. About what comes next."

I stepped back slightly, the cool breeze lifting my hair from my shoulders, a physical manifestation of the distance I felt between us in that moment. "We've already made it, Rafe. We've come so far—together. You and me. We've rebuilt everything."

His hand fell away from me, and I felt an ache where his touch had been. "I know. And I'm proud of us. But there's more. There's always more."

I swallowed hard, feeling the weight of his words press down on me. Was I ready for more? Was I ready to take the leap into the unknown once again?

"Don't pull away from me now, Lila," he said, his voice low, but there was a quiet desperation beneath it, something that cracked through the usual calm he wore like armor. "I need you to be all in. I need you to trust me, like you did before. Like you always have."

I met his gaze, and in that moment, I saw something there—a glimpse of the man I had fallen in love with, the man who had shown me how to build something out of nothing. But there was something else, too. Something darker, something that scared me more than the fire ever had.

"I don't know if I can," I whispered, almost to myself. "I don't know if I'm ready to risk it all again."

The silence between us stretched, thick and heavy. I could see the hurt flicker in his eyes, the way he struggled to mask the disappointment.

"Then maybe we're not ready for what's next," he said, his voice so quiet I almost didn't hear it.

And before I could reply, before I could even think, there was a loud crash from inside the house—a glass breaking, followed by shouting. My heart jumped in my chest as I turned toward the sound, every instinct in me flaring to life.

"What the hell was that?" I breathed, my pulse racing.

Rafe was already moving, his expression shifting from concern to something far more urgent.

"We need to go," he said, his hand once again reaching for mine.

But before I could respond, the door slammed open, and I saw Rick stumbling through it, his face pale, his eyes wild.

"You need to see this."

Chapter 41: The Last Flame

The wind was sharp that evening, a biting chill that nipped at my skin like an unwelcome reminder that nothing, not even the sun, could be trusted to stay forever. The trees whispered in the distance, their branches creaking and groaning with the weight of old stories. I stood at the edge of the porch, looking out over the town below, as if trying to memorize it all—its crooked streets, the tired houses, the sprawl of the hills in the distance that seemed to always hold a secret just out of reach.

The smell of fresh earth filled the air, mingling with the faint scent of jasmine from the garden that Rafe insisted we plant together despite my protests. He had this way of knowing exactly what would make me smile, even if I didn't realize it myself. And tonight, as the last embers of daylight faded, I could feel the weight of the years we had spent apart, and the years still ahead of us, hanging in the air like an unspoken promise.

Rafe was different than I remembered. The years had carved something more into his features—his jaw sharper, his eyes harder—but his smile, that damn smile, was the same. He wore it now, like a rare treasure, one he only gave to me. That smile, always just a little crooked, a little mischievous, was the thing I had been missing, the thing I had never quite been able to forget, no matter how hard I tried to convince myself that I had moved on.

He walked up behind me without a sound, his presence like a warm blanket against the night. I hadn't heard him coming, but I never had to. I always knew when he was near, even if the world was loud with noise and distraction. The world always quieted down when he was close, like the air itself held its breath.

"Thinking about running away again?" he asked, his voice low and teasing, yet there was an undertone of something more, something raw. He always had a way of pulling my thoughts out of me, without me even realizing it.

I laughed softly, glancing over my shoulder at him. He was leaning against the doorframe, his arms crossed, eyes narrowed slightly like he was trying to figure me out. "Maybe. Or maybe I'm just trying to decide how best to escape from you."

He raised an eyebrow, the corner of his mouth curving upward. "Is that so?"

I shifted my weight from one foot to the other, feeling the sudden need to move. "Well, you did just appear out of nowhere after—what was it? Six years?"

"Six years, two months, and twelve days," he said, almost matter-of-factly, like it was just another detail. But there was something in the way he said it—something that made the air between us crackle with tension, with the weight of time spent apart and the knowledge that neither of us could walk away anymore.

I turned fully toward him then, my breath catching in my chest, the space between us suddenly too small, too tight. "What do you want, Rafe?"

He hesitated for just a moment, but when he spoke, it was with a certainty that sent a ripple of warmth through me. "I want everything. All of it. The good, the bad, the impossible parts you think I won't handle. I've been waiting for this moment—for you—to come back. And now that you're here, I'm not letting you slip through my fingers again."

The intensity of his gaze made it hard to breathe. My heart beat harder in my chest, a drumbeat that seemed to echo through the silence between us. His eyes softened for just a moment, as if he was searching for something in me—maybe for the answer to a question neither of us had voiced yet.

"You've never really left, have you?" I whispered. It was a statement, not a question. The truth of it, simple and clear, settled over us like the weight of a forgotten song.

"No," he replied quietly, stepping closer. The warmth of his body was an anchor, a pull I couldn't resist. "I never could."

And then, just like that, he was standing in front of me, close enough that I could feel the heat radiating from him, his hand reaching into his pocket with a careful deliberation that made my pulse jump. My breath caught in my throat as he pulled something small and silver from his pocket.

For a moment, I thought I might be imagining it. It had been years since I had seen that ring, the one I had all but convinced myself was gone forever. But there it was, gleaming in the dim light of the porch, the same as it had been the first time he placed it in my palm all those years ago.

Rafe didn't say anything at first. He simply held the ring out to me, his eyes unwavering, filled with something deeper than the quiet confidence he usually wore. There was a vulnerability in them now, a tremor in his hand that I had never seen before.

I reached out instinctively, my fingers brushing against the cool metal. "Why?" The word slipped out before I could stop it. "Why now?"

His smile softened, a little sad, but still full of that impossible warmth. "Because this time, I'm not waiting for you to choose. I'm choosing you."

The words hung between us, heavy with meaning, with everything we had both been through. With the silence of the years lost and the promise of everything still to come. I felt something inside me begin to shift, as though the very air around us had become charged with the possibility of a future I hadn't dared to imagine. A future with him, where the past was no longer a shadow, and the future was wide open, waiting for us to take it.

I took the ring from his hand, feeling the weight of it settle on my finger, and in that moment, the world outside seemed to fade away. The cold wind, the darkening sky—it didn't matter. All that mattered was the warmth between us, the quiet understanding that no matter what came next, we had already won.

The weight of the ring on my finger was heavier than I had anticipated—heavier than any of the decisions I'd made in my life. Rafe's gaze never left me, like he was trying to burn the moment into my memory, to etch it so deeply into me that it couldn't possibly fade. His eyes held something I'd never seen before, something that was more than love, more than devotion. It was the quiet knowledge of everything we had both endured, of the years spent apart, and of the quiet rebellion of finding each other again. There was a rawness in his look, a tenderness that left me breathless.

I glanced down at the ring, the metal cool against my skin, the stones gleaming faintly in the dim porch light. It was simple, understated—a far cry from the diamonds I'd seen flash on the fingers of other women, the ones who always seemed to have everything figured out. But it was ours, in every sense. It was a piece of our past, our shared history, and it had never been more right. I smiled, but it felt uncertain, like I wasn't sure I was worthy of the moment, of the promise he was giving me.

"Rafe," I said, my voice a little hoarse, the words coming out in a whisper that carried more than I intended. "Are we really doing this?"

He stepped closer, closing the distance between us until I could feel his breath against my skin, warm and steady. "You think I'm the kind of man who doesn't know what he wants?" There was a teasing lilt to his voice, but I could hear the edge behind it—the edge that came from a man who'd fought for something he wasn't going to let slip through his fingers again.

I couldn't help but laugh, despite the emotions swirling inside me. "I think you're the kind of man who makes everything seem effortless."

"Effortless?" He raised an eyebrow, the wry grin spreading across his face. "Now that's a first. I'm pretty sure I've spent the last decade trying to make up for every stupid mistake I made with you."

I felt the sting of his words, even if they were wrapped in humor. It was easy to forget the weight of the past when the future felt so close, so tangible, but there were still scars there, ones neither of us had fully dealt with. The things left unsaid, the promises broken, the time that had slipped away from us like sand through our fingers.

"I never wanted you to make up for anything," I said, my voice softer now. "I just wanted..."

I didn't know what I wanted, not really. I wanted the years back, sure. I wanted to turn back time and undo every misunderstanding, every silence. But what I wanted most—what I had always wanted—was for us to finally be enough for each other. To make it past all the broken pieces and find a way to heal, together.

"Yeah," he said, his voice a low rumble, as if he'd heard the unspoken part of my confession. "I know." He reached out then, taking my hand in his, the heat of his palm searing through me. "But we don't get the luxury of turning back time. All we have is right now."

I looked up at him, my heart thundering in my chest. "And right now, what do we have?"

The question hung between us, fragile and precarious. It was a question I hadn't dared to ask until that moment, and now that it was out there, it seemed like the most important thing in the world.

The way he looked at me, though, told me more than I needed to know.

"Right now," he said, his thumb brushing over the back of my hand in a slow, deliberate rhythm, "we have a future. A future that starts right here, right now. No more waiting. No more what-ifs."

His words were simple, but they settled deep inside me, like a stone thrown into a still pond, the ripples spreading out and touching every part of me. I could feel my heart opening to him again, the tight walls I had built around it beginning to crumble.

I swallowed hard, blinking against the sudden sting of tears in my eyes. "I don't know if I can do this," I admitted, my voice trembling despite my efforts to steady it. "I don't know if I can believe in this... us. Not after everything."

"You don't have to believe in it," he said, his voice fierce, as if the very idea of me doubting us was something he couldn't tolerate. "You just have to trust that I'm not going anywhere. Not this time."

I closed my eyes, the weight of his words sinking into me like a quiet storm, filling me with the rush of relief, of fear, of hope all at once. I didn't know how we would move forward, but in that moment, with his hand holding mine and his promise lingering in the air between us, I knew one thing for certain: I wasn't ready to let go. Not again. Not ever.

When I opened my eyes again, his face was close, too close. His breath mingled with mine, warm and steady. "You're mine," he whispered, the words soft, like a prayer. "And I'm yours. Always."

I didn't know how to answer him. I didn't know what I could say that would be enough. But as I looked at him, all the doubt, all the fear, melted away. What mattered wasn't the past we couldn't change, or the future we couldn't control. What mattered was that, in this moment, we had each other.

"I think I'm ready," I whispered, my voice barely audible, but he heard it. He always heard me.

His lips found mine then, soft and warm, a promise in every touch, in every movement. The world around us disappeared, the sound of the wind fading into the background, the weight of the past lifting as I let myself surrender to the present.

And when he pulled away, just a fraction, his forehead resting gently against mine, I knew, without a shadow of a doubt, that this—we—were worth every risk, every fear, every chance we had taken. Together, we would face whatever came next. Because we were finally ready.

The sound of the door creaking open behind me broke the fragile silence that had settled over us. I didn't even need to turn around to know who it was. The unmistakable scent of wood smoke and earth clung to him, a reminder of the long hours he'd spent in the garden that day, fixing the broken fence that had been hanging on by a thread for far too long. Rafe had always been the type to fix what was broken, to mend what others thought beyond repair.

"You're still here?" His voice was light, teasing, but there was an edge to it, a touch of weariness that spoke volumes.

I turned, half-expecting to find him at the threshold, but instead, he was standing there in the entryway, his silhouette framed by the dim glow of the hallway lights. His hands were stuffed in the pockets of his jeans, but his posture was that of someone who knew he was about to make a decision that could change everything.

"Of course, I'm still here," I replied, my voice a little too sharp for my liking. "Wouldn't dream of going anywhere."

He laughed, low and easy. "Well, that's a relief. I was starting to think you'd run off with some other man, leaving me to pick up the pieces."

I crossed my arms, narrowing my eyes at him. "Funny you should mention that. I was about to ask you the same thing."

His smile faltered for just a second, a flicker of uncertainty crossing his face before he masked it with that same confident smirk. "You know I've never been one for running away," he said, stepping into the room, closing the distance between us in a few long strides. "Not from you. Not from anything that matters."

There it was again, that tension. The one that had always existed between us, no matter how many years had passed, no matter how much we'd changed. It was a pull, a magnetic force neither of us could deny.

I hesitated for a moment, uncertain if I was ready to have the conversation that seemed to loom over us like an approaching storm. "So, what now?" I asked, my voice barely above a whisper. "What does this mean? What do we do with all this..."

"All this?" His brow furrowed as he studied me, as if he were searching for the right words. "You mean the ring? The promises? The years lost and the ones we're about to make?"

I nodded, my fingers absently tracing the edge of the ring on my finger, as though the weight of it might somehow steady my thoughts. "Yes. All of it. I need to know what happens next. I need to know that we're not just... pretending."

He stepped forward, close enough now that I could feel the warmth of his presence. He took my hand, his fingers wrapping around mine in a gesture that felt like both a promise and a plea. "I'm not pretending, Claire. Not anymore. This is real. We are real. And no matter what happens, I'm not going anywhere. Not again."

The words hit me like a tidal wave, crashing over everything I had ever feared. I had spent so many years building walls, convincing myself I was fine, that I didn't need this. Didn't need him. But now, with his hand in mine, those walls felt flimsy, like they were made of paper, ready to crumble with the smallest breath.

"I don't know if I can trust that," I said, my voice cracking with the weight of every doubt I'd carried for so long. "I don't know if I can believe you anymore."

He swallowed hard, the raw honesty in his eyes making my heart stutter. "I get it. I do. But I'm asking you to believe me now, Claire. Just this once. Let me prove it to you."

For a moment, neither of us spoke. The tension was thick, suffocating, and yet, somehow, it was more comforting than anything else. It was a promise of something we both needed, even if we weren't sure how to get there.

"I want to," I whispered, the words slipping out before I could stop them. "God, I want to. But I'm scared, Rafe. I'm scared of what happens if we fall apart again."

His thumb brushed over my knuckles, soothing and steadying. "We won't," he said simply, but with such certainty that it sent a ripple of warmth through me. "We won't fall apart. Not this time."

I wanted to believe him. I wanted to trust him with every inch of myself. But the past had taught me to be cautious. To guard my heart against the possibility of losing it again.

"You can't make promises like that," I said, my voice trembling. "We can't just pretend everything's perfect now."

He smiled then, a soft, rueful smile that pulled at something deep within me. "I'm not pretending. I'm just asking you to take a chance. With me. With us."

There was no more room for hesitation. No more time for questions or doubts. And yet, just as I was about to speak—just as I was about to let myself fall into him completely—the sound of the doorbell rang through the house, sharp and jarring. It cut through the moment like a knife, and my heart skipped a beat.

Rafe looked toward the door, his expression flickering with the briefest shadow of annoyance before it was gone, replaced by something more cautious. "Expecting someone?" he asked, his voice low and controlled.

I shook my head, my pulse suddenly racing. "No. No one."

Rafe's eyes narrowed, and for a split second, I saw a flash of something—something he wasn't saying, something he wasn't ready to confront. "Stay here," he said, his tone firm. "I'll check it out."

Before I could respond, he was already walking toward the door, his footsteps heavy and deliberate. The ring on my finger felt suddenly too tight, like it was a symbol of everything I feared and everything I wanted. My chest was tight with something I couldn't name. Anxiety? Fear? Hope?

I didn't know. But when Rafe reached for the door handle, the last thing I expected happened. The door swung open, and standing there, on the other side, was a face I hadn't seen in years—a face I thought I'd never have to see again.

And in that moment, everything shifted.

Chapter 42: Eternal Fire

that unspoken understanding between us that would carry us through the future. I could feel it, like the steady pulse of a heartbeat, strong and steady, beneath the uncertain skies of a world that had tested us more than once. The embers of the past still whispered in the wind, their heat fading but not entirely extinguished. Yet, in that silence between us, I knew—deep down—that we had earned this moment.

The sun's first rays stretched across the horizon like liquid gold, spilling over the charred remnants of the forest that had once stood strong. It seemed a cruel irony, how fire—something that devoured and destroyed—could now offer warmth and rebirth. But there was beauty in that contradiction. The ashes of the old life were fertile ground for the new one we would build, a life we had claimed from the ashes.

As my fingers traced the worn edges of the porch railing, my mind wandered back to that first night when everything had changed. I had been a different woman then, caught in a whirlwind of doubt and fear, my heart held hostage by the uncertainties that had plagued me for years. But something had shifted, something in me had ignited that night, something that no fire, no matter how fierce, could ever take away.

I turned to face him, the man who had become my partner in every sense of the word. His eyes, those deep, knowing eyes, were focused on the horizon, but I saw the faint twitch of a smile at the corner of his lips. It was small, barely noticeable, but to me, it was everything. In his presence, I felt a sense of peace I had never known before, a quiet reassurance that no matter what chaos lay ahead, we would face it together.

His hand found mine, and for a moment, we simply stood there, the world around us stirring to life. The birds had already begun their morning chorus, their melodies a sweet accompaniment to the soft rustling of the trees. The smell of fresh earth and damp leaves filled the air, and for a brief moment, it was as though the whole world had exhaled, releasing the tension of the night before.

"I didn't think we'd make it out of there," I said softly, my voice breaking the stillness.

He turned to look at me, his gaze unwavering, as though he could read every thought, every fear that still clung to me like a second skin. "We didn't just make it out," he said, his voice low but firm, "we survived. Together."

There was no boasting in his words, no arrogance. Just a simple truth that hung in the air between us, a truth that settled deep inside my chest.

"I still don't know how," I confessed, my fingers tightening around his. "How we made it through all of that and came out on the other side..."

He chuckled, the sound rich and warm, like a promise. "Because we didn't give up. That's how."

I smiled at that, my heart swelling with affection. How had I ever doubted this man? The one who had stood by me, unwavering, through every trial, every fire. His belief in us was as constant as the earth beneath our feet, and it was something I had learned to lean on in the darkest of times.

The wind shifted slightly, lifting strands of my hair and teasing them across my face. I pushed them back with a soft laugh, but the breeze carried a new scent—one I hadn't noticed before. It was faint, just a whisper on the wind, but it was there. Smoke. Not from the forest, not from the distant remnants of our past, but something else. Something... closer.

My pulse quickened, and without thinking, I pulled away from him, my eyes scanning the treeline. It was still too early for anyone to be working that far out. And yet, the smell of smoke grew stronger, more distinct, and I could feel the weight of it settling in my chest.

"Is that—?" I began, but my words trailed off as he stepped forward, his hand brushing against my back in that reassuring way he had when we both knew something wasn't right but didn't yet know how bad it would be.

"Stay here," he said quietly, his tone sharp now, a warning I knew all too well. "I'll check it out."

"No," I said, taking a step forward to stand beside him, my instincts kicking in. "We're not doing this alone."

He didn't argue. Instead, he reached for the rifle he had set down on the porch earlier, his movements slow and deliberate. I could hear the faint click as he checked the chamber, his focus absolute.

I knew what he was thinking. He was worried, and I hated that. I hated the feeling that we were always one step away from losing everything, from being thrown back into the chaos we had just begun to escape. But it was that same chaos that had forged us into what we were now. Stronger, wiser, and more prepared than ever before.

"We don't have to do this, you know," I murmured, taking his hand in mine again. "We can leave. Start over somewhere else. Somewhere far from here."

He shook his head, his eyes dark but steady. "We've been running our whole lives. It's time we stop."

And just like that, I understood. I understood why he couldn't walk away. Because, like me, he had fought for this place. Fought for the life we had made here, even in the shadow of all that had been lost. We were here to stay, no matter what came next.

As we moved toward the woods, side by side, the scent of smoke grew stronger, and my heart quickened. Whatever it was, it was close. And it was coming for us.

the quiet understanding between us that had become the bedrock of everything. It was an unusual kind of strength we had cultivated, one born not of brute force but of patience and compromise. We'd learned to be still when everything around us was in motion. To listen even when the world was screaming for action. I don't think either of us could have imagined how it would feel, this fragile peace. It was like stepping into a world that had forgotten to ask us for permission.

There was something about mornings like this, with the sun creeping over the hills and the soft hum of nature slowly stirring, that made everything seem possible. But we weren't foolish enough to forget that peace was fleeting. It was a gift, a rare treasure, and the one thing you had to fight for every damn day.

"I think we need a plan," I said, my voice surprisingly steady, given the undercurrent of worry tightening my chest.

He glanced at me, raising an eyebrow, a slight smirk tugging at the corners of his lips. "A plan? You?" He leaned in, just close enough for me to catch the warmth of his breath on my cheek. "Since when do you like plans?"

I couldn't help but smile at the challenge in his voice. He was right, of course. I preferred improvisation—making decisions as I went along, seeing where life would lead. But this was different. The scent of smoke in the air had shaken something loose inside me, something I hadn't even realized was still lingering. It was a memory of danger, of things not being as simple as they seemed.

"We don't have the luxury of winging it anymore," I said, swallowing hard. "Whatever's out there, it's not like before. It's not some random fire or an act of nature. This feels... deliberate."

His eyes hardened then, the playful glint vanishing like a shadow swallowed by the dawn. I could feel the shift in him, the way his body subtly tensed, preparing for the unknown. That was the thing about him—he never wore his fears on his sleeve, but I could read the tightness of his jaw, the way his fingers tightened around the rifle.

"Deliberate, huh?" he murmured. "So, you think someone's after us?"

I nodded slowly, feeling the weight of my own words. "I don't know who, or why, but there's something... wrong about this. It's too close, too soon after everything we've been through. This isn't just the land trying to heal anymore. It's something else."

He exhaled sharply, letting the silence stretch between us for a moment. The birds had stopped singing, and the breeze had stilled, as though the world itself was holding its breath, waiting for the next move.

"What do you want to do?" he asked, the question hanging heavy between us.

I thought about it. The decision wasn't easy, not when every instinct screamed at me to stay put, to lock the doors and pretend the world outside wasn't burning. But there was something I couldn't ignore, a sense of urgency that had settled deep in my bones.

"We need to find out who's doing this—and why. We can't just wait and hope it goes away."

He looked at me, his gaze both approving and cautious, the same way he always looked at me when I said something that scared him a little. I could see the struggle behind his eyes—he wanted to protect me, but he also knew better than anyone that we didn't have the luxury of running anymore.

"Alright," he said, his voice low but resolute. "But we do this together. No more going off half-cocked. We get the lay of the land first, figure out what's really going on. Then we act."

His words were a balm to my frayed nerves, but I knew better than to think that any of this would be easy. Nothing had ever been easy for us. There had always been a fight, always been a need to prove ourselves, to survive.

And survive we would.

I reached into my jacket pocket, pulling out the map we had drawn up months ago, when we first settled here—before the fires, before the unknown threats had begun creeping into our lives like dark whispers in the night. The map wasn't much, just a rough sketch of the town and the surrounding forest. But it was ours, a testament to how far we'd come, how hard we'd fought to keep this place safe.

"Let's start with the river," I said, pointing to a spot near the edge of the map. "That's where we saw the smoke coming from. It might be nothing, but it's better than sitting here hoping we're wrong."

He nodded in agreement, and together we began the trek down the familiar path that led to the river's edge. The air had a weight to it, heavy with the anticipation of something we couldn't name, but both of us felt. It was that feeling you get when you're on the edge of something—something big, something that could change everything.

As we walked, the trees closed in around us, the shadows long and stretching, their branches swaying gently in the breeze. It was quiet here, too quiet. The usual chorus of insects and birds had gone still, as though the forest itself was waiting. I couldn't shake the feeling that we were being watched, that every step we took was a step closer to something we couldn't yet understand.

"Think anyone's out there?" I asked, my voice barely a whisper.

He didn't answer right away, but I saw him glance over his shoulder, his senses sharpened. "Could be. Doesn't hurt to be cautious."

I caught the sharpness in his voice, and for the first time in a long while, I felt the weight of his caution settle over me like a blanket. He was always the one to make sure we didn't rush in blindly, but today, something had shifted. Today, we were both holding our breath, waiting for something that neither of us wanted to face.

And I had no idea what would be waiting for us when we reached the river, but I knew we weren't turning back. Not this time.

our unwavering belief in each other that would carry us through anything the future could throw at us. It wasn't the fires that had created this bond between us, but the way we rebuilt from the ashes—slowly, painfully, but surely. I had never thought I'd find someone who could understand me in the way he did, who could sit in the quiet with me without needing words, and yet, here we were.

We walked, side by side, down the winding path that led us to the river. The smell of the fresh earth, the distant scent of pine, mingled with something else. Something metallic, almost sharp in the air, and I couldn't place it. Maybe it was the smoke, but it was too fresh, too pungent to ignore. The sky, once promising a gentle blue, now held a heavy haze, as though it was holding something back—something it was preparing to release.

"Think we're the only ones who noticed?" I asked, my voice a little too casual for the way my heart was racing in my chest.

His lips twitched into that half-smile that had never failed to make me feel like the world was a much better place when he was near. "I'm guessing no one else is this curious. Or stupid."

"Stupid?" I cocked an eyebrow. "I prefer 'brave.'"

"Brave people usually end up with singed eyebrows and half an idea of what's going on." He grinned at me, his blue eyes gleaming like they always did when he was trying to mask his worry with humor. It worked, most of the time. But I knew him too well now. His eyes always told the truth, no matter how much he tried to hide it.

"I can live with singed eyebrows," I said, though the truth was, I couldn't care less about my eyebrows. It was the way he said things that left me uneasy, the way he tried to cover up his own anxiety with that easy humor. "But I'd like to know why this feels like something bigger than we're ready for."

His expression shifted again, the easy charm slipping, and something darker flickered in his gaze. "It always is, isn't it?" he murmured.

The sound of the river grew louder as we approached, the water crashing against rocks with an intensity that mirrored the knots in my stomach. I was starting to realize that we had crossed some kind of threshold, the one where there was no turning back, no going back to ignorance or comfort. The air had changed, the atmosphere had shifted, and now it felt like we were in the eye of a storm we couldn't predict.

When we reached the riverbank, we stopped. The trees around us stood tall and silent, their branches reaching toward the sky as if trying to grab hold of the clouds. But the river itself—unpredictable, unruly—was still. The water, dark and uninviting, flowed with a quiet strength that felt like it was waiting for something. It had been calm just the night before, but now, it was teeming with a force that unsettled me. There was something off about it.

"I thought the smoke was coming from over here," I said, scanning the area. "But I don't see anything burning."

"Maybe it's not fire," he said. He was staring at the river, his eyes narrowed, as though looking for something hidden beneath the surface.

"What do you mean, 'not fire'?" My pulse quickened. Was he suggesting something else? The air around us had felt heavy with the scent of smoke, but he was already looking beyond that, his mind clearly racing ahead of mine.

"You hear that?" he asked abruptly, his voice low. His posture shifted, a slight tension in his shoulders that hadn't been there moments ago. I strained my ears, but all I heard was the rush of water, the hum of nature.

"Nothing," I said, my voice thick with confusion.

He stepped closer to the water, crouching down, his eyes scanning the surface with a mix of suspicion and something else I couldn't place. "No, there's something underneath. Like a hum."

A hum. The kind of sound that settled somewhere deep in your chest, reverberating until it made you question what you were hearing. But all I could hear was the wind and the river, nothing more.

"Are you sure?" I asked, my voice betraying a trace of doubt. "Maybe it's just the current, or some debris..."

He didn't look up, his focus absolute. "No, it's something else. Something's been stirred up. Maybe it's not just the land we need to worry about."

A chill ran down my spine. "You think someone's been here? Recently?"

"I think someone's trying to keep us away," he said, his voice tight. "Or they want us to find something."

"Great," I muttered. "Because it's not like we've got enough going on already."

He turned to me then, his expression as unreadable as the river itself. "I think this is bigger than us. And we need to find out what it is before it finds us."

I nodded, but a deep, unsettling fear gripped me. The tension between us had shifted again, and this time, it wasn't something I could dismiss with humor or sarcasm. Whatever was waiting for us in that river, in the depths of the land, wasn't something we could outrun.

Suddenly, the river bubbled in a strange, rhythmic pattern—a series of ripples that didn't belong. The hum, now unmistakable, vibrated the air around us, sending a shiver down my spine. The water began to churn, and something rose from the depths.

I froze. My heart stopped in my chest as a figure broke through the surface, gliding slowly upward, its movements unnervingly graceful. A long shadow pulled itself from the water, and for the first time in my life, I felt the true weight of what it meant to be hunted.